I0647881

Black Dust

A Partnersverse Story

by Invisiblewolf and Achilles

Black Dust

Production copyright FurPlanet Productions © 2017
Copyright © Invisiblewolf and Achilles 2017

Cover Artwork by Ifus 2017

Published by FurPlanet Productions
Dallas, Texas
www.FurPlanet.com

ISBN 978-1-61450-362-0

Printed in the United States of America
Second Edition Trade Paperback 2017

All characters are © by their creators and are used with permission. All rights reserved. No portion of this work may be reproduced in any form, in any medium, without the expressed permission of the author.

Table of Contents

Acknowledgements

As always, I am truly appreciative of the many people who provide their continual support for my writing; you, who are reading this now, as well as those of you picked up my last book, Partners. Thank you.

There are a few people who deserve to be applauded for their work on this book in particular. Teiran and Ajax from FurPlanet did a superb job to ensure everything in this story was well-written. Their editorial skills improved this story significantly and I am very thankful for their hard work.

I would also like to thank my writing partner, Achilles, whose keen mind has expanded upon my world in ways that meshed seamlessly with the existing characters and settings. I had a lot of fun writing this with him and it seemed like we kept pushing each other to do better as the story went on, which is the sign of a good team. So, good on ya, mate, and so much thanks from me for the life that you helped breathe into this book.

-Invisiblewolf

I am so very pleased that this work is now being published, and I have to add my thanks to everyone at FurPlanet who added to the book that has been a long time in the making.

This was the start of a long collaboration with Invisiblewolf which I hope to continue. He already had a rich and fertile setting, it was my honor that he allowed me to develop it and add to the tapestry with my own characters and drama. I very much feel the essence of this story is the tale of two worlds colliding, and it was so much fun to have brought that to life in our collaboration. Here's to many more stories and new adventures to come!

-Achilles

The events in this story take place approximately two years prior to the events in "Partners"

Prologue: Arrangements

Spiritwolf was on his own.

Three agents dressed in martial arts uniforms – an ocelot and two black wolves – scanned the dojo warily. Their ears strained to catch the tiniest sound, their noses inhaled deeply to catch his scent. They formed an irregular triangle in the room while a fourth person in a *gi*, an elderly fox with golden fur, stood patiently in the center with his eyes closed and his head bowed. Just inside the doorway, the brown bear in the trenchcoat and fedora watched the proceedings with interest.

Without opening his eyes, the fox quietly said, "*Hajime.*" Begin.

The three agents remained completely still for several tense moments before they finally heard footsteps on the *tatami* approach the smallest agent. The ocelot brought his guard up but then he suddenly crumpled over, clutching his midsection and gasping for breath. A swift blow to his back flattened him in the next moment.

The remaining two agents growled and collapsed inward toward the fox but the expected attack never came. A quick glance and exchange of nods sent the younger wolf rushing toward the prone cat, punching and kicking the air as if doing a *kata* demonstration. The elder of the pair kept his eyes on his brother and casually slid forward in his wake, weaving from side to side as though expecting a flanking maneuver. His triangular ears flicked back and forth impatiently.

The younger wolf's foot struck something solid and, caught in that moment of surprise, he was hit square in the chest. He flew backward into his charging brother and they both went down in a heap. The unseen assailant struck each of them just once, knocking them out before they could disentangle themselves.

Spiritwolf couldn't believe it. The timing of his plan had, for once, been absolutely perfect. There was still ten seconds left, according to the clock on the far wall. The invisible wolf grinned wickedly at the lone figure. All he had to do was touch the fox and he would win.

Master Song lifted his muzzle and nodded without opening his eyes. "Very good. But you still make too much noise when you…" The fox suddenly did the splits, dropping down, and simultaneously raising his arms as though surrendering. A sharp, surprised yelp – which did not come from the fox – preceded the loud thud and groan of someone hitting the floor behind.

"…attack." The fox calmly stood and padded to the edge of the mat, then kicked at the air, which responded with another groan. "Too loud," he repeated sternly. He cocked his head toward the ground and then pantomimed helping someone to their feet.

Spiritwolf appreciated the assistance. "Sorry, *sensei*. I'll do better next time."

"It looks like you did well enough," the bear named Zero rumbled from the doorway. He stepped into the room and nodded to the Alpha agents who were slowly getting up. "As did you three. You're dismissed. Thank you for your time, agents."

The defeated trio nodded and grumbled their annoyance in low voices as they filed past the Senior Director. Zero turned back to see the fox calmly approaching with one arm hooked as though being escorted. Master Song's eyes were yellow, like his fur, but they were completely clouded over. Faded scars along his brows and cheeks were etched stories of vicious fighting in his past, despite the serenity now radiating from him. He slid his feet along the edge of the mat until he felt his sandals, which he carefully stepped into as he hummed a soft melody.

Spiritwolf's voice spoke from the air next to the fox. "I guess they didn't like fighting the freak."

Zero raised an eyebrow. "They're the best of the best and they lost. They won't like getting chewed out."

"I never did, either."

The bear frowned. "Then maybe you should be a little more sympathetic, given how often that happened."

"Ah, the good old days. Back when people could watch me getting yelled at by an ex-military tiger with a perfectionist complex. Things have changed since then, though." Spiritwolf's voice had moved toward a small desk where clothes lay neatly folded on its surface. "Nowadays, it's so much easier for me to be overlooked. Less yelling this way." The garments rose into the air one at a time and filled out, reanimating and giving form to the parts of Spiritwolf's body they covered. The clothes walked back to where the other two waited. "At least Master Song doesn't treat me any differently."

The blind fox smiled. "You are no different to me than anyone else."

"See? That's what I like about him. He's obviously an enlightened person if he doesn't care about appearances."

"Master Song," Zero interrupted the wolf impatiently. "Your report?"

"Spiritwolf is much improved. You witnessed his fighting skill. He is fast. Strong. Agile."

"But is he ready?"

Several long moments of silence made the butterflies in Spirit's stomach erupt. "I believe so," the fox said slowly. "But…"

"There's a 'but?'" Spiritwolf interjected.

Master Song swiftly punched the wolf's stomach; the shirt doubled over, gasping for breath. "It is rude to interrupt your *sensei*," he said frostily.

Zero dipped his head for a moment so that his fedora hid his smile.

"As I was saying. One behavior that I have observed is that Spiritwolf continues to rely too much on his invisibility."

"Well, it's not like I can turn this off… sorry!" The wolf apologized before the fox could hit him again.

"Accepted. Spiritwolf. My student," Master Song gently took hold of the wolf's sleeve. "Your invisibility is part of you but it does not define you. It is not all that you are. Do you understand?"

"I… not really. I mean, I think so. The words make sense – I've been making progress, adjusting to what I've become. But there's more, right? Like a deeper understanding of what I've become?"

The fox grinned. "Learning to ask the right questions is a good place to start. I will take my leave, if there is nothing else, Zero?"

"Nothing else, Master Song."

"Good. See you later, Spiritwolf."

"Yes, sensei," Spiritwolf replied.

Song's whiskers twitched at their shared joke before he left the room, pausing only to retrieve his cane at the door.

"Of all the things I've seen in my life," the bear said, watching Master Song go, "I am continually astounded at how easily he gets around despite being blind."

"And I'm constantly astounded at how he can still beat the crap out of me." It sounded like the wolf was grimacing as he spoke.

"You didn't fall that hard, did you?"

"Not really, no. I'm still aching from yesterday's one-on-one session. All this training takes its toll after a while…" Spirit's shirt shrugged. "I agree, though. Master Song is very sure of himself."

Zero nodded. "You never saw him in competition. He was confident. Fearless. And in public, he tried to help where he could and never backed down, never accepted defeat. Even when…" The bear let go of distant memories and smiled a small, tired smile. "Well, that's a story for another day. Let's get you back to your room."

The pair emerged from the multipurpose exercise room that had been set up as a dojo. They were on level eight, as declared by the stylized number "8" every twenty meters, of the Directorate for Advanced Science and Technology's Special Projects headquarters in New Mexico. This level was dedicated to fitness, recreation, and skills training. The corridor outside was carpeted much like a modern office building and the wall coloring was an energetic red. The painter had apparently decided to cut loose by creating murals of white silhouettes in the midst of various indoor and outdoor activities, much like those seen on national or world sporting event advertisements. The images flowed to and from each other seamlessly. The slight breeze of surface air tickled their fur and added to the illusion that they were not at all underground.

Spirit's clothes angled toward the bear as they walked toward the elevators. "So what am I being evaluated for this time?"

Zero chuckled. "What makes you think I'm going to tell you?"

"You did ask Master Song right in front of me. You wouldn't have done that if you were going to keep it a secret."

"True. Well, then. Do you remember what today is?"

"Well, it's one year, two months and five days since I became invisible."

The bear frowned. "You're still keeping count?"

"For anniversaries. You still owe me a one year party, you know."

Zero raised an eyebrow and played along with the sarcastic response. "Dare I ask how do you would celebrate?"

"Don't worry, I won't burn down any buildings. I learned my lesson after the second one. Speaking of fun, you haven't said anything lately about how Canis or the other Ultras are doing."

Zero sighed. "There hasn't been much progress, I'm afraid. Canis is still learning how to… negotiate with the part of him that's nanotech. He emits energy blasts when he gets the slightest bit… distressed."

A visible shudder rippled across the shirt's shoulders. "I remember. Still, if that's all he's doing these days then I'd call that success."

"Agreed. Morey can't stay formed for more than an hour or two. We're thinking of making him a special containment suit to help prevent him from dissolving back into water. The interesting thing is that the idea came from Canis. He invented a new nano-polymer that's completely impermeable to water and has other useful properties." They passed a lapine guard in the hallway; she remained motionless except for her eyes, which followed Spiritwolf's animated clothes as they passed by. "Bal still has incapacitating headaches. When he's alert, he can't handle more than one person in the room at a time."

"What about Topaz?"

Zero sighed and shook his head. "Depends on the day. She's been a big help to Morey, keeping him company when she's in the green, but she still gets disconnected from the rest of us, overwhelmed. We're trying to tweak a class of nootropic drugs to see if it will help her maintain control."

"Can I see them? I might be able to help them with… you know. Adjusting. I mean, it sounds like I'm the furthest along of us."

Zero rumbled. "The last time you saw them didn't go so well, did it?"

"I suppose it didn't," Spirit's voice was low, pregnant with repentance and just a hint of bitterness. "And for the hundredth time, I'm sorry."

"We all have to live with the consequences of our decisions, don't we?" Zero said just as quietly. They turned a corner and walked into the alcove where the elevators were. The bear peered into the retinal scanner mounted between the two sets of doors, then pressed his thumb against the square scanner.

"That's new." Spiritwolf's sleeve pointed to a third device, left of the two scanners. "More biometric security?"

"Not exactly. That's a voice command module. Since your eyes and fingers can't be easily scanned, we need something non-visual to give you access to the elevators."

"Access?" The wolf's hopes began to take flight.

"You know, you never answered my question correctly," Zero said coyly as one of the up arrows lit. A soft chime heralded the arrival of the elevator and with a whoosh, the doors to the right of the scanners opened.

Inside was a cheetah nervously cradling a box about a cubic meter in volume against his lanky frame. He wore only black cargo pants and his hair was disheveled as though he had been running. He peered through his rectangular-framed glasses at the pair as they entered. "Oh, hello. Zero. Spiritwolf. Funny meeting you here. I was just on my way to your place, Spirit."

Spiritwolf's sleeves folded over his large chest. "Did you forget your shirt along the way, Dash?" He sounded amused.

"What? Oh. Sorry about that. I was doing my morning meditation routine when the quartermaster summoned me to get this." He indicated the box with a grin. "I think it turned out well."

"That's the answer to my question, Spiritwolf." Zero turned to the cheetah. "I'll take it from here, Dash. You're free to go."

The cat nodded and handed the box to the bear. "If you have any problems, just give me a shout." He touched the button for the sixth floor and waved to them as they got out on the seventh. The walls on this level were primarily green with imagery of trees and mountains along with the eponymous number 7.

They paused at the third door on the left. Spiritwolf fished a key out of his pocket, which floated over to the lock. "Home sweet home." They stepped inside his apartment, single file through the short hallway, and made their way to the smartly furnished living room. Spirit sat at the end of the sofa while the bear stood opposite, with the coffee table between them. Zero set the box gently on the table. "I wasn't expecting them to finish it on time," Spirit remarked.

"Oh, ye of little faith." The bear opened the box carefully. Inside on a stand was a life-like mask with the visage of a brown wolf and a pair of gloves that looked very much like real hands, wrists, and partial forearms. "Time for the final fit check."

"I hope this is more durable than the last set. I ripped the mask just by yawning." Spiritwolf took the gloves first and slid them on, giving form to his invisible hands. He made fists with them, opening and closing them rapidly. "This feels like silk." His voice sounded startled.

"The material is similar to what Morey's biosuit will be made from, with a few minor tweaks to the polymer. It's not waterproof but it's still lightweight, strong, and it will keep your fur cool." Zero smiled. "You should even be able to eat and drink with it on, though you'll have to clean it regularly."

"Remind me to thank the big guy next time I'm allowed to be in a room with him." Spiritwolf picked up the mask and slipped it over his unseen head. He tucked the lower portion under his shirt collar. "How do I look?"

"Almost normal, except for your eyes and your mouth." The eye sockets were still empty and revealed the inside of the mask, while another gap showed where his teeth should have been.

Spiritwolf peered inside the box again. "More presents." There were three smaller packages taped to the side. He pulled them out gently and opened the first one. "Well, at least I can manipulate items easily with the gloves. That's an improvement." A connected pair of vials fell out of the box and into the palm of his glove. "Interesting. Contact lenses?" He pulled off one glove and gently opened one vial, spilling a lens into the air in front of his sleeve. The wolf turned away and spent a minute fiddling with them before turning back. "At least I don't have to take off the mask to stick them in."

The bear peered again. "Not bad," he said. "They gave you green eyes."

Spiritwolf chuckled. "Well, the fur isn't what my color used to be, either. At this point, I'm just happy to look normal and have people able to see my face when I talk to them."

Zero nodded. "What about your tail?"

"I'll just tuck it into my pants. It's a bit old-fashioned, but it's the easiest thing to do." He opened the second package and held up a 300 mL bottle. "It says 'biodermal compound.'"

"It's an adhesive, to help keep the mask and gloves bonded to your fur." Zero explained. "Last one?"

The wolf opened it and pulled out a pair of veneers, upper and lower. "I guess these take care of my teeth problem." He snapped them in place and ran his tongue over them. "They feel funny, but I can live with them."

"You'll have to." Zero leaned forward and looked steadily at Spiritwolf. "You're being reinstated… on a provisional basis." He paused. "You might want to keep your mouth a little more shut, Spirit." The wolf's jaw had dropped open, exposing the back of his mask in the space between his teeth.

"Sorry, Zero. But… I'm going to be an agent again?"

"As I said, it's provisional. We haven't finished the voice module installation yet and you're not in the personnel files, either."

"So, I'm not in the system. That doesn't sound like I'm even a provisional agent, especially if I still need to be escorted around."

"You won't need that. You're going on a solo mission."

Spiritwolf blinked. "Did I hear that right?"

"You did."

"My first mission… since I became…" Spirit looked down at his hands. They certainly looked normal enough – so much so that he could actually go out in public again. Covered up, no one would ever guess that he was different. *No one staring at me or treating me like some kind of freak. Unless I screw up and get exposed.* The thought made his heart race faster, tied his stomach in tight knots. Most people weren't aware of the assignments he and his former teammates were given. They were the Ultras, a secret "dark ops" team that had been part of the Technology Enforcement Agency – the special projects wing of the Directorate for Advanced Science and Technology – and they had actively worked to counter the threats from terrorists and others armed with advanced technology and malicious agendas. And the general public didn't want to be aware of all that – so much so that it seemed like half of the TEA's work was socially oriented – crowd control, public relations, information filtering, and so on. One mistake on his part, though, and Spiritwolf could easily find himself on the receiving end of a frightened mob's collective panic attack.

No. I won't let that happen. No one will know what I am – it'll be like the old days. This is my one shot, my only chance at going back to what I was before. I have to do this. I have to prove myself again. I can't fail.

Zero leaned forward. "I know what you're thinking, Spirit. You're thinking you might not be ready to go back to active status. Well, I certainly think you're ready, and so does Master Song."

"With a caveat."

"Which you should try to keep in mind when you're in the field." The bear chuckled. "You know, you're right. It's good to see your face again, even if it's different from the one I used to know."

"Thanks. I'll probably be staring at myself in the mirror for the next few weeks."

"You won't have that long." Zero grew serious again. "We intercepted an encrypted email a couple of days ago. Canis managed to decrypt it easily, with his new talents."

"Another reason to thank the big guy," Spiritwolf said with a grin.

"Yes. The message was also the reason we've pushed up your readiness assessment."

"Must have been important."

"It was from someone named Black Dust."

Spiritwolf smirked. "Let me guess… he's a former coal miner gone rogue with outlawed drilling technology?"

"No. He's a trafficker of stolen technical equipment and data. We've had our eyes and ears looking out for him ever since we learned of him several months back. He's apparently been flying under the radar for a long time and he's been adept at eluding even our best investigators." The bear leaned back. "What got our attention was that, just recently, he acquired an encrypted research tablet. From the former Conway National Laboratories."

Spiritwolf did a double take. "That was where… that was the mission that changed me, changed us."

Zero nodded. "The serial number in his communiqué matches one from the partial set of records we recovered after the mission. We think the data on the device has something to do with a synthetic substance that turns biological tissue transparent when exposed to electromagnetic radiation in a specific UV band somewhere between 125 and 170 nanometers."

Spiritwolf hung his head. "I can see why I'm being prepped to go on the mission. Is it… do you think this describes the process that rendered me invisible?"

The bear nodded grimly. "It sounds like it's related, at the very least. Canis and the Sciences team are working on theories to match the concept, but having the actual research data… well, there's no substitute for that. And once we have it, maybe we can find a way to make you visible again." He leaned forward and put his hand on the wolf's glove, squeezing gently. "I know you'd want that, the chance to be normal again."

The wolf raised his head and smiled sardonically. "What, and leave this perfect life I have behind?"

"Spiritwolf, I don't want to give you false hope. This could be fake, or a trap. But still, if there's any chance for you or the others to…" Zero's throat tightened. "You know what you went through before. I don't want you to be devastated if this isn't what we think it could be."

Spiritwolf nodded slowly to calm the *'what-ifs'* ricocheting around his brain. "You're right, and I'll keep that in mind. At the very least, by going on this mission, I'll prove that I'm still one of the best agents around, and that my invisibility is an asset, not a liability. We'll bring this guy to justice and if the data is useful, then we'll use it. If not…" He smiled and leaned back again. "It'll be nice to be out in the world again."

The bear waggled a finger at him. "Just be careful. We can't have you exposed – either as an agent, or as an invisible person. It's not going to be all fun and games."

"I guess hitting the nightclubs is out of the question, then." He held up his hands apologetically when the bear scowled. "Kidding. So what's the plan?"

Zero wrinkled his nose. "First, you need to shower. After that, we'll fly you to ABQ International, where you'll board a commercial flight for Germany. Dresden, to be specific. You're going to be under cover."

"So, traveling with the masses instead of on one our cushy transports." Spiritwolf pulled off the gloves, making his hands disappear again. "Don't you think that's risky?"

"Not unless you do something careless." The bear frowned. "In other words, be on your best behavior."

"It's nice to know that you're still worried about me." Spiritwolf carefully plucked the contact lenses from his eyes and put them back along with the veneers. "I'll be just fine, especially after I sign out a few of my favorite gadgets before heading out. And maybe a few others as well." He pulled off his mask and put it back in the box.

Zero eyed the wolf, now headless and handless again. "About that. This is going to have to be a low-tech op." He unbuttoned his trench coat and unfastened his shoulder rig, which had a Sig Sauer P400-C holstered in it. "I retrieved your piece from storage for your mission. You won't be getting much more than that."

"Really?" Spiritwolf left the gun where Zero put it on the table, a sign of his irritation. "And why are you hamstringing me if you want me to be successful?"

"You don't need a lot of high tech gadgets on this mission to be successful, Spirit. You just need to use your brain."

"Says the person not tasked with finding a well-hidden black market dealer and a tablet." Spirit folded his arms across his chest. "What's the real reason, Zero?"

The bear stared flatly at him. "MI-6."

A low whistle sounded from the invisible wolf. "I'm guessing you mean their Covert Anti-Terrorism and Security division. They're wrapped up in this too?"

"No, but you'll be moving around in Europe and I'd rather not take the chance that our tech could fall into their hands. And there are other organizations than the CATS to be concerned about, not to mention independent actors like this Black Dust person."

"Wouldn't our European cousins have the same problem? Or is this a trust issue with me?"

"It's not a trust issue, Spirit," Zero said gently. "And I'm not hamstringing you. I'm giving you exactly what you need to see this through. Okay?"

Spirit didn't say anything for several moments. "Okay," Zero finally heard him say. "I trust you."

"I know you do, Spirit. And I trust you, or else you wouldn't be going on this mission, believe me."

"Well, any other good news, now that we've established that our mutual trust will win the day for me?" the wolf asked with a soft chuckle. "Any other intel?"

"This Black Dust person is very smart. He moves around a lot and is a master at covering his tracks. After analyzing the few hot spots where he's been active, we think we've correlated his appearances. We think he's part of a band that's about to go on tour."

"'He' could be a 'she.'"

"That's for you to figure out. In any case, Black Dust will be in Europe to auction the data off to the highest bidder, as he – or she – has done before. We've arranged for you to be a personal trainer for the band's lead singer, so that you can snoop around on the inside, so to speak, and find out who the person really is."

"A personal trainer? Good thing I've got a muscular physique, then." Spiritwolf's clothes flexed into a double biceps pose.

Zero nodded and handed Spiritwolf a photograph. "Here's the fellow." He pointed to a shirtless white wolf singing at the top of his lungs into a microphone on stage. He had a flawless, chiseled physique and a tribal fur tattoo of some sort on each arm, with another one sprawled across his chest. "His name is Achilles. We'll get the rest of his file to you before you depart."

Spiritwolf's clothes sank back against the sofa and the invisible wolf studied the photo carefully. *He's… wow. He's gorgeous.* "So, let me see if I understand this correctly. My first assignment, my first time out in the real world in over a year, and you want me to be the personal trainer for a hot rock star wolf that millions of people adore and would kill to be in my position? Without drawing attention to myself?" He pictured the wolf shirtless and sweaty as he lifted weights. *Maybe with the lights out, we could…*

Zero smiled as he got up. "This should be a slam dunk for you, Spirit. Get in, be charming, find out who Black Dust is, and get out. We'll do the rest."

Spirit looked at the photograph again. "But what if the singer's Black Dust?"

"Then it will be a very short assignment." He patted Spiritwolf's shoulder as he passed by. "And speaking of short, I'll be back in an hour. Your transport to the real world leaves in ninety minutes." Zero looked back over his shoulder, suddenly serious. "Don't mess this one up, Spirit. Or it really will be a very short assignment." He exited and left the invisible wolf wondering if he might be better off not going.

* * *

The white wolf cracked his knuckles and coughed.

At the sound of popping bone, the two big cats froze in their tracks. Each was hastily dragging a large, heavy black case across the warehouse floor, making scraping sounds that echoed in the hollow space. They turned to face their irritated-looking employer with reluctance.

"Just stop," the wolf said in a commanding, but genteel tone. The tiger and the panther looked at each other uneasily, and set the cases upright again as he continued. "All right. What we have here, gentlemen, is some of the most sophisticated lighting equipment – and instruments – you'll find in this hemisphere. And you're dragging them like a sack of potatoes!" His eyes were hidden behind a pair of sunglasses, the California sunshine bouncing off their mirrored surface. But they could tell his gaze was unwavering, as was the stern tone in his voice.

"Sorry, sir, we just–" the tiger began.

The wolf held up his hand and cut him off. The flame-like tribal tattoo he wore on the white of his fur rippled upon his arm, exposed by the black tank top he wore. "Stop. Just do me – and the rest of the tour – a favor and carry them. One at a time, between you. No hurry, the plane won't leave without us. And breakages must be paid for gentlemen, and you know how absurdly expensive this equipment is. Slow down, all right?"

The panther – a slim fellow in a khaki shirt and black slacks – breathed a sigh of relief that they hadn't been dealt with more severely. Celebrity tantrums could be hell. "Yes, Mr. Achilles, sir. Slow as you say…" he replied, as disarming as he could manage. Then, with visible care, he stooped down as the muscular white wolf watched, and together with the tiger began to carry the case again toward the waiting truck.

"Roadies…" Achilles muttered once they were gone, his arms folded across his chest as a small army of others around him stacked similar cases, checked guitars, and operated forklift trucks carrying speaker stacks. He stood silent and contemplative, head bowed, watching the touring machine stirring to life once more. Glaring sunshine filtered through the vast skylights above and warmed the fur on the back of his neck; he was just relishing this last taste before they headed off to Europe when a shadow loomed behind him and blocked out the sun.

His ears pricked up as he became aware of the hulking figure that stood behind him. "You didn't tell those boys off too severely, I hope," a booming voice said inquiringly. "That's really my job, you know."

Achilles turned and came face to face – or rather, muzzle to trunk – with the speaker, an impeccably dressed elephant of a fellow with stunning white tusks. He had worked with his manager Regis for many years now – he knew him better than anyone – yet he could not help but feel dwarfed in his presence. At a height of two meters and a half, Regis soaked up the sun that shone upon shoulders so broad they looked padded underneath his steel-grey suit. The man was solidly built, but not really of muscle made – as a manager, he lived far too sedentary a life for that – but possessing sheer mass nonetheless that was built of broad bones, a healthy appetite, and elephantine genes. He had his hands in his pockets and fixed the wolf with an amused smile, the broad chest puffed out. Achilles shook his head and chuckled, impressed as ever that someone so big could still manage to sneak upon him unexpectedly. The man sure knew how to move sometimes.

"Just lending a helping hand. Plus I have my reputation as a… what was it PlayNow Magazine said? As an 'egotistical control-freak' to maintain."

Regis *harummed* deep in his throat, clearing his vast airway. "You are an egotistical control-freak. But don't let anyone hold that against you. It's gotten you this far, right?"

"Mmm," Achilles muttered noncommittally, eying up the tiger and the panther as they returned to collect more cases. "Sure is a big crew you've put together this time, Reg. I've never seen so many workers."

The elephant took the opportunity to slap Achilles' toned back. "You're in the major leagues now, my boy. Sold out shows in each venue, you know. It takes a big crew to pull these things off."

Achilles stepped away, taking off his shades at last. His eyes were piercing blue, radiating wisdom wrapped up in weariness of the way of being famous. "I just hope you've saved enough money for me after you've paid everyone out. I know you'll have saved enough for you…"

Regis laughed. "Don't worry, don't worry." He waved his meaty hand in the air as if physically dismissing the thought. "There'll be enough. You're going to enjoy this tour, I promise. This crew has the works – you've got a caterer, stylist, publicity manager, videographers…"

"I won't need all that, never have before. Get rid of them."

"But…"

Achilles ticked off the reasons on his fingers. "The venues provide food and we order room service. We have our own costumes and we do our own 'styling'. You're basically the publicity manager. And I get enough media exposure without needing a behind-the-scenes documentary. Get rid of the fluff."

"Very well. It will add more to the profit line." Regis folded his arms over his chest. "However, the personal trainer will still come with us, to keep you fit on the tour."

"What?" Achilles raised an eyebrow and the corner of his muzzle curled. "A personal trainer? Again? You remember what happened the last time."

The elephant coughed and looked away. "Yes, well, the trainer was a last-minute addition. Some people have been saying your physique is slipping with your celebrity comforts – and it has become quite integral to your image…"

The wolf's mouth dropped open, as if to object.

"…no, don't argue with me. I'm merely protecting the assets of my client. It's another part of my job, you understand? The trainer will be joining us at the first stop of the tour. It might be just what you need."

"We'll see."

There suddenly came a crash from the other side of the warehouse, and someone swore loudly. That was followed by a bellow from Regis so loud, Achilles' ears rang. "Idiots! Grant, if that was you, I swear… !" His face creased in a flash of irritation; the elephant certainly did not tolerate fools well. He gave a quick sigh as he turned back to his client. "Achilles, please excuse me… don't you worry about this lot. You just get to Oakland. The rest of the band will be meeting you at the airport." He turned back to the commotion and bellowed, "GRANT!"

"All right. Wait – did you bring my personal luggage?"

Regis fished around in his immaculately pressed suit pocket for a moment, then pressed a key into Achilles' hand. "It's in the trunk of the SUV. You take the ride. I'll meet you there with the rest of the gear." He stomped off, trunk swinging and knuckles cracking.

Achilles stood for a moment watching a humbled meerkat getting a decisive shellacking before taking a good long stretch – he'd been standing still for far too long – and heading off to the waiting SUV that was parked by an open shutter door in one of the quieter parts of the spartan building.

He looked over his shoulder, then quietly popped the trunk and looked inside.

Stacked neatly upon one another were a series of black suitcases that contained the wolf's necessary clothes, personal gear, and items that he always traveled with. His eyes sought quickly for the one bag that would be smaller than the others, his carry-on bag. The first stop on the tour was in Dresden, and it would be a long flight. He found the bag slumped in the furthest corner of the compartment and he had to reach in deep to fish it out. He looked over his shoulder again. Grant and Regis were now arguing – a sight to see, given their difference in size. But he turned away disinterestedly and unzipped the bag.

One by one he mentally checked off the different items – laptop, noise-canceling headphones, cell phone, toothbrush… and then his eyes fell upon a bulging compartment within the bag, separated from the rest. He reached inside and pulled out a shiny, flat device the size of an overly large calculator. He examined the tablet computer for a moment, cocking his head. His thumb stroked the dormant touch-screen for a moment, curiously, as if it were something precious, then he slid it back into its hidden pocket, once again surrounded by his other possessions.

Seemingly satisfied, he zipped the bag up again, sighed with relief, and placed the rucksack back with his other belongings. He swung down the trunk door and it closed with a satisfying click.

The wolf smiled. It was time for the show to begin.

Chapter One: Arrivals

Out.

You're out now Spirit. The word rattled around inside the invisible lupine's cranium like the last bullet in a spent box; *out. Out. Into the big wide world again where anyone and anything can happen, full of people, planes and malls… when all someone has to do is reach out, grab that fine silky exterior you're wearing and give it a tug and they'll see that there's nothing underneath, nothing at all…*

"Stop it," the broad-shouldered wolf said aloud, rebuking himself. Opposite him, over the top of a broadsheet newspaper, two yellow eyes appeared and the fox in the business suit they belonged to gave him an unwelcome look.

"I beg your pardon?"

Composed again, Spirit drummed his fingers on the chair and leaned back into the headrest. His gaze was cool and commanding. "Nothing." His features dared the fox to inquire further.

The fox seemed to recoil but a little, then with a crack of rustling newsprint, disappeared behind the paper again. Spirit relaxed, sinking back into the first-class airline seat with an audible hissing escape of air from the fabric beneath him. One lapse, that was all, one small mental lapse…

But he was out, there was no escaping it. He should have been thinking about the mission – digesting all the information from his official briefing with Zero before his departure, thinking about strategy, locality… Instead there was that word, and in it all his unspoken fears about his new state of existence. *Out.* He found himself coming back to it as sure as a tongue teases a loose tooth to see if it's ready to pop. Were they really sure he was ready to get back into the thick of things like this?

Was he even sure?

"Ladies and gentlemen, this is your captain speaking. We're about to make our final approach into Dresden International Airport. The weather here is slightly cloudy with some minor turbulence expected as we descend. We hope you enjoyed flying with…"

Spirit tuned out that gently crackling voice and turned his face to the window, seeing the lights of Dresden appear beneath him in the darkened landscape. Feelings of familiarity stirred in him seeing the city laid out like so many perfect dots, a map of streets and buildings – yes, he had been here before. Not this city – not on this flight. But in so many missions before as an Ultra… a stealthy landing in the dark.

Yes… an Ultra. I can handle this. I can handle anything.

He gazed at the fox hiding behind the newspaper once more and smirked.

And I'm out!

* * *

Achilles looked out the window and frowned. Their chartered jet had already begun the descent into Dresden, passing through heavy clouds that bounced them around a bit. He looked over at the elephant reading a paper at the crew station. "And why did you decide that this would be a good first stop for the tour?"

Regis' gaze shifted to his direction. "Ignore the weather. The venue's indoors."

"I know. That's not what I'm talking about." The white wolf picked up the guidebook from his tray table and waved it. "This place is in the former country of East Germany…"

"They're united now, you know."

"…and they're still recovering from it."

"They 'recovered' from that a while ago. What they're dealing with now is the same recession the rest of the world's had to deal with."

"How many people are going to be attending, at our ticket prices?"

Regis narrowed his eyes. "Careful, there. Money and business is my province. Music is yours. To answer your question," he continued, shifting position, "The arena is sold out and people are paying scalpers well over 2000 euros for a ticket."

Achilles blinked several times. "I would not have expected that."

"It's not surprising – there's quite a bit of industry here now. There's the old car plant – the 'Transparent Factory', I believe it's called. Semiconductors are big here, as are material science and related industries. And Dresden is home to three of the Max Planck institutes: molecular cell biology and genetics; chemical physics of solids; and the physics of complex systems. And they're attracting new business and industry all the time."

Achilles raised an eyebrow. "That's impressive. How do you know all of this? Subscription to Scientific American?"

"Among others." Regis smiled. "As I said, money and business are my expertise, but it helps that I've always had a passing interest in quite a few areas. Music, of course, and the arts, but also engineering and science."

"A jack of all trades."

"I prefer the term 'renaissance man.'" The elephant sighed, sounding more like a rumble as he re-occupied his larger seat across the aisle. "Well, we'll be on the ground shortly. And then I can be out of this damned seat again."

"It will be nice to walk around," Achilles agreed. He twisted around and peered back. Except for the panther, David, and Grant playing cards, the rest of the band as well as the roadies were still asleep in the 'economy class' seats. It was just him and the elephant that had been awake for the last few hours in the forward seats Achilles had christened "first class."

The plane broke through the cloud deck and past the rain-streaked windows, Achilles was surprised to see that a large part of the city was still green with farmland, parks, and trees, in contrast to the large metropolitan areas in the United States. A large river – the Elbe, his guidebook said – flowed through Dresden 'like a silver serpent sliding through grass'. He could see the modern architecture interspersed among the older, stately buildings that still appeared to be standing despite the horrific bombing of the city during World War II. Indeed, several burnt-out skeletons stood silent tribute to that era.

They landed and taxied to a hangar several hundred meters away from the main terminal where Achilles recognized planes from several different European national carriers. A big sign read "*Flughafen Dresden*".

"I know how much you value your privacy," Regis said with a shrug. He stood before the plane stopped; his bulk swayed noticeably when it finally did. "Enjoy it while you still can." The white wolf nodded and put on his black trench coat, then grabbed his carry-on bag and followed the elephant outside.

They were met on the tarmac by several uniformed officials, including a quartet of black and grey wolves toting machine guns. Regis motioned for him to wait while he strolled over to the welcoming party speaking in German. Achilles folded his arms over his chest and intently eyed an overhang as the rain pelted the top of his head.

Regis hurried back a minute later. "They're going to tow the plane inside the hangar so that we can unload the equipment out of the rain."

"That's nice of them."

"Unfortunately, they said that they needed to visually inspect everything for customs. I know, I know," the elephant said, raising his hands to forestall the coming protests. "It's going to take a little extra time, but there's no way around it, I'm afraid. They have instructions to be very thorough. But they did say that some of us could go on ahead."

Achilles' ears had turned back and downward as his patience thinned. He willed them back up and forced a smile. "You and me, then. At least we can get a bite to eat while the crew do what they do best."

"I'm afraid not." Regis shook his head, flopping his large ears. "I have to stay with them." The wolf felt his ears going back down. "Someone needs to be here to bail them out if they run into problems, and that's my job. Why don't you go on ahead and we'll catch up with you? You know which hotel we're at, and you should be able to make your way there easily on the tramway system."

"Are you sure you want your star performer alone in a big city? As much as I enjoy talking to the occasional fan that I meet on the street, I don't exactly want to be mobbed by paparazzi and a screaming horde all on my own in a strange town."

"They'll be looking for a large group, not for an individual." The elephant looked him up and down. "You're pretty well covered up. Put on your sunglasses and a hat and you'll blend in. You'll be fine." He leaned down and whispered, surprisingly soft given his lung power. "I know you're not happy about this, but I'm offering you a way out of having to wait for us for what could be a couple of hours. You'll be able to rest up before we hit the stadium to set up the equipment."

The wolf perched his sunglasses on his head and stared at Regis with his ice-blue eyes. "You promise you won't start the set-up without me?"

"Absolutely. You have my word." They both smiled and the elephant motioned over two customs agents – a black wolf whose uniform read "Ramsden" and a tall, nervous-looking squirrel with the name of "Kurtz". Regis said something to them in German and they nodded. "They'll start with you over at that table, there. We'll unload everything on the other side of the hangar, there." He pointed to where the plane had been towed. "If you run into any problems, have them get my attention."

"Right," Achilles muttered and followed the pair to the table. They both put on latex gloves and the wolf motioned for him to open his bag while the squirrel hurriedly assembled a dozen swabbing devices. Then they started removing the items inside. Occasionally, the squirrel would run the swab over a couple of items and dash back to a larger machine on another table, process the swab, and return for the next set of items.

"You are the rock star, *ja?*" Ramsden asked casually as he pulled out the cell phone.

Achilles smiled as disarmingly as he could manage. "What gave it away?" He shook some of the water off of his trench coat and ran his hand over his head fur.

"You are here, they are there." The black wolf pulled out the tablet next, followed by the laptop. "Very nice. Very expensive."

I don't need to explain myself to you, Achilles thought. His fur bristled under the coat. "Well, you know, I need to have the very best to write and compose my music." He looked over his shoulder at Regis, who was studying him intently. He rolled his eyes and gave a thumbs-up to the elephant; Regis nodded and went back to supervising the unloading.

"*Ja.*" After emptying out everything, including his clothing, Kurtz the squirrel made one last swab of the interior and went back to the machine. Ramsden put his nose into the bag and inhaled deeply.

"Excuse me?" Achilles reached over and tapped the wolf on the shoulder. "Just what do you think you're doing?"

Ramsden lifted his head and met the white wolf's threatening gaze with a cool look from his golden eyes. "Sometimes, our noses are capable of finding things that might fool the machine. You understand?"

Achilles folded his arms over his chest. "This is the first I've ever heard of that. We don't do that in the United States. It's considered impolite."

"It is standard procedure here. Kurtz!" The wolf turned and rattled something off in German. The squirrel's rapid-fire response seemed to satisfy Ramsden. "You are clear. You must come with me to finish the paperwork. You have your passport?" The white wolf nodded as he carefully arranged the items back in his bag. "Follow me. The office is down the hall." Just before leaving, Achilles glanced back and saw Regis waving his arms and bellowing something at David and the tiger. He shook his head and was suddenly grateful for being sent on ahead.

Achilles followed Ramsden inside and then through the first door on the left. The grey wolf padded behind a desk and sat, lighting a cigarette and loosening his tie. "Please, have a seat. Do you smoke?"

"No, thank you. Here's my passport."

"*Danke.*" The wolf thumbed through it for a good couple of minutes. "You are well-traveled."

"Well, it comes with the profession." Achilles was starting to tire of the questions, but he put up a smiling front.

"Of course. It must be difficult, being famous. It is, ah, lonely at the top?"

"I'm always with the crew, so not really, no."

Ramsden grunted and put out his cigarette before stamping the passport. He closed it and slid it halfway across the table. Achilles reached and as he touched his passport, he was surprised by the other wolf putting a hand over his.

"If there is anything else I can do for you – show you around our town, be your escort – you will call, *ja?*"

"You can give me my hand back." Ramsden released his hand and studied him carefully. *Creep,* Achilles thought. "Are we done?"

"One more item of business." The black wolf handed him a business card. "My number is on the back. In case you need me."

"Oh, I'm sure I can find my own way. Thank you and good day." He exited quickly, but not before seeing a smile cross the other wolf's muzzle. He closed the door and stepped to the side, pinching between his eyes. "That was weird," he muttered. Sometimes his fans could be strange but nothing this bizarre.

Achilles turned back toward the door and put his hand on the knob. Maybe it would be safer if he went back and hung out with the rest of the crew, even if it was going to take a few more hours.

But where was the fun in that?

Achilles readjusted his rucksack, turned and hurried down the hallway again. Fortunately, there were English translations underneath the German signage that he was able to follow through the maze of corridors. He finally found a pair of doors marked "Main Terminal, Level 0, Arrivals" and pushed through them.

He was instantly greeted by the sounds and smells of people making their way through the airport. A few glanced his way briefly, but most seemed intent on going about their business, whether arriving or heading upstairs to what appeared to be the departure level. Achilles didn't seem to be recognized but he didn't know long that would last, so he flipped his sunglasses down onto the bridge of his muzzle again.

The smell of food was making his mouth water. The center of the arrival level had a sandwich and café shop with a half-circle of people along the length of the bar eating and drinking. No doubt he could blend in and grab a bite, unnoticed. The front page of a newspaper caught his attention as he passed by a newsstand; it was in German, but there in the center was a picture of him performing on-stage, shirtless and raising the microphone victoriously above his head.

Maybe he could wait to eat until he got to the hotel. He'd had enough celebrity time to last the rest of the day and recognition in the airport could be disastrous, especially without Regis and the rest of the crew. He looked around. No one had picked him out of the crowd yet; a good sign.

"I think Regis said something about a tram system," Achilles muttered. Thankfully, he'd had the foresight to convert at least some currency from dollars into euros. He quickly found the directory and was pleased to find that the transportation area was just downstairs, with an auto-ticket machine near the bottom of the stairs. The white wolf located it easily and sauntered over, putting in a twenty euro note.

'Which line?' the text on the screen read.

"How should I know?" he answered back, faintly annoyed. He searched all the options and selected "Dresden Zone".

'Select time of departure.'

Exasperated, Achilles selected the most recent one and retrieved the ticket. Then he peered at the clock and saw that it was leaving in just three minutes on the departures platform. He kicked himself mentally and collided with someone as he turned to sprint for the train.

"Sorry… I'm in a rush to get to my train…" His voice trailed off as he stared at the large brown wolf that had bumped into him. He was similarly dressed in a buttoned-up overcoat and also wore sunglasses. And this person was staring at him – maybe the rock star had finally been recognized by one of the locals?

"My bad," the other wolf mumbled, sounding quite American. "It's been a long flight and I'm tired. Your train's about to leave." He pointed a finger to the platform and quickly lowered it as his sleeve began to slide back.

"Right. Thanks." The white wolf clutched his carry-on and ran like hell, barely making it inside before the doors closed. He turned and saw through the doors that the large wolf was still looking after him. "First the customs officer, now this guy," he murmured and shook his head. "I guess that's my welcome from the fans of Europe." He picked a seat on the upper deck that didn't have too many people nearby and settled down for the ride into Dresden.

A half hour later, Achilles was checking into his room at the Luxus Hotel Dresden. He thanked the well-dressed leopard behind the counter and strolled past the elevators to where the restaurant Sage was, since the other on-property restaurant, Version, was closed for renovations. The sign to the right of the large double doors showed that lunch had just finished and he would have to wait another three hours for dinner.

His stomach growled loudly. "Maybe they have room service," he snapped back at his hungry belly as he stomped back toward the elevators.

* * *

On the ground, passengers of every size and shape filed out of the plane ahead of Spirit; he let them pass, in no hurry. Those that had been traveling coach at the back shuffled through the first-class aisles at the front. Some stole jealous glances at the opulence here. They first noticed the wide legroom; their eyes trailing across the plush seats, the bigger television screens… and then they would notice the hulking wolf with the dark sunglasses arched against one of the windows watching them pass. They quickly looked away.

As soon as it appeared that the main group of passengers had gone, Spirit hoisted his small carry-on bag over his shoulder, and took a casual, ambling walk off the plane. His head was down, hands in his pockets, seemingly in no hurry at all. Through the thrumming disembarking jet bridge he emerged into a dull gray corridor lined with lifeless indoor plants, jetlagged tourists, and a number of identical doors with secure locks and marked 'Privat' with the English translation of 'Private' underneath. Spirit marched past them all, swinging his head from side to side occasionally. Overhead, signs in bold print and helpful arrows indicated that the passengers were headed toward immigration and customs, where both they and their baggage would be thoroughly analyzed before they could enter the country. The wolf eschewed the sections of traveling floor leading to this destination and instead swung left as a gaggle of cabin-crew passed him by. He stole a single look behind him before walking with purpose right up to a door that appeared no different from the dozens of others in the unremarkable corridor.

Only this one had special locks.

He put his face up to a pinhole barely bigger than the tip of a pencil; a small camera was automatically scanning his mask to create a three-dimensional contour map of his face. The retina scan wouldn't work, of course, so Zero had sent ahead instructions for the contour map to be used along with voice identification; "Agent Spiritwolf" was what he murmured to the hidden microphone. The mechanism took only a second to complete the assessment before a barely audible click from the other side let him know it had been opened. He slipped inside and closed the door behind him, leaving the mundane corridor outside with relief. He was still in the airport but he had entered a different place now, a Technology Enforcement Agency place. A little slice of home, as it were.

He walked down the small corridor; its walls so narrow that Spirit's broad shoulders almost touched the sides. They were white. The carpet beneath his feet – white. Everything was white. And the corridor led to a box-like room, and in that room there was a desk. Sitting at that desk, and watching him approach, was a tigress dressed in a black business suit. She had turned her attention from the television monitors that covered the eastern wall of the room from top to bottom the moment Spirit had closed the door behind him. Each screen displayed the image from a CCTV camera. Hidden ones, no doubt. He walked right up to her and flashed her a toothy smile. "*Guten Tag.*"

"*Guten Tag,*" she answered back, her voice purring in a thick Deutsch accent. She folded her claws neatly together and placed them upon the bare desk in front of her. "Welcome to Dresden, Agent Spiritwolf. We trust your flight was uneventful."

"The flight was fine," came his matter-of-fact reply. To an outsider, this might have appeared to be small talk – but it was all business when the TEA were involved. At least as far as the European divisions went, where formality and custom were still prized. She was checking nothing unforeseen had happened so far. "My bag?"

"As usual, to avoid your armaments and equipment causing a stir in customs, it has already been taken off the plane. You will find it waiting for you in Ixak's office. He's the acting senior director in Europe." Her head indicated a door to her left.

"…beg your pardon?" Spirit asked; for a moment there she sounded like she was trying to cough up a hairball.

She gazed at him unfazed and tapped her claws almost absent-mindedly on the desk. Her attention was drifting toward the monitors again. "Ixak. That is his office."

Spirit couldn't help but blink. "That's… a very unusual name for an agent. That doesn't even sound German."

Just then the tigress' lips curled into a smile, and he was overcome with the feeling that he was in the presence of a man-eater – looking at her, he saw her life, the path that led her here, the struggles she had faced. Once a fresh-faced recruit, she knew she was as tough as the boys in the academy, but for some reason she always felt the need to prove herself just that little bit more - because she was a woman. And this molded her into steel. And there was no greater pleasure to such a woman than having one over the males of the species - like now. "Ixak… is a very unusual agent, even by our standards. You'll see. He's waiting for you now." She smiled more; Spirit wondered what the joke was.

Nonetheless, he gave her a simple nod. "Thank you, agent." His eyes flicked to the panel of screens monitoring the airport inside and out, and then he strode past her desk to the closed door. She swung back on her chair and watched him, striped tail twitching, eyebrows arched into a gesture that read as: 'Well? What are you waiting for?'

To deprive her of further satisfaction from his hesitation, he turned the handle and stepped inside.

He was greeted by an office as plain and ordinary as one could imagine; the furnishings consisted of two gray filing cabinets; low, sickly-yellow lights from old strip bulbs; a kitset desk stacked with a few papers and a computer terminal; a wall clock; another indoor plant; his own large black bag sitting on the floor against the far wall; two metallic office chairs, one in front of the desk, one just behind; and behind that was the… thing.

He didn't recognize it as a person – not at first. He looked again and for a second comprehended that he was seeing the back of a large, broad-shouldered person wearing a black cape. Only not a single crease marked its surface. It was more like a plate of armor. And just above the place where the fellow's head was… danced two pieces of black rope… twitching like they were alive… like they were protruding from him. As he entered, they swiveled toward him – as if they could detect him.

All this in less than two seconds – and then the person himself turned to greet the wolf face-to-face. Any kind of salutation Spirit could have uttered died in his throat; he found himself staring slack-jawed, his vacant insides again on display, this time without Zero to remind him to close it. He was staring in disbelief at a beetle. A two-meter-tall giant *goddamn* beetle! He took a step back as its compound eyes fixed upon him, noticing a speaker strapped to its insectivoral maw; the air was filled with a whirl of sharp, rapid clicks, and then issuing forth from the speaker came a robotic, crackling voice: "Greetings, Agent. I welcome you to Dresden, and to Europe."

Finding himself caught completely off-guard for a rare moment, Spirit found himself lost for words. "I… ah…"

Sharper clicks sounded. Again the speaker crackled into life: "Two things before we get down to business. First, you close your mouth. Then, the door." The insect sat down in the chair and placed scabrous hands – two pairs of them – in front of him, clasped patiently. Spirit obeyed while his mind reeled.

He had never been in the presence of an insect before; few people alive today had. Spirit remembered the history lessons woven through the TEA's tactical training classes. The world was teeming with mammals, reptiles, birds, and amphibians but arthropods were rare. They had nearly been wiped out ages ago when brutal warfare often led to genocide. The truly tragic part was that the last great conflict had been over a simple misunderstanding, rooted in the common belief that they couldn't even speak. Centuries passed and with a strengthening foundation of civilization, researchers uncovered the arthropods' language, their culture – but by then it was too late. They had all gone. And so they were virtually unknown – no more than a couple of thousand left perhaps, scattered among the billions of other species that had emerged victorious. The beetles hid in the shadows and kept to themselves. Anyone could live an entire lifetime not even knowing they were even there, as had been evidenced by the surprise of many in Spiritwolf's class regarding this revelation.

Which was precisely why the wolf found his encounter with Ixak so unexpected and bewildering. But apparently the bug was well used to this kind of reaction; he sat in his chair, cool as a cucumber, until the door was closed. Then he waved his hand toward the water cooler Spirit hadn't noticed behind one of the filing cabinets. "Have a drink if you need to collect yourself. I suppose Clarice just sent you in here with no hint at all who you would be dealing with. Her little idea of a joke – though I am not sure if the joke is supposed to be on you or me." He leaned back a little, carapace clacking together. Was he sighing? It was hard to tell. "We do not always get along, the tiger and I; I think she perhaps likes me having to explain myself."

The idle chatter certainly helped clear Spirit's mind; he sat down in front of Ixak, nonetheless never taking his eyes off him. He said the first thing that came to mind. "You shouldn't have to."

The wolf was subjected to a small amount of pain as the other agent emitted a high series of clicks that alternated in pitch – later he realized Ixak had been laughing - "How funny of you to say so!" The speaker warbled. It was unsettling how devoid of emotion that robotic voice was, when those huge eyes glimmered with such fire and passion.

"Funny?" He eyed his bag coolly. He was more than a little bit curious about the insect – it was the first he had met after all. But he was also keen to get on with his mission. He hoped this chat wouldn't last too long.

There was hesitation from the agent sitting opposite him – the antennae – for that was what the two pieces of 'rope' were twitched violently as he clicked slowly. The voice-machine seemed to take a long time in translating a reply. "…I have read your file."

Immediately, Spirit felt the hackles at the back of his neck stand on end, as he always did when he became aware that someone else knew about his invisibility, and not of his own will. It was like having someone read your personal diary. Not that he had ever kept one of those, but…"That's fine," he heard himself say, his voice growing a little hard and cold. "You did your homework – you know what's passing through your little corner of the world. But what has my… nature got to do with anything?"

"Forgive me; I was struck by the irony when you said I shouldn't have to explain myself. You of all people should realize why I do."

Spirit's jaw clenched. "I don't explain myself."

Ixak rose, his many limbs moving casually, and as the beetle came around the desk, picking up the heavy black bag, full of everything an Ultra could possibly need, and then some. Spirit noticed how the beetle lacked any kind of clothing. The carapace covered everything, and the wolf shivered at how unnatural that seemed. The clicks were low and knowing. "You do not explain yourself because what you are remains hidden." A many-faceted eye settled upon Spirit, and for a moment, it was as if the bug was looking past the facade of the mask and the contacts, and seeing him as he truly was – as no one had seen since his accident. "I have no such luxury."

Now Spirit rose from his chair. He was face to face with Ixak now. He didn't much like the view, and he found the beetle's physical presence as looming as his own. "So I'm supposed to feel lucky, is that it?" He growled sternly.

Two clicks. "You might." The antennae waved as if to ward him off. He raised his claw. "Your bag."

Spirit took it gratefully. He felt his skin prickling under the confines of his accoutrements. "Are you done?"

"Quite." The insect had seated his large bulk again. He appeared to turn his attention to the computer monitor. "Clarice will show you the way out, our organization is at your disposal if you should need anything else during your stay here. You may help yourself to supplies from our stores before you leave."

Spirit hefted the heavy bag over his shoulder with ease. Its contents clanked a little reassuringly. He turned to the door. "Oh no," he replied. "I have everything I'll need right here."

* * *

Topside, the wolf was back in his element, and he swiftly navigated his way to the airport's transportation area; Dresden was an uninspiring place, and the weather outside was as gloomy as he expected from Europe. The civilians passed him by in their gray shawls and rain-spattered jackets, and paid no attention to the wolf in the buttoned-up overcoat and long-sleeved shirt that lumbered through their midst, and he was too lost in his thoughts to pay much attention to them.

I'll have to thank Zero for not mentioning Ixak later – seems Clarice isn't the only one who likes a joke. Am I the only one in TEA that isn't aware that there's a giant cockroach lurking in our basement? He reached inside his pocket and pulled out enough euros to pay the ticket-vending machine in front of him, the lines of the city on the screen already familiar to him.

And he was a moralizing creep too. Shaking his head, Spirit stepped away as another lupine ran up to the vending machine, and looked at the ticket he'd just purchased into the city center. Bare minutes until the next one departed. He glanced at one of the display screens in the terminal and shrugged. Not to worry – he'd catch the next one. These trams departed every fifteen minutes, and he wasn't in any hurry. No sense in running off–

His train of thought – and some of the air from his lungs – was knocked out of him when a white wolf suddenly turned and collided with him. "Sorry… I'm in a rush to get to my train…" came the fellow's swift apology.

It took all his willpower to force down momentary panic of some rip or tear in his outfit when a jolt of energy surged through him, carried by the awareness of just who he was looking at. Oh, the singer had disguised himself all right, if you can call a pair of sunglasses a disguise. But there was no mistaking that body, or that face. He had spent what little time he'd had to prepare by researching the 'mark' he was going undercover with – he just hadn't expected to encounter Achilles so soon. Or like this.

He became aware that he was staring and spoke quickly to cover himself. "It's all right. It's been a long flight and I'm tired. Your tram's about to leave." He pointed toward the platform; his sleeve raised up and exposed the fake fur briefly before he pulled the fabric over it again. The muscular white wolf made a dash for it, and Spirit watched him leave. He was still watching him when the tram left, and saw Achilles staring right back at him. *Well… the connection's been made now – for bad or good.* He would have to ponder the curiosity of the celebrity being all alone and heading to the city by himself later. He had a tram of his own to catch. He could wait.

Fifty-two minutes later, he rose from his seat as the tram rattled to its stop somewhere close to his hotel. A clutch of other passengers – whey, dull-furred creatures by American standards – headed toward the exit at the same time as him. He joined a line of folk alighting from the small step of the tram to the concrete, shuffling along one at a time. A small mouse boy crowded in front of him, while a frail woman, a wrinkled mare who looked ready to be put out to pasture took halting steps just behind.

He had just made the small step for himself, and was allowing himself to look forward to some small measure of respite in his hotel room, when he heard the woman behind him give a muffled "Oh!" of anxious surprise.

He turned just in time to see her mis-time her step, as the elderly are prone to do, and lose her balance completely as she was about to exit. A teenager behind her gave a gasp of horror as they both realized at the same time the old woman was about to fall face-first to the concrete – probably breaking her brittle bones in the process. Only Spirit moved faster. Instinctively he shot out his arm and caught her mid-fall – breaking her momentum and giving her something to grab on to.

That something was his hand.

For one panic-stricken moment, he regretted his swiftness – for as she grabbed hold, he grasped as if her very life depended upon it. He felt the epidermal bio-glue that held the glove on his fingers pull and give way. He felt it going as surely as an egg rolls downhill. *Oh God – she's going to pull it off, pull off my arm – and then they're all going to see that there's NOTHING underneath, and she'll scream and…*

Another voice ricocheted through his mind, even as she caught her balance again and the glue began to snap back, holding fast. This voice was horrified, apologizing, pleading, begging, and it was his own. *"…please. Help… you have to… help me… I can't… be… like this… I can't be nu… nothing…"*

Nothing.

His eyes snapped wide, he took a deep breath. She was all right. Saying something, some thanks in German. He didn't care – abruptly the wolf barged aside those that had stopped to witness the commotion, and took off down the street at a veritable run. A few streets later, he realized he was shaking.

* * *

It was much later when he was finally in his hotel room. The wolf held his head in his hands, looking down at the floor. The voice he had heard was an echo from the past; his despair, his shock and dismay from the aftermath of the accident that had transformed him. Confusion, then the growing fear, the paranoia, anger, and self-loathing, all from the dreading realization of permanent invisibility – it was crushing, a fate worse than he could have imagined for anyone. It had nearly destroyed him but with help, he had managed to rebuild his identity, his very soul. And he had never heard that voice again – those horrified, frightened cries – until today.

He lifted his head again and turned toward the window, looking out at the sleeping city.

All right, Black Dust. You want to hide the information that made me this way? You want to play the game of guns and spies? Well, bring it on. I'm coming for you – and my cure!

Chapter Two: Visages

As exhilarating as it was to walk about again in public, Spiritwolf found himself treasuring every moment spent alone in his hotel room.

He had gone out later that evening, primarily for reconnaissance, but also to immerse himself more deliberately into crowds than he had at the airport or on the tram. Certainly, the less nerve-wracked he was about groups of strangers, the more successful he'd be in his mission. And so very much hinged on the success of this mission. With that in mind, he had steeled himself and, summoning all the confidence he could muster, he had confidently walked out the front doors of the hotel.

Spiritwolf had only lasted a half hour on the outside. He had easily found the gym where he was supposed to meet Achilles – the 'PalaceSport', only a ten minute walk away. It was equipped as well as he remembered; he had been to other franchises in different European cities. Finishing with his reconnoitering, he crossed two more streets and found a corner deli that was still open. Despite the butterflies in his stomach, he had been rather hungry and although the smells made him salivate, he decided to pick up something for later. He reminded himself that he no longer had the luxury of eating whenever he wanted; he would be leaving himself vulnerable by satiating his appetite. He went inside and purchased a freshly made ham and cheese sandwich and a bag of potato chips, along with a bottle of water. He had even conversed briefly with the shopkeeper, a burly bear who had emigrated from the U.K. several years back after a messy divorce. Spirit's encounter had gone well – no alarms, no odd looks, no mistakes. Everything normal.

The wolf left the establishment and wandered into a nearby alley. He was met with throngs of people pulsing their way through a crowded outdoor market. He had only gotten a couple of steps into it before the intense commingling of scents, the rising tide of echoing conversation fragments, the pushing and shoving, began fueling his claustrophobia. Panic set in after getting stuck between a rather obese feline and an older Dalmatian who just wouldn't move out of the way, with a group of shouting college students lumbering right for him. Spirit had nearly bowled the dog over in his run back to the hotel, drawing those stares he had taken pains to avoid earlier. Once he got back to his room, off came his clothes and visibility-rendering accoutrements. He had stood behind the large armchair by the mirror for a good ten minutes, digging his hands into the soft leather and staring at the reflection of the empty room, panting wildly. He should have been able to handle that.

"I am so screwed," his voice muttered. "I can't... I can't do this." Sure, he'd made some progress but maybe Zero really had rushed things along for him. This was too soon, maybe, and it had been too long since he'd been in the world. The TEA were insular to begin with and the incident at Conway hadn't helped with that.

"I can't fail." He didn't sound very convincing. He wanted to succeed, but dealing with others... with normal people... was going to wear him down. There were so many of them and they were all strangers, all of them against him. He couldn't take on the whole world; it would be impossible.

One meltdown, just slightly worse than tonight's, was all that it would take for him to be finished.

"Fuck that," his voice growled. He didn't need to go through the charade of being a personal trainer to some spoiled superstar and skulk around in the hopes that *maybe* he could figure out who Black Dust was and *maybe* find out where he'd hidden the tablet. He was an agent of the TEA, dammit, one of the best in the world. He would just go up there and *take* the damn thing. He was an agent and he was invisible. How the hell could anyone stop him?

A real smile broke across his muzzle for the first time since arriving in Dresden. The more he thought about it, the more he realized that this would, indeed, be a very short assignment.

A short assignment. That was also what Zero had said this would be if he failed. His smile was now gone. He had almost given in to his impulsiveness, almost gone out without a plan, with nothing but his 'who-the-fuck-cares' attitude and a whole lot of invisibility. He had no clue about how he'd get into people's rooms. No thought about how to search bags without anyone noticing. No idea what to do if he got trapped somewhere or accidentally revealed himself. In other words, he had nothing.

This had almost been a lapse in good judgment, not a meltdown but another kind of failure brought about by the overconfidence that stemmed from what he was. He desperately wanted to talk to someone from home. Zero, Master Song, Greystorm, Dash. He knew what each of them would say, though. *Be patient.* Even Morey would tell him that. *Be patient and watch. Learn. Then strike when you know you can't fail.*

He held his hand in front of his face and waved it back and forth. "All of this and I can't do a damn thing with it," his voice said with more than a hint of frustration and impatience. Fine, then. He would wait for an opportunity to present itself.

Day one was concluded with eating the food, followed by a hot shower and peaceful slumber under luxurious covers that didn't care whether or not he was invisible.

Hours later, he was relaxing in the armchair, now moved to the window, and looking out over the busy town below just waking up. Dawn was erasing the night, bit by bit, and giving the eastern sky a healthy rose-colored glow. This was always a favorite time of his to pause and reflect on the coming day, just as twilight was the perfect time to contemplate the break between what had happened in the light and the coming excitement of the night.

It really was a wonder that he ever got any sleep.

Spiritwolf knew that today would be no dry run. Still, he did not completely find fault with his reaction last night; it had at least been an honest one, in the face of returning familiarity in dealing with normal people. He had tested himself and passed, though admittedly not with flying colors. Just facing fear for even a few minutes was a success that he could build on. Crossing the threshold back into normalcy would not be easy. *Be patient.*

For now, he could be that.

The wolf looked down through his hands at the photo that appeared to float just above the oddly flattened seat cushion. It was a picture of himself, before the accident, with Zero. They were a bit younger in the picture but those few intervening years seemed much longer because of his time spent in recovery. Before becoming an agent, he had been ordered to sever any ties that linked to his past and so everything had been disposed of, wiped clean. The irony was that a personal photo should never have been taken in the first place because of that same protocol. Zero had been there for him after his mission at… well, just before he had joined the Ultras and the photo was a reminder of that time, of their friendship. Just like his codename, it grounded him to who he really was, which was why Zero had thrust it wordlessly into his invisible hands not too long after the accident. That was the only time he'd ever seen Zero truly angry with him.

Spirit studied his younger self and traced his outline with an unseen finger. *We never imagine how our experiences change the way we'll look back at our past, do we?*

His own past had been quite the learning experience. Spiritwolf had started off in the TEA with minimal engagement, the barest interaction with other agents. Others thought him aloof but really, he just didn't know what to do beyond what was required because it felt like a façade, like he didn't fit in no matter where he went. He had always been an outsider, so it was easy to keep the rest of the world at arm's length. Then things had changed, first with Zero, and then joining the Ultras. They were the first team he felt like he had belonged to; they were his family. It hadn't been easy at the beginning but he had made steady progress opening up to them, accepting and caring for them as freely as they did for him. And now Spiritwolf returned to those lessons he had learned, vivid in his memory because of the photo. This time, despite his condition and his newfound fears, it would be easier to deal with. Those past experiences in becoming part of a family had laid the groundwork for his new identity as a personal trainer and he felt himself sliding into the role like putting on well-worn clothing. The important thing was that, despite his exterior layers and whatever visage he chose to define his appearance to the world, the core of who he was would remain intact. He could associate with – become friends with – anyone.

He got up and put away the photo, then padded over to the mirror. "One year, two months and seven days," his disembodied voice told the equally empty reflection. *Just one day at a time, Spirit.* Every little bit helped.

Several hours later, after breakfast and a short nap, Spiritwolf re-attired and left his room. He was now dressed in his workout apparel – loose-fitting sweat pants and a sweater, socks, and sneakers. He had paced himself slowly while dressing; he had checked every inch of his appearance in the mirror for chinks in the armor and he made sure to secure his TEA equipment in the locked duffle bag in the closet, away from prying eyes. His wallet, credit card, passport and room key were all accounted for; there was nothing left to do except head out to his big day.

He crowded into the small elevator in front of the well-dressed occupants and ignored their condescending stares; it would have been easy to return the frown and intimidate them, given that he was thirty centimeters taller and probably weighed twice as much as the biggest of the three. Instead, he departed the lift with a snicker and a "Good afternoon, gentlemen," and exited the hotel in better spirits than when he'd arrived, despite the light rain that was falling from the grey sky. His large umbrella would protect the mask and gloves while his sunglasses filtered the natural light to something he could easily tolerate, even without the cloud cover. After a moment enjoying the clean scent of fresh air, he turned left and casually strolled down the street.

The image of Achilles was prominent in his thoughts. In addition to the dossier that Zero had provided, Spirit had found many indie rock video interviews of him on the web. It had not been difficult to find, which he had found amusing. The rock star was very outgoing and confident, as though he owned the world. And he looked it, too.

The white wolf's charisma was hard to ignore. Spirit stopped at the first intersection and pondered his game plan while waiting for the light to change. Watching the videos, he had surmised that Achilles wasn't exactly the flirtatious type – that, coupled with his own condition, made it unlikely he would gain the wolf's trust that way. Spirit didn't know the first thing about music or instruments or singing, so that general area was ruled out. Just about the only commonalities he could leverage were their physiques and working out – weightlifting, cardio, maybe even something more relaxing like yoga. No swimming, though. Maybe their travels around the world would serve as a conversational springboard. Commiserating about foreign locales could be nostalgic. He would have to study how Achilles interacted with people – his manager and his band mates, his confidantes, especially. He would also need to pay attention to what the white wolf said. Anything could provide an opening for him to get closer.

Spirit rolled his eyes. It was like trying on different masks until you found the right one. *If there's one thing I ought to be good at by now…*

The whirl of his thoughts seemed fueled by the exhaust from the automobiles. After a year in isolation, the smell was much more noticeable and, to a large extent, nauseating. How could people stand the smell of oil and gas this close? He made sure to keep a few people between himself and the street – he had purposely chosen to stand toward the back of the impatient crowd waiting to cross the street, anyway. As he surveyed the shivering, wet bunch – all miraculously attired in the same black apparel – he realized that his preoccupied mind had ignored the masses accreting around him. And now? His heart was beating faster but there was no expectation of a sudden scream from someone, no overwhelming urge to run from the press of the crowd, no desire to take everything off and disappear. He was one of them, just another wolf on the street corner, waiting for the light to change.

Score one small victory for him.

Normally, Spiritwolf would have been very concerned about leaving himself vulnerable to some kind of sneak attack from an enemy because of his wandering thoughts. Mental lapses could be fatal in his line of work; he had seen it happen too many times. He was fairly certain that no one, including Black Dust, knew he was an agent and that he was coming for the data. In a way, the anonymity made him invisible. Spirit smirked at the irony.

The light finally changed and it took several seconds for the crowd in front of him to clear before he started walking again. He took care to avoid the puddles and continued toward the gym. Upon reaching the entrance, Spiritwolf folded his umbrella and shook it carefully before entering.

"English?" a female river otter behind the desk said with a beaming smile. The wolf nodded. "I'm sorry, sir. We are closed for the next few hours and will reopen this evening. I can recommend another gym nearby, if you like."

Spirit shook his head. "Thank you, but that won't be necessary. There was supposed to be a private workout session scheduled here?"

"Ah, yes." She checked a clipboard. "Your name?"

"Sean Pellards," he said slowly, to ensure he gave the right answer. As nervous as he was, it would be easy to make a mistake with something as simple as his cover name. That was, of course, the name in his passport and he had it out and ready, just in case she needed identification.

"Mr. Pellards. Of course. You are the last to arrive – the rest of the guests are already waiting upstairs."

Guests plural?

"The men's lockers are on this level, toward the back. The stairs are back and to the left."

"Thank you," Spiritwolf said and padded down the corridor past the entry desk, then made his way up the narrow staircase. He could smell three males, one of whom was wearing expensive cologne. At the top, he heard voices and would have hung back to listen but for one stair's creak, loudly protesting his weight. He sighed when the voices stopped talking and steeled himself as he walked into the room.

The weight machines were all quite familiar, as was the rack of dumbbells by the wall-length mirror. The gym was well-equipped, which was arguably the main reason he had liked this particular chain back in his former life. The lighting was another reason – he disliked being blinded by overhead lights while exercising. Here, the room was illuminated at nearly the same brightness as the dour sky outside. The cool air was refreshing; gyms could sometimes be much too warm and it had been one of the million smaller worries that had run through his mind in the last couple of hours.

"Are you going to just stand there or are you going to come over and introduce yourself?"

The familiar sound of the white wolf's voice brought Spiritwolf's attention back to the trio standing in a far corner near the flat benches. He noted the emergency exit in the wall opposite from the stairway – just in case a hasty exit was needed – and snaked his way through the labyrinth of workout equipment. He appraised each member of the group in turn. Achilles was instantly recognizable from their chance encounter yesterday at the airport. The white wolf was dressed in a black tank-top which partially revealed the tribal tattoo design on his chest, not to mention his well-toned body. His smile was genuine and there was an air of curiosity about him as he peered back at the large wolf approaching. The large pachyderm in the business suit was also difficult to miss; his demeanor suggested intense scrutiny though he was far less subtle about it as Spiritwolf was. It wasn't too difficult to guess that he was the source of the cologne smell. The third was a badger, attired in was could only be considered classic "rock wear" – jeans, an old T-shirt with grease stains on it, and sandals. He was big enough to have lifted at some point in his past, but his midsection showed that he was pretty far out of shape.

Nothing to worry about, thought Spiritwolf as he approached. *You've got them right where you want them. Just remember to keep your cover, literally and figuratively.*

"You must be Mr. Pellards," the elephant said in a deep voice and stepped forward to shake his hand. Spiritwolf nodded and hesitated, thinking about his glove being pulled off. His fear grew as he waited for his hand to be released from the strong grip. "My name's Regis."

"Spiritwolf," he blurted, to everyone's surprise. *Shit, shit, shit. Calm the fuck down before you completely lose it, agent.* "It's, um, my stage name. Just call me by that name, okay?"

"As you prefer," Regis said without missing a beat. "That's not uncommon for the rest of our entourage. Single-word names are all the rage these days, it seems."

"Didn't I see you at the airport yesterday?" Achilles had also stepped forward. He clapped the wolf on the back and Spiritwolf winced – not from pain but from the sudden contact. Despite its brief duration, it felt rather intimate and therefore unnerving.

"He doesn't say much, does he?" asked the badger with his arms folded over his chest.

"I do," Spiritwolf finally mumbled. "Achilles… ?" The white wolf nodded. "Yes, that was me at the airport."

"Well, then, thanks very much for the advice."

"My pleasure." Spiritwolf noticed that Regis was watching the exchange closely and kept his muzzle down to keep his mouth from opening too much. Being taller than Achilles and the badger helped, though the same could not be said of the elephant.

"Advice? At the airport? He's not a stalker in disguise, is he?" the badger asked.

The white wolf turned slightly. "Cain, this is my new personal trainer." That elicited a snort from the badger.

"He's certainly big enough."

"I've checked his references thoroughly." Regis' quiet assurance seemed to unnerve Cain as much as it did Spiritwolf, though probably for different reasons. "You started off at Gym Mania but only stayed for a year before leaving to give lessons to private clientele. You fractured your clavicle a year ago and only recently recovered from the surgery."

"You've read my website," Spiritwolf said with a smile.

Regis stepped closer and stared down the length of his trunk at the wolf. "You were also in several bar fights during college, one of which caused both retinas to detach, which is why you're sensitive to light and usually need to wear sunglasses, even at night or indoors. Before Gym Mania, you were dismissed from several other jobs for reasons ranging from insubordination and excessive tardiness to destroying property – an executive chair and desk, if memory serves – and verbally abusing the CEO of Java Time."

Spiritwolf shrugged. "He deserved it – he was an idiot and tried to bully the rest of the staff where I worked." Cain was now smiling along with Achilles and Spirit silently thanked the Sciences team for putting the bad boy stuff out in places that only a determined search would find. The background was a personal touch from Zero.

"The reason why I agreed to your hiring, Mr. Spiritwolf, is because of your impeccable record as a personal trainer since then." The elephant's warning tone was unmistakable. "If I find that you've engaged in… tantrums that affect the band's publicity or cohesion negatively in any way, you will not only be fired, but I will sue your ass for every penny you have and then some. I will make it a personal project of mine to have you destroyed and humiliated. Have I made myself clear?" Regis stared hard; with his tusks fronting his bulk, he appeared formidable even to Spirit.

"No clearer than I am right now," the wolf replied smoothly. "I'm here to help Achilles get into shape, nothing more. I haven't been to a bar since working as a personal trainer and I am not very keen on large groups of people, so you won't have to worry about me going out and embarrassing the band."

"Ah, he'll fit in just fine," Achilles said, almost lazily. "What do you think, Cain?"

"Sounds like he's ready to roll with the tour," the badger replied. He began padding to the exit. "And now, if you'll excuse me, I need to get tuned up for the show. That, and I'm allergic to exercise." He waved. "Welcome aboard."

"Thanks." Spirit turned to the elephant and took off his sunglasses, squinting against the sudden brightness at the imposing figure. "Are we good?"

Regis regarded him thoughtfully. "Yes," he said and followed the path Cain took toward the stairs, though considerably more effort was spent squeezing his bulk between machines.

"Try not to be offended by Regis; he said pretty much the same to me and I'm supposed to be the star of the show!" Achilles unfurled his towel to lay it on the bench. "Let's get started – I've been dying for a decent workout!"

"Hold on a moment." Spirit set down his umbrella and then put on his sunglasses again before facing the other wolf. "We should take a few minutes to see where you are in your workout level, what might work for you given your concert schedule. Things like that." Inwardly, Spiritwolf was amazed at how well things seemed to be going; his earlier panic seemed to have disappeared upon crossing the initial threshold. His demeanor had thus far betrayed nothing of his true mission.

"And here I was hoping to start pumping iron," Achilles shrugged good-naturedly. "Well, let's get it over with, then. Ask away."

"I'm not familiar with the life of a rock star, so you'll have to educate me a bit. What's your typical day like?"

The white wolf laughed. "Well, most of it's spent in preparation, really. The roadies and Regis start early, the band wakes up later in the day – this early afternoon workout is akin to a morning workout for anyone else. We go down to the venue late in the afternoon to do some tune-ups, as Cain mentioned, and sound checks and maybe rehearse a song or three. Then it's off to the dressing rooms for a light dinner in and then we typically hit the stage by about eight or nine. The set's a good hour and a half to two hours, then another ten minutes for encores. We decompress and some of us hit the town but we eventually go back to the hotel; it's usually dawn by the time the last of us stagger back. Then it begins all over again the next day, unless we're traveling to a different city."

Spiritwolf nodded. "Busy, then. It sounds like you don't have much time to yourself?"

"Oh, here and there," the white wolf waved his hand. "After a show, I usually just head back to the hotel and stay there, and I usually get up earlier than everyone else, except Regis. But yeah, life on the road is demanding. Which I guess is one reason why I need to keep up with my workouts – enhances my personal appearance, I suppose."

"..."

"Hey, are you there?" Achilles waved his hand in front of the other wolf's muzzle, startling him from his thoughts. Spirit had been putting together a mental profile of everyone and their interactions; it had distracted him to the point of ignoring his 'client'. He berated himself wordlessly and chalked it up to being out of practice while promising to tighten it up.

"Yeah, sorry about that. I was trying to come up with a workable routine for you." He took a deep breath. "One more pair of questions – how long and how often do you want to work out?"

"Well, I usually lift weights for about an hour. Somewhere around that should be fine."

"Good, because that's probably about all we're going to have time for." Spiritwolf scratched his chin thoughtfully – he used a light touch, ever aware of the mask he was wearing. "You're wanting to keep toned rather than build muscle mass, right? I think if we do cardio every other session, mixed in with weights, it should be good to start with. We can adjust the routine after a few days if we need to."

"Well, I get a fair amount of cardio while on stage." Achilles' grin was infectious and Spiritwolf remembered the photo from the paper, showing him in mid-leap. "So maybe I should bulk up a bit, more like you." The white wolf was now unabashedly studying Spiritwolf, making him feel suddenly self-conscious.

Don't panic, don't panic, just stay calm and maybe…

"How on earth did you come up with the nickname of 'Spiritwolf', anyway?" Achilles suddenly asked.

The bigger wolf laughed, more relieved than anything else. "Sorry, it's not you. No one's asked me that before. Everyone just assumes that I…" He suddenly realized the door that was being coaxed open by the conversation. *Shut it. Now. Don't do this to yourself, Spirit, don't let down your guard.*

"Well?"

"Oh, nothing," Spiritwolf said nonchalantly.

"It's not nothing," Achilles insisted. "There has to be something behind it. You want to be called that and not 'Sean' for a reason."

"Says the person called Achilles with a badger named Cain in his band. What were your real names, again?" Spiritwolf saw brief annoyance flash across the other wolf's face and attempted to mollify him. "There's not much to it, or to me, for that matter. Seriously." *Yeah, I really should have stuck with my original cover if I'm trying to keep from being discovered. Might as well have put up a flashing neon sign above my head with the word 'INVISIBLE' in big bold letters. I am such an impulsive idiot sometimes…*

"Huh. All right," was Achilles' eventual response, paired with a nod that relieved Spiritwolf. He lay back on the bench and looked up at the bar, not seeming to see the other wolf getting set to spot him. "I've already put the weight on for my first set and increment by about five each thereafter."

"Seems kind of light, don't you think? I'd recommend ten instead. After all, you said you wanted to bulk up a bit, right?"

"Only a bit. I don't want to end up as big as you." The white wolf unracked the bar and drew it down to his chest and back up for the first repetition. Spiritwolf watched the rhythmic motion, noting Achilles' breathing, making sure his form was proper. A few reps into it and his attention diverted to the last few exchanges and Mr. Rock Star's sudden bivalve imitation. The assignment was a tricky one – he knew that going in – and his first snag had already unraveled their initial trust.

"Eleven… twelve!" Achilles heaved the last one and Spiritwolf caught the bar, guiding it back to the rack. "How am I doing so far?"

"You're looking fine," he said absently. The white wolf smirked and raised an eyebrow. Spiritwolf waved his hands. "No, no. I meant that your form… dammit!" Achilles grinned even wider. "I didn't notice any mistakes. You've got the hang of it, for sure. Next set?" he pleaded, throwing himself on the mercy of his audience of one.

"Of course," said Achilles and waited for his trainer to put the appropriate amount of weight on. "Are you sure you can remain focused?"

"I… yes, of course."

"Good." The white wolf adjusted his position on the bench and then looked up. "Because my last trainer decided to admire himself flexing in the mirror and I nearly tore a pectoral muscle because he'd missed the spot. He was fired as soon as Regis found out, of course."

"Oh. Sorry to hear that."

"Don't think that will be a problem with you, though." Achilles grunted as he unracked the bar again. "Not with the way you cover yourself up."

"Yeah." It hadn't even been meant as a jab, but Spirit felt his mood immediately plummet. After that, he mumbled acquiescence to Achilles' directions and answered sparingly about other kinds of chest exercises. In between dumbbell flys and the wide grip press machine, Spiritwolf took a moment to stare at the mirror as Achilles went for a water break. His masked face frowned back at him and spoke volumes of the walls he'd built for himself. He recognized them, the old foundations upon which this new layer was being constructed and knew he'd have to open up somehow if he was going to gain the wolf's trust. But how could he? There was no clear path forward through the layers of secrets that made up his life now. A soft growl of frustration escaped and he attempted to cover it up by coughing before finally meeting Achilles at the machine, this time with more of a smile. *A fake smile for a fake muzzle, I guess*, he thought darkly.

"Something wrong?" Achilles asked after the first set.

"Am I going to get fired if I admit something's on my mind?"

The white wolf laughed. "You've been paying attention while spotting, so, no. But you do seem preoccupied and I really appreciate honesty with my mates in the band. You're part of the team now, so I kind of expect similar from you." Spiritwolf nodded, a little more stiffly than he would have liked, but at least he smelled like he was being earnest. Achilles continued when nothing further was said. "Do you need to work in a few sets with me? I suppose that I should have asked you about that from the start."

"No thanks, I'm fine. I keep my workouts separate." Spirit winced at the flicker of annoyance that crossed Achilles' face. "With good reason."

"Which is?"

Spiritwolf thought for a moment and when he spoke again, this time his smile was genuine. "I'll tell you when we're done with your workout. It's wrapped up in your original question about my nickname." *And I think Zero would be just about ready to kill me at this point.*

That seemed to have completely stunned Achilles; Spiritwolf saw it only for the briefest of moments before he began his second set with more determination. The bigger wolf added five more kilos for the third and final set. Strangely, he had no sense of worry despite not knowing how this was all going to play out. Improvisation was a game that he played well. Usually.

Achilles finished and emerged from his seat in the machine, toweling his shoulders vigorously for a couple moments while Spiritwolf returned the plates, neatly avoiding the temptation to ogle. "All right," the white wolf said, sitting back on the flat bench where they'd started at, ears perked forward. "I'm ready."

Spiritwolf took off his sunglasses and took a deep breath. The smell of the gym, of working out, sweaty canines prickled his nostrils as he launched into his story. "I... when I was getting into fights and all that... I was a bit of a loner, never really fit in, couldn't connect with anyone," he rambled awkwardly, weaving fiction with personal memories. "I began to lose myself."

"Go on," Achilles prompted, listening raptly.

"One day, after a really bad night where some things from my past came to a head, a good friend of mine paid me a visit and we got to talking and he... helped me. He set me on a better path. He was the one who nicknamed me Spiritwolf and the name's stuck. It's a reminder of his kindness to me."

"But why? Why the name Spiritwolf? Why not Thunderheart or Swiftriver or some other name like that?"

Spirit sighed and considered the irrepressible white wolf who, despite his own fame and fortune, seemed to be greatly interested in his rather personal story. *Can't stop now, he'll be too suspicious.* "My friend told me that I was moving through life as though I was a spirit, rather than as a real person. I was confused at first but the more I thought about it, the more I realized he was spot on. I had withdrawn – I was never very social to begin with, but, in the weeks leading up to our talk, I had well and truly isolated myself from life. You can't really live that way for very long, you know? Anyway, afterward, I tried to change that, in small steps, and it got better. I made new friends when I joined a new group at one place I worked, and opened up to them. It was one of the best times of my life. So, it's taken a while and although I've grown accustomed to people, sometimes I still prefer to be by myself. That's why I still exercise on my own. I promise you, Regis doesn't have anything to worry about." *There, that should help get me into his inner circle.*

"I think," Achilles said quietly, "you'll find that most of us in the band have faced these kinds of situations before. I'm pretty sure that Cain recognized it in you, as did I. We're not anarchists, but we do rebel in our own way, which had the effect of bringing us together and using our expertise to make, if I may say, some of the best damn music on the planet. When we're performing, our band is our family."

Spiritwolf nodded. The Ultras had been much the same way, oddly enough. They had been his family.

"Though I think you're going to have to get out a little more often than you do. And I know just the thing." The white wolf grinned that charismatic grin again. "You ought to come to the show tonight."

Spiritwolf's face would have gone white if it hadn't already been invisible. He forced his features into a smile so that he wouldn't appear taciturn. "I don't know, rock star. Crowds really aren't my cup of tea."

Achilles shook his head. "Spirit… do you mind if I call you that?" Spiritwolf nodded acceptance. "I meant a backstage pass. That way, you can meet the rest of the band and some of the roadies while avoiding the screaming thousands."

Thousands. Spiritwolf barely repressed a shudder as the other wolf continued. "You can stay in our dressing room and watch the concert from there – we've got video feeds set up and everything. Just kick back and enjoy yourself. No one will bother you, I promise."

This time, Spiritwolf was first to offer his hand to shake. "Sounds like a fun time."

"Great. I need to shower before the concert – you don't have to wait for me, big guy. "I'll have the pass set up for you by the time you get there."

"Are you going to be okay on your own? Shouldn't I escort you back to your hotel?"

Achilles pondered that. "Technically, I don't think that was part of your contract, but I'm sure Regis would throw a fit if you didn't. Tell you what. I'll skip the shower until we get back. You didn't know I was in the same hotel as you?" He seemed amused at Spiritwolf's surprise.

"I hadn't, but I guess that makes sense." Actually, he had known that Achilles was in the same hotel, up on the suites level; that had been one of the first things he'd looked into, in order to go searching for the tablet. "I'm ready to head back whenever you are."

The white wolf nodded and started walking toward the stairs. "I just need to get my duffel from the locker downstairs."

Spiritwolf cursed his shortsightedness; if Achilles had just gone and showered, he could have simply stripped off his clothes and searched the bag here. If only he'd had the foresight to realize that the white wolf would have a bag with him, it would have meant one less thing to search. *Other opportunities will come*, he reassured himself. *In fact...*

"Fine. We'll meet at the front desk, then?" Achilles said from the stairway and then descended without waiting for the answer. Spiritwolf followed, albeit more slowly. He felt unsure about attending the concert, even if it was well away from the stage, before the screaming throng of faceless fans. After all, his successes in the last twenty-four hours had been interlaced with failures. But, with Achilles and the band on stage, it would be a prime opportunity to scout around. If nothing else, he should stick close to Achilles so that he would be there when Black Dust made his move. He wasn't sure whether the rock star was the seller, but he couldn't disprove it, either. Spiritwolf was beginning to like Achilles, which meant with his luck that the rock star probably was the seller.

"All set!" The white wolf had changed into a leather jacket, jeans and some kind of industrial-looking boots. The duffel bag was slung over his shoulder and Spiritwolf tried to not look too longingly at it. What he wouldn't have given for a handheld scanner just then, to check the bag remotely. Canis' symbiotic nanites probably could have infiltrated the bag – probably could have done the whole hotel, come to think of it. *No, those things would probably devour the tablet after they found it, and who knows what else...*

"Earth to Spiritwolf!" Achilles appeared a bit perturbed at being partially ignored yet again. "What am I, invisible?"

That one word caught his attention like nothing else and he had to surreptitiously take a deep breath to put a lid on his rising panic. "Ah. Sorry. I was just thinking about the concert. Never been to one before."

The white wolf's jaw dropped. "You've never been to a concert? Of any kind?"

"I... don't get out much, as you said." Which was true. The TEA taught him and the other agents various aspects of culture, and the latest trends and fads for their deep cover assignments. But, as it had been demonstrated before on other missions, it was one thing to watch it on a screen and another to experience it. "Sorry," he said and sheepishly shrugged his shoulders.

"Then it'll be a learning experience for you. Don't worry – if it gets too much, you can take the van back to the hotel. I'll let Grant know."

"Thanks. I might take you up on that." Achilles exited through the glass door and Spiritwolf followed. They didn't say much on the short walk back to the hotel other than chitchatting about the weather and their next venue, in Rome, but Spiritwolf got the feeling that Achilles was really warming up to him, despite his earlier misstep. *Seems like a nice enough guy,* he mused as he got off the elevator and waved to the white wolf before the doors closed. But there was something nagging at him about this whole thing, some veiled truth he couldn't quite penetrate. He knew it was his training that was telling him this, his instinct that sensed the discontinuity. His rational mind couldn't grasp it, though, and rather than force it, he filed it away and entered the sanctuary of his room.

A few hours later, after a luxurious hot shower and another nap, he dressed in his casual attire of a black polo shirt and matching slacks with soft shoes that felt more like sneakers. Like the other field agents in the TEA, his clothes had been engineered to be light and durable, allowing him to move easily while making barely a whisper when moving against his fur. Canis had apparently come up with a few improvements to them recently; the new coat, for instance, wouldn't quite stop bullets, but it was now difficult for a knife to slice through. No doubt this tech would also make it into the public domain in twenty or thirty years and get branded with some nonsensical name, its true usefulness lost to the secret history of the TEA.

Spiritwolf performed a final check of his appearance after concealing a few small must-have items on his person as well as his pistol, and then made his way into the lobby where the driver was waiting. The rest of the band would have gone ahead, according to Achilles, so Spirit relaxed and enjoyed the quiet ride over to the arena. He looked out the window when they unexpectedly passed the main entrance and forced himself to remain calm until the driver circled around to the back, where a meerkat was jumping up and down excitedly and chittering away at a rhino carrying a large trunk over one shoulder. The van stopped near a side entrance to the arena and the driver handed him a lanyard with three laminated cards that identified him and the areas he could go. The van sped off as soon as the agent stepped out and shut the door.

"Valet parking certainly has changed since I've been away," Spiritwolf said with a bemused grin and checked that his Sig was still concealed before marching over to the guard at the arena entrance. The black bear perused the pass for a moment before buzzing the door open for him. No metal detectors, thankfully.

"Glad you could make it." Achilles greeted him in the large lounge area with a friendly clap on the shoulder that set his insides fluttering again. The white wolf was doing warm-up stretches in his concert attire, looking very much like he did in the newspaper photos, although with a mesh shirt instead of bare-chested. "Welcome to the band. Guys, this is my new trainer, Spiritwolf. Spirit, you've already met Cain." The badger waved lazily from a couch where he was flipping through channels with a bored expression. "This is Garrick," he pointed to a cat tuning his guitar and ignoring them altogether. "And Les."

The green-scaled gecko was in front of a portable keyboard and played a quick five seconds of 'Flight of the Bumblebees', which his incredibly long fingers blurred through, and then straightened and bounded over to the bigger wolf. "Hey there," he said in a slightly raspy voice and lightly punched Spirit's chest. "Solid AND gorgeous. Wanna get together afterward for a private encore?" the lizard asked, licking his lips.

Spiritwolf smirked. "Thanks, but I wouldn't want you to bite off more than you can chew." The reply was enough to get even Garrick to snicker.

Les was about to volley back a retort when Achilles put his hand over the lizard's mouth. "Okay, you're done with the flirting. And yes, he doesn't know what he's missing," he added in response to the muffled squeak that escaped. "I'm sure he knows that. We're on in less than ten minutes, now, so make sure you're ready to hit the stage. Got it?" Les nodded and winked at Spiritwolf before bounding over to a wardrobe rack and putting on a vest to match his white pants.

"I'll just stay in here, then?" Spirit said slowly.

"Nah, if you do that, you'll be bored in about five seconds." Cain found his drumsticks and pointed them at the door. "You should walk around. Don't buy from the concession stand, though – we get everything we need brought here. Just ask Theo outside."

Achilles nodded and finished off with one final stretch. "And like I said, if you need to go back to the hotel, just have them get the van. Everyone ready to hit the stage?" His band mates nodded and filed out into the staging area where people had already congregated – there were security and other venue staff speaking in odd mixes of German and heavily accented English; photographers with wildly snapping cameras; the stage manager, a tall heron perfectly suited to her role; other musicians that appeared to be the warm-up act coming off stage; and a few other privileged super-fans with all-access passes patiently waiting to get decent footage of the band on their cell phones. Those in the last group were starting to scream and yell and it looked like the band members were feeding off of them – Cain raised his sticks and bellowed and Les was bouncing up and down. Garrick's tail was waving. Even the white wolf's eyes gleamed as he turned back. "Are you… ?"

"I'll be fine. Go!" Spiritwolf shooed him with his hands and Achilles turned toward the thundering masses. Spiritwolf took off his sunglasses and watched the monitors closely: the other band members had assumed their posts in the dark and when Achilles leapt onto the stage, the whole arena suddenly flashed with pyrotechnic brilliance that saturated the video equipment for a good five seconds. Spiritwolf chuckled quietly and leaned back in a chair to watch the concert.

The first couple of songs were interesting but he could already tell that the music wasn't quite his taste. It had a good beat but he couldn't quite make out all of the lyrics and some of the performance seemed a little avant-garde, even for him. Halfway through, after he was sure that the food and water he'd had at the hotel had been digested, he decided he would scout around. Achilles' duffel was the first thing Spirit had looked for, of course, and he wasn't surprised that it wasn't around; it was no doubt back at the hotel. He considered going back sooner rather than later; it would be relatively easy to break into Achilles' room and everyone was here at the concert, so there wouldn't be any surprises. Or would there be?

You must be patient and study your enemy. Impulsiveness can lead to reckless behavior. That hadn't been Master Song speaking to him; it had been Zero, lecturing to him in the Ultras' operational briefing room. Spiritwolf nodded in agreement with his memory – reconnoitering the tour's logistics to understand who did what when would be invaluable later. Spirit doubted that Black Dust was going to be active tonight; his modus operandi suggested one of the upcoming events would be when he'd hold the auction. He still had time.

Spirit opened the door and nodded to the guard standing outside. "Need to stretch my legs," he smiled. The German Shepherd beckoned him to come over and checked his pass before closing the door behind him. The wolf gave him a quick salute, and then padded off. *No easy exit through there. I need to find a place where I can take off my clothes if I need to.* He casually strolled down the hall past a few people still lingering, including a couple making out at the bottom of a stairway. He ignored the heavy breathing and slight moaning and forced his senses to sharpen into the empty area ahead. No one seemed to be there and he checked for security cameras before proceeding cautiously. The first door that he came to opened into a broom and cleaning supply closet, a perfect place for changing, especially since it had no lock on it. The next couple of doors were locked, unfortunately. As he approached the corner, he heard the soft tread of feet that were not his own and he sidled up to it, heart pounding, nerves ice-calm. He pulled out his sunglasses and angled them toward the edge.

The curved reflection showed someone moving further down that corridor, away from him. He withdrew the shades and peeked like a kid on Christmas waiting for Santa. A black wolf was at the end of the hall, muzzle sweeping from side to side as though searching –

– Spiritwolf's memory triggered. The wolf was a security guard he'd passed earlier on the way to the dressing room, 'Ramsden' had been the name on the tag –

– before rounding the next corner.

Spiritwolf froze, his mind processing the moment like a camera snapping a captured image. Was this Black Dust? The fur color was right – but then, fur coloring might have nothing to do with it, unlike his own weirdly appropriate code-name which had been chosen almost two years before that fateful mission. If his target really was the black wolf, though, then what part was Achilles playing in all this? Was he innocent or was he in league? Or could the rock star be Black Dust? The name seemed sufficiently avant-garde; societally contrarian for a white wolf. Too many possibilities and not enough data.

The roar of the crowd surged behind him and the agent suddenly realized he didn't have the luxury of asking questions – the answer was in the form of the black wolf growing more distant with each passing second.

Chapter Three: Static

The line between Germany and the United States was hazy, shrouded in a whispering hiss that made normal speech difficult to hear. But the artificial mechanical voice came through loud and clear. Discarded were the clicks. "It has been a long time. Too long."

"Yes, old friend," came a tired, rumbling voice on the other end of the line. "If you'd still consider me such." A dismissive, but nonetheless embarrassed cough sounded from the American speaker, causing a crackle and a roar across the wire. "You can probably guess why I'm calling you now."

"Yes, Zero. Your agent landed here yesterday. I would have known he was one of your men even if I had not read his file."

There came a disembodied growl. "That information was *supposed* to be internally classified to the highest level and sealed. How did you…"

"Do not worry about that now," the robotic voice interrupted. "I have my ways. They do not call us 'bugs' for nothing, after all. But I know your man, yes."

A moment's quiet. The lull filled by a hiss. "What did you make of him?" the gruff speaker finally asked.

"He seemed capable." It was a cold statement, removed of emotion. But then he continued. "A bit stand-offish, but considering his background, not surprising. He was not here for long. He is flying solo on this operation, is that not so?"

"He is, for the first time in quite a while. And…"

"Even you have your concerns, alpha-bear. I understand."

There was another distinctive grumble from the American, though laced with more humor than the last. "Well, you seem to have kept up your habit of interrupting me, at least. Glad to know you haven't changed. But yes, I do have concerns. And so, I'm about to ask you a favor."

"And this is?"

Zero sighed. "I need someone to keep an eye on him for me. I don't want him to know – this is why no one from our side of the world can go. Least of all me."

There was a pregnant pause. The background noise took sway. And then the crackling speaker came through again. "This is what you want me to do? Watch Spiritwolf?"

"I wouldn't trust or ask anyone else," came the reply, punctuated with sincerity. "He mustn't know about any of this. You'll have to be discreet."

Now it was Ixak's turn to grumble. This didn't translate through the crude technology of his voice-speaker, but it came through as a vibrating drone like the hum of a wasp. "I do not often go into the outside world. Secrecy for a giant beetle does not come easily."

Zero chuckled. "But you didn't immediately say no, which means you're going to do it. Don't worry, I'm sure you have your ways. They don't call you *bugs* for nothing, after all..."

"You presume much." Cold. "But I will do this. For him, however, not you. We have not made our amends yet. But there is still time for that, once your man's operation is over."

"Yes Ixak. I understand. Soon, then." The older bear's voice became tinged with sudden humbleness.

"Then I shall make preparations to depart. Goodbye, alpha-bear."

"Goodbye... and thanks."

But his words went unheard; the line from Dresden was already dead. And across the world screamed the static.

* * *

One of the first lessons given to TEA field agents when they enter reconnaissance training was that of speed; Master Song in particular was also a strong advocate for lack of hesitation, despite his relatively recent employment with the organization. So when Spiritwolf saw the incongruous sight of the black wolf disappearing from view, he seemed to actually hear the old fox snarling in his ear. "*Move quickly!*" the sensei urged.

And so he did.

Amazing how it all comes back. Amazing how I've missed it, Spirit allowed himself to muse as he lightly but assuredly strode down the corridor with the guile of a predator. One moment relaxed, now his body was on edge, nerves tight as a wire in an instant as swift, sure adrenalin surged into his blood. Already as he walked his senses were attuned to everything in his environment, which had narrowed to that corridor and the interconnecting rooms. His own footfalls and the feet of his quarry were his main focus but there was the rest: the sound of thundering applause way in the distance, the gossip of roadies, hairstylists, and stage crew muffled behind dressing-room doors; a toilet flushing; ice in a glass; breathing. But it was all static, static, nothing to hear and nothing to do with the sound of two feet marching ahead of him. He felt a small breeze that tickled the follicles of hair even under his masked muzzle, a whisper of air from an open doorway somewhere in this windowless, grey place. He had the scent.

As he got to the corner that he had first sighted his quarry disappearing around, he instinctively flattened against the wall, ears raised. The footfalls were continuing their steady pace, which meant the fellow had no idea he was being followed and was completely unaware of Spirit's presence. The agent was just considering risking a glance to check upon where the wolf might be headed, when abruptly he heard Ramsden stop. Then came the distinctive clunk of a door-handle being turned.

He resisted the urge to then look around the corner to see *which* door; that would have been a crass mistake. The first thing anyone up to no good would do, just before going where they shouldn't go, is to check that the coast is clear. He could still remember the time during one of his earliest missions with the TEA, that one of his rookie teammates *had* poked his head around in a similar situation, and had gotten his muzzle blown off for his trouble. That little mistake had made the job rather messy and complicated from that point.

Better not to look, then. Unless…

What if he just took off his mask and peeked around the corner?

In the two-second pause as he waited and held his breath while Ramsden decided to go through the door, Spirit was struck by the thought that, for the first time, he was entering a situation where his current… condition could assist him in a way that had never been possible before. He could now look openly down the passageway without getting his face shot, and why stop there? Strip down completely and follow everywhere, just two steps behind. The target would never even know.

The old fox in his memory spoke up again; he remembered the words clearly. They were spoken to him right at the very start of his rehabilitation, and they formed the root of every lesson his sensei had to teach him after that. *"You have a condition Spirit; but it is an ability,* not *a crutch. And one day, you will understand the difference."*

His ears tingled as he heard Ramsden go through the door and he winced as Master Song's words suddenly struck deep, so long after being spoken. Of course he knew how to tail a target without being seen, invisible or not. In the arts of stealth, he had excelled as well as any other – and that was *before* the accident. It had taken from him so much. He would not allow it to rob his skills and training, take away everything that made him who he had been.

He heard the door swing closed on its hinges. Spirit chuckled and rumbled softly, readying himself. His target would not see him.

He turned the corner and followed.

* * *

"Fuck you! Thank you! *Danke* and Goodnight Dresden!" Drenched from head to toe, eyelids dewdropped with water, Achilles stood before the baying audience panting and barked his final words. They ricocheted about the stadium like a shotgun blast and left behind an echo of his final *fuck* long after he had left the stage.

He half-tumbled down the stage steps and disappeared behind the double doors that led to the artist's backstage area in something like a daze, a clouded state brought on by the exhaustion and excitement of the performance. People were clapping him on the back, congratulating him on a great show. Someone was jabbering something in German in his ear – a fan, a member of the press? He didn't know, didn't care what was causing the commotion all around him. He pushed them away and staggered on until he reached his dressing room. Once there he found the nearest chair and collapsed.

"Oh… God," he panted, chest still heaving. He closed his eyes and let the chatter swell over him like a wave. He was only gone for a moment. When he opened them again, his drummer, guitarist, and head technician had crowded into the dressing room with him.

"Encore tonight, chief?" Cain, his rhythm-maker asked. The badger was a broad fellow, carried a bit of extra padding around his waist, but man could he bang those cans like a mean one. Even though they had played for nearly two hours solid, and Cain was looking more disheveled than Achilles was, behind his eyes he was still wired and raring to go. The stage manager waited expectantly for the answer, while Garrick, still cradling his instrument, looked distinctly nonchalant about the whole affair. That was just like Gar; onstage he was a real demon, a wild unpredictable cheetah shredding chords and tearing around the place with an unpredictability that kept each performance fresh – that was precisely why Achilles had hired him. But when he wasn't under the lights, he was the quietest, passive thing. In fact, he could be so taciturn and blank that it was unnerving to spend much time around him. Now they were doing their second tour together, the wolf could see why the cat's stint with his previous band *The Black Spots* hadn't ended well. Only the fourth member of their outfit, Les, the keyboardist, was absent. And that was just like Les too; the lizard was probably already off somewhere getting blown by the guy (or girl) with the hottest lips.

"Not tonight, boys," the white wolf replied, gesturing toward the doorway where the sound of thousands of hands clapping for more sounded in unison in the distance like thunder. "I'm broke. First night – we did good. Right? Next time. Man, those Germans were crazy! I'm beat."

"Me too," Garrick grunted and then sloped out, squeezing past the hangers-on crowding outside the doorway.

The stage manager followed him, already speaking to the rest of the crew through her head-mic. "*Nein.* You heard me, no encore. Stage lights down, guys. Burt, house lights on. Let's get this shit broken down. *Was ist… ?* You there. Grant, is it? I don't care what happened earlier – you need to stop messing around with those people and get your own team organized…"

Cain surveyed Achilles with his arms folded across his chest and rolled his eyes in a conspiratorial fashion. "Getting too old for this eh? I thought with that fitness-freak body of yours, you'd have *heaps* of energy… quitter." He emphasized his point with a grin.

"Cain, buddy, I'll never understand where you get your energy from." He sunk deeper in his chair, the buzz starting to lift from his over-stimulated brain. He massaged his temples and grabbed a nearby towel, drying himself a little.

"One day I'll tell you, boss. Les and I – when I find ol' bug-eyes that is – we're gonna see the nightlife, check out what this place has to offer. Sure you won't come with?"

Achilles looked up from his post-show toweling and smiled back, which from his bent-over angle momentarily looked like a leer. "One day, I'll come. But that's not going to be today. You guys have your fun; I'm going to go back to the hotel, as usual."

Another trademark eye-roll from the mustelid. "As usual…" He ceased leaning against the wall, and shrugged his shoulders, straightening his sleeveless leather jacket as he went. "Night, boss."

Cain's exit signaled the arrival of a dozen more people, an entourage he could not name – fans, record-label guys – he sighed and closed his eyes and went away again. And suddenly – surprisingly – found himself wondering what Spirit was up to now.

* * *

Midnight in Germany; a black night in Dresden, streets empty save for the hauntings of the homeless, who lurked in vacant doorways and under bridges like ghosts in the shadow. Achilles stood alone, a silhouette in the window of his hotel, looking down upon them from the thirteenth floor. The room behind him was dark and dimly lit, shaded flickering blue from the light of the lone television set in the corner, soundlessly playing out a 24-hour news channel. From a war in a desert far away, grainy footage of soldiers fighting in the sands came and went; protesters marching in the capital followed; men in suits in the seat of power shook hands, looked soberly out into the camera lens and promised either one of two things – death or peace. But Achilles ignored them; he rested his forehead upon his arm and, muzzle pressed against the glass, watched an old fox in a greasy grey coat rummage through a dumpster in an alley. It was some kind of world they had created, all right.

He turned away, feeling like a voyeur, and looked at his unused bed and the clock on the bedside table. Rubbing the side of his face, he sat down on the side of the bed, and clicked off the television. He started to take off his boots, slowly unlacing them as if he were in no hurry. Nothing in the room changed, but suddenly he paused halfway anyway. For a moment he sat still, fingertips still wrapped around the laces, knee pressing against the muscles in his chest. He looked at the clock again, then began to tie his boots back up again, reversing the movements he had just made.

With the certainty of an insomniac, the white wolf rose, collected his wallet and keys, put on his sunglasses, and silently slipped out of the door as if he feared that something would follow.

In the lobby, the night concierge raised an eyebrow, but said nothing as the rock star strode past, and disappeared into the night.

He did however, reach for his phone.

* * *

Two blocks away from the hotel, walking past shutters scrawled with unintelligible graffiti (*WEISEN WAHN* cried one; *Schwarze Staub-Aufstiege* another), Achilles began to feel the inexplicable ennui that traveled with him on tour lift a little. Yes, he had done this before – often, in fact. Stardom was a gilded cage; to walk in the street unaccosted a privilege renounced with the signing of contracts and compensated with money. Money! Was it for that sake that he performed, or art? The line had been blurred; and so he would walk, for hours, in countless cities down countless streets trying to find the pattern to his thoughts; to be alone.

To feel normal.

He turned the corner at a boarded-up gas station, the pumps in the forecourt ripped out and missing, the bare, cracked concrete looking raw like a gum line missing its teeth, and found what he was looking for. Just down the road there was only one light shining forth, the unmistakable yellow tint of neon upon plastic laminate, the cheap plastic glow of 24-hour dining at its finest. He eagerly approached; it was not shelter or food he was looking for, but a finishing point. Somewhere to pause for a while. It was a small building but from the large window you could see that it had a line of plastic dining booths disappearing down the back.

He entered the shop, the door creaking in a protesting whine, as if disgruntled to be disturbed at this hour. He was blasted by fresh, humid warmth, and the aroma and tang of stale fryer grease. Standing on the floor – already noticing how it stuck to the sole of his boots when he shifted his weight – he stared up at a menu made only comprehensible through the application of pictures. He licked his lips and became aware of the server behind the counter, a rough-looking gorilla, looking at him expectantly. "*Guten Abend*," the beast grunted.

"*Guten Abend*," Achilles dryly responded in kind. He stood in silence examining the menu for some time, hands in his pockets, trying to figure out what he could get that would keep him here for a while. He noticed that he wasn't alone; two teenagers, their faces mostly hidden by their hooded sweatshirts were occupying the nearest booth, eating something that looked like a burger, but still nothing like any of the photos proudly displayed on the neon menu. The gorilla grew tired of waiting first, and leaned over the counter at the wolf expectantly.

"*Was wünschen Sie..?*"

"*Ein… Ein Würstchen…*" he replied with only half confidence. He squinted at the menu again. "*Mit Zwiebel… ?*"

This seemed to be enough, because then the tired-looking ape punched up the purchase. "*Gut. Neun euro, bitte.*"

Handing over a few notes from the roll Regis had indiscreetly shoved into his hands after their arrival, the gorilla in turn handed him a few coins as change for his trouble; then turned his back upon Achilles and began to make a racket with the clutter that passed as the kitchen. Feeling assured that this was normal, the wolf sloped past the teenagers and secreted himself in the booth that was at the very back of the shop. He had his back to the door, and occupied himself with a newspaper he found under his table; he couldn't read it, but at least he could look at the pictures. Unsurprisingly, he turned a page and found himself staring at his own visage, a photo accompanying an article promoting the concert he'd just performed in full color. He'd been captured vaulting across the stage at another gig, midway through a cry into the mic with his lips curled into a snarl, looking fierce. Making himself comfortable inside the diner, he chuckled.

Yet he had only been there for a minute when he heard the door creak open again, and someone stepped inside. He resisted the urge to look around; he turned the page away from the picture of himself and sat staring at a wall of German text even as footsteps creaked stickily but assuredly toward him. His skin prickled in instinctive surprise and he recoiled as the newcomer didn't stop, but actually came and sat down opposite him; he saw in one moment the large, broad shape approaching out of the corner of his eye; the next, he was looking into a familiar face looking unimpressed and seriously into his.

Spiritwolf.

Achilles blinked in surprise, taking off his shades at once. "Spirit? What are you…" he began to say, but then noticed something amiss. Apart from Spirit's stern expression, the corner of his muzzle – right at his lower lip – was puffy and swollen as if it had been struck with a good amount of force. The large wolf was holding his arm stiffly, as though he'd hurt it somehow. Yes, in fact, it looked very much like the wolf he'd been thinking about earlier had been involved in a fight. "What are you doing here? What… what's happened to you?" he continued.

Spirit cracked his knuckles just by clenching and unclenching his fist. "Wouldn't you like to know," he replied darkly.

* * *

Under the plush lighting, across polished marble floor, the feline concierge paced, checking he was alone. The line rang once, twice, and then was answered. He took his place behind the desk again. Everything was still.

"Yes, it's me." His words echoed. "Your man, the one you wanted me to keep tabs on for you. Well you were right – he just left a few minutes ago." He looked at the clock, as if checking something. "He was alone."

There was a moment's pause. Outside, across the street, he watched a fox in a dirty grey coat shuffle under a streetlight, and bury himself under a pile of discarded boxes. "Thank you. Yes, I understand. A good night to you too, sir."

He hung up, looked around the empty lobby once more, and discreetly began to look pleased with himself.

* * *

The gorilla came over; placed the '*Würstchen Mit Zwiebel*' upon the melamine table that stood between them with a wet thump; and then slowly walked back to the counter, giving the teenagers something that looked like a scowl as he went. Achilles was distracted from Spiritwolf's piercing glare just long enough to peer down at what he had ordered. The greasy mess appeared to be imitating a hotdog with onions, though he was sure it was a poor tribute act.

He cracked his knuckles in response and faced up to the larger wolf. "Why yes, I *do* want to know what you're doing here. Otherwise I wouldn't have asked. My crew don't usually stalk me when I…"

"Vanish? Go wandering in a city you don't know all by yourself, without protection?" Spirit interrupted. His words were clipped, and his swollen bottom lip throbbed painfully.

Achilles stared at the other wolf's mouth. That was some bruise… or was it? Something about it wasn't right; the absence of black and blue under the fur, no discoloration whatsoever. But Spirit was talking and wincing as though it were a bruise. "I was going to say, when I have something to eat. But if you want to call it vanishing, go ahead…"

There was a moment of silence between them then that grew. The two wolves sized each other up, staring. Wondering. Investigating. A conversation without words. Achilles folded his arms. Spirit ground his teeth. Then something unexpected happened – something changed within the larger wolf, as if he had suddenly decided something. Achilles flinched back as Spirit leaned forward and placed his hands on the table. He took a deep breath – and then began to speak. "I was following someone. And this is what happened…"

Achilles' ears pricked up and he listened. And as he listened to Spirit tell his story, he looked into the canine's eyes and realized that there was a mask there that was beginning to slip.

* * *

Following Ramsden through the door undetected was easy; it was merely a matter of timing. Before it had even started to close he'd sprightly darted down the corridor, positioned himself to one side, and stopped it from shutting fully with the toe of his boot.

Listen to the footsteps on the other side; count to four.

He nudged the door open just wide enough to pass through, checked both directions down the corridor once, and slipped inside.

He instinctively concealed himself in the shadows against the wall; this room was unlit, but just ahead was another room whose light bulbs

61

were on. It was this light that Spirit shrank back from, the immediate darkness allowing him a moment to observe. It was a medium-sized room, smelling mustily of dust and mildew and chemicals. Against his back, he could still faintly feel the awesome reverberation of the thundering crowds and drums that accompanied Achilles' show, still in progress. In this room were two lawnmower-sized motorized floor buffers; shelves of cleaning chemicals, mops, and buckets against one corner. And as he lurked among the bleach, he observed Ramsden moving with purpose down the next room of the same size – lights on – which seemed to lead to another room, and perhaps one after that, all connected. They all had high ceilings; in Ramsden's room there were looped, dull strings of Christmas lights and faux Santas hanging from the rafters. Spirit glanced over and saw another neon-cutout of a grinning Jack-o'-lantern propped against the wall, which the black wolf brushed against as he hurriedly made his way past. This was obviously storage.

Uncertain whether Ramsden would be doubling back, he remained in position, but crouched lower so as better to conceal himself. He saw his quarry enter the next room and disappear into darkness, where his sight could not penetrate. Without hesitation, Spirit reached into a pocket deep inside his coat, and produced the small, lightweight pair of binoculars that he held to his eyes. He tapped one button on top, and they became his night-vision, the next room leaping alive in a wash of green and black after compensating for the nearer light sources.

All he saw was a brick wall. Adjusting his focus, he clearly saw that the room was empty – unless Ramsden was immediately to either side of the doorway. He remained silent and frozen in position like a statue until his ears detected an unusual sound, like furniture being moved around ahead, a rough scraping noise like a bolt being drawn back in a rusty lock. The distant pounding on the walls matched that of the blood in his veins as he listened very closely, trying to determine what could be afoot. He counted to twenty, but still Ramsden did not emerge from the seemingly deserted room.

"Move quickly, indeed," he muttered before rising to stealthily slink into the next room, skirting past Saint Nicholas, the Easter Bunny, and Mister Jack Hallowe'en. His fingertips twitched as he finally stowed the binoculars, pulled out his Sig, and shifted mental gears from recon to combat. He preferred to avoid a fight that would invariably leave a mess; mission success was also measured in the scale of the clean-up afterward. The further Ramsden went, the more likely it was that he really was somehow involved, and Spirit needed to at least protect himself. He flattened against the next wall before risking a peek around the doorway.

His eyes adjusted to the darkness; he saw that this room was much barer; one desk had a few discarded tools and screws scattered upon it; against the eastern wall, out of sight from his previous position, was a garage work shelf that large piles of boxes of light bulbs rested upon. Only this shelving was at an angle – as if it had been shunted out of the way – and from behind there was a very thin sliver of light. Spirit cracked a wry smile.

Concealed passageway then. Not just for creepy old houses anymore.

He casually strode into the room and kept an eye on the light. Going over to the desk, he checked for other impromptu weapons he could use. He picked up a box-cutter, its edge glinting, and stowed it in his pocket. Next to it was a flimsy-looking hacksaw that he ignored at first sight. On a whim, he pulled open the top drawer of the desk, and found it empty. In the second drawer was an oily cloth; the last drawer was also empty. He'd just have to make do with his gun and the box-cutter.

Turning his attention back toward the hidden doorway again and the crack of light, he readied the weapon and counted to three. With a crouched gait, he used the tip of the gun to nudge the opening in the wall – a doorway that would have blended in perfectly with the rest of the brickwork had it not been just opened – to risk a peek inside.

This next room was more brilliantly lit than the humble storage closest, and Ramsden was highlighted in detail, crouched upon red plush carpeting next to a dresser lit by dozens of shining white globes around huge, vacant mirrors. Half-filled bottles of water were haphazardly scattered around the rest of the room, which consisted of a couple of couches, a miniature fridge, two chairs and little else. On top of the table were a few personal items – an iPod, some magazines, and a cell phone. It didn't take Spiritwolf long to surmise that this was Achilles' private dressing room, off the main lounge area. What he had to think about harder was what Ramsden was doing. The wolf was fiddling with something that lay on the floor by one of the chairs. His work must have been swift however, because Spirit only got a momentary glimpse at the scene before his quarry rose to his feet again.

Immediately, Spirit backed away from the door. Trigger-finger steady and cool as ice beneath the mask, he retreated further into the storeroom and then further still into a deeper darkness. Crouching low, he stared intently at the secret opening, calmly holding his gun at head-height. He waited a moment, and listened to the footfalls coming closer. Became one with the static.

Ramsden emerged, oblivious. The moment was perfect, and so was the shot…

The black wolf looked *directly at* where the agent lay in wait and could have, should have, seen him. And in the second that his target looked at him and ignored him so utterly, his world suddenly lurched into a moment of unreality. *Even when I'm here, I'm not here... even when I'm around I'm... oh God, oh no... I should have known...*

A deep, black hole of panic opened at the edge of his mind and threatened to swallow him. Even as he fought the irrational urge to make his presence known, he heard a familiar voice from the past crying out from its dark depths.

"I can't be nu... nothing. I can't b-be... gone... Please... I'm sorry... oh, God... I'm sorry... so sorry..."

It took all the mental effort he could muster not to cry out; and as Ramsden closed the hidden door behind him again and strode past where he lay, he remained on edge, stunned at the force of the mental shock he'd just given himself. Slowly the mental hole closed itself back up again, preventing the voice from speaking again. The black wolf walked back down the corridor of rooms then exited the final doorway to the main corridor again. The latch closed behind him with a click. Spirit exhaled a breath he'd been holding in for a stupidly long time, and slumped down against the wall.

He put the weapon away and looked up at the ceiling. He could analyze what the hell just happened inside his brain at a more convenient time; right now, however, he desperately needed to know what Ramsden was doing inside that dressing room and what the connection was to Black Dust and the stolen information he so desperately needed.

He stood and swiftly went to work. The doorway opened with a barely-audible squeak; it was surprisingly well-maintained. Perhaps its original function had been to allow the stadium's stars to get away unnoticed if fans began to congregate outside their dressing rooms. That might explain how Ramsden knew about it, at least. Spirit slipped inside, closed the door behind him, and examined the dressing room for himself, first-hand.

Everything was as ordinary as it had seemed when he'd first looked inside; there was nothing on the dresser of interest among the personal items. He then bee-lined for the place he had seen Ramsden crouching by the chair, and unexpectedly came across a pair of black boots. He picked them up and examined them by smell first – some kind of rubber and microfiber combination, it seemed. The boots were probably expensive and could likely be sold as a "concert souvenir" previously owned by the singer, but that didn't explain why the security guard would have left them there.

Spiritwolf picked up each one individually; he felt around inside the left one first, but the inner-boot was empty and slightly unpleasantly sweaty. He withdrew his hand and when he lifted the right one, he noticed a faint light blink on the floor, a reflection of some kind that was gone half a second later. He turned the garment over and focused his attention. The soles were made of a thick rubber, the grooves only slightly worn. But he was turning it over in the mirror's light when he noticed something small that caught his eye – another momentary blink of a red LED. It was tiny compared to the boot itself, but he brought it to his face and saw that something had been inserted deep into the heel of the sole, and the only sign of its protrusion was this singular light which blinked every twenty seconds by his timing. He spent perhaps two minutes looking at it this way, before finally realizing what it was.

"Ah," he said aloud to the open air. "A tracker. Clever…" *Advanced design, too*, he mused. *More like something TEA would use than something on the open market…*

The next second, the hidden doorway behind him squeaked. Spirit spun around with surprise and looked at the equally shocked visage of the person who had just stepped through the door – Ramsden.

For some reason the black wolf had doubled back – ostensibly to check something. He took one look at the muscular brown wolf already getting to his feet with the boot in his hand – and turned and ran.

Shit. So much for going unseen. Spirit growled and reached for his gun. He leaped forward in pursuit; the boot fell to the floor next to its companion. He thundered out the door, slamming it shut behind him, and bounded into the dark storeroom. Ahead, charging under the low-hanging Christmas lights, Ramsden had a solid head start and was making the most of it. Without even giving the black wolf a warning – that stuff was for movies and cops – he took his first shot. His attempt to aim carefully and just wing the wolf made his shot go wide; instead, a nearby figure of Saint Nicholas exploded in a shower of plastic. Ramsden reached the opposite doorway and was out.

Despite his pounding heart and the adrenaline surging through his veins, Spirit slowed and checked the other side of the door for an ambush. With none present, he ran into the main corridor but still on guard with his gun low and to the side. The hall was awash with the sound of hollow thunderous cheering as Achilles played out his final song of the night in the stadium, then it was broken by a piercing scream as, up ahead, Ramsden charged into a beaver who happened to be in his way, her tray of makeup scattering everywhere. The wolf was fast, Spirit had to give him that. The black wolf ran like an athlete and shoved aside another pair of rail-thin guys, now heading unimpeded for the backstage exit and his freedom.

Swearing, Spiritwolf put all his energy into the pursuit, breezing past the bewildered people just as his quarry jumped out the back door – literally jumped into the open air like an experienced parkour practitioner. Ramsden broke his fall on a pile of autograph hunters and press who had gathered at the back door beneath the raised steps. They went down en masse, crying out in surprise and dismay amid the chaos. Then the black wolf was on his feet again and charging toward a black SUV parked under a streetlight.

Spirit thundered out of the doorway, weapon raised, but there were too many people in the way to take a shot. Even as Ramsden had opened the passenger-side door, the vehicle was in motion, and he was barely inside before it took off with a screech of rubber. Charging forward, Spirit jumped down into the already-spooked crowd and ran toward a ferret with a camera slung around his torso standing astride a sleek red motorcycle. The photographer had been caught off-guard by the commotion, his muzzle hanging open, but his instincts were kicking in and the camera was already being raised as Spirit charged at him. Paparazzi to the core.

"Get off. NOW!" Spirit bared his teeth, pistol flashing. He didn't wait for compliance. With one shove, the considerably smaller ferret tumbled from the vehicle. The guy landed with a squeak of indignation; his camera going off with a flash. He recovered just in time to witness Spirit slamming the bike into life, the engine roaring as he kicked it off its stand, and then speeding up the tarmac in pursuit of the SUV.

The wind whipping at his fur, the mask and the unseen, Spirit smiled for the first time that evening. Now things were *really* getting interesting.

* * *

Across the road from the diner, crouched in an alleyway, eyes were watching a conversation they could not hear. They spied on Achilles and Spirit through binoculars, easily penetrating the yellow glare of the diner window. Little scripts of data ran down the side of the image, identifying the targets, specifying environmental information. Spirit's lips moved constantly as he explained something at great length. Achilles sat there passively, arms crossed, but looking more and more concerned with each passing moment.

A walkie-talkie was hissing and crackling its silent vigil in the alley as they watched. The observer pressed a button and the static disappeared. "He's here. Someone else with him too. Do we proceed?"

A hiss before a deep voice on the other side answered. "Proceed. Get in there, and get them both. We want him *alive*. You may terminate the other one if necessary."

"Understood. Radio silence from now. Over and out."

The static vanished forever as the radio was deactivated. Guns were drawn. And in silence beyond the window, Spirit talked on.

* * *

Over the meaty roar of the motorcycle's engine, the world began to shudder and blur. For once, the old fox who had taught Spirit most of what he knew was silent in his memory; it seemed the sensei had little experience with vehicle pursuits held at a hundred-plus kilometers an hour.

The black SUV cruised through the inner-city traffic like a barracuda, intimidating other road-users to the sides, swerving past slower trucks with a threatening growl, and all the time getting faster. Spirit's reactions were tested to their limits, zipping past cars, then suddenly diving between, leaving stunned drivers with shocked passengers in his wake. Even another wolf riding a motorbike ate his dust as he tore off in pursuit of his quarry. The objective now was to get them off the road and get them contained. Once he did that, he could find out what they knew and who they worked for.

Easier said than done. He kicked the bike into a higher gear as streetlights whizzed past, the buildings getting smaller as they receded away from the inner city. The SUV was still six vehicles in front when Spirit came to a sickening realization that made his heart sink.

The Autobahn. They're heading for the Autobahn. God help me.

There was a conversation he'd had long ago with a very mean, very fast, and very experienced jackal who'd taken all of the TEA agents on their advanced vehicle training. Fast pursuit had been one of the lessons. *"And so, you can take down anyone with the trainin' you've had today. Anyone, anywhere on the planet…"*

"Anywhere, huh?" one of the young recruits had questioned skeptically.

"That's right, well, 'cept maybe on one of those damn German Autobahns I s'pose… no speed limit y'see. Crazy buggers! Tryin' to get 'em on one of those would be suicide near 'nough, not that it's likely yer gonna be in that neck of the woods if yer lucky…"

For once, Spirit considered aborting the pursuit; just for a moment. His right hand twitched almost imperceptibly upon the brakes – but his left hand twisted and cranked the bike faster still. In a few more moments they turned a corner, and began sliding into the Autobahn itself.

No going back now.

The SUV sprung upon the unsuspecting flow of traffic like a wraith, and like a dagger Spirit came after, again cutting between the cars with deadly precision. He needed it; just one false move on this hair-trigger motorcycle and the mission would come to a rather messy end. The cars were not as thick as rush hour, but still in the dull glow of the nightlights the asphalt was cluttered with vehicles, churning along at their own comparatively slower pace. He stole glimpses of tired commuters sitting up in surprise as first the quarry, and then the hunter, sped past them.

Suddenly, the SUV looked to be in trouble; a red BMW in the fast lane wasn't getting out of the way quickly enough and there was nowhere else to go. Spirit readied himself for the SUV to slow down, maneuvering the bike between a rumbling tow-truck and a family sedan to prepare to pull ahead of the pack. What came next was a move of ruthless desperation; instead of slowing down, the target instead sped up and rammed into the BMW's rear, clipping it on the right. The response happened in an instant, as the unfortunate driver of the vehicle screamed, his car jerking forward and veering toward the barrier at an incredible speed. He applied the brakes and tried to steer back onto the road, but overcompensated; there was a smash of metal and shattering of glass as he collided with a silver Porsche in the next lane over, the momentum carrying his front end first over the hood of the car, and then *over* the car itself. Suddenly the road was filled with jagged debris, the SUV was roaring ahead and the two smashed cars were barreling directly into Spirit's path.

Oh, shit.

Two things happened simultaneously with blinding speed: the tow-truck slammed on its brakes and Spirit accelerated as much as he could to escape the trap. The sedan went into a panic and jerked violently to the left, faintly grazing Spirit's rear end. The ferocious wobble this caused lasted only for a moment, but it was nearly enough to finish him; at the last second he regained enough momentum to squeeze past the sedan and the wreckage of the crash; an airborne wheel passed so close to his head that even by ducking he felt the wind of it passing beneath his mask.

Dripping determination and perspiration, he spared a moment's thought for the carnage behind him before re-fixing his eye upon the SUV that was now making serious headway on the road ahead.

All right then. No more of that, you German bastard.

He moved the bike to its highest gear and weaved between the cars in a blur. The jackal's lessons had been true and soon enough he was pulling enough speed to draw alongside the SUV. Nearly there, with no obstacles ahead, he kept one hand on the bars and with the other he reached into his jacket and drew out his gun. He was sweating bullets but kept his nerve somehow. *Inches away now.* Soon he was going to be alongside the passenger-window; he accelerated in order to line up the shot.

He turned his head and prepared to pull the trigger, but instead found himself staring into Ramsden's mocking face and gun-muzzle. He screeched sideways in time to dodge one bullet, and then exchanged fire. Now a lane of traffic was between them, cars bustling past like blurry shapes of color. Inside them, terrified occupants screamed as bullets clouded the air, shattering side-mirrors, piercing hoods. One of Spirit's shots got close enough to penetrate the SUV's windscreen; it left a snowflake of a bullet-hole right next to Ramsden's head. He looked unimpressed by the gesture and responded by taking shots at Spirit's tires.

Good idea, the invisible wolf remarked to himself. *I should have thought of that sooner.*

The deadly twin dilemma of trying to operate a motorcycle at top speed with one hand, and exchanging gunfire with an enemy agent on a suicidally fast stretch of road was not lost on Spirit, however, and he forced himself to slow down and let the SUV pull ahead a little again to plan his next move. He put his gun away and with both hands in control of the bike again, he took a moment's breath to steady himself for the next assault.

He blinked and the next moment his vision was filled by a swarm of flashing blue lights winking in the sky in front of him as well as clouding the reflection in his rear-view. He turned his head and looked in dismay at an approaching BMW with *Bundespolizei* stamped upon its doors. The police had come – just what he didn't need.

From the helicopter above, a beam of light swung upon him with blinding brilliance. "*Anschlag sofort!*" a voice barked from the skies. "*Wir schießen Sie!*"

Despite the light upon him and the seconds he had left to bring this chase to a conclusion, he swung his view to the black SUV ahead of him again in time to see one of the rear doors thrust open. There crouched Ramsden again, wearing a sly smirk, with something bulky and cylindrical perched upon his shoulder. Something that almost looked like…

… *Oh, Scheiße!*

If Master Song hadn't honed his reflexes to a hair-trigger, he would have been blown to kingdom come that night, and in other universes that is exactly what happened. But in this one, Spirit veered sideways as soon as he recognized the rocket-launcher pointed at his head, and the projectile streaked past him with a piercing shriek. From behind him there was an explosion of terrible proportions as the rocket instead impacted with the lead police-car on his tail. There was a rush of heat and a roar of sound and color that filled him with dread. The last sight he caught of the SUV was of Ramsden's satisfied and grinning face as he put the heavy-weapon down. Then the force of the blast inexorably lifted the rear of the bike into the air, and he found himself staring at the road in front of him as he pulled the most terrifying front wheelie known on earth, struggling to resist the momentum that would push the rest of the bike over the whole way and leave him a bloody smear on the Autobahn's surface at two hundred kilometers per hour.

By some miracle, the bike stayed on course and then the rear began its fall back down to earth. It landed with a terrible smack that sent shockwaves jarring through Spirit's bones. His teeth clicked together and his hand clenched around the brake out of pure instinct to prevent himself from flying off into the oncoming lane of traffic. His luck ran out, however, as the force of the braking locked out the bike's wheels, and with inevitable dread he felt it slipping out of control underneath him. He at least did the decent thing, which spared his life: getting the bike to stay upright as it slowed for long enough that by the time it topped over and skidded onto its side, it had lost enough speed for him to tumble from its chassis to the side of the road where he landed with a bone-jarring thump. The bike continued screeching with a flash of sparks for several meters ahead while he rolled several times before coming to a halt next to a barrier, his arm pinned painfully underneath and the wind knocked out of him.

Dazed and dizzied by the crash, he felt lucky to be alive, but only for a moment. As he lay struggling to regain his breath, the helicopter blinded him with its radiant light, hovering over him. Tires screeched as other cars came to a halt and the law pounced upon him

"No, not me… go after the SUV, you idiots… !"

The blue lights surrounded him, swarming his vision. He tried to get up, started scrambling to his feet but the officer first on the scene, imagining he was about to make a run for it, socked him in the jaw and sent him sprawling back down to the ground again. The large lion turned the wolf onto his belly, pinned his legs, and cuffed him without leaving room for any more of a fight.

Then the others hauled him to his feet, shouting things at him above the din of the helicopter blades. Telling him his rights no doubt, that he was under arrest. He looked for the SUV but there was no sign of it, only the chaos it had left behind. His jaw throbbed painfully from the punch; it was already beginning to swell up. Fighting dizziness, first came the frustration that his mission had, literally, been blown up. But gnawing at its heels came a familiar fear and voice of panic welling up from inside, mocking him with insecurities. *You're not cut, are you Spirit? Are you sure you're all there, have you checked? What if part of your attire came off in that little spill back there… you'd better hope not, or answering these officers' questions will be the least of your problems…*

A lump welled in his throat. He struggled more but by the might of many hands he was bundled into the back of a police van where he was left to ponder his next move alone.

* * *

"This is bullshit," Achilles spat. "I don't believe any of it."

Spirit smirked, cradling his sore arm reflexively. "I didn't expect you to." He looked a little more weary than when they had started the conversation.

"Mmm. Well. I think I've heard enough. It's a nice story. You should try pitching it to Hollywood sometime. Is that what this is? Some kind of… weird pitch for a movie you want me to be in?"

"No."

"Whatever. It's late. I'm going back to the hotel and you're officially off the tour come morning." Achilles began to stand, feeling righteous and in control. He was stopped halfway however when Spirit leaned over the table, put a hand firmly on his shoulder – and pointed a gun discreetly at the star's midsection. In plain view for them both to see but obscured from the rest of the diner.

"You're not going anywhere," Spirit growled. "Not until you've heard the rest. Not until I figure out if you're Black Dust or not."

Achilles looked confused, then began to protest. His eyes flicked to the gorilla at the counter, who was by now passing the time engrossed in a late-night German talk show. Then they flicked back to the gun.

"You're insane. But I can see the gun was one thing you weren't lying about." He sat down stiffly, regarding Spirit guardedly, searchingly.

"Believe it. Now shut up and listen to the rest. We're nearly done."

From outside, a red laser-dot settled upon the back of the gorilla's head, then moved ominously away.

* * *

There were worse things for an agent of the TEA than being captured by local law enforcement, but not many. Apart from the indignity of being hauled before a bunch of desk jockey soft-asses like your average petty criminal, it raised flags you really didn't want raised and put you on a grid that you really didn't want to be on. From one mug shot in one county, you could appear on any criminal database in the world, a very handy tool for old enemies to find you and settle the score. Failure propagated quickly; the mission would be dead in the water within hours if not minutes, and then there was the inevitable reaming you'd get from your superiors at the TEA once they busted you out and got their hands on you. More than one agent had been demoted thanks to getting nabbed by the boys in blue. Getting caught by your supposed allies was a serious brood of bad news.

But none of this was at the front of Spirit's mind as the police van rumbled back to the station; these worries were somehow insignificant compared to the irrational fear that some part of him was missing. It was hard to check every last inch with both hands cuffed firmly behind his back. But eventually he concluded that everything was intact and he allowed himself to relax a little. Relaxed enough to then remember that the only way this bad night was going to get worse was if he made it to the station; he'd have to escape before then.

Fortunately, these officers were so stunned by everything that had happened – they'd just seen a car literally blown up before their eyes, after all – they had just dumped him in the back with no one to keep watch. Unfortunately for him they had little need to; the truck was built like a tank: thick steel plates on every wall, the floor, and at the door. Getting out by force was not an option.

He swiftly surmised that the only chance he had was to surprise them when they got to the destination and make a break for it. As much as he didn't want to rely on stripping down to get away, this time there wasn't going to be much choice. To do that, he'd first have to deal with the handcuffs. No problem. With what little maneuverability his wrists had left, his hands lifted the back of his coat and began feeling their way up the fabric. His fingertips felt along until they found the few artificial strands that had been planted there. With a sharp tug, he held in his hands a thin pick made of carbon fiber, just the right thickness to see to a lock of cuffs.

He set to work immediately, nimbly maneuvering the stashed tool into the lock. It was a tricky procedure made none easier by the momentary distraction of a bug flying at his face, landing upon his nose. Some kind of small beetle. The agent shook his head and it flew off in another direction; he lost it in the darkness. He sneezed, fumbling quickly, listening to the clicks as the catches turned. He was listening for the final master click that would signal his release but the next moment there came a louder *clack* from the door of the van – and it swung open.

He shifted the final catch from the cuffs and released himself just in time to see the inner city of Dresden appear before him again with the van still in motion. Was this some kind of trap or an overly fortuitous mistake? He didn't intend to stick around to find out. Immediately Spirit bolted for the door and landed with a thump on the road, staggering only slightly. With no other vehicles following behind, he was able to dash away off the pavement to hide behind a dumpster, heart racing fast as he watched the police van recede from view. Soon they would realize he was no longer their cargo, but by that time he would be long gone.

Already thinking ahead, he took off at a quick march down a side alley cradling his sore arm and feeling his bottom lip throb with a painful bruise. It didn't feel like the arm was broken, but no doubt he had injured himself, perhaps strained a muscle. It could have been a lot worse.

He reflected that luck had been with him frequently tonight. He could have died a half a dozen times on that crazy chase, could have been bloodied to a pulp when he crashed. And then the door to the police van… how had it opened? That was the strangest piece of luck of all. But bad luck had been with him as well. He still knew nothing about Ramsden, only that the wolf was part of an organization that meant serious business. That rocket-launcher had been some damned heavy firepower, not the sort of thing he had expected to see in Europe. This thing was swiftly escalating beyond his control.

But still, everything came back to Achilles. The whispers of the tablet, allegedly somewhere among all of the tour's bags and boxes. The interest Ramsden had showed in him. The tracking device. Spiritwolf jogged on, his course suddenly determined. It was time to go right to the source of it all and stop beating around the bush.

It was time for a little chat with Achilles.

* * *

"And, here I am. Talking to you."

The words hung in the air like a threat. Achilles sat with his back pressed up against the squeaky plastic lining of the booth, watching the gun pointed at him with calm disquiet. "You're still a fantasist," he muttered. "You-"

"Stop." Spirit interrupted coldly. "You want proof. You want to know how I found you tonight? Check your boot."

Achilles rolled his eyes. "Sure. Which one? The right or the left?"

"Right," the larger wolf said with narrowed eyes. "He put it in the right boot. In the heel."

"Of course he did," the singer replied. But Spirit didn't look moved by his assurance. He looked so *convincing*. So slowly, Achilles reached down to his feet… fumbled down the boot, still keeping one eye on the gun he felt and squeezed the heel intently… and found a small lump where there should have been none. His eyes widened out of curiosity. Spirit seemed to nod a little. His fingertips probed further and then pulled out a tiny object, a cylindrical piece of metal with a blinking red LED on the end. He held it up with the skepticism slowly draining from his features. "What is it?"

Spirit lowered his gun slightly. "A sophisticated tracking device. Part of it has been co-opted from a device we use ourselves at the TEA, which is why I was able to track you tonight. The frequency is the same." His hand dove into his pocket and flourished an advanced-looking cellphone for a moment. "Which means someone is interested in you, Achilles, *very* interested in you. And I want to know why."

The wolf threw up his hands in disgust. "Are you kidding me? I'm famous. I'm on a world tour. *Everybody* wants to know what I'm up to, especially the paparazzi. You wouldn't understand."

Spirit smirked. "Try me."

Achilles opened his mouth for another retort, but he never got the chance. A small red dot appeared upon his forehead, unknown to him. But Spirit saw it, and he reacted as swiftly as a praying mantis. "DOWN!" he yelled, diving across the table, shoving condiments everywhere, and tackling the wolf to the floor with him. A fraction of a second later, a bullet embedded itself in the plastic where Achilles' head had been with a dull *thunk*.

"What the *fuck!*" Achilles yelled, collapsing to the floor with the full weight of the trench coat clad wolf landing atop him. Meanwhile, the teenagers had fled screaming and the gorilla had snapped out of his reverie in time to witness the laser dot on his shoulder get replaced by a bullet. He went down with a roar of pain.

Spirit was icily cool under the pressure, his gun now pointing away from Achilles for the first time as they lay sprawled beneath the table, out of sight from any windows. With no visible movement to the outside, they were safe for the moment but the agent still readied himself for the inevitable attack. "Stay down," Spirit hissed. "Keep quiet but get ready to run when they make their move."

"Who… are they?" Achilles wheezed from underneath.

The agent slowly rolled off him. "Don't know for sure but they planted the tracker on you and nearly killed me earlier tonight. Guess they're after the tablet, too."

"What tablet? What the *fuck* is going on?" Achilles whispered fiercely. The agent was about to answer when the main window of the shop was smashed by a large metal canister hurtling through it. Then another. They spun fast and whined, releasing a payload of white gas.

"Rear exit. Don't breathe. Follow me. *NOW!*" Spirit seized Achilles by the lapel, hauled him to his feet, and began shooting at the figures clad in black uniforms and gas masks who were already then swarming toward the diner. He struck one in the chest, the man falling to the ground with a yell. *Kevlar armor, probably.* The others ducked for cover and in that moment, he shoved Achilles backwards toward the door at the very back of the diner that he had first taken note of upon arrival. In an agent's line of work, you never went into a place unless you knew all the ways in or out, and one thing Spiritwolf had always been very good at was reconnaissance. Their escape route was thankfully unblocked from the inside and Achilles stumbled through the rear exit first.

Spirit saw that the gorilla was unconscious and got off a few more shots at the masked assailants advancing before the door swung shut again. He spared a second to give a nearby dumpster a shoulder-shove in front of the doors to slow them down before he grabbed hold of Achilles again. "Get in the shadows. Don't let anyone see you." He gave the white wolf another push in the right direction but did not see the black silhouette in the shape of a rotund crocodile up on the roof taking aim upon him. Achilles did.

"Above you – there!" he yelled, pointing. But it was too late to stop the reptile from taking the shot and the next second there was a hiss of white light and the crackle of electricity as a pair of wires shot out from the gun and embedded itself in the agent's exposed neck.

"Bastard!" Spirit cursed, feeling the hot prickle of the charge upon his skin through the material covering his person, the next moment grabbing hold of the wire and giving it a sharp tug. The croc was so surprised that the stun gun hadn't worked that he kept hold of the other end. He ended up tumbling to the ground for his foolishness. Spirit finished him off with an expertly placed kick to the head, knocking the lumbering reptile out cold. "Might have worked better on someone whose fur was actually connected to their nervous system," he muttered.

Meanwhile, Achilles' muzzle was hanging open in surprise. Spirit saw him standing there and shrugged his broad shoulders. "Don't sweat it. Just run until I tell you to stop."

Hammering at the door emphasized his point as the others tried to burst through. Just as they ran down the alley away from the diner, two more agents appeared at the mouth to the street and began firing at them, but they weren't quick enough. Achilles and Spiritwolf disappeared into darkness.

The leader lined up another shot, but a digitally altered voice crackled over the radio, bringing the attack to a halt. "Alive, you fools, alive! Stand down. The assault has failed. Acknowledge!"

The gun slowly lowered. The agent in the mask raised her radio to her muzzle grudgingly. "*Ja*. We let them go. Now what?"

"Patience. We wait until the next moment presents itself – it will come, rest assured. We know his itinerary, so round up everyone and report back to base. Leave for Rome immediately; when he arrives after, your team will keep an eye on him and be ready to strike again."

The agent nodded, and removed her mask. The tigress smiled in satisfaction, looking at the cloudless sky above her. "Yes, we will," Clarice purred. Then she walked away.

* * *

The two wolves ran several blocks without exchanging a single word; Achilles too shocked to speak, Spirit too preoccupied with the turn the mission had taken. But as they emerged to the main street again the opportunity arose to hail a passing cab and Spirit took it. They threw themselves inside.

"*Sprechen sie Englisch?*" Spirit asked immediately.

"*Nein*," the otter replied grumpily.

"Okay. Luxus Hotel, *bitte*," he instructed. The driver nodded and began to move off. Spirit then turned to Achilles. "Means we can talk freely, at least."

"Talk? What's there to talk about?" the rock star replied dryly. "I've just been shot at. You're apparently some kind of super-agent who's either out to kill me or protect me; I haven't figured out which yet. And… whatever the hell is going on, I wish it wasn't." He covered his face with his hands for a moment, as if fighting off the onset of a strong headache. When he removed them again, his eyes were wild with approaching fear. "Where are we going now? Back to the hotel? Are you crazy, they know where I'm staying, they'll-"

"Not lay a finger on you. Not tonight. If they'd wanted to take you out at the hotel they could have easily done so before tonight. They either attacked just now out of opportunity alone or it wasn't really you they were after."

"This is all so confusing."

"Yes. And to top it all off, I have a conundrum. Either you *are* Black Dust, which means those men were after you to get the tablet for themselves, and now that you know my identity you may try to kill me. Or, you are *not* the person I'm after, but you still now know who I am, which means the whole mission is compromised."

Achilles snorted. "Then why did you tell me in the first place?"

Spirit smiled. "To see what would happen. Things could have been brought to a swift resolution if by some slip of the tongue you had absolutely proved you were Black Dust, or you weren't. I admit I was taking a short cut, but after being shot at and nearly blown up in one night, I was in the mood to shake things up. I didn't plan on those soldiers crashing the party, though."

Achilles spared a flashing glance at the city outside; the orange lights reflected upon his calm features coolly, the scent of exhaust fumes wafting through the air-vents. They were almost back at the hotel. "So what are you going to do about your conundrum?"

"Oh, I have the solution for that," he muttered and silently slipped a needle into Achilles' neck as the wolf looked outside. Spirit injected him with the thin capsule of solution he had produced from his coat without the singer noticing – the last bit of kit that had survived the crash other than his gun.

The white wolf felt the pinprick and instinctively covered the needle-hole after slapping the agent's hand away. "What did you just…"

"Methyl caudate. An experimental drug cooked up by some of the Sciences personnel who work for DAST. It's going to go right for that wonderful creative brain of yours, and get inside the para-hippocampal cortex – that's the part of your noggin that deals with intermediate term memory – and break down all the neurons that have formed in the last three or so hours. Come morning, you're not going to remember any of what I've told you, and I'll just go back to being your personal trainer, continuing my investigation at a more leisurely pace."

Achilles' eyes grew wide. "You fucker!" he snarled, teeth flashing. "You can't do that to me! I'll write it down! I'll… put it on my computer… or… speak… on the… phone…" His rage subsided as swiftly as it came on. The world began to darken. "You…" he began, but never finished, succumbing to the approaching darkness.

Spirit caught him as he pitched forward and propped him back in the cab seat, smiling all the while. "The Sciences team also mixed in a potent sedative, just for good measure. Sweet dreams, rock star."

The cab driver glanced up in the rear-view mirror, cocking a curious eye at Achilles' sleeping form. Spirit rolled his eyes and made the 'drinky-drinky' gesture to the driver, which was apparently universal. The otter nodded and carried on paying attention to the road.

Spirit sighed and leaned back in his own seat, his eyes feeling equally as heavy. What a night. So much had happened, so many mysteries to uncover. There were more parties now at play with than he was comfortable with and he was so very tired. And sore. He looked at Achilles' dead weight and groaned inwardly a little. First, though, he would have to haul the wolf back to his room – he'd have to spare the rock star the indignity of being placed on a luggage cart, in case any paparazzi were around. He didn't want to destroy the poor guy's career. Back door, then, and up the hotel staff elevator. Only then could the agent return to his own room and sleep a little. As much as he would have taken the opportunity to search Achilles' room, he needed rest and besides, something in his gut said that the singer couldn't be the black-market technology dealer he was looking for. The agent yawned – keeping a hand over his muzzle – which confirmed his course of action. With the sedative, they'd have seven hours of rest, maybe eight, before they were all off to Rome. No doubt the other players would follow, and whatever form the next attack took, whenever it happened, it was likely to be worse than tonight's.

Amazing how it all comes back, he mused, fighting somnolence. *Amazing how I missed this… I must be insane.*

That night, he dreamt of the beetles and the static.

Chapter Four: Entropy's Dance

The hues from the rising sun stained the Colosseum's dirty walls pale red, leading Spiritwolf to wonder how just many gladiators had died within it two thousand years ago. He sat in the open-air rooftop restaurant of his favorite hotel in Rome, gazing at the magnificent structure while slowly stirring his coffee. *Look upon my works and despair*, thought Spiritwolf as he sipped the strong brew. Its bloody history made it a monument to killing and death, and yet, Achilles' next concert was to take place in the very same spot as a different form of entertainment for the masses. He smiled into his coffee, his gaze lingering on the image of his mask reflecting back from the dark liquid. There was an example of rebirth, good coming from bad, life from death. Second chances were rarely given in his line of work and he truly felt fortunate that he could be sitting there, enjoying the warm breeze which brought the smells of meat, cheeses, and freshly baked bread from up the street. The accident seemed so far away; it had happened to someone else, not him. Here, he was in a different world and could feel comfortable in the pretense of normalcy.

He finished his coffee and the mustelid waiter was immediately there to retrieve the cup. *"Prego."*

"Vorrei un espresso, grazie. E una bottiglia di acqua."

"Frizzante o naturale?"

"Naturale."

"Sì."

Spirit dipped his sunglasses down the bridge of his muzzle and watched the lithe male walk away in that unhurried pace that exemplified Italian life. *Ah, I could get used to this.* After a few minutes the waiter returned with his espresso and water. He downed the coffee in one gulp, taking care to not get any on his mask, and chased it with the glass of water.

He leaned back with one elbow crooked on top of the chair and stared over the rooftops, letting his thoughts drift back two nights.

My first real action here on the outside and I almost wind up as a smear on the Autobahn. Spirit sighed. He needed to find less lethal ways of shaking the rust off. His jaw was still sore from the lion officer's punch and his arm was not quite one hundred percent. There were spots of road rash that his clothing somehow hadn't protected – or maybe where his clothing had chafed against his fur while tumbling at two hundred kph – and it had been difficult to find them all. He had meticulously noted each one's location and would inspect them twice a day by touch, the same protocol he followed after Master Song's workouts. Thankfully, they felt like they were healing; some of them seemed to have scabbed over.

His mask, though, was another problem. Although it had protected him from the electrical jolt, the electrodes had burned a small pair of small holes in it. Normal skin would heal, the synthetic material wouldn't. It had already been a couple of days since he'd been zapped; another few days and people might start to get suspicious if they were looking close enough. Hell, they might start asking uncomfortable questions or insist that he go see a doctor… and tag along. That was, of course, unacceptable and it meant he'd have to keep the back of his neck angled away from others as best he could.

The wolf sighed. He needed a new mask, no doubt about it. Just before he'd checked out in Dresden, he'd sent a text message to Zero on his TEA-encrypted phone explaining the problem and asking for a new mask. The bear would probably be pissed, given how difficult (and expensive) they were to make. He just hoped they could make a new one quickly – without his mask, without everything that covered him, he was nothing. Literally.

Still, despite the injuries to himself and his mask, it had felt wonderful to be in the middle of danger. The thrill of the chase, escaping from the police, talking to Achilles, and then nearly getting killed again in the ambush. So much more exciting than the ordinary, plain, and mundane chartered flight to Rome with the band. Now they had to wait an extra day while the equipment was driven down by the roadies in large trucks. It felt like there was too much time going to waste and Spirit had no choice but to sit on his hands and wait.

Very well, he thought. *If I must wait, then I will plan. I will be ready.*

His first thought was of Achilles. He was pretty sure that the white wolf wasn't Black Dust. Spirit had really started to like Achilles, particularly after their conversation in the diner and in the taxi. The white wolf had shown some moxie and though he had only just been exposed to his world, he'd still demonstrated some smarts and hadn't panicked too badly during the attack. Sure, it might have been an act, but his gut was telling him that Achilles wasn't anything more than he appeared to be. It had taken some effort to come to that conclusion; the incredibly charismatic white wolf was distracting and he'd made sure to avoid Achilles for the last day or so, claiming fatigue while he made his assessment. His excuse wasn't far from the truth; Spirit had been well and truly exhausted, getting up only a couple of hours after leaving the sedated wolf back in his room. It was difficult to sleep during daylight hours when you could see through your eyelids, and he'd been too exhausted to put on the blindfold he sometimes wore. So, he'd begged out of the workout session with Achilles yesterday, to which the equally sluggish white wolf had agreed. Twelve hours' sleep in Rome had helped immensely but it had also left his body clock slightly askew. He was grateful for the restaurant's early opening.

So, if his instincts were telling him that Achilles wasn't Black Dust, then who could the dealer be? Spiritwolf wasn't sure, and there were so many people on the tour. He could at least narrow the list by discarding the people who were brand new to the tour. Still, that would leave about half of the people that had traveled to all of the cities on previous tours where stolen tech had changed hands. It sure would be easy enough to deal; auctions, payments and deliveries could be scheduled during the downtimes between cities. That meant that something might already be going down, right now, but no one at the TEA had yet cracked the mystery of how the bidding announcements were being made. Canis had cracked the encryption on the intial email to start the bidding but there was a different communication scheme for the actual bids, perhaps something that had been pre-arranged. So again, there wasn't much he could do beyond keeping tabs on where the tour members went and try to get wind of unexplained absences. He drummed his fingers on the table. That would be impossible for him to do exhaustively, by himself, so the best thing to do would be to narrow it down.

How to do that, though? What information was he missing? Spirit's thoughts went over that last night in Dresden again. There was the black wolf that had planted the tracking device in Achilles' boot. Could he be Black Dust? He had thought so – at least the fur coloring was right. He wasn't a member of the tour group, though; he was a security guard employed by the arena. Whoever he was, he had nearly killed Spiritwolf; the agent would have to keep an eye out for him, in case he was in disguise or showed up again.

Then there was Achilles' somewhat atypical behavior of leaving the hotel after the concert. Was the diner supposed to be a meeting place for a buyer? Spiritwolf still hadn't found the device, either. A tablet could be hidden just about anywhere and everyone these days carried some kind of portable computing device that masqueraded as a "tablet" – large smartphones, e-readers, small notebook computers. Regardless of its significance to him, it was just another part of the mission's bigger picture; he couldn't just recover the tablet and disappear, so to speak. He would also have to make sure that Black Dust couldn't traffic in stolen technology that dangerous ever again. That was the TEA's charter, after all, and Spirit wanted to leave no doubt regarding his ability to perform as an agent. It was about more than just himself.

What else? There was the diner. Aside from the attack itself, the one odd thing about that was that it had not been reported on the news at all. A disturbance like that should have been extremely newsworthy but it had been sanitized – cleaned up and kept quiet. No media chatter, either. The police chase hadn't been caught on camera, thankfully, but the chagrined police chief having to explain their prisoner's disappearance had. Spirit was just glad no one at the airport had detained him upon departure. Maybe he had Ixak to thank for that.

And speaking of which, there were the doors to the police wagon. It had been a little odd that they hadn't been locked. Despite it helping him to escape, it was still out of the ordinary. Could that have been Ixak, too? He wasn't sure. Fast forward again to the diner – those people who'd attacked had been pros and the whole thing didn't at all fit Black Dust's M.O. of being ultra-secretive. Which meant there was a rival group after the tablet.

There were so many possibilities. Spiritwolf sighed and shook his head. How the hell was he supposed to make sense of it all? The string he followed only led him deeper into the labyrinth. *You're right, Zero,* he thought ruefully. *I never was good at planning.*

The sunlight had crept along the table during his cogitations and was warming his left sleeve when his ear swiveled toward the faint *ding* of the elevator at the other end of the restaurant. He heard the heavy tread of someone in boots clomping toward the buffet. *He's up early.* Spirit distinctly kept his attention focused forward but his ears continued to track the sounds of food being gathered onto a plate while he watched early morning exercisers jogging through the *Arco di Constantino* toward the green lawns of the *Circo Massimo.*

"Good… morning." Achilles hadn't quite shaken the sleep from his voice yet. "Mind if I join you?"

"Please."

Achilles sat and poured himself a cup of regular coffee from the carafe. "You're dressed rather well. Trying to get in good with Regis after postponing our scheduled workout?"

Spirit looked askance at the white wolf, attired in a tight T-shirt, black jeans and boots. The odd-looking tattoo on his arm drawn like a stylized 'B' peeked out from under each sleeve. "This is the way most of the people dress here." It felt strange to be talking to him as though the events at the diner hadn't happened; Achilles wouldn't remember it, but Spirit did. *The perils of our work.* He remembered those words that Zero had spoken to him, years ago.

"Ah, trying to blend in, then?" Achilles began eating the thinly sliced meat with cheese rolled together on his fork. "This is amazing!" he said, chewing slowly to savor the taste.

"It's what I do," Spiritwolf replied dryly and pointed to the plate. "Try the fresh mozzarella – you'll probably like that, too."

"Already ate one at the spread back there. So what's your plan? Why are you up so early? A morning workout routine? You didn't mention one yesterday, I don't think?"

"Actually, I was thinking of heading out and stretch my legs a bit. I didn't get much of a chance to do that in Dresden, so I thought it might be good to do in Rome, since we're here through tomorrow. I'm very familiar with the city, visited here several times before. Even stayed in this hotel."

"When in Rome, eh?" Achilles said, chomping on a breakfast pastry. "Well, as long as you have me back in time for the group meeting later this afternoon, that should be fine."

Spirit nodded, and then did a double-take. "You want to join me?"

"Why not?" The white wolf grinned and stabbed some fruit with his fork. "I have some time before the rest of the equipment arrives. You know the city and I'd like to see some of the sights as well. Unless you don't want me to come along for some reason."

"Well, no, it's not that." Spiritwolf foundered for the right words. Achilles' blue-eyed gaze was focused on him and he suddenly felt awkward. "I just… prefer doing certain things by myself."

"I see. You've been away from people because of your accident and you got used to doing things by yourself." Spirit fought down sudden fear of having been discovered before reminding himself of his cover story. "Well, I can certainly empathize with you."

Those words clarified something for the agent. "Because you can't be normal. You're a world-famous rock star celebrity and get recognized no matter where you go. And it's going to get worse, isn't it?" The shocked look the other wolf threw him was answer enough. "I think I've been there before. Tell you what. If you change your attire into something nicer, you can join me."

"Nicer?" Spirit watched the wolf's face take on a pale imitation of the anger and slight arrogance he saw two days ago in the diner.

"Yes. There's a practical reason for my demand. Your fans have seen you in your concert attire and what you've got on now is about the same, so it will attract attention. They'll be looking at you regardless, but if you wear different clothes, people are much less likely to recognize you. I don't know whether the average everyday citizens of Dresden would know you at first glance, but in Rome, you're more likely to be noticed. And mobbed. This way, you'll be hiding in plain sight."

"I suppose you're right." Achilles' plate was now devoid of food and he set his fork next to it. "Then you're coming down to my room to help pick the right clothes for me to wear." Spirit flushed at the sudden thought of watching the handsome wolf doing more than just changing clothes and immediately buried the image as deep as he could. It was a temptation he did not need to battle right now. *There's no way he can be Black Dust.* It was more of a plea than an actual assessment.

Spirit noticed that the white wolf was watching him with sudden intensity. "Oh, of course," he replied with a smile he hoped wouldn't be taken as predatory. "I'm ready when you are."

* * *

A few hours earlier
The soft voice had answered his call. "Talk to me, Ramsden."

"I have some bad news." The wolf relayed what had happened, trying to ignore the listener's heavier breathing as he told his story across the encrypted link.

"So the tracking device isn't on him?"

The quiet response was only focused on his failure. "We lost the signal at 12:47 A.M., at the same time the diner was attacked the night before."

"You're only telling me this now?"

"We had to stay under the radar, because of the police."

The soft grumble sounded quite loud over the phone. "What's your backup plan?"

"I cannot leave the country right now, so I've made the arrangements with our contact in Rome to continue surveillance."

"Eriz Blanc?"

"That would be the one. He'll keep a close eye, you have nothing to worry about."

"I am not worried. I am rather concerned about your miss, Ramsden. It's very unlike you to chalk up a failure." The black wolf's fur prickled and the room suddenly felt very cold as he listened to the resonant voice soften to an angry whisper. "You would do well to remember what happened to Forzata."

"*Ja.* I have not forgotten, sir." The raccoon had missed his rendezvous with a buyer by thirty seconds and had been thrown from the roof of the Hotel Cien in Arenosa – a hundred story fall. "The unit is still safe, I am sure."

"It had better be; the initial arrangements have already been made. But first, there is something I want you to tell me." Ramsden straightened up attentively at the pause in the speaker's voice.

"Tell me everything about the wolf who chased you at the concert."

* * *

Spiritwolf followed Achilles downstairs, past his room, which still had the *Si prega di non disturbare* sign outside. They went into Achilles' suite in the corner of the building and Spirit peered around the spacious accommodations. "Do you always carry so much stuff with you?" The temptation to search the singer's bags was rising.

"I have to. A lot of it is gear for the concert and personal effects." The white wolf was looking through a closet, glancing back at Spirit every few seconds, then rummaging again. From where he was standing, Spiritwolf could see that the closet was full; including the floor, where boots and shoes of all kinds occupied every last inch of space. The agent padded over to a stack of suitcases near the window. A quick sniff brought more of Achilles' scent than anything out of the ordinary and he fought his subconscious' attempt to unbury his earlier thought.

"How about these?" Achilles was holding a dark purple dress shirt and black slacks. Shiny black dress shoes had been extracted from the closet as well. "They're what I would wear to an award ceremony." He flashed a cocky grin.

"Yeah. That's fine." Spirit nodded and leaned back while the white wolf disappeared into the spacious marble bathroom, closing the door except for a crack. He shook his head and gently rubbed his temples to keep his mind focused on the task at hand, rather than on the rock star changing his clothes.

And then his gaze fell upon the rucksack hidden behind the pile of suitcases.

He reached for the bag and had almost extricated it when he heard the soft click of a belt fasten into place. Spiritwolf pulled his hand back just in time to hear the bathroom door open again. *God DAMN it*, he swore silently. So close! The tablet had to be in there – why else would the rucksack be hidden behind a ton of luggage? For the briefest moment, he contemplated killing Achilles anyway and just taking the bag…

NO! His stomach did a few somersaults and his legs suddenly felt wobbly. *No.* The one thing he was NOT going to become was an assassin – invisible or otherwise. Armed people, people who were going to kill him – sure, he'd killed dozens. Maybe over a hundred. Or other people who'd planned to unleash technology to kill or terrorize the unsuspecting populace. Maybe Achilles was Black Dust – even though the pendulum seemed to be swinging back in that direction, he didn't have proof, and he was NOT going to kill an unsuspecting, unarmed person on a hunch. Not again. How could he have even thought about that? Spiritwolf felt his breakfast start to make its way back up to his throat. He had made that promise to himself another lifetime ago and he was not about to break it, even to have his visibility restored. Never.

But the thought had entered his mind, temptation seeping through a tiny crack of his will that never should have been there to begin with, would not have been there except for the accident. And if it happened once, it could happen again.

Master Song's lessons found their way back to his thoughts. *Find your center. Stay calm.* It was easier said than done.

"Ready to go, Spirit?" Achilles asked with a broad grin as he stepped into the room and spread his arms to show off the new threads. The smile faded and Spiritwolf realized his nausea, coupled with the effort of restoring equanimity, must still have been apparent on his masked features.

"Are you okay?"

"Ah, no. Sorry. I had a bit of an upset stomach just then, but I'm fine now," he replied with a slow cadence so as not to appear curt. A wan smile made it all seem fine. "Might have been the espresso."

"Mmm. The clothes are suitable, then?"

"Yes. You look outstanding in them." That admission seemed to help his mood. "I think we should do the double-decker bus tour first." The ride would buy him time to conceive a plan to allay his suspicions once and for all. Unless…

"Don't forget your bag, there," he blurted, pointing at the rucksack.

"What? No, I won't be needing it."

Spirit carefully appraised the white wolf's demeanor; the singer had casually dismissed the bag, which settled the matter for the time being. *Back to square one. I guess I need to stop jumping to conclusions.*

"In any case, the bus tour sounds like a great idea." Achilles extended his arm to the door. "After you."

The bigger wolf slowly nodded and stepped outside the room. They emerged from the hotel into the warm sunshine and Spiritwolf paused a moment to catch the scents on the wind. He turned left to head up the street toward *Stazione Termini* with his companion in tow.

* * *

Three floors up, the figure that watched them depart pulled his head back in the window. "I can't believe how much time they're spending with each other," Les pouted.

Cain looked up from his smartphone, where he was busily posting a new entry on his touring blog. "Jealous?" the badger smirked.

"Not really." The lizard shrugged and leaned against the wall. "But ya gotta admit it's curious. Our fearless leader, who never does anything with us, suddenly takes a shine to someone we barely know? Always going places in secret."

"You think Spiritwolf's trouble?"

"Why, no!" Les batted his eyes. "I think he's in a secret love relationship with our boss!"

Cain let out a loud guffaw. "C'mon, kid. You need to find a new hobby." He looked down at the screen and set about composing a response to *SDUrsine0*'s queries about kickoff night in Dresden and some of the rumors that were going around regarding a chase between a couple of people and gunfire.

The lizard looked out the window again and his eyes narrowed. The newcomer, that big wolf, a personal trainer – the disjointed thoughts blossomed into the beginning of a plan to be hatched and he licked his lips with that long tongue of his.

"Or a new person."

* * *

"Amazing!" Achilles was quite taken with the sight of Castel Sant'Angelo, just across the river from where the bus was traveling. It was indeed a rather magnificent old fortress but Spiritwolf had seen it many times before, including areas outside the usual tour boundaries, during a past mission. He was instead preoccupied with untangling the various threads of investigation from his earlier musings, combining the relevant ones with the discovery of the rucksack to see if any new theories resulted. The white wolf had been marveling all morning at the ancient buildings and grand statues the bus had paused at, giving the agent the opportunity to think. Nothing really substantive had emerged, except for a persistent feeling that Achilles was perhaps not the bad guy. He glanced at his tour companion snapping a picture of the building with his cell phone camera. They were sitting on the upper deck, where there were fewer people. Spirit felt more comfortable, and thinking about the rucksack kept his mind occupied enough to forestall any panic attacks about being discovered.

"Magnificent," Achilles sighed and slumped back in his seat. "I'll have to come back some day when I have more time. Maybe I should toss a coin in the Trevi Fountain to ensure it. Hey, are you getting at all hungry? You've been quiet for most of the tour."

"That's because I've already seen it. But yes, I could probably stand a bite to eat." Truth was, Spirit was famished. He hadn't been able to eat anything at the hotel; the espresso was supposed to have been a prelude to carrying his breakfast back to his room, where he could take off his mask and eat, but the rock star had co-opted his plan and so he'd been forced to wait to get food. He wasn't sure he wanted to risk eating with his mask on in front of Achilles – much less anyone else – and he wouldn't be able to be completely unseeable again for at least an hour until his metabolism assimilated his meal. He would not sacrifice his last-ditch method of escape. Besides, he very much did NOT want to see, hear, or smell someone eating in front of him while he himself was starving, but he didn't see any polite way out of it. He'd already used up some of those nicely crafted excuses in the last twenty-four hours, anyway.

"Shall we get off at the next stop, then?" Achilles stood and held onto the back of the seat while lazily brushing away a bug that had landed on his shirt sleeve. Spiritwolf got up as well and squeezed through the tight aisle and down the stairs. He glanced back at the rock star and nearly had a heart attack upon seeing everyone looking at him before realizing that they were merely curious and not staring for other reasons. Thankfully, Achilles had remained unrecognized in his new clothes, as Spirit had predicted, and for one moment he had the silly thought that his invisibility might have somehow been extended to the white wolf as well. Two male ermines, a teenaged white mouse, and a pair of shiba inus with cameras slung around their necks queued behind them. The large wolf studied them all cautiously; he didn't want a repeat of the near-disaster coming off the tram in Dresden.

The double-decker bus stopped and the driver, a bored-looking calico, opened the doors. Spiritwolf stepped out and focused on the street signs on the buildings well above the threatening throngs of tourists. He found the street leading to the *Fontana dei Quattro Fiumi* in the *Piazza Navona* and threaded his way into the larger open area. There, his pace quickened, becoming a brisk walk toward the south end of the *piazza*.

The white wolf kept in stride alongside him without much trouble. "Why are we passing all of these restaurants here?" Achilles asked, glancing at patrons of all sizes and species laughing, chatting and, most importantly, eating at the multitude of outdoor tables. The angry gods resident in Spirit's stomach growled in agreement; the smells of freshly prepared Italian food made him acutely aware that he hadn't eaten since last night. The gods demanded sacrifices and their patience was growing thin.

"Because you want to eat at a decent place, right?" Spirit automatically muttered *scusi* after nearly bumping into a white fox dressed in dark blue construction clothing and continued past the other fountain at the far end of the piazza. He followed the street as it angled from the south toward the southwest.

"Ah, they're for the tourists, then." Achilles smiled. "Well, I appreciate that you're taking me to an authentic Italian restaurant."

"Sure." Spiritwolf continued on as they made a couple more turns. "There're a few exceptional ones I know just slightly off the beaten path. Ah, here we are." The sign outside said "*L'Anima Vive*", a phrase from one of Michelangelo's writings which had intrigued Spirit upon his first visit to Rome. The two wolves entered and seated themselves at a table in the back.

* * *

"Hello, boss."

"Status report."

"All set up. 's like you wanted."

"Good. Call me when you've found the target."

"Don't need to. Already have."

"You're sure it's him?"

"Ya ya. They just went into a restaurant."

"Did they see you?"

"Nah."

"Follow the target and keep track of him."

"Ya ya. And th' other guy?"

"If he gets in your way, kill him."

The click in the earpiece abruptly ended the conversation. The white mouse shrugged, flipped his hair out of his eyes and began texting, though every few seconds, Eriz Blanc looked across the street at the pair of wolves he'd followed from the tour bus.

* * *

Clarice looked down at the white mouse from her position on the roof across the street. She wrinkled her nose distastefully. The kid was a gypsy with a strong aptitude for technology and although his operations had gotten him listed in the TEA database as a wanted suspect in various thefts and a few killings, he was still an extremely small catch compared to their real target.

"Do we attack now?" The American crocodile at her side was itching for revenge; despite his fall, he'd only suffered bruised ribs, thanks to the reinforced suit that they all wore.

"Of course not." The tigress seemed surprised that he would even make such a suggestion and the tone of her voice was enough of an admonishment. The reptile shrank back with uncertainty in his eyes. "Surveillance for now," she purred. "We'll strike when the situation favors us."

* * *

"Are you sure you're not going to order anything, Spirit?" Achilles appeared genuinely concerned for the larger wolf, who had been content to sip *acqua naturale* through the whole meal. "I mean, you recommended this place, so I figured you'd be eating, too."

Spiritwolf smiled. "Thanks. I'm getting something to take back to the hotel. In fact..." He motioned to their waiter, a tawny-furred muscular Cane Corso with striking green eyes. Spirit pointed to the pizza margherita and asked how long it would take to prepare one for his trip back to the hotel. *Quindici minuti*, was the gruff reply and Spirit nodded and asked for the check. "We can go in fifteen," he told the other wolf.

"That's good. That will get us back in time for the pre-concert meeting. You're still welcome to join us."

"I appreciate the offer. Maybe the next one." The water was only barely keeping his hunger at bay. *Maybe I should have ordered two pizzas*, he thought.

"And you've been rather distracted all day." The sterner tone snapped his gaze back to the blue-eyed countenance. "Maybe you didn't want me to come along, but I'd have expected at least some pleasant conversation from my trainer instead of being treated rudely."

The sudden arrogance in the younger male's voice combined with his hunger was a toxic mix. Spiritwolf's temper flared and he slapped the table – the sudden pain cut through his anger nicely while making the rock star jump in surprise. "Sorry, Achilles," he replied. "You're absolutely right and I suppose I should tell you what's on my mind." *Time to make up another story to appease the rock star.*

"Go on."

"I've been thinking about my past." Achilles opened his mouth as if to say something, then thought better of it. "As Regis and I discussed a few days ago, there are things I've done that I'm not exactly proud of. Other things, I wish had never happened." His voice softened. "I feel like I'm trying to figure out who I am, in the face of all that."

"Wow. That's pretty deep thinking, all right." Achilles nodded – whether sarcastically or sympathetically, it was difficult to tell. "What brought all this up?"

"The last few days, getting back to the real world, as it were, following my recovery. Talking with people again who aren't doctors, nurses, or… other specialists has been both good and bad. And different, compared to where I was in my life before my injuries. So, you could say I'm preoccupied with where my future seems to be leading from my present. It just… feels so chaotic and random."

"Okay, that makes sense, I guess." Achilles leaned back and closed his eyes. Spiritwolf stared at him, wondering what had made him admit all that. Had to be the wolf's charm. Granted, Achilles would be taking it in the context of his cover story but like before, it still had truths woven throughout. Dropping the barriers was becoming a little too uncomfortable.

"Do you regret your past, then?" The white wolf was looking at him again and this time, it was Spirit who paused to search for the answer.

"A wise lioness once told me, 'Without what we were, we are not who we are, and can never be what we are meant to be.'" *Topaz was always right, even before the accident,* he mused.

"You know, your deep thinking might be a condition caused by the people you associate with," Achilles chuckled. "Perhaps you should try simplicity for a change."

Spirit broke into a grin. "My goodness! Why didn't I think of that?" He smacked his forehead and quickly put down his arm after feeling the bio-glue under both his glove and his mask dislodge slightly. "And what about you? I'm sure you have no regrets in your past."

"You'd be surprised." Achilles looked like he'd eaten something sour. "I think maybe one of my biggest regrets turned into one of my greatest strengths. Years ago, when I was just getting started, I opened for one of my favorite bands in Sydney. 'The Cockamamies', they were called. I put on what I thought was a pretty good performance and ended it with a cover of one of their songs – to get the audience in the mood for the real thing."

"Uh-oh."

"Uh-oh is right, but maybe not for the reason you think. The audience loved my version and it pissed off the band. Their lead singer came up to me after I got off stage and socked me in the jaw. He told me I was a no-nothing piece of shit that didn't compare to them, so don't go fucking around with their music. At first, I was devastated. Here they were, some of my idols, talking to one of their biggest fans, me, like I was scum of the earth." The white wolf's eyes were blazing. "But then I realized that the audience had liked ME. Not them. ME. I left school and began performing full-time in just about any venue I could find. I told myself I was going to prove those fuckers wrong and, about a year later, I finally got a request from THEIR manager to open for one of MY shows."

Spiritwolf was listening raptly but broke in to ask, "And did you let them?"

"Nope." Achilles smirked. "But I stole their manager by offering to pay him more than they were."

"You mean Regis was their manager?"

"Yup. He knew they were on the way down and, I think he knew I was going to say no. Hell, it wouldn't surprise me if he orchestrated his transfer of employment. He's a savvy businessperson, to be sure."

"Yeah, I noticed. So the band ended up driving you forward despite them attacking you."

"Oh, don't get me wrong, Spirit. The majority of people who have helped me to get where I am have done so in friendly fashion rather than by trying to hurt me. But when someone comes after me, I can't give up. I just can't."

"Yeah, it's not in me to do that, either," Spiritwolf chuckled. "So, I guess, whatever my future may be, I shouldn't give up."

"Even if life hands you lemons. Making lemonade and all that. Ah, here's your food." Spirit turned and took the box of pizza and the bill. He fetched a couple of 20 euro notes from his wallet and noticed another piece of paper in the folio. He waited until the white wolf had turned his head before swiping it and pretending to fumble with the wallet in his lap while reading the hastily scribbled note.

Your old friend wants to see you. Be at 14 Via dell'Acqua in Trastevere at 22h.

* * *

That evening found Spiritwolf standing under a street lamp as he glanced at the note again and checked the address against the map that displayed on his cell phone. 14 Via dell'Acqua. Morey would have been amused at that. He smiled. The otter had a great sense of humor, despite what had happened to him and even though he was still recovering, Spirit knew Morey would keep going no matter what. It was in his nature. Meanwhile, Spirit was left to puzzle out the same lesson with the help of Achilles in an Italian restaurant while watching him eat pizza.

He checked the time on his phone. It was only 21:47, but the wolf had wanted to arrive early and do a little informal recon, as was his habit. He could have arrived much earlier but there wouldn't have been much point. He knew he was being tailed, ever since reading the note. It wouldn't be anyone he could see; the European agents wouldn't be that sloppy. And there wasn't any need to cause excitement by trying to find out who, or by disappearing. He couldn't afford to draw too much attention to himself.

The wolf stood in front of number 12 and he could see "15" on the next building down. So where the hell was number 14? Spirit looked across the street. Nope. A pair of young women – leopards, he recognized as they approached – giggled and dashed past him toward the Ponti Garibaldi as they made their way from Trastevere and into Rome proper. He exhaled and studied the buildings in front of him carefully.

Perhaps the number 14 wasn't an address at the street level, per se. There were some buildings large enough to encompass several street numbers; in fact, their addresses were listed as a range, say, from 10 - 20. But then why hadn't the note's author put that down? Was this a test of some kind? *One problem at a time.* The wolf walked to the corner of number 12. Like many of the buildings, the adjacent buildings shared a common wall. There was no way that number 14 was in between.

Spiritwolf frowned and kept his senses alert for movement all around and above him. He knew Zero would have already forwarded his itinerary to the European branch of the TEA; Ixak had gone a step further and somehow pulled his personnel file. Though protocol normally required at least one local agent to assist in any operation, undercover assignments would bypass coordination rules as long as Zero provided information to his counterpart and assured them his agent hadn't gone rogue. Still, it was common courtesy to check in with the locals at the point of arrival on the continent as he'd done in Dresden. Travel in the EU made subsequent check-ins unnecessary.

So, Spirit *should* have been left alone, but someone had made contact anyway, against protocol. And until he figured out why and resolved it, it would be a threat to the operation to be shadowed.

Who in the TEA would behave like this? He doubted Ixak would have had him followed. Despite the giant bug's outward appearance, Spiritwolf had gotten the impression that he was an honorable fellow. That meant it had to be someone local to Italy or Rome, or maybe someone passing through. The wolf sifted through the memories of his training in Europe from five years ago. He hadn't worked with more than a handful of agents but he couldn't narrow down the list at all. They hadn't been more than casual acquaintances and he'd kept his distance, staying in and studying while the rest of them went out and formed bonds of friendship. He had been the outsider, as had been the case so often in those days.

And then a glimmer of insight made him pause. He had looked different, the last time he was here. No one would have recognized him visually in his mask. And he'd had a different codename – it had been changed just before he'd joined the Ultras. He should have been completely anonymous. The only thing that hadn't changed was his voice. Someone must have overheard him talking and recognized him that way. But maybe they didn't know for sure, and that's why they'd purposely given a wrong address.

He remembered one part of his training that involved reversed or inverted numbers as an easy way to give someone a coded message that would appear like normal information to anyone else reading it. It wasn't strong encryption by any stretch of the imagination but it would do for situations where an algorithm or a cipher couldn't be set up beforehand between sender and receiver. And Spirit knew the encryption keys in his old TEA file would have been wiped out with the rest of his background, once when joining the Ultras and again following the accident.

Spiritwolf walked casually past number 15 and pretended to enjoy the nightly stroll. It wasn't difficult; he was somewhat pleased with himself for figuring out the little puzzle. Mostly. There were still the questions of who had discovered him and why they wanted to talk to him despite orders to the contrary.

The wolf approached number 41 on Via dell'Acqua and rapped on the door. "Chi è esso?" was the muffled challenge from inside.

"The note was well-received."

The door opened and Spirit looked down at a white fox dressed in the dark blue uniform – a construction worker, in fact. The hazel eyes regarded him with intent curiosity; the scent was no different. "Are you… ?"

"I was."

"Do you remember me?"

"Inverno."

"You look different."

"Otherwise, I'm the same person you knew."

"And what should I call you, if not… ?"

"Spiritwolf will do."

The fox nodded. "A good name. Please, come in." The wolf entered and saw Inverno holster his gun after closing the door. "It's been a long time and you've been off the grid for a few years now. What happened?"

The wolf felt his temper rising again, despite having eaten. Memories of his past were adding fuel to the fire. "It's none of your business, agent," he said coolly. "And I sure hope you've got a better reason for contacting me and possibly blowing my cover."

"Well, your attitude hasn't changed much, for sure. But just because you don't have any manners doesn't mean I have to be the same way." Inverno beckoned him to follow and together they went into the kitchen. The fox pulled a bottle of dark beer out of the refrigerator and popped the cap off. "Can I get you something to drink?"

"No."

"Don't sulk. It's unbecoming." The fox took a long swig from the bottle. Spiritwolf remembered Inverno as one of the bright stars of the Euro TEA agents and although the wolf had been overly competitive in just about everything, the popular fox had just been content to do his best and look outstanding while doing it, which had annoyed Spirit even further.

"You're right, Inverno. I apologize." A tiny spark of satisfaction buzzed his synapses upon seeing the fox almost drop the bottle in surprise. "And I wanted to thank you, for trying to help me back then, even if I was an ass and treated you badly."

"I take back what I said. You've changed a lot." Inverno took another sip.

More than you'll ever know. Spirit kept his expression neutral as he nodded.

"So what's happened to make you more humble, agent?"

"Will you please just tell me why I'm here? No more games. No more stalling."

"*Certo.*" Inverno finished the beer and when he did, there was wetness in his eyes that caught Spirit off-guard. "The professor is dying," he replied in a raspy voice.

The wolf felt his knees go wobbly and he leaned heavily against the doorframe. Professor Jacques du Nord was easily the most beloved person in DAST-Europe. He had been a researcher in the R&D branch of DAST and had voluntarily given up his life's work to teach the best and brightest agents of the TEA about the science and technology they would be guarding against. And not just the cutting-edge tech but also the stuff that was mere speculation; how the concepts and ideas could be realized into solid theory and from there, to practical implementation. This was what had allowed the TEA to anticipate malicious use of technology and be proactive instead of reactive. Spirit had been lucky enough to be one of the few agents from the Americas chosen to learn from him and the quirky, affable black wolf had been one of the few people who had broken through Spirit's aloof exterior and engaged him. The professor did that with everyone, instilled not just knowledge, but also the love of math and science, engineering and research into every agent he taught. In return, they made him an honorary member of the TEA, and gave him his code-name.

"What? Noir? Dying?" For several long moments, it felt like the world had gone stupid and absurd around him. "How long does he have?"

"Honestly? I don't think he'll last the night." The fox was staring at the empty bottle in his hands. "Though I'm sure he'd tell you otherwise."

"Why didn't you just tell me instead of going to all this trouble?"

"I…" Inverno pinched the bridge of his muzzle and gulped down a sob. *He's not taking this well at all*, the wolf thought.

"Sorry… it's been a rough couple of weeks. I wasn't sure whether it was you, when I heard you speaking. I had to know, I had to be absolutely sure."

"I know. I have a mask on. And before you ask, I'm not going to take it off. I have my reasons." The fox just nodded and looked down at his feet. "Is anyone else here?"

"No. Just me."

"What? Didn't anyone else want to see him?"

"Of course they did. They came, said their goodbyes and went back to their assignments. But he doesn't have any family, you see… so I… I mean… he doesn't deserve…" The fox's voice was breaking from bitterness.

"You wanted to stay with him until the end." Spiritwolf's voice was little more than a monotone. "To be with someone who he knew." *This is so much like… when I woke up after the accident. People coming in, talking for a few minutes, then leaving me to go about their business. I felt so lonely when they left…*

"Yeah, you know the professor." Inverno hiccupped and forced a smile. "He sent the medical staff away last week, said he didn't want them screwing up his chances to recover."

"What's wrong?"

"Brain tumor. Inoperable."

"Fuck." Spirit exhaled and shook his head. He felt so helpless to make things right. *Keep steady*, he told himself. "I'm so sorry – that's got to be rough, what he's going through. May I… see him?"

Inverno nodded again. "After I left the note on the tray, I came back and told Noir I thought you had returned. You should have seen his face – it was like he'd invented something new, right on the spot. He was so happy..." The fox turned his head out of view and coughed. "I'm sorry. You're right. I should take you up to see him now - this way." He left the beer bottle on the counter and moved past the large wolf. At the end of the hall, they climbed the creaky staircase and made their way to the first door on the right. The fox knocked lightly and entered after a brief pause.

The sight of the black wolf in the bed was like someone had punched Spiritwolf in the gut. Noir had never been a muscular person, thanks to a lifetime of study and research, but the gaunt figure with paper-thin flesh and fur stretched tight over very visible ribs showed how far his health had deteriorated. His eyes were closed – that, and the lack of medical equipment and doctors made it seem like he was already... departed.

Spiritwolf suddenly knew what it must have been like for Zero, Corona and Greystorm standing over him in the medical bay after the accident.

And then Noir's eyes opened, those piercing yellow orbs that absorbed and analyzed everything meticulously and could make even the most entrenched debater seem unsure of themselves. Those eyes were a welcome sight; it seemed that the professor's illness hadn't robbed him of everything.

"Who the hell are you?" The voice was strained, hoarse, but it still had energy behind it. It was still him, French accent and all.

Inverno cleared his throat. "Sir, this is your former student, the one I told you was here in Rome. He goes by Spiritwolf now."

"What's in a name, anyway? Spiritwolf, is it? All right. Come closer." The bedridden wolf never took his eyes off of him as he padded to the side of the bed. "Well? Aren't you going to say anything?" There was a small sliver of hurt edging into his voice.

Spiritwolf coughed. "My apologies, professor. It's good to see you, even under these circumstances."

"And the same for me. Inverno, leave us."

"Sir?"

"I must speak with him in private. No listening at the door, or anywhere else. Understand?"

"Of course, professor." Spiritwolf glanced behind him and mouthed a silent apology, which elicited a small, sad smile from the fox. He nodded and closed the door behind him; Spirit heard him going down the stairs.

"Now, then." Noir took a deep breath and pushed his stick-like arms to sit himself up. Spirit automatically reached down to help him, gently cradling him and rotating up. The lightness of the other wolf made his stomach turn.

"That's better." Noir closed his eyes and took as deep a breath as he could manage. His hands were trembling. Spiritwolf put his gloved hands over the older wolf's fingers and sat on the bed next to him.

"Thank you," he whispered. "At least the tumor hasn't destroyed my cognitive faculties. Now, to business." Noir's voice grew steadier. "I have some information that will help your investigation."

Spiritwolf chuckled. "I won't ask how you know about my assignment. You always put two and two together faster than anyone else I knew. And that's still true today." *And Canis doesn't count... he's in a class by himself.*

"You remember well." The old wolf smiled toothily.

Spirit returned the smile; fond memories blossoming warmly. "So what it is that will help me?"

Noir's eyes narrowed to triumphant slits. "In a moment. First, I want to see for myself."

"See... what, exactly?" The nausea in Spirit's stomach had returned.

"Your condition."

How the hell... ? "Why?" The word came out harshly.

"Young wolf." Noir tsked put his hands over Spirit's. "I am the one who is dying, yet you are the one who cannot accept what has happened to him, his destiny. Why is that?"

He sounds exactly like Master Song. It must be something they pick up after so many years of being a teacher. "I am under orders to keep it secret."

Noir barely managed a squeak in place of a snort, but Spirit saw the old fire in his eyes. "Oh, pardon me. I have mistaken you for another person who notoriously had problems with... how was it described? 'A deep and abiding dislike of superiors who give stupid orders.' No, there is no need to explain further. I remain sympathetic to your feelings, even if you cannot express them adequately and have to make excuses." Noir cocked his head. "But did you not realize that is why I told Inverno to leave? So that you could be comfortable around your old teacher?"

Spiritwolf sighed. "I did not realize it, no. Sorry." He shrugged. "So you won't help me unless I show you?"

"I did not say that and I would not do that to you, in fact." The black wolf appeared tired. "There has been some chatter about someone offering some... shall we say, interesting technology. Preliminary bids have already been solicited and very soon now, it will be auctioned off to the highest bidder. The TEA didn't catch it because the message is being broadcast with a primary decay signature ranging from -1.035 to -6.993 Joules per Kelvin."

Spiritwolf's forehead creased in thought. "Spread spectrum entropic modulation?"

"Very good. It appears as thermal noise, but there are a few organizations out there with the expertise to decipher it. And myself, of course."

The agent grinned. "And how did you discover it?"

"I was researching tachyon detection by monitoring fluctuations in the quantum field and came across the messages. Anyway, those idiots in the TEA Sciences group would never have found it – they only ever listen to single points in the spectrum at a time and I keep telling them to check whole bands and perform mathematical operations on them. Their variable bandwidth integrators should be able to lock onto it, once they insert the correct parametric function into the receiver's datastream."

Spirit nodded, focused on memorizing the technical aspects of the conversation, minus the personal commentary about his friends in the Sciences organization.

"So, when Inverno told me you were here, I knew that you were following the trail."

"I am. Did the message indicate what kind of technology?" Eagerness crept into Spirit's voice.

"Only that it had stealth applications." Noir was panting, wheezing, and he turned his head slightly. "I am sorry. This is the most I've spoken in days. I need to rest soon."

"It's all right, sir." Spiritwolf squeezed the old wolf's hands with familiar fondness and then let go. "Thank you for telling me."

"My last chance to help an outstanding former student." Noir managed a weak smile. "It was good to see you again, even if the fur is a different color than I remember. The person I knew is still beneath the surface."

"Yes. And I am in your debt for helping to make me a better person, back then. So…" Spiritwolf hesitated before pulling off his right glove. Noir raised his head from the pillow, his rheumy eyes widening and riveting upon not seeing the other wolf's right hand. "You have to promise to not tell anyone."

"I promise." The black wolf seemed full of life again and he gingerly reached out, found Spirit's invisible hand, felt it all over and looked inside his sleeve. "*Mon dieu.* I am very, very sorry that this has happened to you."

"Me, too." Someone holding his hand – not his glove, his actual hand – was the strangest sensation. It felt almost intimate due to his near-lack of anything but the occasions of brief physical contact since the accident – he idly noted that there had been a few of those with Achilles in the last couple of days, though that had been through his clothes or the gloves. Now, there were no barriers; there was nothing to hide. They were connected, in those moments, and the sympathy from the dying wolf filled him with the hope that, just maybe, things were all right no matter what he looked like. Acceptance of his condition would be a final lesson from his teacher.

And then Noir was speaking again, rapidly, excitedly. "It seems so natural, so much a part of you. *Incroyable.* You will forgive me for saying this, but I wish I could have done a full analysis, learned more about your condition and what caused it. Maybe even I could have found a means of undoing it."

Spiritwolf smiled gently. "Your information may do just that, sir. In the meantime, I'd like to stay and chat for a while. If you wouldn't mind." He put his glove back on, re-establishing the presence of his right hand at the end of his sleeve.

Noir nodded, blinking back tears. "I would like that very much, *mon ami.* As long as you don't screw up my recovery."

* * *

The ferret entered the small, dark room and closed the door behind him. His hand unerringly found the switch and a red light blossomed overhead like a baleful eye. He massaged his bruised shoulder while surveying his kingdom and then went to work.

The first eighteen photos had resulted in a few titillating concert images that could go toward paying his rent. Many of the others were unfortunately out of focus or obscured by some idiot stepping in front of the lens at the wrong moment. The next photo, for example. Some goddamn wolf… an American… had brandished a gun, pushed him to the ground, and stolen his motorcycle. It had been recovered by the police in pieces and the wolf had somehow escaped custody. The ferret's lower lip curled as the image began to appear. At least he had snapped the mug shot at the right time – if it was in focus, he could take the photo to the police and have them look for him. And then he'd sue the wolf for everything he was worth.

After several more minutes, the ferret picked up a pair of forceps and pulled the photo from the developing tray. He scowled; the wolf's arm was partially blocking the top of his face. It wasn't going to be of any use to the police.

"*Scheiße!*" he growled and threw the photo toward the wastebasket. As it frisbeed through the air, he saw something that made him leap after it and dig it out of the trash. The ferret sat heavily on the floor and held up the photo. He squinted at the image, rubbed his eyes, and then squinted again. His muzzle opened as if to say, "What the hell?" but no words emerged. He scratched his head and then the light bulb in his mind clicked on. He pulled a jeweler's eyeglass off the shelf next to him and studied the magnified part of the image thoroughly. The moment caught by his camera showed a clear shot of the snarling wolf's muzzle.

Up inside past the wide-open lips, there was no tongue, no mouth, no head whatsoever. It was not a trick of the light, nor could it be attributed to a problem with his camera. There was simply nothing in the interior except the back side of the wolf's head, like some kind of empty mask. An empty mask that had somehow yelled at him to get off his motorcycle.

The ferret's eyes were like polished, sparkling opals as he pulled out his cell phone and began to dial.

* * *

Spirit shuffled back to the hotel sometime after midnight. He had stayed with Noir, holding the old wolf's trembling hand steady until the professor had fallen asleep. He had hugged Inverno afterward; their shared grief of knowing the old wolf's time was almost up locked them in place for several minutes before Spirit felt strong enough to depart, sure that the white fox was also sufficiently steady. Outside again in the real world, there were lights, distant laughter, and then silky shadows murmuring nonsense. Life flowed around him and trailed a forgotten wake, dispersed by the city at night. He walked on ancient stone roads, numb, unable to think, slightly askew from reality. Nothing seemed right.

A very long day, he told himself wearily. *I just need it to be over.*

He wandered into the lobby, nodding at the desk clerk – a stylishly dressed vixen with rectangular glasses who pursed her lips in a smile that befitted her narrow muzzle. And then he paused.

"*Buona sera.* Anything for room 304? I'm expecting a package."

"One moment, please, while I check." She disappeared into a side room and emerged scant moments later. "I am sorry, Mr. Pellards." Spiritwolf didn't realize at first that she had used his alias and it added to the unreality he was already feeling. "There is no package for you."

"That's all right. Maybe it will be here tomorrow."

"I will ring your room if it arrives. Is there anything else I can do for you?"

"No, thank you. Good night."

"*Sera.*"

Spiritwolf sighed as the elevator doors closed. Obviously, it was too much to ask for his replacement mask to already be here. He leaned his forehead against the cool metal and pretended that, for once in the last few days, everything didn't seem to be falling to pieces around him. Moments later, the elevator stopped and he emerged onto floor 3. The concert was long over, which meant that Achilles was likely asleep. Or maybe he was out again, walking around the town. He paused and turned toward the rock star's room. Should he knock? Or wait for him to return? It would be so easy to just strip down and follow him around, watching everything he did, waiting until the right moment. Whoever was behind planting the tracking device would be interested in Achilles and make their move again.

The wolf clenched his fists. No, he needed to complete his mission without resorting to that temptation. He would not be so reliant on his... unique nature. The problem was that he needed to figure out who Black Dust really was and end the mission fast, preferably before the auction started. The information needed to cure his condition would slip through his fingers and be lost forever.

Tomorrow, he promised himself. He would formulate his plan tomorrow, when his head had cleared.

Spirit entered his room and texted Noir's info back to the States and to Ixak so they could start their monitoring while he slept. He stretched and was about to take his clothes off when the knock sounded at the door. Maybe Achilles was up after all. Spirit gazed longingly at the bed for about five seconds, then sighed and padded over to the door.

It was not Achilles who was waiting for him in the hallway. "Hey, gorgeous guy," said the lizard named Les. He was dressed in a loosely wrapped bathrobe that exposed most of his chest and abdominals, and he wore a huge grin that nearly split his snout into upper and lower halves as he gazed admiringly up at the shocked wolf. One end of the robe's tie was curled idly around his long forefinger.

"I figured it was time we got to know each other much better, don't you?"

Chapter Five: Hungry Is The Night

Three heartbeats; the moment that passed while Spirit unexpectedly appraised the nearly naked, lithely muscled visitor at his door. Les leaned forward into him.

Spirit held out a hand and resisted the reptile's push. "You need to go back to your room," he admonished, his voice sounding unwilling. And yet a familiar, animal flicker of desire ran through him and made his already weak resistance more susceptible than it should have been. Les wouldn't have noticed; the fellow found himself defied by an arm that could have held back a man three times his size. But he'd been around the block enough times to know when 'no' really meant 'yes.'

"Only if you come with me…" he murmured, silkily, while feeling up the forearm that was attached to the hand pressing against his exposed chest. "Man you're thick…" he mused, exploring the girth of the muscle and the synthetic fur that the agent was wearing.

Another flicker of emotion clashed with desire; this one was anger. "Let go of my arm," he warned. His eyes flashed with dangerous intent. And yet bubbling through his veins, desire met anger, clouding his judgment more effectively than any counter-agent, and gave rise to their child, *need*. It had been a long time. A *very* long time. Not once after the accident in fact had he…

Les let go, as intended. He gazed at Spiritwolf with lust and expectation. Spirit surveyed the hallway in a calculated, trained manner. Abandoned. Alone.

He grabbed the lapel of the lizard's robe and without saying another word, hoisted the smaller man off his feet and back into the near-darkness of his room.

Need would not go hungry this night.

* * *

Five footsteps; the distance from the mirror to his bed. Achilles groaned, fighting the pangs in his head, behind his eyes, and closed them. It was only darkness now but bright indeed was the pain that afflicted him, still prickling at his mind. He crawled between the cold sheets, threw the pillow over his head, and groaned.

It had started in the Colosseum. The area of ancient bloodletting had been turned into a sea of writhing bodies of another kind, the concert. On stage he was emperor; the noise they made, their edicts, accompanied by songs of fear, joy, and sex. He executed his role perfectly, as he always did. Ringmaster; freak; master; slave. Thousands of Italians had come to witness the spectacle of *Achilles*; this was one of the biggest nights of the tour. He gave it everything. Pushed himself. Snarled, spat, roared and demanded. Such was the energy of the live concert experience, he even ended up breaking one of Garrick's guitars. But that was it. That was *always* it. The moments that he lived for.

The cacophony had brought on headaches before, of course. The punishing volumes and chaos of the experience made the brain cry out for mercy from time to time. But this one was different. A sudden knife that came down, like day turning to night.

He was at the fore of the stage; bathed in light. It was the encore. Second to last song of the night. Beneath him, separated by a barrier, a sea of baying faces swam. The hunched forms of security guards managing the melee stood impassively against the audio assault, only the backs of their heads visible. He was singing one of his moodiest songs – a tale of addiction and withdrawal. It was brilliant. A soaring crescendo. And then he reached the first line of the second verse.

"And if you put that needle in my veins… I swear I'll see your face again…"

His tongue tripped over the word 'needle', and it was as if a bubble burst inside his skull. He choked out the word 'veins', as the sudden memory of something being injected into his neck flooded his senses. He staggered forward, eyes bulging, but the song continuing. "I swear…" *A cab. Silently looking out of the window. Dresden. Night. The pain!* He had lost the rhythm now. Missing words. Someone would notice. "Face… again…" He slapped at his neck, as if feeling something anew. His head suddenly flickered with a dull fire. Mouth dry as sand.

The rest of the song he carried on, fumbling through until the climax. As he collapsed, panting and against a mic stand, he caught sight of Cain picking up his sticks, waiting for the signal to play the last song. Eyes watering, he waved the badger and the rest of the band off with the pre-determined *show's over* signal, and then staggered offstage to his waiting entourage. The applause turned to baying, and then another kind of chaos surrounded him.

The phantom needle had become a stain on his consciousness, something that he saw again and again. Not knowing what was happening, or what the image implied, he threw off all attempts by his band and crew to coddle him, and instead demanded that he go straight back to the hotel. He got his wish.

Upon his bed now, he groaned. Two ibuprofen consumed, he wanted desperately for the pain to stop, and for sleep to take him. Things were always better with sleep. He was just over-taxed, that was all.

But sleep would not be a refuge from this night.

* * *

Spirit's trembling fingers fumbled with the cords of Les' robe and pulled the lapels open. The lizard smirked and opened his mouth to say something; he was instantly silenced by a commanding kiss that threatened to suck the breath from his lungs completely. The surety of the embrace only masked the fleeting terror the wolf was battling.

So what – he'd not been in the sack with anyone since the life-altering circumstances of his accident. Some nights – after seeing to his needs alone – he had wondered with dull bitterness whether he ever could ever be intimate with anyone again. That had been but one inconsequential part of his rehabilitation that no one had even bothered to consider. It seemed to be an inevitable fact; and yet, somehow, he didn't plan on becoming a monk to see out the rest of his days.

Nor did he expect someone to offer themselves to him on the fourth night of his mission, but they did.

And yet, even in the rising heat of determined passion, there was that fear. Such familiar anxiety. The perpetual *what if…* and *how can I…* screaming out for answers, conjuring awful scenarios.

The lizard was already naked and beginning to deftly remove the wolf's clothes. Too bad he didn't know this wolf had layers. *And he never would.*

"No," Spirit said, breaking the kiss.

"What the…"

"Not yet," Spirit rumbled huskily. "Gotta get something. Wait here." Les shrugged and got on the bed, tending to his own arousal while the wolf went to the duffle bag in the closet. He extracted something and brought it back.

"What's that?" Les asked warily.

"A blindfold."

"For me? No way." The lizard scooted to the edge of the bed. "If I'm gonna play with someone as hot as you, I get to watch."

"You don't. You put it on or else you get to leave, right now." The wolf unwrapped the blindfold and turned it around on his hands like kneading pizza dough. "I told you that you were going to bite off more than you could chew with me." He wrinkled his snout to look as arrogant and condescending as he possibly could.

Les' mouth opened and then his eyes danced with amusement. "You egomaniacal asshole!" he laughed, surprising the wolf. "You need that to fuck, well, put it on me, then. I can take what you got, blindfolded or not."

"We'll see." Spiritwolf slipped the blindfold he used for sleeping over the reptile's eyes; Les would not see a thing in it. He tied a slightly complicated version of a square knot to keep it secure and then sat back while the lizard tested it.

"Kinda kinky." Les reclined on the pillows and kept stroking himself. "Your move, big guy."

Spiritwolf silently studied the lizard, doubts raging through his head. His head, his face – it was the mask that the agent remembered looking at for the first time in his room with Zero, the lifeless thing that he made real and made him real. Spirit looked down at his hands, covered in the fake fur that the TEA had made for him. Earlier, Noir had touched his real hand, had made that connection to who he really was, past the lies of his exterior. There was acceptance of what the agent had become.

That was the moment the fear lifted from the wolf. That was when he knew how things had to be. *Lifeless, fake, am I?* he said silently. He steadied himself on the edge of the bed and stared at the lizard. Les, who had come to *him*. Who had put on a blindfold at Spiritwolf's command and waited for *him*.

No. Not lifeless. Not fake. Beneath this – I live.

"Ready whenever you are, wolf," Les finally said with a hint of impatience.

Spiritwolf peeled off a glove and watched his hand disappear, as it had earlier that evening. He was ready.

* * *

Two scenes plagued the rock star in his sleep. Two images. They danced a merry dance through his dreams and forbade him any rest, as his brain slowly rejected a chemical interloper meant to harm. The pain was a healing pain.

He was sitting in a movie theatre. It was dark; abandoned. Rows of dusty red seats sat empty, while he sat in the middle, alone, bathed in the silvery light of the screen. A film was playing out before him – the image blurry around the edges, somehow, and even as he shoveled buttery-tasting popcorn into his maw, he couldn't help but feel he had seen the story somewhere before. He was watching a long, pale line of corridors, the camera looking over the shoulder of a shadowy black wolf. He had a gun ready. Achilles knew what kind of movie this was. A *spy* movie. He could tolerate that. And the familiarity… yes… it was so familiar because the corridors were like those backstage at one of his concerts. They were all the same.

He was no longer alone. There was someone whispering in his ear, telling him the story of what was transpiring onscreen. Narrating. Informing. The camera panned over a long highway – the Autobahn – and it was a chase scene. The whispering continued. The black wolf was on a motorbike. Lights flickered and flashed by. Whispering. Instructing. At first the voice speaking of things that had happened; then it seemed to speak of the events onscreen unfolding… and finally, out-of-sync, it spoke of things that had yet to come to pass – and then did.

The dream-Achilles put down his popcorn. Turned to face the whispering figure over his shoulder – and cried out in pain from a needle jaggedly being inserted into his neck. He felt the poison pumping and flowing down into him, and screamed.

Darkness followed.

* * *

Both of Spiritwolf's gloves were on the floor. The agent slid his bare hands along the lizard's legs, slowly moving up from tight calves toward the quads. The touch of the slick scales on his palms was electrifying but the wolf still carefully watched Les to see if he could somehow see the empty sleeves reaching out for his legs, feel the lupine's ghostly touch. Quite the contrary, the gecko lay back and was breathing hard, evidently enjoying it just as much.

Les suddenly sat up. Spiritwolf froze, unsure of the lizard's impetus for doing so until Les reached for him, crooning, "Wanna taste you." He stayed unmoving while the gecko found his trousers. Even blindfolded, he expertly undid the belt and then unfastened the pants. Spirit let them be tugged down and felt his erection spring free. He watched in near-disbelief as the lizard found his balls, cupped seemingly air in his hands, and then leaned in to take the unseen shaft fully in his mouth. Without a word, Spirit carefully wormed the rest of the way out of his trousers and let the cooler air play over his invisible lower body.

"Oh, man," Les mumbled. Again, the agent froze, not knowing why he had stopped. "You taste awesome."

The reptile went to work on his unseen sex again. Spiritwolf unbuttoned his shirt eagerly, disappearing more as he went. Finally, the mask and contact lenses were cast aside, leaving Les as apparently the only person on the bed, appearing to be giving someone the best blowjob of his life. The last of the invisible wolf's fear surrendered to the inevitable need for release – his first taste of freedom that he could truly enjoy as himself. And with that blindfold on the lizard, he could do whatever he wanted.

A few minutes later, the lizard flipped onto all fours and rocked back and forth in a quick staccato rhythm, moaning his desires in equally fast cries of pleasure. A few minutes after that, he began a series of miraculous contortions and impossible, gravity-defying positions that, had he been able to see himself, he would most certainly have been in awe of.

* * *

One…

Achilles was sitting in a diner. It was abandoned. Decaying. The walls yellowing with grease and age. Perched upon a booth whose fabric had been torn long ago, he stared down at the table in front of him. Upon his plate was the half-eaten remains of a hot dog. It was moldy; green and black – and for a moment, it was as if he saw it crawl. The white wolf shoved it away from him in disgust, revealing a paper placemat beneath. Upon it, the sunken face of a sullen gorilla stared up at him. *And then it spoke.*

"*Was wünschen Sie?*" came the disembodied voice. Achilles gasped in a nightmare with no reply. "*Was wünschen Sie?*" it asked again.

He grabbed the face and crumpled it up into a ball before it could ask again. He threw it against the wall opposite – which promptly collapsed backwards in a pile of dust, revealing itself to be as fake as a prop on a television set. In horror, Achilles stared as the other walls came tumbling down, revealing that he was sitting on a giant soundstage, like the ones used when he shot one of his infamous music videos. A figure stood hunched behind a video camera, its leathery hide absorbing the light that poured down upon them both from the spotlights above. The white wolf stood up reflexively, knocking over the table. A glass smashed, as from behind the camera out slid a mean-looking crocodile. He cradled some kind of gun within his claws.

A grin flashed. Sparks flew, and Achilles raised his arms to defend himself. The gun fired a projectile of two wires that shot right past his head. He spun, gasping, as the black wolf from the movie caught them within his hands. The wolf was a shadow, a walking silhouette, absorbing all light. Just an outline. An enigma. He stepped toward the wolf, a needle in his hands.

You… you're the one…

The needle flashed; the crocodile, the soundstage, gone. There was only the wolf. And then there was something else. *A cab. Silently looking out of the window. The orange lights reflecting upon his features, the scent of exhaust fumes wafting through the air-vents. Dresden. Night. A wolf at his shoulder. The needle going in. The pain.*

One…

The black wolf was upon him. The instrument in his neck. *The anger! He heard a voice – his voice! – snarling dire threats. "You fucker! You can't do that to me! I'll write it down! I'll… put it on my computer… or… speak…"*

In his dream, Achilles seized the needle. Tore it from his neck, and faced his assailant down. The black lines slowly peeled themselves away, like the layers of an onion, lifting away the wolf's pain. Revealing the face beneath.

"You… it's you… you're the one…"

The white wolf recognized Spiritwolf. Remembered *everything*.

And opened his eyes.

* * *

Dawn broke.

Sickly yellow sunlight crept into the room, filtering through the curtains restlessly, the space seeming now to be less luxurious, hospitable. Overnight it had become seedy, dirtied. Discarded garments lay here and there. Socks. Pants. A face. A snoring gecko with a blindfold over his eyes lay on the bed. On the sofa, a large form in a blanket moved; the sheet rose like a ghost before falling away, the form gone. The depression that remained in the cushions rolled itself to the edge and disappeared. Footsteps in the carpet; and then the wolf's mask floated from the floor. Suspended in mid-air for a moment, absent hands examined the material and empty sockets before a great sigh swept throughout the room.

"What have I become?" Spirit's moody voice asked; the sound soon muffled by the soft furnishings.

There was no answer.

The invisible wolf gathered the rest of his things, and padded into the bathroom, stepping over the debris of clothes, pillows, and blankets strewn about like the aftermath of a tornado. *Some night,* the wolf mused. *Some wild, passionate, messy night.*

But somehow unsatisfying.

In the solitude of the bathroom, he applied his disguises once more. For some reason, the mask and gloves felt more ill-fitting than before, as if their time on the floor had somehow caused them wear or distortion. The agent examined them carefully in the mirror – they looked fine. But the feeling that they were sullied somehow could not be shaken. He put in a fresh pair of contact lenses and sighed anew, tearing his gaze from his unwelcome reflection.

Checking himself, he exited the bathroom and peered at the clock. Nearly seven; he had an appointment with the white wolf in the downstairs gym shortly. *Just another distraction.* He wrapped himself in workout clothes and checked for gaps; as usual, there were none. Suddenly the oppressive feeling that he was wasting too much time crept upon him. Sex. Secrets. Subterfuge. Damn cunning; damn protocol. He wanted this mission to be over already.

He looked down at the lizard, who was slack-jawed, naked, and sprawled out on top of the bed, and visibly shuddered. Funny what the light of day brought. He untied the knot and pulled off the blindfold. In two more steps, he had found the keyboardist's robe, and had flung the velveteen garment at the fellow.

Les' dreams were finally interrupted when Spiritwolf smacked him gently on his leg. The lizard sat up groggily and as swiftly as his addled brain would allow. "Snuh... huh... wuh?" were his first expressions like words.

"Home time," Spirit rumbled, grabbing the few items he needed – room keycard, phone – from the bedside tabletop.

"Man..." Les groaned, rubbing his head, feeling over his teeth with his impressive tongue, and fumbling at the robe. "What did we... last night... I..." He paused, looked around the room, the sheer disarray of the room, and again at the muscular wolf looming over him. He widened his eyes. "Did we do all *that?*"

Spirit coughed, doing up his shoelaces. "Yes. We had sex. Quite vigorously."

Les slid out of the bed, and put his robe on. "But I didn't think we... I mean, I couldn't see what you... what we were doing..."

Spirit bit his tongue. "You didn't mind last night."

"Uhh…" Les muttered, suddenly feeling sore. "I think I need to go back to bed." He lifted the covers to crawl back inside.

Spirit caught his skinny arm. "I'm afraid not. I need to get going, which means you do too. Sleep it off in your own bed."

He pulled the lizard out of the door before the fellow knew what was happening, and closed it behind him. Then he walked purposefully down to the elevator without even looking back over his shoulder. Les swiftly followed.

"Damn, you're an asshole in the morning," Les sulked. "So you wanna get breakfast?"

The imposing wolf turned around, faced down the lizard and spoke sternly. "Les. Listen to me. Last night was fun, but don't ever come to my room again. Don't come to *me* again. And don't expect a Christmas card, either."

With that, he shook his head, strode away from the elevator, and disappeared through the door to the stairwell.

For a moment, Les merely stood there in the corridor, still half-naked in his robe, stunned. "Fucker!" he spat at the direction the wolf had disappeared through. A petite female mink passed him in his diatribe. "What?" he barked at her, stomping off back to his room.

* * *

Down the hall, in his corner suite, the white wolf was ready.

Ready for the day. Ready for action. Ready to put someone in his place.

As dawn found him, he was already awake; and as he dressed into his workout gear, he felt like a gladiator putting on armor to step into the arena. Anger had carved itself upon his features and left gravelly creases that were unknown to all but a few. He studied them intently in the mirror – before purposefully, slowly, forcing them to relax. Smooth. Calm. He put on the disguise of normalcy to convince the world that everything was fine.

But it wasn't. Not for him. *And certainly not for Spiritwolf*, he growled mentally.

He exited his room. Lost in a haze of narrow-minded scheming, he practically bumped into the white mouse that was pushing a cart of towels down the corridor.

"Housekeeping?" He muttered to the mouse, noticing how she kept her head down, black bangs of hair covering her features, green uniform failing to disguise a pair of breasts that were anything but unnoticeable, even to Achilles.

"Ya, ya," she squeakily replied, still keeping her head down. "Want towels?"

"You're early," Achilles muttered, beginning to walk away. "You can go in. Don't touch any of my things." He found the elevator at the end of the corridor waiting for him. Before the doors closed, he glanced up at the housekeeper again, and could swear he caught her smiling.

* * *

Spiritwolf arrived in the hotel gym first; it was a fairly small room, with only the minimum in terms of equipment, but it would do. Mirrors on every surface. At this hour of the day, it seemed none of the other hotel patrons were using it, typical of the Italian laid-back philosophy of life. *La vita dolce.* Or maybe they too had indulged themselves last night.

The brown wolf had a momentary flashback to a debauched moment with Les and relived its physical pleasure but felt nothing emotionally. *Time to shake off the cobwebs,* he thought, heading over to a chin-up bar and taking hold. Carefully and deliberately hanging on to it to stretch out his back, after a few minutes he began to lift himself up slowly and with purpose; he could feel the cobbled muscles of his lats and biceps rippling with effort. He found himself admiring his reflection in the mirror for a moment just long enough for Achilles to slip into the room unnoticed. Enough time for the white wolf to throw the lock on the door from the inside.

"Morning, Spirit," he said with a shrug of his shoulders. "Getting started without me, are you?"

Immediately, the brown wolf let himself drop to his feet. "Just warming up," he said with a smile, a little off-guard. Was there something different about Achilles this morning? He studied his training partner intently for a moment. When he had last seen the rock star at *L'Anima Vive* before they parted company, he felt like some barriers had come down – maybe not all of them – but a window of familiarity at least. He glanced at the wolf who now had his arms crossed over his muscular chest, and could see that the old barriers were back up again – and more besides. "How was your night?" he asked, pleasantly.

Like a ray of sunshine, Achilles brightened. "Wonderful," he answered, lifting his arms animatedly. "I'm afraid that beautiful Italian food will go straight to my handles, however; no holding back on the workout today. How was yours?"

Spirit smirked, unable to shake the feeling that something was amiss in all the mixed signals the wolf was giving him. "Mmm… all right. I had a bit much from the minibar, I'm afraid."

Achilles chuckled, jumping up on the chin-up bar himself and cranking out some reps of his own. "Careful," he said through gritted teeth as he went through the motions. "Those things are expensive – even on my wage. We must be paying you too much."

Spirit puffed out his chest as the rock star dropped. "Time I earned my keep, then. Are you ready?"

"Are you?"

The brown wolf smiled and clapped Achilles on the shoulder as they headed for the treadmills together. "That's the spirit," the singer muttered.

* * *

Forty-five minutes later, Spirit was panting and sweating desperately. Thank goodness the bio-mesh that made up his disguise was porous; otherwise, he was sure that his feet would be four times the size from all the bodily fluid his fur was secreting. They were approaching the end of the session, yet Achilles seemed to have boundless energy. It was like he was a wolf possessed this morning. Perhaps his wild night hadn't helped his performance that day, but he couldn't shake the feeling that the rock star was deliberately pushing him hard, trying to outperform him in some way.

"Gods," he panted. "I thought I was the one who was supposed to be training *you*."

"You're not helping your argument that you're worth your pay," Achilles chuckled, slyly. "Don't disappoint me now." He sat down at the bench press, which had an empty bar waiting upon the rack. Then he slid off again, as if changing his mind. "No. Here. You go first."

"Phew… naw… clients first…"

Achilles shook his head. His smile was so friendly. "I insist… I want to see how you ended up so big. Show me how much you can press."

"My max?" Spirit said cautiously, looking at the nearby plates. "I don't know if they have enough…"

Now Achilles smiled for real. It was wide. "Now that sounds like a cop-out if ever I heard one…"

Coughing loudly, Spirit sat. He puffed out his chest to its full size. "Fine then. Load me up. Let's see how long it takes you to rack up 170 kg, rock star; this can be part of *your* workout."

The brown wolf waited, getting his breathing under control and preparing himself as he watched the plates being loaded up. It took a little while for the right plates to be found... his attention began to drift, as he wiped his forehead with the back of his hand. The bio-glue slid too easily. *Damn*, he thought. *I guess this much sweat isn't good for it. Memo to self...*

"Ready, big guy," Achilles said, interrupting his reverie. "Let's see what you're made of."

"Spot me," Spirit instructed. "It's been a while since I've done this much."

The white wolf sauntered over to hover above the bench and bar adjacent to Spirit's head. As the wolf lay down, he saw Achilles staring at him intently. "I can't wait to see this," he muttered.

Spirit grinned, taking hold of the bar, readying himself. "Prepare to be impressed!" His hands gripped the metal tight. He planted his feet firmly either side of the bench, and looked up at the ceiling. The fan wobbled lazily on its axis. He focused on the sound of his breathing as the bar went up, and with huge effort slid from its rack. Muscles bunched and groaned impressively under the weight, and as he began to lower the staggering weight down to his chest, his eyes flicked to Achilles' face and he glimpsed a devil's wicked satisfaction. An alarm bell rang in his head, as he tried to halt the weight's inevitable decline and rest – but found that he was not strong enough.

"F... fuck!" He said, arms shaking, unable to move the bar from his neck, where it was perilously resting, but with enough strength remaining to keep it from crushing him completely. "How much... ?"

"About 200... maybe? And that's not including the bar," Achilles sulkily answered back. "Sorry, I was never any good at math."

Spirit tried to give a heroic push, which nearly ended in disaster. Unable to lift the weight, he only lost more of his stamina, the cold iron bar pressing ever more firmly upon his neck. "Stop..." he croaked.

The white wolf leaned forward and took hold of the bar with both hands – putting in just enough effort to allow Spiritwolf to lift the bar off his neck – but keeping him otherwise pinned. "I'm not going to do that, *Agent* Spiritwolf," he growled. "You picked the wrong wolf to mess with this time."

Now Spirit's eyes bulged with dismay. How could he have... how was it that... the methyl caudate had worn off! "So... it's you... Black Dust..." he gasped.

Achilles snarled. "For *fuck's* sake! I'm not Black Dust! Never was! I'm just the wolf whose trust you betrayed. Who you tried to make forget. Do you have any idea how fucking... *violated* I feel? And I trusted you!"

In a heartbeat, Spirit thought of the little black case. Thought of what he had done to the white wolf. He gritted his teeth, arms losing more of their strength, finally a feeling of helplessness washing over him. He fought it – but answered honestly as he could. "I was just… doing my mission… didn't want…"

"Didn't want what? My help?" Achilles said, calming himself. "This is *my* tour. If there were something going on, I would know about it."

"No…" Spirit groaned. "Please. Stop."

"I'm no assassin. Not like you probably are. But how do I know I can trust you?" He let the bar slip a little further, pressing down on the brown wolf's neck.

Calmly fighting panic, the detainee spoke quickly now. "If you remember what I did to you… you must remember what I did *for* you. At the diner. I *saved* you from those goons. I'm not going to hurt you."

Achilles narrowed his eyes. He left a pregnant pause. "If I let you go, can I trust you?" he answered at last.

Spirit quivered. He steeled his gaze, faced the wolf, and braced himself. The quivering stopped, in a remarkable display of strength and will. "You can, if I can trust *you*."

The rock star seemed to consider this indirect phrase for a moment, before he leaned in and hissed. "Push. Now." And began to strain and haul the bar up with all of his effort. Sighing relief, the agent pushed up at the same time, and together – and not without effort – they managed to place the bar back on the rack.

Achilles stepped away, as Spirit sprang from the bench as if it were a vicious animal that would bite him. Across the gym, the two wolves faced each other warily.

Silence reigned for a time.

"There's more to you than I gave you credit for," Spirit said at last. "It's been a long time since anyone got the drop on me. *And* you resisted the methyl caudate."

"And you're nothing what you appear to be," the white wolf said sternly, arms folded across his chest. "From everything I remember now… you could probably kill me with your bare hands if you wanted."

Spirit glowered. "If it makes you feel any better, I don't kill innocent people."

Achilles stood his ground. "But that's not all I remember. You told me in the diner what you were looking for. A tablet." He managed to lift his frown to a wan smirk. "I know where you can find it."

"If you're not Black Dust, then how… ?" Spirit asked.

"Later. But for the price of never seeing you again, I'll show you where it is."

"Done," Spirit said, brushing himself down. "Lead on, rock star."

Achilles unlocked the door.

* * *

Eriz Blanc was very happy.

Eriz Blanc was going to be very *rich*.

The white mouse tumbled out of the service exit of the hotel, and tottered past the abandoned bags of refuse upon indiscreet high heels. A black rucksack retrieved from the white wolf's room was clutched firmly in his hands; within lay his prize. His assignment had been surveillance but someone else made a better offer, one that had been very easy to accept. The buyer was going to be very pleased, which made Eriz very happy. Sell it quickly, leave quickly, and have enough money to never take orders ever again.

He sauntered a few steps further, before tiring of his disguise. "Ya ya…" he crooned. "More towels…" he snickered, shucking off the housekeeper's coat, revealing the obviously fake breasts, dumping them in with the trash. He shucked off the heels and sighed in relief, resting against a wall despite the place reeking of piss and garbage.

"Eriz Blanc?" A booming voice suddenly spoke, snapping the white mouse to attention. A large figure was walking down the alleyway toward him. The man was soon looming over him.

"Ya ya… it's me. You are here to pay?" The mouse nervously answered, gulping. He held out the rucksack.

The man looked over the mouse and the bag. Paused for a moment, then advanced with a snarl. "I'm afraid not. I'm *Black Dust*, you worm, and you have taken something that belongs to *me!*"

The mouse squealed in terror.

And then he screamed no more.

* * *

Riding the elevator together – Achilles made sure they got on an occupied one – the two wolves stood shoulder to shoulder, stiff-backed and facing ahead. A caribou and a zebra were their lift-mates, who were staring silently ahead.

"We're going back to your room, aren't we?" Spirit hissed.

"Well done," Achilles spat, eliciting an odd look from the herbivores. "It's a wonder you haven't found what you're looking for already with acumen like that…"

The agent was quieted to silence again, chagrined. Only the zebra coughed in the uncomfortable silence that followed.

When they reached the third floor, the wolves exited and the other passengers rode on. Achilles led the way, passing by the abandoned housekeeping cart outside his room. Spirit looked at it askance. "That's odd. They don't usually leave them…" And then he saw the open door that Achilles was heading purposefully toward.

"Wait!" He shouted, bounding ahead of the rock star. "Something isn't right."

The white wolf found himself blocked by a meaty arm and rolled his eyes. "Is that what your super-spy senses are telling you now? Because of a stray cart? Please…"

"We're going to your room. *Fine*," Spirit said, losing patience. "At least let me go first."

He marched on before Achilles could answer – peered into the doorway – and then pushed it open, aghast. "I'm too late. I don't believe it." He felt the dismay washing over him and inwardly groaned at the scene before him.

"What? What's happened?" Achilles gave him a shove, stepped into the room, and found his dismay to be of equal ferocity once he was among the carnage.

And it was carnage; everything had been ransacked. Every drawer tipped out and its contents strewn like a rummage sale on the floor, the bed. The bed itself had been split open from tip to toe, as had the pillows, a dusting of feathers everywhere. Suitcases belched thousand-dollar Armani suits, and even the minibar had not escaped the thieves' prying hands, all-too-expensive miniature bottles of finest cognac smashed, seemingly for no purpose, upon the plush floor. "No… no… no no!" Achilles cried, clambering over the mess.

"Is it still here?" Spirit barked, eyes flicking over everything. His heart was pounding in his ears. His vision contracting with anger that was building for release.

The white wolf examined the corner, looking about for the concealed rucksack. "It… I can't… *shit.*" He answered.

"*Damn* it!" Spirit roared, punching a nearby dresser. The wood splintered a little at the force of his blow. "If you're not Black Dust, then *how!*"

"Fuck me, I don't know! Your tablet – the one you were talking about – it just appeared in my personal rucksack as the tour began. It wasn't something I'd seen before – I tried to get it to work one night, but it was encrypted. Bricked, I thought, by whoever made it…" The white wolf was pacing now, picking up things that belonged to him and looking about forlornly. He caught Spirit scowling at the thought of what he'd lost, and who might have it now, and defended himself against critical questions that weren't even being asked. "A lot of shit gets packed into the wrong bags when you're on tour, okay? How the *hell* was I supposed to know it was some secret-spy tech? If you had…"

But Spirit wasn't listening. He was trying to think of how he could possibly describe his failure to everyone that had put faith in him in the mission. How he could face them.

And how he could go on knowing that the only chance he had to find his cure had slipped by right under his nose.

* * *

Half a continent away, someone else was having a bad night of their own.

Milan Bosley sighed, shook off the rain from his umbrella, and entered the lobby of the glinting MediaCentury Corp tower still drenched from head to toe. The slender ferret had probably doubled his bodyweight from the sheer volume of water his clothes and fur had taken on; at least it felt like it. The storm had hit London suddenly, too sudden for the photographer to take note and retrieve his umbrella from his luggage as he walked through the clean, but abandoned business center of Canary Wharf until it was too late. The first downpour had been the heaviest. He cradled a briefcase against his chest; within were contents too precious for the elements to ruin. Ignoring a curious, unimpressed look from the late-night security guard manning the desk at the lobby, the first thing he did once inside the shelter of the glass walls was to throw his flimsy umbrella to one side, crouch down, and peer inside the briefcase intently. He prodded some papers and moved about a half-eaten packet of nuts, but seemed satisfied that everything was in order. When he stood up again, the guard had left his post and was looming over him. Milan gulped in alarm at the broad, sharp-suited ram and blinked expressively.

"I hope, for your sake, you are the photographer," the sheep rumbled. He spoke in English – the universal language of Europe – but his accent betrayed his Russian heritage.

"I am," the ferret replied crisply, his Germanic tones flat and unwavering. "I was sent for."

The ram did not move. "It is a bad idea to walk into this place and be seen to pull something from a briefcase. I will see your ID now."

For the first time, Milan noted that the guard was armed; from the folds of his suit, a holstered gun was peeking out. When he looked up into the ram's eyes again, he was unable to hide the shock on his features, and retrieved his passport immediately – but slowly. The ram examined it dutifully. "Very good," he said at last. "Mr. Murdock is expecting you. Follow me."

He handed back the passport. The ferret put it away again, into his trouser pocket. Then he noticed how much he was dripping onto the black, expensive marble floors at his feet. He looked about himself abashedly. "Excuse me… I should freshen up before the meeting… do you have a towel, or something I could…" His English rusty, he struggled to find the right word to use.

But the guard looked at him coldly. "Does it look like we're running a day spa? Come, rodent. He does not like to be kept waiting." The heavyset ram then turned upon his heel, and walked toward an elevator across the lobby.

Bristling with perspiration and quiet indignation, Milan followed dutifully. He stepped up to match the guard's pace. "He's working late tonight," he muttered.

"Boss works late every night," the fellow stoically replied, putting a key into a slot by the lift. The gold-paneled doors slid open obediently – revealing two more mean looking men in suits who were standing inside. The bear and the crocodile both nodded to the ram, who took Milan's arm and escorted him inside. Dwarfed, and beginning to grow a little afraid, the ferret tried not to notice that both the other men were also carrying weapons and instead focused on the array of gently ascending numbers in front of him. Nobody spoke. He didn't even notice the bear eyeing up his coat over his shoulder.

Eventually, they reached the top. "Thassa nice coat," the bear muttered as the doors slid open. "It would fit my son perfectly."

"Um, thanks," Milan nervously replied. "I'll give you the number of the tailor on the way down…"

The bear gave an ugly, broken-jawed grin, which made the ferret's skin crawl. His escort shook his head, took Milan's arm again, and with firm insistence walked him from the confines of the elevator, onto the top floor of one of the tallest skyscrapers in all of London.

The white marble floors reflected orbs of light from ostentatious fixtures above; the walls themselves were windowless, so that one could not see the night-sky outside; only covered with an array of flat-screen televisions, dozens of them, seemingly tuned into every possible channel imaginable. Upon them flickered news stories from around the world, dramas, movies, cartoons, and music videos. It was a cacophony of color that struck Milan's retina like a fist; thankfully they all were silent. The ram walked on with echoing, heavy footsteps toward a figure seated behind an expansive desk at the other end of the long room; the ferret followed, only a glance over his shoulder confirming that there were two more men guarding either side of the elevator as it clanked shut behind him.

He walked on, and heard the man behind the desk speaking in irritated tone, a one-sided conversation drifting across the empty room to reach the ferret's ears. "No. That's unacceptable... of all the incompetent... ! Tell me... wait. You'll have to excuse me – something I have to deal with personally." At that, the voice stopped. A high-backed chair swiveled around as the photographer and the guard approached.

"Ah, Milan," a well-dressed lion purred, revealing himself. "So glad you joined us on such short notice." He spoke English flawlessly; in fact, there was a hint of plumminess in his voice that was unmistakably upper-class. He was solidly built, and stood, holding out a golden-furred hand to the smaller man across the desk. The ferret shook it, and the ram melted away discreetly back the way they had come, his job done. Silver cufflinks in the lion's white shirt glinted noticeably; they were in the shape of a cat's skull. This did not make the ferret feel any easier as he sat in the chair proffered to him at the lion's bidding.

"I hope you had a pleasant journey. Sorry about our weather, by the way."

"It was fine, Mr. Murdock," the photographer replied, gripping the attaché tightly between his drying hands.

"Oh, please," the lion said, waving a remote. With one click of the button, all the television sets winked out. Suddenly, the tycoon's office had become much darker. "Call me Blair. How long have you worked for us now?"

"Five years," the ferret nodded. "You bought out the newspaper I was working for at the time."

"Ah yes. *Die Moderne Welt*. Great returns. You've provided us with some wonderful pictures, too; I've seen your work."

The ferret smiled weakly. "Thank you... Blair. But that is not why you summoned me here, no?"

The lion smiled toothily. "Straight to the point. You Germans! I like that," he leaned back in his chair, folding his hands over his stomach. "You told your editor you had something unusual to show him, from the Achilles concert. Once you sent a copy to him, *he* contacted me immediately. Do you know why?"

"*Nein*. I mean, no."

Blair smiled all the more. "Because I tell all my editors to keep an eye out for such things. Show me what you sent to him."

The ferret nodded obediently, bent down, and retrieved a sheaf of A4 glossy photo prints from the film he had developed the night of the Achilles concert. There, in monochrome glossy glory, was the impossible image of a wolf that had shoved him with no head inside the mask, snarling with a mouth full of emptiness and rage. The photographer handed them over to the mogul, who took them eagerly. Blair put on a pair of glasses and rubbed his chin. "Ah… and so there he is…" he whispered to himself quietly. He looked up at Milan again, slight dissatisfaction in his eyes. "A pity he was covering the top half of his face."

His visitor nodded. "Yes, indeed. I could have pressed charges otherwise."

The lion's expression grew serious. He put the pictures down again. "Did you bring the negatives?"

"Yes…" he said, retrieving a small black canister from the case. It was such an outmoded way of photography now; but the only one he was used to. Milan enjoyed the solidity of the negative print, the tangible nature of it. Take a digital photo, one false click and you could delete it forever. But a negative you could hold… a negative you could bargain with. He held it in his hand for a moment, took a deep breath as he sized his employer up one final time, and then said, "But I'm not handing it over until we agree on a price."

For a moment, the lion looked shocked and outraged; flickers of anger ran across his handsome, tufted features. And then he burst out laughing. "My dear fellow – what a businessman you *are*! You Germans…"

"I'm serious."

Wiping his eye, Blair calmed himself. "Of course you are. You have a price in mind too. Don't keep me waiting – out with it."

"Five million."

The ferret jumped back as the lion slapped the desk in front of him. He was laughing again. "Five million – I see! Pounds or euros?"

"Euros, *bitte*."

"Of course. A princely sum!" And then he leaned over and said, darkly, dropping the humor from his voice as swiftly as a burning coal. "And what makes you think your little picture is worth that much? For a trick of the light?"

The ferret's gaze was unwavering. "No, sir. Because I know it is no trick of the light. Because you wanted to make sure I came straight to you with the negative. You're going to buy this photo because you want him not to exist. And I will charge you that much, because I know you can afford it – you own the largest multimedia corporation this world has ever seen - and you don't want me to take it to anybody else."

The lion looked unsatisfied. He leaned back in his chair again, claws drumming upon the arm. "Is that all?"

"Not quite. You also revealed to me just now that it was someone you were looking for. That added another million to my asking price."

For a moment, the lion looked as if he were within inches of spitting rage. But then his features relaxed. Some kind of peace seemed to settle upon him. "Of course," he smiled. "Germans. Such cunning bastards, aren't you? That's the way the war went on, isn't it?"

Milan didn't rise to the bait. "The money, please, sir."

"Fine," Blair coughed. He retrieved a checkbook from his desk. "You'll have to forgive me – I don't carry that much on me. This will have to do."

The photographer watched with wondering, wide eyes as the check was written out in front of him. Mentally, he was doing cartwheels of relief and joy. *Holy scheiße*, he thought. *I did it.*

There was a dull, metal thud as the lion placed his pen down. A slight ruffle of paper, and then Milan found himself holding a piece of paper that had suddenly become worth one hundred times more than his entire annual income. Numbly nodding approval, he slid the negatives and the prints over to the lion's desk. Blair wasted no time in removing the film, and examining it carefully in the dull light. Satisfied, he nodded, replacing them in the canister. Then he cocked his head at the ferret. "You're still here. I think we're done, don't you?"

"Of course," Milan nervously answered back, standing. A dark shadow of dampness was left upon his chair after he stood. He reached out to take the feline's proffered hand to shake upon the deal. The shake was firm, as the men looked keenly into each other's eyes. And then Blair gripped him tighter.

"You were wrong about one thing though," the lion rumbled ominously.

"What is that?"

"Well. It wasn't *me* who's been looking for this wolf. No. It was my employer."

Milan's eyes widened visibly. "*Your* employer? But you… you're…"

"One of the most powerful men in the western hemisphere? Oh, I know. And doesn't that just make your blood run cold that I'm under someone's keep as well?" Still holding Milan's now-shaking hand, he leaned in close – so close now that his mane was brushing against the photographer's shoulder, and whispered hauntingly, "Which means you're worth to him *absolutely nothing.*"

Blair pushed the smaller man away and his last two words were punctuated by a pair of silenced gunshots. The ferret gasped his dying breath – and then collapsed like a sack of potatoes, eyes bloodshot and wild. Blood began to pour from the two wounds in his back, which had severed his spine and exploded into his lungs.

From behind a hidden alcove in the wall, the goon whose duty it was to perform the deed stepped forth. The elevator opened, and the men within stepped forth. The mogul sat back in his chair, and casually wiped his hand with a white handkerchief produced from his pocket. Flecks of red stained his shirt from top to bottom, but they did not seem to trouble him. "Dispose of it. And then do not disturb me again." He looked down at the photo of Spirit and scowled. "I have business to arrange."

"Yes, boss," the bear said, looking down at the pitiful corpse of the ferret at his feet. "Damn," he muttered, looking at the holes in the photographer's back. "I really did like that coat…"

* * *

Achilles punched the wall of his hotel room. Scooping his belongings back into their cases, he'd been about to look up and tell the brooding spy clogging up his doorway to get lost, get gone, and not come back – when he realized that Spirit had already disappeared, robbing him of even that privilege. Despite the secrets that he knew now, anything that got Spiritwolf away from him was a *good* thing. So the bad guys got the tablet they wanted. *Big deal.* It wasn't his problem – he was just a fucking musician. A *prima donna*, the press liked to say. An artist. He didn't need people running around with guns, planting tracking devices, hiding things from him. His ears flicked, shoving an expensive suit into a case when really it ought to have been folded. He just wanted to know one thing now – *who was Black Dust?* Someone had planted that tablet on him; made him their mule to carry around God knows what halfway around Europe. It had to be someone on the tour. One of the techs? The drivers? Could they get that close to him? Had they?

He frowned and picked up the tour contact sheet. God, there were so many names here. Did he really need so many people with him? How much was he *paying* for all this entourage? Next time he had Regis' ear, he'd have to ask – he'd already told the elephant to get rid of some of them. Speaking of which, where was the elephant? There'd been a major fuckup in their schedule this afternoon, and he couldn't wait to inform him that he'd hired an actual bloody spy to be his personal trainer. Maybe he'd fire Regis too. He fumed.

Just then there was a knock at his door. "It's open," he growled, figuring it was probably the elephant now, or one of his bandmates. There was no answer. And then it knocked again. "I *said* it's... ah, for goodness sake!" He waited for a moment and then in swift strides he crossed the cluttered room and flung the door open.

Only an empty hallway greeted him; empty all except for one thing – his rucksack.

"No bloody way..." he said, looking about and picking it up. The hallway was silent; there seemed to be no possible clue as to who had left his bag for him to find. Seething at the cowardice of it, he closed the door again and with fumbling hands looked inside. All the contents had gone – including the mysterious tablet. But at the bottom of the bag, a piece of paper caught his eye. He retrieved it and unfolded it for inspection.

"Dear Achilles; you won't know who I am, but I have taken back something that belongs to me. The people that ransacked your room should bother you no more. It is done." And there, beneath, it was signed: "Black Dust."

Heart pounding in his chest, Achilles slowly found himself sinking to sit upon the edge of the bed. Then he tossed the piece of paper to one side, put his head between his hands, and growled a cry of silent anger and frustration.

"I can't do this," he huffed pointedly. "I can't tour knowing... *not* knowing who the... who..."

His voice trailed off. Lifting his head again, Achilles swallowed hard. Diving across the floor, he picked up the scrap of paper again and held it before him. His eyes flicked over every line of the message. His face creased deeply with disbelief and worry. Still holding it, he walked over to a case, and pulled out a photograph of the band, that each member had signed. He held the paper before him with a shaking hand, comparing the two. His friends in the picture smiled up at him; but he was not smiling back. "No..." he whispered. "It *can't* be..."

He threw the photograph and the note back down again with pain in his heart, and marched toward the door.

* * *

Spiritwolf was walking down the corridor toward his room, when he stopped in his tracks. Leaving the rock star, his head was swimming with the combined miseries of a mission in failure and an identity blown. It was a mess of the worst proportions. Could he erase Achilles' memory again? If it hadn't worked the first time, he was doubtful it was worth a second attempt, and it could cause permanent damage. He hated to think of it, but the rock star might need to be neutralized in other ways – brought in, to remain a 'guest' for the foreseeable future. It was what his training told him to do… and yet, it was uncomfortable to think about. He pushed that thought aside for the time being; better to concern himself with the possibility of picking up the thief's trail, finding out who had stolen the tablet from right under his nose. As for Black Dust himself, the identity of the tech-peddler was the very minimum he could return back to Zero with, at this point.

That, or the bastard's head on a plate.

That was when he halted. No, he had this all wrong; he was walking *away* from the scene of the crime. He should go back… perhaps there was something he'd missed. If Achilles got in the way again, well…

He would have to deal with him.

* * *

Bam bam bam.

Achilles knocked on the door of room 303 tersely. It was just down the hall from his own ransacked abode. His hand twitched; body shot with adrenalin, his eyes were glistening with contempt and disappointment. He kept looking thinking about the note; kept hoping he remembered things differently; but the text remained the same. In his mind he screwed it into a tiny white ball and knocked again. "Cain!" he bellowed. "Open the door! Get your ass out of bed…"

With satisfaction, he heard heavy footsteps approach the door. The portal swung open, only to reveal a rather large and surprised pachyderm in a business suit, his trunk waggling disapprovingly. "Good morning Achilles," the elephant rumbled. "We didn't expect you to finish your workout so soon."

"Regis?" the wolf muttered disjointedly. "What are you doing here?"

"I don't know if I should say," the elephant replied darkly. He appeared to be blocking the doorway.

"It's all right," Cain said, appearing over the elephant's shoulder. "Let the boss in. He would have found out anyway…"

Regis nodded, and stepped aside. With a curious glance, Achilles began to enter… but was stopped as a brown hand reached out and took hold of his wrist. With dismay, the rock star turned to find Spiritwolf holding him back. "Sorry, *boss*. But I really wanted to have a word with you."

"Now isn't a good time," the white wolf hissed. He saw Cain cocking his head in curiosity at the two wolves.

"You don't want to do this," Spiritwolf said. He held the note, hidden in his hand. He had read the contents and feared what they meant.

Achilles made to admonish the muscular wolf again, but that was when Regis intervened. "Who *is* that… ah, Spiritwolf. It's you," the elephant tersely snapped. He appeared displeased by something. "I've been looking for you. You may as well come in."

Unable to refuse – skin prickling with concern underneath his disguise – the brown wolf merely nodded and followed Achilles into the badger's room. He closed the door behind him, keeping it just a little ajar.

Cain leaned against a dresser, his paunch hanging over the edge of a black belt. He looked different this morning, somehow. Collected. Happy. Achilles walked between them, head bursting with questions, and looked from Regis to Cain, and back again. "So what's this about?" he glowered. "What was it I walked in on?"

"Ah boss… you see…" the drummer began, awkwardly. "How can I put this…"

"He's decided to leave you, Achilles," the manager blurted, obviously offended by bashfulness of any kind. "He wants to form his own group and he wondered if I might be his manager too. After the tour ends and my contract with you has expired, of course."

"Reg!" Cain moaned. "Don't sugar-coat it for my sake, will ya?"

Achilles looked impassively from the elephant to the badger, feeling his temperature rise sharply and hotly.

Spiritwolf, meanwhile, had kept his arms crossed, hovering at the side of the room and was silently observing the group. In particular, he was considering the badger very closely. Regis saw that look, and walked over to the wolf. "As for you, Mr. Wolf, I wanted to ask you something. Les didn't make it back to his room last night. This isn't unusual for the lizard. But there was *some* speculation about whose room he *did* end up in. Noises were heard through all hours of the night. Do you know anything about this?"

"Of course," Spiritwolf said quietly. "He was in my room."

The elephant narrowed his eyes. "Indeed. Well, I consider the band members to be my property, Mr. Spiritwolf, insofar as our contract allows. If someone borrows something that is mine, I expect it to be returned in good condition. This morning, when we found him in his room, Les was quite agitated about something – he was yelling at everyone and fortunately, we stopped him before he could throw any expensive equipment or furniture around. To have one of our key players misbehave like that is absolutely *unacceptable*." The manager wandered over, and using his trunk, prodded the wolf squarely in the chest. "Do not provoke him or anyone else on the tour – remember; you, too, have a contract, and as they say in the trade, *you break it, you bought it!*"

The brown wolf resisted the urge to growl. "I think I understand," he replied, unable to hide his contempt. *Remind me not to go undercover as an employee in the future*, he mentally admonished himself.

The elephant, meanwhile, seemed satisfied that the point had been made. His shoulders relaxed, and he turned back to the two musicians in the room. "So Achilles, I hope you're fine with Mr. White's decision. I've heard his demo – did you know how well this man sings? Keeping him behind a drum kit would be a travesty…"

The white wolf looked directly at the badger – gazed into his friend's wondering eyes. As he spoke, his face was a mask of distaste. "Get off my tour," he spat.

"…what?" Cain said in disbelief. "You can't mean…"

Furious, the wolf turned to his manager. "Did you hear me? I said I want him *off* the fucking tour!"

The elephant blinked. "Why would you say a rash thing like that?"

"Because…" Achilles began. Dozens of sentences formed in his head. He wanted to shout aloud. *Because he's Black Dust. Because I know his handwriting. Because he's a traitor, an arms dealer, a fraud, a…* but he saw Spiritwolf looking at him with stern warning. The brown wolf's eyes bored into his gaze, as if he were silently communicating a very specific message. *No*, the agent seemed to be saying. *You can't do this.*

Cain, wrong-footed, couldn't bear the delay. "Because *what?!*"

Achilles turned back to the badger, snarling. "Because *you know* why! We're done. Fucking *done!* I don't want you anywhere near me."

He marched toward the door as if to leave. "Now wait," Regis said, pulling him to one side. "If you really want to fire him… this can happen. But not now; the contracts… the penalties. Are you sure?"

"Yes…" Achilles hissed.

"Boss, *please!*" Cain pleaded. He moved toward the white wolf. Achilles drew back, as if he were going to punch the mustelid. This time, it was Spirit who held the drummer back, for his own sake.

"Very well," Regis replied gloomily. "But he'll have to play the next stop; we can't afford to cancel the whole gig. And maybe, by then, you'll have come to your senses."

"I *have* come to my senses," the white wolf said calmly. "That's why I haven't fired you as well."

His manager looked truly shocked – the first time he could ever remember seeing that. "You'd fire *me* over this?"

"Best that you don't question that decision just now, Reg," Achilles replied sternly. "And on that note, I think I'd like to be left alone for a while." He pushed the elephant aside, and barged out the door.

Spiritwolf took off after him, leaving the badger and the elephant to argue angrily over the remains of the morning.

* * *

Achilles had made it to the elevator by the time his 'trainer' caught up with him. He jammed himself inside the doors as they closed; the two wolves were occupied in the elevator alone as it began its journey.

"When I said I wanted to be left alone," Achilles growled, seeing that he had been followed, "that included you. You're fired too, by the way; I don't think I'm going to need you on the next stop." He huffed disdainfully; it was impossible for him to feel any more ticked off than he did right now.

Without warning, Spiritwolf jabbed the emergency halt button on the elevator's controls. The carriage jerked to a sudden halt, and a tiny little alarm bell rang out.

"What the f-" the rock star began to utter. The large wolf shoved him back against the elevator wall, silencing his protest.

"Listen to me," he growled throatily, holding on to Achilles tightly. "You're not nearly as clever as you think you are. One wrong word in there, and it would have meant the end of more than just your musical career."

"But Black Dust…" Achilles protested.

"*Isn't* Cain," the brown wolf answered. "You were played for a fool." He held out a tiny slip of paper. The note. "I went back into your room, and I found this. I also found your band photograph; you were *meant* to compare the two. Black Dust – whoever they are – only wanted you to *think* it was Cain."

The rock star pursed his lips. He pushed Spiritwolf away from him. "But why?"

The agent smirked. "To sow confusion among us; he knows someone is on to him. Confusion means he can hide himself better. The note was actually great news for me; it means the tablet is still here."

Achilles narrowed his eyes. "No," he growled.

"No? Look, I'm telling you…"

"No. Just *no*, all right? I don't want this. I don't want these secrets and spies. I just want to go back to playing music, and entertaining people. I want my tour back."

Spiritwolf folded his arms. "You want Black Dust off the tour, then, don't you?"

"Yes. And if firing Cain hasn't done it, then I'm lost."

Spiritwolf tried to relax his posture. Tried to think back to when they had first met; how they had dined together in the café; how friendly things had been then. There was a chance this could still work… if he could get the rock star to trust him again. "You'll have to keep me around a little bit longer, then."

Achilles bit his lower lip. He examined the brown wolf guardedly. "If that's how it has to be."

"It is."

The white wolf held out his hand. "Then we work together to bring this son of a bitch out into the open, so that you can find what you're looking for, and I can get my life back."

With dry amusement, Spiritwolf examined the proffered hand; and then grasped it firmly. "Agreed." They shook, neither one taking their eyes off the other. Not for the first time, the white wolf felt a sliver of admiration for how strong the brown wolf was. *Better to have this guy for me than against me, anyway*, he mused in the moment they shook.

The deal done, Spiritwolf turned off the alarm. With grinding gears, they were soon in motion again.

Now things were really getting under way.

* * *

By 10 A.M., the band, the roadies and the crew were at Fiumicino airport, waiting to board their flight. Achilles had arrived alone; clothes all packed into bags again, he had a cloud over his mood that matched the storm that was descending upon the city. There were grey clouds upon the horizon. As he approached the check-in counter, he caught sight of Cain leaving the clerk with his carry-on bag. The badger looked at him for a moment, gave an ugly, wretched frown, and stomped away.

"Ah… shit…" Achilles whispered, putting his bag down.

"He'll be fine," Regis muttered, appearing at Achilles' side. "I hope you won't let it distract you from giving the Spaniards what-for tomorrow. I've made some calls; apparently Bill Stix is available, to pick up for Cain in London."

Momentarily forgetting his troubles, the wolf cocked his head at the elephant. "That's excellent. I always wondered what the old bird was doing after he left *Feathers of Fury*. Let's hope he's a fast study."

Regis shook his head. "You really know how to throw a spanner in the works, boy. I have enough to deal with as it is."

Just then the singer spotted Spiritwolf enter the lobby. "I'm sure you do; but I pay you enough. But if you'll excuse me a moment…"

He left his manager standing idle, as he approached the brown wolf. "You're very nearly late," he muttered. "Don't they teach timekeeping at spy school?"

The large wolf smirked. "This plane won't leave without me. Believe me, I know; the pilot is a *DAST* European agent."

Achilles' eyes widened. "You're kidding," he ventured.

"That's for me to know. Now, quit talking to me so much; Black Dust still being around, we don't want them to get suspicious."

Shaking his head, Achilles muttered "You're not making this easy. I feel like quitting and going back home."

"Hey, no more of that," Spirit said, slapping his arm. "You don't want to disappoint your fans. Now… call of nature before we fly. See you on the plane."

Spiritwolf walked away, rolling his eyes as soon as his back was turned. At least he still had the tablet in his sights; once again, he could feel how close it was. Just work with the rock star a little more to bring the bastard into the open, and this would all be over.

He ducked down an empty corridor of the building, and entered the dingy men's room. He fumbled with his trouser fly for a moment, and then all that could be heard was a stream of fluid that the eye couldn't see. He was just about done with his unseen business, when in his back pocket he felt his smartphone vibrate urgently.

Pulling it from his pocket, he looked at the screen – recognized the *DAST* code encryption – and answered, expecting to hear Zero's voice. It was not.

"Spiritwolf!" a fox's voice blurted, his voice crackling faintly with static. "Thank God I caught you."

"Inverno… how did you… well, never mind that, I guess," the wolf muttered, zipping himself back up again. "You can't just call me like this."

He heard the other agent sigh. "I know… but I needed to tell you. It's Noir; he's gone."

A stab of pain and regret struck the wolf through the heart. He exited the stall and leaned against the grimy sink, looking at his false reflection under the pale lights in the mirror. He closed his eyes. "I'm sorry to hear that. He… at least his suffering is over."

"I know you will miss him, Spirit…" the fox said, his voice restraining emotion. "But that isn't why I called you. There was something else. Something much more important."

Spiritwolf's ears flicked, and he straightened himself. Still reeling from the sad news, he tried to focus on what the agent was telling him. "This is about the mission?"

A pause on the line, as if the fox were suddenly afraid. "No, Spirit. Just before he passed, the professor intercepted another message. Some new chatter, from a group no one has heard of before. He wasn't able to show me how he broke their encryption, but we're talking some very, *very* advanced algorithms. He was more concerned that I got the message to you… and I've been trying, but you're not easy to find…"

"What, Inverno!" Spiritwolf said, growing impatient, as if he weren't so sure of the plane not leaving without him after all.

"This group – they call themselves *Rising Force* – they're not after the tablet. They know you're in Europe, and somehow, they know whatever your secret is. Spirit, you're in great danger – these guys are after *you!*"

And that was when all the lights in the bathroom went out.

131

Chapter Six: The Fabric Of Shadows

Spirit immediately dropped the phone in the sink and in the moment before the LCD screen darkened, he caught a glimpse of himself in the mirror, surprised as all hell that the lights in the bathroom had gone out. That image remained burned on his retinas as he lurched back toward the stall and crouched inside to give himself as much cover as possible from someone aiming at chest height. He slowly drew his gun and held his breath, waiting as precious seconds ticked by. His advantage was erased by the darkness and he was in a place with only one, maybe two exits. And he didn't know who or how many there were. Movement could lead to death, so waiting was all he could do.

The silence teased his paranoia and after ten seconds, he slowly let out his breath to minimize any sound. Another fifteen seconds and he heard a door to his right open. The entrance he'd used was on his left, so this person must have been hidden in the janitor's closet. The wolf held his gun sideways under the edge of the stall, ready to shoot his assailant's legs. The approaching footsteps clicked on the tile. He frowned, trying to categorize the sound and link it to a type of shoe. A woman's high heels? Odd for someone in his line of work, but not unheard of. He timed the release of the safety with one of the footsteps, yet they still stopped as soon as he moved the catch.

Familiar clicking preceded an equally recognizable mechanical voice. "Agent Spiritwolf?"

"I'm here." The wolf immediately rose and went to retrieve his phone from the sink. He had the sense of a large something next to him and for a moment, wondered whether others felt the same when he was standing nearby and invisible. He tapped the screen with a fingertip and it came to life. The mirror now showed a large insect just three paces to his right. "Good to see you again, Ixak."

"Your tone of voice does not suggest such."

Spirit inwardly grimaced at the admonishment. "Well, you did catch me in the middle of important business. Why are you here?"

"To give you this." One of his four hands held a metallic briefcase, which he swung up to the counter that ran above the sinks. Spiritwolf had a brief irreverent thought of imagining the beetle's arm breaking off under the weight, as some children might do to torture innocent insects. Another hand came up and worked the catch on both sides to open it.

Inside was a flattened version of a familiar wolf face – a spare mask; dead, de-animated twin to the one he wore. Along with it were gloves, extra contact lenses, and a small bottle of the adhesive that bonded the items (except for the contacts) to his fur and flesh. Spiritwolf immediately pulled the mask out and began unbuttoning his shirt to loosen the collar. Then he pulled off his old mask and put on the new one.

The beetle made a flurry of clicking noises to express his surprise at the sudden beheading and re-heading of the lupine. "That is very strange to watch," he said and added, "But also very interesting."

"Glad I could entertain you," Spirit muttered and buttoned his shirt up. He placed the old mask carefully in the briefcase and spied a piece of paper inside.

Hope this reaches you in time. Take care. - Dash.
P.S. Zero said not to go through these like toilet paper.
P.P.S. The code to unlock the briefcase is 12357.
P.P.P.S. The original's underneath.

Spiritwolf smiled fondly, imagining the cheetah jotting down the postscripts in quick succession. It was chaos within the barest of frameworks, something that resonated with Spirit.

Zero's message told him that the bear wasn't too pissed, thankfully. Then the wolf read the final postscript and frowned slightly. He pulled up the briefcase divider that his new mask had rested on; below was another familiar face; this one, a grey wolf.

It was the mask had been the one he'd tried on a month ago, which he'd torn with a mere yawn. He picked it up and examined the left side of the jaw and cheek. There was no sign that it had ever been ripped. Dash must have found someone to fix it – maybe they had woven the new polymer into the material like a fibrin scaffold embedded in a wound.

The mechanical voice broke his reverie. "How many masks do you wear?"

Spirit glared sidelong. "Just one. Thank you for this. But you could have had another agent bring this. Clarice, for example?"

"She is on leave, attending to a dying member of her family. This is too important to be trusted to any agent."

He means the mask. And my secret. "What do you know of a group called *Rising Force?*"

"They are a very new organization, mostly from nations in central and western Europe. Not much is known about them. They appear to be interested in biotech."

"Huh. And their agenda?"

"Unstated as of yet. Why do you inquire?"

"I heard a rumor on the wire. Oh, crap! I need to board my plane!" Just then, an announcement for his flight blared over the loudspeaker. He shut the briefcase and paused.

"Thanks, Ixak."

"The best way to repay me, agent, is to be successful in your mission."

Spirit nodded curtly and donned his sunglasses as he stalked toward the door. It slammed open, startling the TEA plainclothes agent outside guarding the door.

Ixak stared thoughtfully at the void left behind by the wolf. After a few moments of contemplation, he turned and went into the janitorial closet again. The darkness swallowed him and left no trace of his passing before the lights came on and returned everything to normal.

* * *

"Where the hell have you been?" Achilles snapped at the agent's easy jog toward the waiting Sky Freedom business jet.

"The restroom. Important business."

The white wolf glanced at the briefcase while following the larger wolf up the stairs. "I'll bet. Do yourself a favor and don't be late again. Time is money, as Regis would say."

"Of course. Sorry." After a brief nod to the pilot, Spiritwolf squeezed down the single aisle and ignored the varied looks from the band, especially Regis, as he made his way to the back. Well, only Cain and Regis were giving him looks. Achilles was behind him, Les was pointedly ignoring him – as did Cain to Achilles – and the inattentive Garrick was fiddling with some kind of midi program on a laptop.

The interior of the bizjet had first class seats up front, one on each side, with plenty of room to stand and even swivel the seat. There were motorized bins for luggage in the floor and widescreen video displays in front of every seat. The LED lighting system overhead was a brighter blue, roughly corresponding to the time of day. Spirit passed through the lounge area and found the pair of seats at the very aft of the airplane. He stowed his bag in the bin corresponding to his seat and carefully put the briefcase in the one across the aisle with extra blankets on top of it. The shade was already down, so he sat and buckled his seat belt. There was plenty of room to stretch his legs. His seat was large enough to accommodate his muscular body; it was certainly better than the first class seats he'd been in on his flight to Germany. The thought of stowing away invisibly on business jets for the rest of his life brought a slight smile to his face as he surveyed the plane's luxurious interior with a calculating eye. There were many places where he could be out of the way and it would be rather easy to dodge around an approaching executive. The fantasy slipped away as the airplane backed away from the terminal and then moved forward, rolling slowly along the taxiway.

"Folks, from the flight deck, this is your captain." Spirit's ears perked up. "We have a strong tailwind that will cut our flying time in half. The tower's asked us to hold for takeoff to let eastbound planes get out early, so it'll be about thirty minutes before we're airborne." There were several groans from up front. "We'll still be arriving in Arenosa a half hour ahead of schedule. In the meantime, we're moving off to the side. You can feel free to get up and move around, but be prepared to return to your seat immediately if we're cleared to take off. I'll inform you if we receive any instructions from the tower."

Spirit leaned back and puffed an exasperated sigh. All that hurrying for nothing. Well, at least he could try to relax a bit before they arrived. After all, there hadn't been much in the way of sleep last night and the workout had been rather exhausting. Noir's passing. Rising Force. Achilles' ransacked room. Black Dust. Too much going on and he was too tired to think, too tired to reason, didn't want to…

His room was cloaked in shadows, yet he could still see the lizard naked and reclining on the bed, stretched arms welcoming him toward unspoken promises of fulfillment. Heat rose in him. Unsubtle need. Raw, primal desire. Articles of clothing dropped from him and in the haze that shrouded his reasoning, he realized the lizard hadn't put on the blindfold after all, yet was smiling and entranced by the disappearing wolf, by him, his true self. He got on the bed, unseen body pinning the other man down and entering him, hips thrusting until his release. And then the badger was there at the side of the bed, stroking himself as the lizard rolled off and disappeared. Strong arms pulled the mustelid down, flipped him over and then he filled the larger man, pounded harder against the heavy thighs until he came a second time. Next was the cheetah, then the elephant, the lizard again, everyone had their turn with the invisible wolf, they wanted it and he gave it to them again again again…

And suddenly it was Achilles on the bed with…

Spirit jerked awake. His mind was still attempting to process the sheer weirdness of the dream. His disorientation was quickly replaced by a hard, lingering fear that crept through him. *What was I thinking, having that one-night stand with Les?* The answer was as obvious as it was immediate – there had been no thought whatsoever. Too long without sex, too many things in a short span of time eroding his defenses, and too much temptation from the lizard. *Maybe it wasn't my smartest decision, even with the precautions I took, but done is done. I got what I needed, and he got what he needed.* The only thing Spirit could do going forward was to stay sharp and make sure there were no further lapses in willpower.

The problem was that the genie was now out of the bottle. Yielding once to temptation had thankfully brought no significant consequences. *Yeah, except for hurting Les' feelings afterward. It's not like other agents haven't ever slept around, left broken hearts when their missions ended.* His situation, though, was unique. It would be easier now, like going down the proverbial slippery slope, and what would be waiting at the bottom? Maybe not the sex-crazed monster from his dream. But maybe it would be someone who would have to deal with the repercussions, more than just hurt feelings. And perhaps it would be too much to bear.

Spirit took deep breaths, closed his eyes, and allowed the discordant thoughts to drain. He pushed away the dream, his memories of last night, and his fears. He imagined them like balloons in a persistent breeze, gently guided farther away; he watched them recede until they were out of sight, leaving him with the cool, quiet peace of assuredness. Master Song had taught him the basics of meditation in his first lesson, which had helped re-equilibrate and re-orient his often-panicked state of mind. With his calm demeanor restored, Spiritwolf opened his eyes and flicked his cell phone on. Only twenty minutes had passed between falling asleep and his meditation. Another ten or so to go until the plane would take off. He took the bottle of water from the side tray and drank half, saving the rest for later.

The captain came back on the intercom and, with some surprise, announced their immediate departure, which brought cheers from the rest of the band. The plane started moving again and Spiritwolf caught sight of Les returning from the lounge with Regis behind him. The keyboardist scowled at him and threw himself in his seat. The elephant stared at him for a moment before also sitting. Spirit did his best to ignore both and looked out the window to watch the plane taxi to the runway. He let his mind drift as the plane finally went wheels-up.

After leveling off, Spirit heard noise up front again. Regis was lumbering his way to the rear of the plane. "Let's talk," he said abruptly and motioned to the lounge area.

The wolf sighed, got up, and sat opposite the pachyderm. "Look, about Les…"

"This isn't about Les," Regis interrupted. "This is about my star performer."

"Achilles?" Spiritwolf asked, incredulous. "What, are the workouts too hard on him?"

"If only they were. Then I could fire you." Regis let that sink in for a moment before continuing. "He's been extremely temperamental and confrontational, and right now, he's sulking in his seat like a five-year-old. I don't know if him being around you has caused this change of behavior, but whatever the source, it has to stop or else he'll spiral out of control and the show will suffer. So, I'm going to give you a last chance. You talk to him and get him to behave before our next concert."

"Me? What makes you think he'll listen to me?" He flashed back to earlier this morning in the hotel gym when Achilles had caught him off-guard and had been content to let him choke to death under the overloaded weight bar – and had threatened to kill him by pushing down on it.

"Because you're the only one he's talking to right now, the only one he's listening to. Our next concert is very high-profile and if it goes south because of him, you're through. Talk some sense into him and I'll consider that you have some usefulness to me. Are we clear?"

"I don't have much choice," Spiritwolf glared at the elephant.

"No. But lucky for you, you have some time. Thirty-two hours, to be precise." Regis stood and helped himself to a glass of Twin Seraphs liqueur and a large bag of peanuts before slowly making his way back to his seat.

Spiritwolf remained in the lounge and stared moodily out the window at wispy clouds unraveling in the noontime sky below. The situation just kept getting worse. He'd have to go on the offensive in a big way if he was going to overcome inertia, shift the momentum back in his favor, and complete his mission. But how?

Maybe it was time to be more direct.

* * *

The city of Arenosa was primarily a high-end business and resort area in southeastern Spain on the shores of the Mediterranean, much like St. Tropez was along the Côte d'Azur, or Dubai in the UAE. The rich and famous would fly or boat in year-round from all over the world to see and be seen: royalty, heads of state, billionaires, reclusive mad-genius artists, famous actors and actresses, power couples, sports legends, and of course, music stars. Decadence littered the streets, opulence was on display on the sandy beaches, and excessiveness could be found in all forms and shapes, from the world-class Zemina Cul restaurant at the top of the 700 meter Torre Azul building, to the simply named but high-powered Arenosa Casino, built on a sea cliff overlooking the town.

Spiritwolf saw it all from above as the plane circled during its descent, including the Zoloja Grande arena. The largest stadium in Europe was originally designed to accommodate two hundred thousand screaming fans of the national soccer (or as the Sciences Director, Greystorm, called it, "proper football") team, Los Dragones. This would be the venue of Achilles' next concert; it looked very *grande* indeed from this vantage point. The plane landed five minutes later and Spirit waited in the back while the others up front gathered their bags in uncharacteristic silence. He was the last one off, exchanging a knowing nod with the pilot.

"At least I understand why you spent the money to arrive on a bizjet," Spiritwolf told Achilles upon disembarking. "Arriving in style in Arenosa would seem to be mandatory."

"It is," the white wolf nodded with a faint grin. With his shades on and his dark blue silk shirt open to expose his chest ruff and abs, along with his white slacks and dress shoes, he was the spitting image of himself from the cover of *Rock On* magazine. At least he seemed to be out of whatever bad mood the elephant had described him being in earlier; the confident swagger was back. They walked across the tarmac and entered the main terminal, where the gate agent waved them through.

"Shouldn't we wait for the rest of your band?"

"No." His muzzle curled in momentary distaste. "Regis suggested that we catch a cab to the hotel together."

"Did he, now?"

"Yes. And don't think that we're going to go on a nice little tour of the city like we did in Rome. We're going right to the hotel and then you and I are going to figure out what to do next before we part ways."

They got on the escalator going down to baggage claim, hotel shuttles and taxis. Spirit chuckled. "I'm just glad you're not a control freak."

Achilles actually smiled at that and dipped his muzzle down. "It's a hazard of the job. Regis may oversee the business end, but I make sure everything else is taken care of. Granted, I don't do it all myself, but that's why I have folks who keep me apprised of what's going on. With this." He held up his smartphone and waggled it. "I expect no less from you."

"You're the boss." At the bottom of the escalator Spirit looked back up and stopped, thinking for several long moments as the white wolf continued, unaware that the other wolf wasn't with him.

"Hang on."

"What?" Achilles turned and saw the larger wolf waving at someone still on the escalator, obscured by the overhang from the floor above. His mild annoyance turned into surprise as Cain emerged, chatting with Spirit and not realizing that Achilles was waiting impatiently just ahead.

The singer's ears went flat. "What are you doing?" he finally snapped, causing the badger to register his presence.

"Cain's coming with us," Spirit said firmly.

"What?" The stunned badger stopped in his tracks. "I'm not going anywhere with him."

"Sure you are. Achilles and you need to work this out."

"We don't have anything we need to work out..." the white wolf began.

"Yes, you do." Spiritwolf gave him a meaningful look, much like the one in Cain's hotel room earlier in the morning. Then he took the badger by the elbow and guided him back into walking. Spirit tried very hard to not think about the dream he'd had earlier.

Achilles followed them outside and into a waiting taxi-limo. He noticed that Spiritwolf kept his carry-on bags with him, so he did the same, as did the badger. There was plenty of space inside for everything. Achilles and Cain appeared riveted on something just outside their respective windows.

"See?" Spiritwolf smiled as the taxi drove off. "You're getting along already."

"What the hell are you doing?" Achilles muttered.

"My good deed for the day. Your firing him was based on an incorrect conclusion, wasn't it? A misunderstanding?" The badger looked up in surprise.

"So?"

"So are you still going to fire him? Or are you going to let your pride drag you down a road you'd rather not go down?"

"Is this true?" There was a hopeful undercurrent in Cain's speech.

Achilles' gaze bore right into Spiritwolf's eyes and his back teeth clenched. "Yeah."

The larger wolf continued. "Even I can tell Cain's a good drummer. You don't want to lose him. If he wants to go solo after this, let him. Hell, you can even help him get started. Let him sing one of your songs." Spirit folded his arms across his chest.

"Like hell I will. You don't tell me how to run my show and no one sings any of my songs but me."

"Okay, fine. But you need to listen to counsel from the people you trust. And my advice is pretty damn good. You know that. So where's the harm?"

Achilles ground his teeth. "No."

Spiritwolf pulled a wadded up piece of paper from his pocket. "So you really want to throw this away?" he said softly, passing it over. Achilles opened it and smoothed it down; it was the band picture he'd used to determine Black Dust's handwriting had been Cain's. There he was, in the middle of it, with the badger smiling next to him.

The agent remembered the photo he'd pulled out to look at, back in Dresden. Other memories of his team played in his head like flipping through a photo album, and he smiled wistfully to no one in particular.

"Aw, c'mon, boss," Cain said, also looking at the photo of the band. "I'll give you back a cut of my pay."

"It's not about the money!" By now, the white wolf's tail was rigid with anger.

"Then what's it about?" Spirit stared at him. "Give me one reason, one valid reason why you shouldn't let him get up on stage with you."

Achilles opened his mouth, ready to retort, but then appeared to think better of it. "Cain can play. As for singing… no. That's my gig. No one else's."

Spirit looked at the badger. "You fine with that?"

"Yeah, I think so. Thanks, boss. And for what it's worth, I'm really sorry you had to find out the way you did." Cain held out his hand.

"Nothing to apologize for, I guess." Achilles shook the badger's hand. "As Spirit said, it was based on bad information."

The larger wolf nodded and looked at the driver, a rat, through the closed glass divider. They had turned from the airport express bypass and were now on the coastal super-highway that paralleled the high-speed rail system which eventually linked up to the Arenosa light rail network. Ahead were the skyscrapers and various monumental edifices – hotels, business offices, luxury apartments, and so on – that stretched up toward the sun and out along the coastline. At night, the city would be lit up with all sorts of images along the buildings; dazzling art, sometimes live, would attract and inspire tourist and local alike. The nightly street vendors were already out at this early hour selling mouth-watering morsels and tasty treats near the white sugar-sand beaches; further out, magnificent yachts were moored in the azure and emerald waters of the Mediterranean and smaller watercraft darted around them daringly. For a moment, Spiritwolf permitted himself the firm belief that he should retire in this place, right now.

His attention returned reluctantly to his fellow passengers and the work he had to finish. "Great. And now that we're all friends again, I need to ask you a few questions, Cain." Both of the other passengers started in surprise, the badger nodding a few long moments later. "You were in your room all morning, this morning?" Another nod. And the beginning of comprehension from the other wolf. "Did you hear anything out of the ordinary, outside your room?"

"No. I didn't. Why?"

"Achilles' room was broken into and ransacked. Keep it to yourself, all right?"

"O-of course. Are you… a policeman?"

Spiritwolf looked at Achilles. "No, I'm just a personal trainer. But after this morning, Achilles asked me to be his bodyguard. And I accepted. So, I'm just trying to piece together what happened and make sure it wasn't someone from the tour that did it."

"That makes sense. Well, the morning was pretty quiet. I slept in, then Regis stopped by and we were discussing how to transition to my solo career when you guys came in."

"Huh. Well, it sounds like whoever went through his things was a professional, kept it quiet. I guess there isn't anything else I can do right now."

"I appreciate you taking your new role seriously, Spirit." The agent glanced at Achilles, who gave a small, tired smile in return. His ears were no longer flat against his head and he appeared more relaxed as the taxi exited from the coastal highway. The hotel was already in sight, the Estrella del Oro, but the passengers were instead staring at the various boutiques, the beautiful people dressed in everything from business suits to swimsuits, the high end sports cars darting in and out of lanes. The last brought Spiritwolf back to the Autobahn chase and he was once again thankful that he had survived that night.

Their conveyance pulled to the front of the hotel and Achilles pulled out a couple hundred euro notes for the driver. They retrieved their bags and entered the lobby, ignoring the attendants asking to help them. As with the rest of the city, the interior of the hotel was a study in lavishness: large columns, marble floors, an open courtyard, and a fountain in the middle. The clerk at the front desk, a lion, had an air of disdain about him, until Achilles removed his sunglasses and mentioned his name. Then suddenly Arzalin the lion was pleased to make their acquaintance, glad to help and of course, they could have their rooms ready right now. Upon receiving their keys, they shuffled along through the expansive lobby and took the shiny elevators to the 30th floor – a relatively low number given the building's height, but one whole wing on the floor had been booked for the band. Cain made his way into his room, waving goodbye to the wolves.

"So what now, boss?" Spirit asked with a cocky grin. "More planning about how to get rid of your new bodyguard?"

Achilles yawned. "I think I could do with a nap instead. After that, a tour of the arena and then the lads and I start our equipment checks on the stuff we brought with. The bulk of it arrives tomorrow afternoon. Question is, what are you going to be doing in the meantime?"

"I have an idea."

Achilles nodded. After several moments, he asked, "Are you going to tell me?"

"Nope."

"I thought you were going to keep me apprised of what you were doing."

"I will. As soon as I find something." Spirit fingered his cardkey. "How I go about my business, out there," he pointed toward the window at the end of the hall, where the view extended toward the sweeping beach. "That's my jurisdiction. It has nothing to do with your concerts. Out there, I am in charge." He smiled grimly. "That was our deal, was it not?"

"As long as you don't keep secrets. You'll report what you find?"

"Of course."

Achilles searched his features and, satisfied, nodded and entered his room.

Spirit went into his as well, carefully placing the duffel on the luggage stand and leaving the briefcase on the executive desk. He drew the curtains, pulled out a small black box from the bag and clicked the device on. It made a soft squealing noise which modulated in frequency as he swept it around the perimeter of the room, as he had done before in Dresden and in Rome. When he was convinced there were no monitoring devices, Spiritwolf put the box back in the bag and pulled out a good-sized stack of 500 euro notes, a different cell phone, and a small device that looked like an old-style USB capsule. The money was placed into a leather zip-fold; the rest of the items went into his pockets. Then he pulled out his contacts, dropped them in the case, and pulled off his mask and gloves. His headless reflection casually regarded himself and his disembodied voice said, "One year, two months, ten days." Then the odd figure moved toward the briefcase and started laying each extracted item carefully on the desk.

Thirty minutes later, a well-dressed grey wolf with blue eyes sauntered through the lobby of the hotel like a high-roller going out on the town, talking on his cell phone and making preparations to put his plan into motion.

* * *

Lunch in the restaurant had been a pleasant affair: a filet mignon cooked rare; a salad with bleu cheese, pears and candied walnuts; warm bread with hints of rosemary and garlic; and a small chocolate torte for dessert. Blair Murdock wasn't the sort for overindulgence when it came to eating; many bad deals usually started somewhere with indigestion and he hadn't had very many of those in his life. This meal was nothing compared to the feasts they would have every so often. Biology was an irresistible force that couldn't be bargained with; his owner's biology certainly demonstrated that.

The stately lion returned to his office with an easy walk, nodding at the security guards flanking the doors. His secretary, a top-heavy hyena, presented him with his afternoon callback list as well as a sealed, unmarked manila envelope. Blair waited until the doors were closed before loosening his tie and perusing the list. Requests for interviews. Requests for donations. Requests for his approval on various business decisions. Nothing out of the ordinary for the man at the top. He smirked and tossed the list onto his desk; the A4 sheet swooped like a skimming bird and settled onto the polished wood. The manila folder, by contrast, demanded his attention with its anonymous exterior and he slit the top with a manicured claw tip and a hint of anticipatory impatience.

His expectation of success was unfulfilled by the contents. Worse, it indicated that he had been dealt a setback. He re-read the summary slowly, mining every word for subtle knowledge, anything to indicate that something positive could be gleaned from this. His frown deepened; he shuffled the papers, bypassing the autopsy report and focused instead on the picture of the dead mouse, Eriz Blanc.

Bruises and lacerations tattooed his face, and there were more disfigurations along his throat where his windpipe had been crushed. Blanc was supposed to have delivered the stolen tablet to one of Murdock's proxies in exchange for payment. Instead, someone had beaten the mouse to death and hadn't even had the courtesy to leave any forensic evidence or CCTV footage that would allow the killer to be found. And so, Murdock had no idea where the tablet had disappeared to, either.

It was intolerable and inexcusable. The lion felt the heat rise in him and he wrung the papers in his hand. It had been a long time since a mistake had led to outright failure. He snarled aloud at the word, heretofore excised from his vocabulary, and slammed his other hand on the desk. The problem, he realized, was not that the help was incompetent.

Blanc's talents should have easily put the tablet into Murdock's hands. No, this was different. There was another player, hidden from view; the whole thing felt similar to how his owner operated. It was this person who was outmaneuvering his pawns. Someone who was very, very crafty, and who knew when to strike from the shadows. The molten anger in his golden eyes hardened into resolve.

Starting from this moment, Blair Murdock would have to be extremely careful in handling the operation. The situation could still be salvaged, but it would require a slightly different way of going about it. As in chess, the best way to win was to draw your opponent out into the open by appearing to give him the advantage and then start shutting off avenues of escape.

The lion hummed softly and turned on the array of television screens embedded in the wall. They flickered to life in silent greeting while Blair Murdock pulled out his cell phone and voice-dialed the one person who could sniff out this hidden player and get him what he needed, in one fell swoop.

"Gareth Zirkowski."

* * *

The tigress marched down the jetway; her uniform had been swapped out for a smart business suit that resonated with the air of authority that she projected. Her assistant, a bruiser of a crocodile with a decent-sized belly that threatened to burst from his own suit, followed her in silence and surveyed the posh crowds with narrowed eyes. "Where to now?" he asked in a voice that was oddly quiet for his size.

"We don't have to go far," Clarice purred. She fiddled with her datapad for several moments, then showed the screen to him. The Achilles concert tour blog's latest entry had a picture of the white wolf screaming on the stage in Rome, followed by, "ARENOSA, HERE WE COME!!!" The date shown indicated the concert would be tomorrow. "It is obvious, *nicht wahr?*"

"Well, why couldn't we have just snatched him in Rome, if it was so obvious?" her companion grumbled. "I'm just about out of leave for the year. And then they'll start getting suspicious when I ask to extend it. If I'm lucky, I'll just be rotated back to the States."

"Darius," Clarice replied in an overly sweet tone of voice, "You don't realize yet that your precious career is already over. So please do not speak of nonsense and keep your focus on the task at hand. Or I will *replace* you with someone willing to do what it takes to successfully complete our mission."

"Can the euphemistic bullshit," the croc replied with an impressive snarl that showed many of his teeth. "I get your point."

"Good. And now, we need to find where our target is staying."

"How do we do that?"

Clarice tapped the pad and opened a window of arrayed webcams across the city. One showed a cheering throng in front of a four-star hotel. "We follow the fans."

* * *

"It's so nice to meet you at last, Mr. Thomas!" The tall, thin sable offered a hand and a broad smile to the person that sat to his left. He lifted his cards after the dealer flipped him his second one and tapped the table for a hit. "I haven't heard from you in quite a while. What have you been up to, hmm?" He seemed pleased by the third card.

Spiritwolf peeked at his cards. *Seventeen. Bleah.* He left them down, passing a hand over it to indicate a stand. "Call me James, Carlos," he replied with an equally large grin.

The dealer turned over a ten to match the two that was showing, then hit with a six to make it eighteen. Carlos laughed and turned over a twenty – a king, a three, and a seven. Spiritwolf showed his cards and chuckled ruefully as the dealer scooped up his wager of a thousand euros and put down a thousand more, the table minimum. "Yeah, I dropped off the grid for a bit. Too much heat over a deal with a couple of punks living in Bumfuck, Illinois. So I decided to get out and see the world for a bit. But I'm back, looking at what's changed and who's still around." *And who might give me a fresh lead.* His good fortune returned with both wins on his double-down. Carlos also won and finished off his mojito in celebration.

"Sounds like you're well on your way, James." The sable winked and rung an imaginary bell with his finger at a passing leonine waitress. She nodded and immediately turned to get him another. Another round of cards, another win for Carlos, another loss for Spiritwolf. "Can I get you something to drink?"

"Nah, I had my fun earlier." He peered at his next set of cards, a jack and a five. *Perfect. Why couldn't this be cribbage?* He decided to stand. The waitress brought Carlos' next drink just as the dealer busted. The sable let out a celebratory whoop and drained his drink in one long swig.

Spirit didn't have to hide his amusement. "Looks like you're living it up."

"Hell, yeah." The sable eyed his next set of cards and immediately frowned. "I spoke too soon. Hit me." This time Carlos gritted his teeth at the sight of the nine that gave him twenty-two.

"Fuck." He tilted his head at the sight of the wolf raking in the large stacks of chips given him by the dealer for his blackjack. "You up or down?"

"I'm up now. And I think it's time for a break."

"What? You've only been here five minutes."

Spiritwolf grinned. "I stop when I'm ahead." He nodded to the dealer and received in return a plain-looking card with a chip embedded in the middle. The wolf put the card in his wallet, threw a hundred euro chip to the dealer, and knocked on the table as he got up.

"Wait a sec."

The agent paused while the sable cashed out his chips as well – his stacks were smaller but the value of the chips were higher. He linked his arm with Spirit's and tugged him through the ringing and chirping of the rows of slot machines with such force that the wolf was thankful for having reapplied the bio-glue liberally. Once again, the close contact brought that certain hunger of his to the fore and he had to pretend the sable was really a buxom woman and the thought of sex with a female… He shuddered. *Maybe I really should have been a hermit.*

Together they marched through the casino until they reached the restaurants; Carlos led him into a teppanyaki restaurant and, nodding to the maitre'd, finally stopped the excursion by sitting in a lonely booth near the back.

A waiter, this time a tiger, appeared within seconds. "Two menus and a 'dark and stormy' for me."

"Water for me, thanks." The waiter nodded and went off to the bar.

When they were alone, the sable's demeanor turned serious. "So what the hell are you really doing here, James?"

Spiritwolf didn't have to fake the look of shock that creased his features. "Excuse me?"

"You've always done business over the phone, or by instant messaging. Never in person. You almost seemed averse to being seen." The sable put his elbows on the table and laced his fingers together, under his chin. "So why are you here, now? You must want something from me – pretty badly, I'd wager, if you're here now."

Spiritwolf stared back at him with his blue-eyed gaze. "It finally sank in, did it?" he asked with a contemptuous sneer. "As I recall, your thick-headed insistence on transferring merchandise in person cost me a million-dollar deal that ended with two of my best operatives in bodybags." The sting had been one of Spirit's better plans and had neatly caught Carlos' top three lieutenants. The two TEA agents had been freed en route to the morgue.

The sable's eyes blazed with fury. "You ass. You were the one who fucked things up. The feds were waiting when we got there!" He snarled and swiped the air with a clawed hand.

"So we both got our tails handed to us." Spirit leaned back and folded his arms across his chest. "I'm not here for revenge, if you're worried about that."

"Worried? Who's worried?" Now it was Carlos' turn to favor the other man with a sardonic smirk. "I could have you killed before you reach the casino's doors."

"But not before I leave the restaurant, I hope!" The joke brought the sable 'round and they shared a laugh as the waiter returned with two beverages and two menus. Carlos took a sip of the amber drink and savored the taste on his tongue before swallowing. "Oh. That's really good," he murmured.

Spirit nodded and sipped his water. It tasted pure; he doubted Carlos would attempt to poison him here. Their exchange told him that it wasn't the sable's intent to off him and he had similarly let him know that bygones were bygones. Now it was down to business.

Spiritwolf leaned forward again over the table. "I really don't have anything that I'm looking to get from you. I've moved on from the mid-level tech to something a bit more lucrative."

"Oh? What's that?"

"More… exotic forms of tech." The sable's expression remained impassive, but the agent could tell from the subtle changes in his scent that he was interested.

"Like what?"

"Futuristic shit." Spirit grinned and took another sip of water.

"You mean like integrated weapons platforms? Orbiting lasers? That kind of stuff?"

Spirit laughed and shook his head. "No, no, you're thinking of the old me. I'm talking about biotech. Theoretical physics. The stuff you see in movies. Or not." He let that last bit linger over a coy smile while he pretended to peruse the menu.

"Huh. You know that stuff's monitored pretty closely by the Directorate, right? And their dogs in their Enforcement agency?"

"Yeah, so?" Spirit shrugged. "How's the sushi here, anyway?"

"Pretty good. So, what, do you have a means of escaping detection? An inside person?"

"If I did, I wouldn't give him or her away, would I?" *Baiting the hook was never my specialty.* Carlos was hitting uncomfortably close to his cover, so he steered the conversation in a different direction. "It's unlikely you have what I'd be looking for, anyway." The tiger returned and Spirit placed an order for a large bowl of ramen while Carlos ordered the Sushi Combo B.

"I just might have something, James," the sable said, swirling his glass and listening to the ice clinking against the sides. "But it's probably more than you can afford."

Spirit smiled. "Times change, my friend, and I have some very wealthy clients."

Carlos laughed. "I'm not surprised, especially since you're playing in the casino these days." His voice lowered. "I can't give away much. Someone's looking to offload some top secret hush-hush stuff."

Spirit's face soured. "Yeah? Like what?"

"Experimental research notes."

"When I said 'experimental physics', I meant working prototypes. Not some egghead's scribbles," the wolf snorted. *Reeling in the catch, on the other hand…*

"They include working plans to build the shit. Or so I'm told." Carlos finished off his drink and signaled for another.

Spirit stared at him. *How the hell can he still be sober, guzzling booze like that at his body weight?* "You mean you don't know?"

"Not for sure. The data's encrypted." Carlos appeared to be studying him closely now.

Spirit laughed, remembering to keep his muzzle down. "Let me get this straight. You want me to pay a large sum for encrypted data my clients might not be able to break?"

"If you do have a person inside DAST, it should be no problem," the sable replied with a sly grin.

"And just how is this data supposed to be delivered? I'm certain my clients would not want to share. They pay me a lot of money so that I can guarantee their selfishness."

The sable leaned back. "It's a security feature. You can't get the data off the tablet without decrypting it."

And there we are, Spirit thought.

"So? You up for it?"

The wolf tilted his head and splayed his ears to indicate his concern. "Huh. I'm not really sure. It sounds pretty risky.

How much?"

"Bidding starts at 500 million euros. Would have been more but for the encryption."

So now I know how much I'm worth, Spirit thought irreverently. "This person looking to offload… they're looking to weed out all but the serious, right?"

"*Sí. ¿Hay problema?*"

"What was that?" the agent asked, pretending he didn't know Spanish.

"Oh, sorry," the sable said with just the tiniest slur. "Is there a problem?"

"None. My clients can play, for sure. The risk is still tough to stomach."

"Well, I wouldn't want you to ruin your digestion. Tell you what, James. Let's enjoy our meal and you can give me an answer by the time we're done."

Now Spiritwolf snarled. "You're a crazy little fuck, you know that? Why not give me until tomorrow?"

"Because if you're not who you say you are, it's risky for me to stick around and let you get your backup in place. Either way you decide, I'm gone after I'm done eating." The sable leaned back, eyes narrowed from knowing he had the wolf by the balls.

The agent forced himself to calm down. "All right. My answer after the meal." They made polite small talk in the charged atmosphere until the food arrived just three minutes later. Spirit carefully slurped his ramen; even though it was a second spare mask, it was the only one that gave him complete anonymity where Achilles and the gang were concerned. Carlos, on the other hand, was shoveling all of the food from the bento-style tray as quickly as he could and making quite a mess doing so. *Asshole,* Spirit thought. *Trying to force me into making a quick decision.*

"What's taking you so long?" Carlos leered, barely three minutes later.

Spirit smiled. "A lovable sensei of mine taught me the wisdom of patience, and of slurping noodles to enhance the experience."

"Sure, sure." Carlos finished off his latest drink with a look of bored indifference. Spirit smiled and felt a certain zen-like calmness wash over him as he kept eating at his unhurried pace until he finally drank the last of the broth from the bowl and put it down. He licked his lips, hoping it wouldn't appear overly bizarre.

"Well?" The sable asked. "What's the decision, Mr. Thomas?"

"The decision is that I need to contact my clients. However, I recognize your concerns about me and I'm willing to let you be the driver on this, if you're still interested."

Carlos motioned for him to continue.

"I shall call them later this evening." Spirit pulled out a gold business card case. "My current front is a personal trainer." He hadn't had time to make up new cards; most of his time eating had actually been spent whether to risk discovery as part of Achilles' entourage. "My cell is there.

Ring me after midnight and I'll have your answer. You'll be in control and I won't know where you are, so there's no way for me to try anything funny."

Carlos took the proffered card and stuffed it in his pocket without looking. "Very well. Then our business here is done." He stood and threw a hundred euro note on the table. "You will wait here for five minutes before departing. He'll see to it." He pointed to the tiger, who nodded and flashed a Glock under his apron.

"Ever the trusting soul, aren't you?" Spirit smirked. "It was a pleasure meeting you in person, Carlos." The sable grunted and stalked toward the restaurant entrance, then out to the casino's main area.

After the designated time was up, the tiger waved nonchalantly at him and Spirit got up, leaving in the same manner as his dining companion. He made sure to head in the opposite direction than Carlos had and, after a perambulatory route around the machines and tables, he found his way outside and hailed a taxi to the Oro. Once he was safely inside the car, he pulled out his cell phone and pretended to fiddle with it, answering his email or trying to find the right link to follow in his browser.

The screen was replaced with a map overlay of the city. A bright green dot showed where the sable was, his position routed via satellite reception of the wafer-thin transmitter embedded into the fibers of his business card. A little more sophisticated than the tracker that had been implanted into Achilles' boot, but more or less the same concept.

At last, events were proceeding according to plan.

* * *

Achilles waded through the hotel lobby, surrounded by security to fend off screaming fans so that he could go have his dinner in peace. The press conference had gone strikingly well; the band had all pulled together as though the last day's worth of weirdness had never happened. Cain had even stuck up for him when a journalist had asked about fumbling through his last song in the Colosseum. The badger had waved aside the question, saying that he'd lost a drumstick and the wolf had been magnanimous enough to halt the performance for him. And then they'd moved on to the next question before the completely pole-axed questioner managed to recover.

As the white wolf was escorted toward Regis waiting in the limo outside, a familiar-looking figure caught his eye. He nearly called out before realizing at the last second that the other muscular wolf was grey with blue eyes, instead of brown with green eyes. Still, the man could have been twin to the person he was thinking of.

And then he caught the wolf's scent.

His eyes widened and he turned, but the other wolf was already sauntering past and staring at his cell phone screen. Achilles thought about stopping him, demanding an explanation, but he was already being swept toward the front doors like a surfer toward the beach on the incoming tide. He kept his surprise and his curiosity in check and recovered his composure in time to make it appear to the waiting elephant as though nothing was out of the ordinary.

Nothing out of the ordinary, that is, other than Spiritwolf appearing to be a completely different person.

* * *

Evening had cooled off the city but not enough to chase the beachgoers from the sand and surf. Amethyst skies pursued the ruby sunset with the crescent moon in tow to create a postcard-perfect moment over the water. Couples and groups of looking-to-get-luckies paraded in a never-ending stream along the well-lit boardwalk. Restaurants, shops, and clubs just off the crowded path were the destinations of choice, though many others, especially the nocturnal species, strolled to join the daytimers on the sand in crepuscular activities – bonfires, grilled dinners, and night sports were the main draws.

A lone figure watched across the street from the Cyberstalliano Café, keenly aware of his distance from the crowds. Spiritwolf looked again at his tracker; the sable was still in the hotel room about a mile away and whether he was resting or having sex, he had no idea. That accidental thought slanted his memories toward Les again and he immediately quashed the temptation back into the hole it had crawled from. The genie would stay bottled.

An encrypted text message announced itself with a friendly chime. He read it and raised his eyebrows.

What do you MEAN you want five hundred million euros?? - SDUrsine0.

Yup, Zero's pissed. Even a Senior Director in DAST like him would have trouble authorizing that much bank.

That's the price to buy into the auction. A billion for our final bid. Go or no go? - Sprtwlf.

Answer should be obvious. - SDUrsine0.

What's the spending authorization limit for my cure? - Sprtwlf.

There. That should make him come around.

Need to get approval from committee. Will take time. Stall. Need to go to meeting. Talk later. - SDUrsine0.

Spirit didn't bother to look at the waiter, who'd come to replenish his water. The response had been five minutes in the making. Spirit hated guilting Zero into doing it; he knew the bear still blamed himself, and probably would for the rest of his life. But the wolf also wanted to be seen again without having to cover himself in order to appear normal. He didn't want to have to be on guard every moment, have to worry that he was going to do something stupid that would reveal his secret. It was fatiguing to constantly keep up the pretense and there would always be the worry of some little thing that got overlooked that would do him in. And maybe, just maybe, the data on the tablet would turn back time and allow him and the others to be like they were before. *So many ifs and maybes*, he thought. *One step at a time.*

He went back to the tracking program; still no change.

"Care to explain yourself?"

Spirit jumped at the seething voice next to him and stared incredulously at the white wolf dressed so uncharacteristically in a baseball cap, short-sleeved T-shirt, jeans, and an apron around his waist. The analytical part of his mind was quirkily assessing Achilles' biceps and triceps growth and his id patted himself on the back with a hearty 'well done!' at the quick results of his training.

"Wait, what? How did you find me?" And then he remembered he was wearing his other mask.

"How did you find me?" he repeated.

"Caught your scent in the hotel lobby," the rock star replied with a victorious smirk. "When you said you were going out, I didn't think it was like this." He peered at the other wolf. "How the hell do you have that stuff on you, anyway? Isn't it hot in there?"

"Very." Spirit pulled his cell phone back toward him; the movement caught Achilles' eye. "I'm tracking a lead right now," he said quietly. "You need to go back to your hotel room and let me do my job. Go talk to some reporters or some fans."

Achilles shook his head. "No. This has gone on long enough. I'm coming with you."

"This isn't a game. Do you remember what happened in Dresden?"

"I remember you injecting me…"

"Cripes… forget that already, will you?"

"Why don't you give me another injection? Problem solved."

"Don't tempt me." He knew the methyl caudate wasn't likely to work again, not to mention the risk of causing permanent damage, but he sure wasn't going to let him know that. "No, I meant the hit in the restaurant.

And being chased afterward. You almost got yourself zapped with the stun gun."

"Yeah, you took it for me. How's your neck, by the way?"

"Doing fine." He'd examined himself before going to meet with Carlos earlier and was pleased to feel that the bruises were healing nicely.

Achilles stared at him again and this time, Spirit growled from the discomfort of the close scrutiny. "Your lip's better, too," the white wolf noted.

"Yeah. So I can't risk you getting injured or killed. Regis will have my head for the former and my boss will have my head for the latter." He paused. "How did you get out, anyway? The lobby of the Oro and its parking lots are a madhouse of fans."

"Same way I got the apron," Achilles pointed to his outfit. "I turned on the charm and gave an autograph or three. You'd be surprised what people will do for you if you ask nicely."

"That's what I'm doing. Get back to the hotel where it's safe. I promise I'll tell you everything I find tonight."

"No way. You never said anything about going out in this new face of yours. Who knows what else you're keeping from me." Achilles paused at the approach from a shirtless serval who, with his relatively bulky frame, was about the same size. The wolf smiled and unwrapped the apron.

"Thanks, *amigo*," he said; the serval nodded and grinned back, surreptitiously fingering a signed glossy as he headed to the back of the cafe.

Spiritwolf started up again when he was out of earshot. "Look, I don't have time to argue with you. I can't have you coming with me. You're a liability."

"Bullshit. You could always use someone as backup."

"I. Don't. Need. Backup."

"Your dot is moving."

Spirit blinked. "What?" Then he looked at the screen, which showed the green dot moving rapidly away from the hotel… and the cafe. "Fuck," he muttered as he got up and began running.

"See? I can keep up with you." Achilles was loping behind him and weaving through the crowd just as he was. "All that working out must be paying off."

"Fine. Whatever." Spirit growled. "Just stay the hell out of the way if the bullets start flying."

"I'm not that stupid."

The agent didn't say anything in reply, choosing instead to focus on the sable's route.

"Damn… he's getting away, and fast. Must be in a car, or riding a motorcycle." He immediately began searching along the row of parked vehicles for one that would be easy to steal.

"Taxi!"

Spirit turned and saw the white wolf flagging down an approaching cab. It stopped and he piled in. "Coming?"

The agent grudgingly nodded and slammed the door shut after he got in. "Up two blocks and make a right," he ordered.

The driver, a friendly-looking cougar, nodded. "Any particular destination, sirs?"

"I'll let you know when we get there."

Within ten minutes the pursuit had left the touristy environs of Arenosa and had entered the inland part of the city, where the working class lived. The lights were not as bright here; wan streetlamps provided faint illumination of sullen residential houses. The cougar drove where Spiritwolf directed and after another minute, they crossed a pair of railroad tracks and made a sharp turn to the north. The rail lines led into a large tunnel through the hills that served as the northern border of Arenosa proper and into an adjacent valley. This was a warehouse and distribution area, where shipping and railways converged and cargo was commingled prior to separation and transfer to their destination. The businesses obviously wanted the place out of sight to attract the elite citizenry but close enough to keep transportation costs down and profits maximized.

The signal led them to an industrial park about a mile from the tunnel. When Carlos appeared to moving slowly again, Spiritwolf told the cougar to turn down a side street a couple of blocks away and then pull into a parking lot. Newly downloaded map data indicated that his quarry was in a warehouse of furnishings and decor for the wealthy and glamorous.

"Stay here," Spirit told the driver and handed him a fifty euro note. "I'll be back in twenty minutes. That goes for you, too, rock star." He exited the vehicle quickly.

"The hell it does." Achilles did the same but before he could start walking, Spirit was already in his way.

"Do you want to get killed?" the agent asked in a low voice.

"No. But the person you're tracking…"

"Isn't going anywhere. And this could be a trap, set up for me." Spirit pulled his gun from the back of his waist and popped the clip in. The white wolf's eyes stared unbelievingly at the weapon. "When the area's clear, I'll come back for you. Deal?"

"Fine." Achilles got back in the taxi while Spiritwolf went around to the driver.

"*Si no estoy detrás en veinte minutos, vuelva al Oro con el lobo. ¿Entiende?*"

"*Sí.*"

Spirit ran back toward the street where Carlos was. He could have ordered the taxi driver to take off with Achilles in the back right then but he didn't want to deceive him again, not when the wolf's trust of him was hanging by a thread. It wouldn't be a threat to their safety if he cleared the way and then led him into a controlled situation. The main thing was that he couldn't afford to be seen with a world-famous rock star.

He smiled. Then again, having Achilles with him would lend credence to the cover story he'd given Carlos earlier.

Spirit sidled along the edge of an adjacent building and peered around the corner to his right. The street was completely deserted and a minute's worth of searching the surrounding shadows didn't yield any new discoveries. Was Carlos really that careless? Or was something else going down that he didn't know about?

And then he spotted the two jackals in a parked car at the end of the next block and almost around the corner, which explained why he hadn't noticed them before. Spiritwolf caught the glint of a gun muzzle and backtracked, then turned left so that he could come up on them from behind. He carefully fitted the suppressor to the end of his gun and saw that one of them had gotten out and was facing the wall to take a piss. Spirit carefully watched both of them as he approached, moving as quickly as he could without causing too much of a distraction. Fortunately, the person still in the car seemed to be more intent on his laptop than what was around them. The other jackal zipped up and was turning around when Spirit made his move and put the suppressor under his throat pointing up. In the car, the man had dumped the laptop and was reaching for his gun when the wolf leaned in around the collapsing body of the first jackal and fired, catching him square in the chest. He added one more in the head to be sure and pulled out the laptop before dragging the first jackal back into the car, rolling up the windows and locking the doors. He caught the sable's scent – Carlos had been in the car, all right. Spirit saw that the screen had been password locked, so he closed it, tucked the laptop under his arm like a football, and sprinted back to the taxi.

"What's that?" Achilles inquired upon his return.

The agent shook his head and motioned for the white wolf to come out. "You, go. Now." He barked the order to the driver, who nodded and started the engine.

"Hey, wait!" Achilles waved at the driver then turned back to Spiritwolf. "Are you nuts? How are we going to get back? It's got to be at least a couple of hours if we have to walk."

"We'll walk."

"No way. Hey, buddy. *Amigo.*" The cougar looked at the white wolf waving a hundred euro note. "Yours if you wait for us to get back."

"That buys you a half hour, my friend."

"I have more…"

"We don't have time for this," Spirit interrupted, glaring at Achilles before turning back to the driver. "You leave, now. And don't speak to anyone about this." He snatched the bill from the singer, exchanged the laptop for it, and crushed it into the cougar's hand while bringing the gun into view. "Understood?"

The feline gulped and nodded, zooming away from *los dos lobos locos.*

"Oh, that's just brilliant!" Achilles nearly dropped the laptop by throwing up his arms in disgust. "Why'd you do that?"

"Because I took out a pair of armed jackals waiting in a car not too far from here and I didn't want our driver to get caught up in my business." He glared pointedly at the wolf. "I told you, I'm in charge when we're out here."

"Yeah, whatever." The rock star pointed to the cell phone. "Let's go meet your contact and get this over with."

The green dot was still stationary and, using some downloaded construction plans from the European TEA servers, Spirit found the nearest back entrance to the warehouse the sable had stopped in. They proceeded warily with the agent peering up, down, and all around for other lookouts. There were none to be seen, so they went inside after Spirit picked the lock. As they passed a row of lockers, Spirit took back the laptop from the singer and shoved it inside an unoccupied one for safekeeping. His gun was out and at the ready in one hand and he was tracking the sable on his cell phone with the other. Achilles trailed a meter behind him, surprisingly quiet in his movements.

The first bay they emerged into was full of office furnishings, presumably for dwellings that doubled as businesses. Their target was still seventy meters ahead and to the left, so they didn't bother giving anything more than a cursory glance before passing through. After findings rugs, drapes, and bathroom furniture, they came upon the "beds room". Everything from four-post beds with mosquito netting to sleek modern frames which integrated beds, bookshelves, and an entertainment center, to faux caves and the suggestively erotic, were strewn across a football pitch-sized area. Spirit looked back at Achilles to make sure he was still there and then listened very carefully for any sound. Nothing but silence reigned until the air conditioning unit kicked on, providing them with some cover for continuing.

They crept to within ten meters of the signal and stayed out of sight behind a stack of mattresses. Spirit gestured with a finger pointing down to tell the white wolf to stay put. Achilles nodded and peeked carefully to watch the other wolf weave through the obstacle course, then pause before a black-sheeted bed.

On top and nearly invisible was the sable's naked body, all appearances suggesting he was sleeping peacefully. His clothes were even stacked neatly on a dresser. The drool from his mouth, though, was a dark crimson-black and another pool had formed near his left chest.

Achilles saw Spirit drop down before losing sight of him. He came crawling up to the white wolf a half minute later; Achilles knelt down, too.

"We're in trouble…" was all the agent whispered before shots erupted and tore up some of the pillows on a display stand to their right. Spirit moved, still hunched over, pushing Achilles along and keeping himself between the shooters and the rock star. Achilles was no doubt terrified by what was going on but if the agent could keep him moving, maybe they could get out unscathed. The white wolf hadn't yelled or screamed when bullets had started flying, and he hadn't been paralyzed with fear, which was a good sign.

There were at least two pursuers that Spirit could distinguish from the rounds that were fired; looking back over his shoulder confirmed four large shapes dodging and crashing through the furniture. A lion and three zebras running through a warehouse… there was a joke in there somewhere.

The bullets coming toward them, on the other hand, were no laughing matter. Every dozen seconds or so, Spirit would fire his own gun, just to keep the pursuers on their toes. At this point, every moment of delay would help the two of them and yet he still had to balance that against his remaining ammunition. One of the first things taught to the newly minted TEA recruits who didn't count military or law enforcement as part of their background was that real life was not a video game and you could run out of ammo real quick if you weren't careful.

The next salvo destroyed the lamp immediately to his right. Thankfully they were near an exit from the room; Spirit growled, "There! Left!" and the white wolf plunged headlong through the opening with the agent on his tail. They straightened up and began sprinting down the hallway for the opening to the next room and dove into it just as the quartet had emerged and began firing.

This room was much smaller; in fact, only a wooden service bar with four stools was in the room. Spirit nearly cried out in frustration at the lack of an exit and led Achilles behind the bar. He positioned himself at the side just as one of the zebras came into view and fired. The zebra's right eye became a void and blood and brains sprayed out the back of his head.

One down, three to go. The remaining three stayed back out of sight and then the two zebras stuck their hands and weapons around the corner, firing furiously.

* * *

Outside the room, the lion speed-dialed the first number on his cell phone and spoke hurriedly after the recipient picked up. "Sir... we took care of Carlos, just like you wanted. But two more came in after him." He let off a couple of rounds himself and turned around, ignoring the dead body while his remaining men kept going. "What do you want us to do?"

On the other end of the line, Gareth Zirkowski smiled. "No witnesses," he said as if he were ordering a birthday cake. Then he clicked his headset off and peered outside his office window before returning to his desk to finish typing the report on his computer. No one else was staying late at work; the deputy director in charge of MI-6's CATS unit had sent everyone home early for a well-deserved night off. After all, the investigation into the Arenosa killings would make for a very long day tomorrow.

* * *

Spirit ducked as another angry swarm of bullets embedded themselves in the walls, barstools, and the bar itself. There weren't any security cameras in here, so all he needed to do was... *No! I have to find another way. I have to.*

"Goddamit! Don't just sit there... DO something!" Next to him, Achilles was curled around his knees, ears flat against his skull and looking every bit as though he wished he hadn't followed the agent. Spirit cursed and racked his brains; it was his fault they were in this mess and he had to protect the white wolf. He was the agent, he was supposed to know what to do to get out of this hopeless situation. He couldn't let them die.

Could he?

The problem was, there wasn't a way out. They barely had cover while the gunmen blocked the only exit from the room and had them outnumbered and outgunned. And if Carlos was any indication, they weren't likely to accept a surrender; if they did, it wouldn't be pleasant for the two wolves. Living beyond this night to see the next sunrise would be a miracle. They had to survive, despite having no tactical advantage whatsoever, and there was only one way that would happen.

The silence surprised Achilles. He pried his arms from his legs, half expecting to be fired upon yet again when he did so but nothing came. It seemed like an eternity since the last volley of gunfire – maybe the agent had done something after all. His ears were still ringing like one of his more impassioned performances and he shifted position to see Spirit still sitting beside him. The other wolf's head was down; he was peering at... a contact lens case?

"Spirit!" Achilles hissed. "What the fuck are you doing?" A few more shots rang out and he flinched. Without moving his head, Spiritwolf arced his gun arm horizontally until it was alongside the edge of the bar. He returned fire with a few blind shots that seemed more like casual suggestions than anything authoritative. Then the agent put the case on the ground and turned his head up to look at him. The blue eyes were gone from his face and while Achilles expected to see his real eyes – the green irises he'd gotten used to seeing – he was surprised he didn't see those, either. There wasn't much more than shadows; his eyes were sunken in too far, it seemed.

Well, his trainer-slash-agent did say that he had been in an accident. Maybe he hadn't been lying about that and his sensitivity to light. Spirit put a finger to his lips and Achilles nodded agreement, faintly annoyed and still trying to puzzle out the other wolf's plan.

Spirit put down his gun, reached behind to the back of his neck, and tugged. Now Achilles understood what was going on. Obviously, his disguise as a grey wolf meant he was in a mask. Maybe shucking it would somehow give them an advantage? No, that didn't make sense. Maybe he didn't know what was going on.

And then Achilles watched Spiritwolf complete the motion and pull off his head completely, leaving nothing above the shirt collar.

If the rock star hadn't already been white, he would have been so now. The headless thing next to him was busy removing gloves that served to mimic hands and forearms; off they came and fell to the floor. Then the clothes started a weird dance of opening and undressing and doffing – first the shirt, then the loafers and socks, and lastly, the pants. And then, just like that, Achilles was alone and more confused than ever.

"Stay here and keep quiet." Achilles stifled a gasp; Spirit's gruff voice had come from the air somewhere nearby; exactly where, he couldn't tell. But the words elicited another round of bullets and this time, two actually penetrated the wood between them... well, between Achilles and the pile of Spiritwolf's clothes. And his gun. And his face. It was creepy, looking at the exanimate and distorted visage, not unlike peering into a funhouse mirror.

Achilles picked up the weapon and was surprised to see his hand shaking. His other hand covered it reassuringly and his grip steadied. Soft footfalls made his ears prick up and then the two zebras came into view on either side of the bar, their guns pointed right at him. "Drop it! NOW!" Achilles obeyed immediately, putting it carefully on Spirit's pants.

Where the hell had the wolf gone off to? Did he desert him, leave him as the sacrificial lamb? It was a chilling thought.

"Lay face down, arms over your head." Achilles nodded and moved forward slowly – he didn't want to move suddenly or do anything that might get him shot at. As he got to hands and knees, he heard a sudden "erk," followed immediately by a loud crunching noise, and then the zebra to his right was falling parallel to him. He landed heavily on the floor – his neck flopped about too easily before it finally settled to rest with his eyes permanently unfocused. To the wolf's left, the remaining zebra snorted in surprise and he immediately ducked back behind the bar.

"Stay down," Spiritwolf's voice whispered in his ear. Achilles felt a light touch on his back that was gone a moment later. He waited for what seemed like forever, hearing little other than the faintest of footsteps in the room. And then a loud thud, followed by a feline roar of pain, more thuds and grunts, the sound of the zebra running toward the door, another cry, and a final crunching similar to the one he'd heard when the first zebra had died. One lone shot from a gun was the final sound before silence reclaimed its authority.

Achilles heard the padding footsteps again and as he turned, he watched a slower version of the previous dancing clothes put themselves back on over air. He sat up, with his back resting against the bar, mesmerized by the strange sight of empty clothing filling out, topped off by Spirit's mask and gloves and, lastly, the contact lenses.

When the agent stood whole before him again, he opened his mouth to speak. "Shut it," Spirit said tightly. "We're leaving."

"Hang on…"

"I said shut it."

Perhaps it was the bizarreness of the last half hour – the last couple of minutes, really – but the younger wolf decided not to challenge the tone that brooked no discussion. Certainly Achilles didn't want to to challenge the person who had left the four corpses in his wake – six, counting the two jackals. They slipped back through the rooms, with Spirit making a stop to visit the sable and search for anything in his clothing. Only Spiritwolf's business card in the left pants pocket was even remotely of interest – there was no wallet, no keys or anything else. The large wolf snarled and kicked over an armoire, sending it to the floor with a loud crash. He took the card and stalked from the room with Achilles in tow, stopping only to retrieve the laptop before heading outside and beginning the long journey back.

* * *

"And you're sure it's taken care of?"

"Of course."

Blair Murdock sighed, relieved at Gareth's reassuring tone. "I'm dispatching a team to Arenosa in the morning to clean up loose ends. And then I'll personally see to it that this Black Dust fellow becomes his namesake. You'll have it within a week."

"Good news. I knew I could count on you." The lion hung up and stared back at the shadowy alcove in his large office suite. "Sir? Are you sure that it will have the information you need?"

He couldn't see anything moving in the darkness, but the whispering voice replied, "Oh, it will. This proves it." A shiny piece of paper slid along the floor out of the darkness and the lion picked it up.

It was Milan's odd photo of Spiritwolf.

* * *

They walked in silence and even seeing the 'Glittering Jewel of the Mediterranean' upon emerging from the tunnel did nothing to dispel the cloud of gloom that appeared to have taken hold of Spirit. Each wolf was lost in his thoughts; each step carrying them further away from the agent's world of dark intrigue and death, each step bringing them closer to the bright lights and throngs of people that were part of Achilles' life.

The road meandered toward the city, curving off in one direction to follow the water's edge and another to join up with the super-highway. Along the way were turnoffs that beckoned toward the secret places off the beaten path. Their passage was largely unnoticed at 2 A.M. on the darkened roads until they crossed into the city line, still in the outskirts of Arenosa. Cars zoomed by more frequently as they got closer, and every so often, cyclists, gliders, or walkers would pass by without much fanfare. Spiritwolf guided Achilles off the main thoroughfares where crowds still held sway and they instead slinked along through back alleys populated by all-night eateries and, occasionally, less savory businesses.

They were still a bit more than a kilometer out from the Oro with no one around when Achilles finally spoke up. "Look, about what happened back there. I just wanted to say… thanks for saving my life."

No reply.

"Didn't you hear me?" Still nothing from the brooding wolf. "Well, anyway. That was absolutely spectacular, the way you took down those guys. I don't know how you did it, but it was phenomenal, never seen anything like it. What was it, some kind of super-secret gadget? Maybe you could let me borrow it sometime… I bet that would make for a great special effect on stage… hrrrk!"

Spirit had lunged at Achilles and slammed his forearm across the white wolf's throat to pin him against the side of the building. He leaned in close until he was almost nose to nose; Achilles squeaked and then sucked in some air as the pressure let up a bit.

"You don't get it, do you?" Spirit was seething and the younger wolf was taken aback that it was being directed at him. This wasn't just anger or annoyance, it was hatred. Of him.

"What you saw tonight… me… that's how I am. All the fucking time." He tucked the laptop under his arm and tugged his free hand with his teeth; off came the glove and with it, all sight of his hand. The white wolf looked into the sleeve and saw nothing, only the fabric that enwrapped the invisible wolf and allowed him to be seen.

Achilles gulped as the agent continued his quiet, murderous rant. "You want to know what I'm hiding from you? Okay. A freak accident a year ago made me like this. No special effect. No device. No 'OFF' switch. And no fucking way back. Except maybe for some data on a stolen tablet." Achilles' eyes widened as comprehension seeped in and filled some pieces to the puzzle. "And my only lead to where it might be and who might be selling it got himself killed. My only lead to restoring my body to what it was. And you think this is all a fucking joke." Spirit let him go with a disgusted look on his face and calmly replaced his glove while Achilles coughed violently and wheezed as he sucked in precious air. "You saw something tonight that you weren't ever supposed to see. Don't tell anyone about me, or about anything else that happened tonight. Or people more secretive and less tolerant than I might come after you." He adjusted the laptop under his arm and began to march toward the hotel.

"Sorry… I'm so sorry, Spirit… look, I didn't know about any of this… what you've been through…" The white wolf stumbled after him until he caught up and put his hand on the other wolf's shoulder.

Spirit wrenched his arm away and kept going. "Don't bother, rock star. From now on, I'm doing this by myself, my own way, like I should have from the start." Then Achilles paused, stunned at the wolf's next words.

"I quit."

Chapter Seven: For Heart And Voice Would Fail Me

A young, teenage white wolf padded down an empty school corridor. It was night. The lights were all out; there must be secrecy for this mission. He was dressed in black, traveling lightly. Wan yellow light from the quad rippled over him as he treaded stealthily toward his goal. In the heart of the multimedia department, he passed by numbered locked doors, silently counting them off one by one. Eventually, he reached number fifteen. Out of hopeful, instinctive habit, he grabbed for the handle and jiggled it. Locked. This was expected. From his pocket, he produced a key that had been craftily stolen from a desk drawer during daylight hours, and with a satisfying click, gained egress to the seemingly forbidden room.

Inside, it was utterly dark – no windows here. His hand fumbled against the wall for a fleeting second, and then he found the light switch. There was an expectant buzzing sound as the solitary light bulb warmed to life, illuminating the small room. Before the wolf was a large desk; it housed a behemoth of a mixing desk, green LEDs awaiting his hands like the eyes of invisible sprites – faders and dials for every level and channel of the auditory spectrum. A glass window above the desk looked out into a cramped, but empty padded room, a lonesome untouched microphone resting within, like the prized exhibit of a museum. The white wolf rubbed his hands expectantly, and threw himself down upon the chair in front of the desk. *I made it*, he thought, in awe. His heart was beating at a hundred miles an hour. *Nobody discovered me. Holy shit... I did it again.*

He was able to savor the success of breaking into the school's tiny recording studio for a moment; the faculty itself was renowned for the arts, and this equipment had been a generous gift from a wealthy alumnus. In fact, it was called the "Trent West" room in his honor. But its use was heavily supervised; a kind of supervision the white wolf did not care for. Immediately, surely, and confidently, the wolf began to do his work; hands

163

moving over the dials. Plugging things in. Headphones on, so that nobody could hear the sounds he was making, he began to mix his music. One note at a time, pulled from the bottom of his soul. He'd already done his illegal work recording his music earlier in the week, tonight was the night he mastered the tracks. Soon, his demo would be ready. And he could begin… *something*. He wasn't sure what, exactly. But there was music in him that needed to be released.

His guard dropped completely, the wolf buried himself in his work, listening to every note with crystal clarity, hearing his own voice growling and speaking of things that nobody else had ever heard him say. Fifteen minutes had passed before the door behind him clicked open again. He didn't even hear the footfalls upon his back, until a heavy gold hand settled upon his shoulder. With a single yelp breaking the silence, the white wolf was sharply startled, and he tore the headphones from his ears. As they released themselves, some wailing, frenzied guitar riff could be heard echoing through the space, while his own voice crooned from the muted speakers: "I will show you the way… it's my way, my way…"

"Shit!" he cursed, facing the newcomer. He turned, and in the dim light stared directly into the eyes of the head of the arts department, Mr. Bailey. The large, middle-aged lion was looking at the student with a quixotic kind of amusement and annoyance, down the rims of his silver spectacles.

"I might have known," the feline rumbled. "Achilles. That's the name you prefer outside of class, isn't it?"

"S-sir," the teenager began, fumbling and killing the sounds coming from the headphones. "I… I can explain."

"I'm sure you can," the professor patiently replied, staying absolutely motionless as the wolf went this way and that, turning things off, protecting his secret. "But trespassing? Breaking and entering? Unauthorized use of school equipment? Those are serious things, pup. Your explanation would have to be an excellent one." The older lion was dressed in a knitted blue vest, beige trousers. It was an old-fashioned look, but one he wore remarkably well. He stared directly down into the wolf's eyes again. "Well?"

"I…" Achilles found his cheeks feeling hot, as his embarrassment caught up with his shock. "Just… I should go…"

"No," the lion growled, a little forcefully. He was blocking the doorway. "Not until I find out what you've been up to these last four nights of furtive recording. Do you think I wouldn't have noticed someone had been coming in here at night? That my spare key had gone missing? I knew you had a rebellious streak; I never knew it went so far."

"Please," the wolf begged. His eye went to the multimedia stack, where his nearly finished CD lay waiting, needing to be retrieved before he could go. "I just wanted to work on some… stuff. Away from prying ears and eyes."

The lion folded his arms over his chest, and looked all the more sternly at the delinquent in front of him. "You could have booked a session with the department. *Properly*. You didn't have to risk expulsion to gain privacy."

"Sir!" Achilles begged, the emotion and fear welling up inside of him. "Don't… please, I can't be expelled… my parents… !" his breath was coming in short burst. He feared he might start crying, in spite of his supposed age and maturity, which made his cheeks burn all the more.

"I'll cut you a deal then," Burt Bailey fixedly replied. "Let me in on what you've been doing in here, and this goes no further."

The wolf's eyes widened. He wasn't ready. "I… I just… I'd rather…"

The lion rolled his eyes. "Listen, you're a gifted musician, pup. One of the best in my class, but I've *known* you've been holding back from me, from your peers. There's something you feel you're not ready to share yet. Something you're *embarrassed* by. And that both intrigues and infuriates me. You're better than this. You could be great. He eyed the stack, where the CD lay. "Is this subterfuge worthy of greatness? What do you think?"

"No," the wolf said, lowering his head. "It's not great at all," he replied, mumbling to the floor.

"Liar. You don't even believe that. You just don't want anyone to hear; well, tough, because I am." Commandingly, he eased himself past the young canine, and into the chair, which creaked slightly under his weight. He picked up the headphones, and settled them past the flecks of his golden mane to his ears. All the time the wolf felt his stomach tightening, but could do nothing to stop the man. Instead, he hung back, horrified, embarrassed – but strangely, amazingly, desperate for approval. He put his hand to his mouth, and bit down upon the knuckle from stop himself moaning aloud as the professor pushed 'play', and the tiniest traces of music escaped from the space between the speaker and the older man's ear.

The song only lasted three minutes; they were the longest three minutes of the wolf's life. The lion's expression was inscrutable. He wore a slight frown the entire time; obviously he was extremely annoyed by his student's actions – but somehow, his innate curiosity won out. But did he enjoy it? Then the three minutes passed, and the next song began to play, and still he listened. Achilles eyed the door; he could run for it. But then, he would never know… fighting the urge to escape, the wolf crouched down, and waited. He buried his head in his hands, and knew that a mighty judgment was about to rain down upon him, whatever the outcome.

Finally, the lion slipped the headphones from his head, and slowly turned to face the errant musician, who stood to attention as if he had just caught the glance of his drill-sergeant. Slowly, he shook his head. "Oh pup… if only you knew how little you had to be embarrassed by."

The wolf scratched his slender arm, but said nothing. He felt so exposed, no words would come out.

The lion sighed. "Listening to you… I feel so old. Make the most of this time Achilles. Stop hiding." He placed his hand upon the wolf's shoulder again, and squeezed insistently. "If you have something to say, you *must* say it! Do you understand me? Your work is crude; you must find some way to refine it. But stop silencing yourself; stop sneaking around in the dark. Go find your light." Numbly, the wolf nodded as if he understood; yet he did not. All he could comprehend was that on some level, he had impressed the lion. And that was good. Perhaps he could go, without consequence. He nodded, but there was no comprehension in his nod, which the lion immediately recognized.

The lion paused, and shook his head one more time. "I should know. For I can no longer sing the old songs I sang long years ago, for heart and voice would fail me, and foolish tears would flow. Don't fail me, Achilles. Now go."

* * *

Spread upon the backseat of the taxi, with the late morning sun upon his face, Achilles had no idea why that memory, of the furtive encounter with his old music professor, should have come unbidden to his wandering, tired mind. He missed the cryptic lion, in his way; he'd been kicked out of that institution not two months later, for not showing up to any of the classes. By then, things were already in motion; his demo was getting attention from some larger industry players, big dollar checks were being waved in front of his eyes, and suddenly his musical education began to seem strangely irrelevant. He wondered sometimes what the man had made of his success. Had he found his light? Had he failed him, or pleased him? Before he could ever summon the courage to reach out to him, some other distraction came his way. A new album. A new tour. It was all the same, stuck in the fame machine.

Except, that morning, it wasn't all the same. The machine had fallen apart.

First, he'd been shot at – he'd never been shot at. And he'd survived. And seen… what, exactly? Some drugged out illusion? Some super-secret spy tech? Something mad, something incredible? His mind, creative as it was, struggled to rationalize it. *Yup. Just your average personal-trainer-*

turned-secret-agent who's invisible. No big. I've seen weirder mutants backstage at a music awards ceremony, right? The wonders of plastic…

But no, he couldn't convince himself to dismiss it like that. Not when the taste of fear was still in his mouth; the risen acrid spittle coated with the certainty he was about to die, back in that warehouse. He'd wanted to help; wanted to do something outside the machine. But he'd gotten more than he'd bargained for; nearly gotten himself killed. He should be thankful the agent said they were done. Thankful he could have his life and tour back. Except that it was all still going to be going on, around him, in spite of him. The secrets. The battles. The deaths. And he couldn't stop it, not even if he tried. He was just a singer. Just a pop-tart. Right? The taste had been in his mouth even when Spirit had snarled at him, abandoned him upon that street. He had no idea where the wolf went after that – he'd walked away, turned a corner, and then seemingly vanished. Shocked, bereft, the celebrity had been forced to hail a cab all on his own, making his own way back to the hotel. Numb. Trying to figure it out. He'd gone up to his room to sleep, only to find – unsurprisingly – that he couldn't, despite being dead tired. He wasn't hungry, so he'd finally decided to hail another cab and had the driver take him around the town while his mind just drifted along…

"Your stop, *señor*," the donkey driving him gruffly said, bringing the vehicle to a halt. Already, one of the posh footmen stationed outside the hotel was at the cab door, holding it open. Nodding, Achilles thrust a fistful of euros at the equine, before swinging out to the open. As usual, a gaggle of eager, patient fans who had been camping outside the entrance flocked to him. He found camera phones flashed in his face; he flashed smiles instinctively. His hands didn't even have to look for the autograph books and papers, he just put them out, and they were there. He signed his scrawl automatically, not even listening to the chorus of excitement that surrounded him. "Thank you," he muttered, his mind still chewing over the events. "Thanks for coming. Goodbye."

He stalked away, leaving the fans behind him like driftwood. He entered the hotel unhindered, and even inside the elevator, he found himself daydreaming about the past and his present. *"If you have something to say, you must say it."* The sentiment was insistently bouncing around his skull.

Heart set upon action, the wolf breezed down the corridor, and marched up to Spiritwolf's room. His hand banged upon the wood, a summoning knock poised in his fist, but the first moment his knuckle struck the portal, it swung lazily open, revealing a distressing sight.

The room was empty; what's more, there was no trace of it having been occupied at all. No clothes; no luggage. Not even a whisper of life; Spiritwolf, whoever or whatever he was, had gone. Leaving him to his fate.

Alone, and exposed.

He sank down in a defeated mode onto the plush bed; suddenly, he felt very tired. He leaned back, arms splayed out to his sides, and rested upon the dark red spread, eyes wandering over the shimmering halo of the ceiling-fan. Eyes that had seen much of late; too much. Where could the wolf have gone? Should he even bother to try to track him down?

No, an inner-voice countered. *Fuck him. Fuck this whole deal.*

"So what do I do?" he moaned aloud. His feeble sentiment was absorbed by the drapes, the empty room.

You're a singer. His unconscious hinted again. *If you have something to say…*

Eyes jolting wide, the next moment, the wolf sat bolt upright as if a switch had just been thrown inside his skull. He gripped the bed with his hands as the idea blossomed. "…Sing it!" he cried out, inexplicably. In that moment, Spirit's abandoned room held nothing else for him; he was already off, sprinting out the door. He did not stop running until he reached his room. Garrick, his guitarist, was silently slinking down the corridor as he passed; the feline gave his boss an indecipherable stare, his black fringe obscuring his left eye. The wolf charged right past him. Then, in an over-animated scramble, Achilles doubled back and practically pounced the musician.

"Garrick!" the canine barked, seizing the troubled feline by the shoulders. "Where are you going?"

"L-lunch…" the slim cheetah replied, swallowing hard.

Achilles shook his head. "Lunch is cancelled; grab something from the vending machine and then come to my room. Oh. And I want you to round up Cain and Les. Everybody come – band meeting."

"W-what's going on?" his band-mate replied. "Are you going to fire us?"

With a devilish, almost manic grin, the wolf leaned in close. "No, not a chance. But it is big; we're going to do a new song tonight."

At this, the guitarist's eyes lit up like lanterns. He loved new material. "Fuck yeah! How does it go?"

The wolf shrugged, and began edging back toward his room, where his laptop and his portable studio awaited him. "I don't know – I haven't written it yet. But," he continued, as Garrick looked at him like he'd grown a second head. "It does have a name. *Black Dust*, my friend – and trust me, this one's going to bring the house down!"

* * *

High above the city, a ghost looked down upon the streets of Arenosa and despaired.

Spiritwolf has shed his accoutrements; his second skin and disguise. His exit from the hotel had been perfunctory, brief, and unnoticed. He'd not even checked out with the clerk; let that uptight pachyderm deal with the mess. Let them all wonder where he'd disappeared to. The person he'd created to run his ruse had never existed anyway.

Did he, himself, exist?

In the brightening afternoon light, he looked through his hand and saw the world, a dry chuckle rising in his throat. It was fitting that his first mission since his 'evolution' required him to cloak his identity, layers upon layers of dressing, covering the empty core. He felt emptier than ever now, with the sting of failure surrounding him. But better, more focused. Determined. He was done playing the game now, watching from the sidelines. He could see now his folly in trying to fit in with the tour from the beginning; the mistake in allowing the singer to get so close to him. *I'll tie up that loose end later, perhaps.* It seemed bitterly irrelevant to him now. All he cared about was the tablet.

And Black Dust.

He ground his teeth and from the hotel roof, glared at the people walking below, small as beetles to his eye. *I swear I will find you,* the wolf silently vowed. *And by the time this day is done, your head will be on a plate.*

Grimly he turned, and made ready to begin his real work.

* * *

"I'm tired of waiting," an oversized ursine rasped, picking at his claws beneath the shade of a sloping fig-tree that grew on the other side of a crumbling red wall in the city-center. "We should have grabbed him as soon as he landed."

A tigress, resplendent in a white Versace suit and Gucci sunglasses slowly shook her head, barely even looking at the bear, pretending to read a newspaper instead. "Brennan, how many times must I remind you that patience is a virtue?" she purred. "We know where the mutant is. Following along and gathering information on how he operates has been invaluable."

The bear sneered again, and folded his arms. "I think you just like shopping. Rising Force doesn't have unlimited funds, you know. What happens when our paymasters find out?" There was a third person on the team; Darius, the crocodile, who was out hunting down a fresh cache of weaponry in the city.

Clarice lowered her sunglasses and favored him with a withering look. "You think I'm that stupid? I've been pushing my expenses onto the TEA – I am still an agent, after all. They do have the World Nations Reserve Bank in their pocket..."

Still dissatisfied, the beast grunted. "Fine for you, but I'm not getting paid until we have him. I want to act. Now."

Sighing again, the tigress picked up the paper once more. "He's gotten himself into quite a mess, you know – whatever it is he's after, it's brought a lot of dangerous individuals into play. That white mouse was just the start. Trust me, we've been better off keeping clear of the crossfire so far. But you're right; time waits for no woman, so tonight, you'll get your wish."

"You mean, we're going to take him? You have a plan?"

"Oh yes," Clarice purred, smiling at a handsome Spanish stallion that walked past in the street and gave her an appreciative stare. "Tonight's the night. By the time Achilles begins his encore, Spirit will be ours!"

And then she laughed and the horse shivered and quickly turned away from the predatory leer that had appeared upon her face.

* * *

"This isn't good, Gareth," Blair's schoolmasterly tone rumbled, pitch perfect with displeasure and foreboding. "You're making me very unhappy."

"No, it's not good. I'm dealing with it," the deputy director of MI-6 answered back. His voice was steady, but unseen by the lion on the other end of the phone, his body temperature was rapidly rising in response to the stress. "I can clean up after my own."

"So you're good at protecting your own hide; but I expected better than that of you. What was it they call you overseas? The jihadists and the peasants of revolution? 'Merchant of Death,' wasn't it?"

"Only as much as they call *you* the 'Prince of Darkness,'" the polar bear growled in reply. "So spare me the lecture."

Blair gave his own rumble in response; the two men of power circling around one another with barbed words. "So, what are you going to do about it? Something that will prevent me from needing to use the 'insurance', I hope..."

"I'm going to deal with it," the director said, crunching his fist, thinking about the sword the tycoon was holding over him, to keep him in line. He could not fail. "Personally."

There was a moment's pause of breath and silence from the lion. This statement seemed to mollify him. "You had better," Blair cautioned one more time. "I expect results."

"Don't worry. You'll get your tablet. I'll see to that."

Without the courtesy of a farewell, he put down his phone. He stroked its polished surface one more time, staring into his warped white reflection in its black exterior; then he picked it up again, pushing a number on speed-dial. His next words were icy cold with determination.

"It's me. Assemble teams *Romeo* to *Victor*. Yes, all of them. Departure from Knightsbridge in an hour. Briefing will occur at time of departure. Yes. This is prime importance. All other missions are rescinded." As he spoke, he spun a globe upon his desk around until his hand rested upon Spain's sun-kissed coast. He tapped it once and smiled a cruel smile. "The Merchant is coming to town."

* * *

A raccoon news anchor on the television was saying, "…and finally, we hope you've all got your tickets, because the big show tonight is sold out. There's only one gig in town that everyone's talking about, as Achilles serenades our good city for the first time. Talking to the people on the streets, there's a clear generational divide between who's going and who's not, but there's a definite excitement in the air for his frenetic, often unpredictable show."

The ferret entertainment correspondent next to the raccoon smiled as she turned back from him to the camera. "That's right, Jude; the singer himself was sighted yesterday landing in a private jet at Arenosa airport. He's known for keeping to himself while on tour, and not giving interviews to the press, but surprisingly he did agree to a few words this afternoon, as he headed out from his hotel to the stadium."

"…guys, hi. I'm not going to… wait, I *am* going to say something. Listen up Arenosa; I can't wait to see you at the show tonight. I have something I want to show to you. Something new. I have just two words for you: *Black Dust*. That's all. I hope you're listening, and if you're not, that you're there with me in spirit. Goodbye…"

"So there you have it. What new tricks could he be up to? Tonight's the night we find out. Now, over to Rosa on the weather desk…" Jude said as Achilles walked away on the screen behind him.

* * *

Backstage, Achilles paced within the small dressing room. A light bulb above his head was flickering, seemingly in sympathy with the distant swell of cheering voices that enveloped the room like a cocoon. Lined up in front of him, like a row of anxious soldiers about to go over the top of the trench, were his band. Cain, Les and Garrick were watching the singer walk from one end of the room to the other. They shared between them the bond of anticipation that stirred within them before the show, but this time was different. They'd performed together so many times, and yet they'd never seen Achilles as tense as this; he was normally the ocean of calm, the professional, the businessman. But he was clearly worried about something; it made them all nervous. And at the forefront of their gestalted mind was the new song.

"Are you sure about this, boss?" Cain rumbled, his voice cutting through the tension. "It's not too late to drop it from the list. It's a good song and all but… don't you think we've rushed it? We only got to play it through the three times this afternoon. That bridge in the middle…"

The white wolf chuckled, and gave the badger a reassuring pat on the shoulder. "You're going to nail it Cain, trust me. We all are. I'm not worried about the song. We can play it. I just hope… it's received how I intended it."

"An' how's that, exactly?" Les chirped, his long tongue lazily flicking out of his mouth, curiosity bubbling through his words.

"I need a reaction," Achilles cryptically answered, unconsciously cracking his knuckles. "Any reaction…" He lapsed into a moment of silence, looking down at the floor in thought, and the three supporting musicians took the opportunity to exchange uneasy glances between themselves.

An ocelot wearing a head-mic strode into the room. "Five minutes, guys. Ready to walk?" he said, nodding toward the corridor.

"Ready as ever…" Achilles mumbled, striding out in front. He tried to control his breathing, and wondered why his heart was beating so fast. *Keep it together*, he chided himself. *This will work. You're going to get this right…*

Down the empty corridor, they all ambled. The supporting band was just heading down toward them as they walked, and though Achilles could barely remember their name – they were some local outfit Regis had booked, though he'd never heard of them – he shook their hands and congratulated them on a job well done. Just as he was pressing palms with a rail-thin otter in *KISS*-style makeup, his thoughts turned to the elephant briefly. It wasn't like Regis to be absent preshow; but the pachyderm had informed him in the afternoon him via text that he'd had business to attend to, wished them well, and that he'd see them at the hotel in the evening. Shortly after the impromptu television interview went out though, Achilles had received another concerned message asking what he was up to, but by then he was too busy to respond. Oh well – his manager would find out about the new song with the rest of the audience. The publicity would make him pleased, no doubt.

The aspiring band drifted away and in front of him the roar of two hundred thousand voices and stamping feet grew louder, as the pitch of the crowd swelled with their own zeal for the main act's appearance. At the edge of the stage, the musicians gathered. Automatically a fox appeared at Achilles' side and began wiring him with his earpiece, so he could hear cues from backstage. He nodded to Cain, who nodded and smiled back, but with a forced kind of earnestness. *He still distrusts me after I nearly kicked him off the tour. I've been such a fool…*

"Achilles…" a whisper of a voice said over his shoulder, practically inside his ear. He spun, and saw Les standing there, looking out from the curtains to the crowd. The lizard noticed the singer was looking at him, and swiveled his own reptilian eye to the wolf.

"What?" the white wolf asked, looking down at the keyboardist.

"Huh? I didn't say anything," Les answered, having to raise his voice as the crowd erupted into another spontaneous cheer at something; they might have even spied movement in the wings, believing the time for the band's appearance was nigh.

"Never mind, then," the singer replied, but still a shiver ran down his spine. Perhaps the invisible wolf was here after all…

"Ready guys?" the stage manager's voice chirped into Achilles' ear. The wolf turned and flashed him a thumbs-up, before walking out onto the dark stage, where only the shadows could hide.

* * *

Deep under the New Mexico mountains, the TEA Sciences director marched through vacant corridors, his pace quickening. The snow leopard wore a white lab coat and a concerned scowl, neither of which suited him particularly well. All was silent in the research department as well; there was just the thud of Greystorm's feet and the whirring, clicks, and chirps of scientific instruments. Even on a weekend, at least someone would usually be working away, but not today, it seemed.

By the time he reached Zero's office, Greystorm was feeling out of breath but did not let it show. He opened the door without knocking, faced down the surprised ursine, and then shut it behind him again without saying a word. The Senior Director himself was about to protest the unannounced intrusion, but as soon as he saw the look upon the agent's face, the words died in his throat. He immediately gave the feline his full attention, sitting up straight and ignoring the report that had been bothering him. "Problem?" he uttered, but it was more of a statement than a question.

"Huge," Greystorm replied, sliding into the chair opposite and leaning in close across the desk. "You're not going to like it."

The bear narrowed his eyes. "Go on."

"Someone's broken into my account. I've just discovered it. It was an internal job too, and what they were after was quite specific…"

The director bristled, and put his hand upon his chin. Greystorm could tell he would be absorbing this information, and planning an immediate response. "What did they take?"

"They tried to cover their tracks, but I'm guessing they were in a rush; this was amateurish. I've got the logs; they swiped a copy of the SDS suite. The thermal algorithms. *Everything.*"

Zero's eyes flashed. "God damn!" he growled. "They took that? The timing can't be an accident; and Spirit hasn't checked in for a while. What else? Internal, you say?"

Greystorm nodded. "Yes. I've already traced the hacker back down the line to one of our outposts; they couldn't hide the fact that they used our credentials to gain access to the mainframe. Someone in Europe; specifically, our offices in Germany."

"Ixak's region. Someone's gunning for Spirit… *hell…*" Without hesitation, Zero picked up his phone, and pushed a number on speed-dial. There was a moment's pause as the tones rang across the continents; and then all Greystorm could hear was one side of the conversation.

"Ixak, this is Zero. A serious breach has occurred… yes, from your office. Someone's got the SDS algorithms… the *Spiritwolf Detection Software*, dammit! Get to his position. Get him extracted. I asked you to keep tabs on him… what do you mean he's vanished? Christ! Pull together all your agents. Have them converge on Achilles' position and… what? You're missing an agent? Who?" Greystorm watched the bear write down a name on a piece of paper. The writing was jagged, and from upside down looked like 'CLARENCE'. "It's her. It has to be! Find Spirit and find *her.* Quickly and quietly. You know what's at stake."

By the time he put the phone down, he could feel his temple throbbing, and the temperature of his body rising. Greystorm was cracking his knuckles, which did nothing to break the tension. "So what happens now?"

Zero glowered and stood up. "Now we hope that Spirit can capture Black Dust and the tablet before someone gets to him… and if someone knows about him, and is after him, it's our job to figure out who."

"I thought we were supposed to let him fly solo?"

"That was for his original mission; the game has changed and we're playing catch-up, so let's get to work."

Understandingly, professionally, Greystorm nodded and cracked his knuckles once more.

* * *

And once more, the baying mob roared.

They were a wall of faces, sound, passion. Achilles could no more make out an individual in their midst than he could identify a grain of rice in a sack, but together he knew they were larger and more powerful than any person could ever hope to be. Together, they could raise a man up to the heights of fame and glory... or bring him down again. He stood under the stage lights, panting, holding on to the mic-stand as if it were the only thing that could keep him upright. The cheering applause was erupting below, ripples of excitement flooding through the air. The band had just played his breakthrough hit, 'The Falling', the last chords dying away, each of the musicians panting and pacing, glad to have made it to the end. It was an intense song; fast, energetic, moody. Cain felt like his arms would drop off if the piece had been only thirty seconds longer. He reached down to a bottle of water at his feet, snatched it up, and did not so much drink as spray himself with its contents, gushing over his face. He shook the moisture from his face and fur, and peered over his kit toward the white wolf. Achilles was standing rigid, hands clenched. Flexing and unflexing, his fingers sought to release the tension within him.

But he was not alone.

Unseen and inscrutable, Spiritwolf stood onstage next to the singer, eyes wide, taking in the scene before him. *All those eyes,* he was thinking. *All those eyes, and nowhere to hide. How does he do it? How does anyone do it?* It went without saying that the idea of being so much in the public eye was anathema to him, but to stand there, to catch a *glimpse* of what that was like...

He suddenly had more sympathy for the white wolf than he could have ever thought possible.

The very fact that he was onstage at that moment was a mere diversion; for the afternoon he'd been an unseen ghost floating through the corridors of the hotel. Slipping in and out of roadies' rooms; hands rifling through luggage, mattresses, clothing, anywhere a secret could hide. Once he entered a bathroom and found a well-built ram pleasuring himself in the shower; he would be lying if he said he hadn't taken a mental snapshot and grinned to himself, letting temptation carry him only so far. But it still wasn't what he was really after. With a fruitless search behind him, he caught up with the band as they were leaving, and tailed them to the venue. All the time he couldn't take his eyes off Achilles; the white wolf seemed nervous, tense… but otherwise continuing as normal. *The show must go on, eh?* he mused, oblivious to what the musician could have been plotting behind those eyes. He'd known they were rehearsing something in one of their rooms, which didn't seem all that unusual. *But there's something I'm missing. Black Dust is close. I can tell…*

By the time the show began, he was moving through the stage equipment in the wings, observing the movements of the roadies, the lighting technicians, the security guards. Everyone was maddeningly focused on the work at hand; if someone were hiding something, they were doing it very well.

Though the harsh sounds the band was producing made his ears ache, and the frenzied action onstage caught his attention in glimpses, he eventually grew curious enough to wander out onto the stage itself. His heart had beat faster, as he spurred himself to do so; being invisible was still relatively new to him, and his body instinctively reacted to the thought of walking out onstage in front of tens of thousands of people. Adrenalin kicking in; the temperature of his fur rising. But soon enough he was there, right there alongside Garrick, watching the guitarist sway – and all eyes were glazing over him. He laughed, and for a microsecond the cheetah had flicked his eyes in his direction. Then he continued playing, as if the ghostly laughter had just been a figment of his imagination.

Spiritwolf shivered, suddenly feeling more liberated than he could have imagined possible. He should have been terrified, reeling, worrying that if he couldn't be seen, he couldn't exist… but this was different. This was being where thousands would give their left arm to be, and getting away with it. Being in the center of attention without *being* the center of attention. He stood alongside Achilles, watching the singer pant as he finished his song, and smiled. *All those eyes…*

And yet, if he thought no one was looking at him, he was wrong.

So very wrong.

He appeared to them as a shimmering white outline on a canvas of green, like a specter of burning ethereal fire. "And there he is," Clarice purred, staring through the lenses of some particularly advanced-looking augmented reality binoculars. "The protocols have done their job."

"Let me see," Darius growled, eager to catch a glimpse of the phantom they had been chasing with his own reptilian eyes. The crocodile held his hand out expectantly; the tigress smirked, paused, and handed the device over, before looking down at the stage from the lighting rig they had sequestered themselves into before the show begun. Her henchman raised the spying device to his own eyes, looking down below before his jaw visibly dropped as he saw the blazing wolf standing next to the singer. "Holy shit," he muttered, flicking the binoculars down, and then back up again. "That's some grade-A freakiness right there."

"Are you done?" the black-clad predator hissed. "Focus now; our moment is at hand."

"So you knew he'd be here; that's swell. But you want to snatch him, here, *now*, with all these people watching?"

Clarice chuckled. "And what, exactly, would they see, hmm? You can't steal what doesn't exist. After the next song, when the lights go out. That's when we strike." The reptile nodded, and raised the tranquilizer gun with almost murderous intent.

It was at that moment that Achilles turned to the drummer, and slowly gave a knowing nod.

It was time for the new song.

Taking in a deep breath, Cain readied himself, and stretched out his arms. *Here goes nothing*, he thought. He raised his sticks; brought them together to make a count of three, and then smashed them down upon the skins.

Immediately, the lights flashed red, like the stage had been washed in blood; the badger was striking a pounding beat like a military march; Garrick's guitar began to growl, a softly syncopating rhythm, while Les leaned on the keys and began to slowly build a jagged melody with notes that sounded like a string orchestra. And through it all, Achilles began to chant: "I am dust, I am dust, I am I am Black Dust… I am *dust*, I am *dust*, I am I am *Black Dust*…"

With a look of horror and surprise that could not be seen, Spiritwolf's muzzle fell into a wide 'O' of shock. "What are you doing?" he yelled, but he could not be heard – already the crowd had gotten the idea. Achilles flashed a grin at them and began to pump his fist as if commanding a legion of revolutionaries as thousands of people began to chant as one, the music slowly building: *I am dust, I am dust, I am I am Black Dust!*

Like he were trapped in some kind of bizarre nightmare, Spirit turned and looked at the band who were growing louder in their playing, even as the projector above the stage flickered to life. Images began to play upon it, changing in time to the music. At first it seemed random; darkened alleyways, abandoned urban decay, slogans of corporate America. The typical alternative rock backdrop. But then, for a nanosecond, other words flashed through the black, there for a moment and then gone again, a dog-whistle that only a specific audience would hear.

DAST.

Spirit reeled, as this was followed by SECRETS. There was a video snippet of a building on fire, and a clip from some 1970s TV series about an invisible scientist, followed by the word FOR SALE.

And that was when the introduction reached its crescendo. "I'm motherfucking Black Dust!" Achilles roared, and suddenly Garrick's guitar melody exploded into a rapid, fierce tune, Cain stopped the marching and began to charge; wild-eyed Les' fingers flashed over the keys, and the wolf began to sing in earnest.

"I've been around, I've been locked down, carrying something that I shouldn't see."

"Yeah yeah yeah," the rest of the band intoned.

"But pay the price, you'll get something nice, the secrets unseen for all to see."

"Yeah yeah yeah."

"It's *here*. Right *here*. The place where you and I ought to *be*. I'll be waiting for you on the count of three."

Spiritwolf couldn't take his eyes off the screen to see what words might follow next – and he was glad he didn't, because come each time the wolf uttered the word 'here', a photograph of a distinctive statue appeared. Arms outstretched, an ocelot carved in bronze presided over an abandoned city square. There was some kind of clock-tower in the background, half-hidden in shadow like a ghost.

The agent had heard enough. Whatever the singer's plan was, it was madness. He turned back to the shouting wolf, and for a moment considered the possibility of punching him in the face, right then and there. Achilles was soldiering on, repeating the chorus, and the crowd was lapping it up, faces upturned aglow, proud to be the first to hear his new song. They were getting more and more energetic; Spirit could see the security guards struggling to hold the front row back, as if they had been imbued with some inhuman energy by the song.

But it wasn't a song at all, it was a message, and a dangerous one at that. It had some very specific intended recipients, yet even the uninvited guests heard it plainly.

"I don't believe it," Clarice hissed, teeth flashing. "He's outing himself."

"Who?" Darius said, oblivious.

"*Black Dust*. He's the focus of Spiritwolf's mission. And… of course. No wonder the TEA was so interested in the singer. Now it makes sense."

The crocodile readied his gun. He could still see his target, but already some members of the audience were overcoming the security at the front of the stage, and were beginning to climb up to meet their idol, to experience the incredible moment firsthand. "Does it matter? I'm ready to shoot…"

"Hold your fire!" The tigress suddenly barked. "We wanted the mutant – but the information *Black Dust* purports to be selling could be even more valuable. No. We wait and we collect *both*."

The reptile growled. "A fuckin' bonus, eh?" he looked down; the song was nearly over, and Achilles was being mobbed. Spirit's outline flickered again, and in seeming disgust the invisible wolf ran offstage, into the wings, where he was lost from sight. "Great," he muttered. "Lost him."

The feline smirked at him. "Not to worry. Thanks to *Black Dust*'s song, I know exactly where he – and our target – will be." She clicked her teeth and smiled triumphantly. "*El Cuadrado Del Santo.*"

* * *

Backstage, after the deed was done, Achilles staggered into the wings, the final cries of the crowd still baying behind him, pleading him for more. But he had no more to give; he was done. *Not just with the set*, he realized in an inescapable bout of clarity that gripped him as he grabbed a towel being proffered by one of his assistants. *Maybe with this whole touring deal. Not for a while. After something like this… it'll be time to rest. Get off the radar. That would be just fine…*

But the hard work was still to come. The song was just the first piece of the larger trap; if anything, coming up with the music and the message was the easy part. What was to follow tonight… was beyond anything he'd ever attempted before. Probably out of his league. Probably get him killed. *But I have to try.*

"Fuckin' A!" Les rasped in his ear, pouncing upon him and breaking his concentration. "That was *awesome*. You gonna put that out as a single, chief? You gotta… love it!"

"Maybe," Achilles replied coolly, peeling the skinny arm from his shoulder. "Everything's up in the air at the moment." He spied Cain out of the corner of his eye, the badger already slinking away to the dressing room. His old friend no longer enjoyed his company, it seemed. "So many things…"

As they talked, he walked, swept along by a corridor of people and well-wishers. Some fans who had been lucky enough to receive backstage passes immediately thrust out their autograph books to him. One after another, he signed his name in a nonchalant scrawl, moving down the line and exchanging fewer pleasantries than normal. As he reached the end of the row, instead of looking into a cheerful, glowing face of admiration, he found himself staring into the granite-like visage of his manager. The elephant was standing with his arms folded over his chest; he was wearing a dark blue suit now, his face creased with caution. For some inexplicable reason, the wolf found the sudden appearance of the pachyderm unsettling, like a child whose hand has been caught in the cookie jar. He could tell by the businessman's body language that he was in trouble for something, but not yet what for. Nonetheless, he flashed Regis a cheerful grin and greeted him in the same manner. "Hey… how's it going?" he chirped. The lizard at his side melted away and by some unseen arrangement, so too did the fans. Though the backstage was still a hive of activity, and the crowd could still be heard, it was as though Regis had arranged for a cocoon of privacy to descend upon them.

"Things are going fine. Just fine," the elephant muttered. "I came back, you noticed, when I heard about your new song. I just had to hear it for myself."

"Did you like it?" Achilles muttered, scratching behind his head.

"I was surprised by it," Regis cryptically replied. "I hate surprises."

"Way to dodge the question," the wolf hissed. This side of the biz always troubled him; and though he usually had the patience to work with the elephant, in light of everything else he had going on, he just couldn't be troubled to be polite. He shrugged like a distempered teenager. "You knew what you were getting when you signed me up. I would have thought you knew that by now."

He moved to brush past the broad shoulders of the pachyderm, disgruntled, when an unforeseen force stopped him; he found his wrist bound by Regis' vice-like grip, pulling him back into the conversation. "But do *you* know what you're getting? That's the question," the elephant replied, practically hissing in his ear. In all the time he'd known Regis, his manager had never so much as laid a finger on him. Why mess with the goose that was laying the golden egg?

"Let go of my arm," Achilles growled in the darkest voice he'd ever heard himself produce.

Immediately, Regis complied. When Achilles next looked at him, he found the elephant's frown gone; replaced by an eerie expression of placidness. "Of course. Whatever the star wants. You'll be all ready for your next stop, then? Paris awaits. I trust you'll be well-rested."

"Absolutely," the white wolf replied with great reluctance. Still stunned that Regis had even dared to try to stop him, and what it could possibly mean. "I'm looking forward to it."

"Very good," Regis replied. "Oh, speaking of which. We've received word that a lunatic fan might be trying to break into the hotel; one of those crazies. You know the sort. I've hired some men for tonight; they'll be outside your hotel room to make sure you don't get any unexpected visitors in the night."

Achilles stiffened immediately. "I didn't agree to that!" he barked. He wanted to act cool about it, but he found himself unable to when it meant the ruination of his plans. "I don't think that's necessary."

"You don't have to agree to it; it's in your tour contract that I can enforce additional security measures if your personal safety is deemed at risk. I know it curtails your freedoms a bit but it's just business. If it's for your own good, it's for my own good as well, and everyone else who has money involved in this tour. So you can argue and pout all you want but you're getting bodyguards tonight – and for every night from now on, actually. Ah, and speaking of which, here they are now."

Regis stepped aside, and his large form was replaced by two larger ones, as two heavy-set brown bulls stepped into view from the shadows. They were dressed in suits, and wore sunglasses in spite of the darkness, which would have been comical were it not for the seriousness of the expressions they wore.

"Mr. Achilles," one rumbled, introducing himself by extending a meaty hand. "I'm Lars and this is my brother David. We'll be looking after your protection for the remainder of the tour."

"I don't need protecting," Achilles complained. "And I don't want you around. No offense."

"None taken," Lars responded nonchalantly, indulging him with a smile as if to say he was used to this response. "But Mr. Castellanos here has decided otherwise and it's his call. Fortunately, though, you should be able to go about your business for the night; you'll never even know we're there."

"But you won't let me out of your sight either, right?"

"Wouldn't be doing our job if we did, no," the younger muscular bull replied, sounding just as patronizing as his sibling. David flipped up his shades, and saw his perfectly blue eyes for a moment. "But you just carry on as normal, and let us worry about the rest."

Though the bodyguard seemed sincere, Achilles knew he was being sat upon in a way that rankled him to his very core. He looked between the three of them one last time, and then shook his head. "Fuck you all," he rasped before turning his back upon them and stomping away.

Behind him, Regis exchanged a single nod with the two men, and immediately the bulls began trailing in his wake.

Fuming and scattering people out of his way, Achilles made his way down the stage corridors, thinking of what he could do tonight to lose the two burly bulls that had suddenly become attached to him, when he reached a door leading to the bathroom. He pushed open the door to go inside – then turned back to the two shapes he saw lingering over his shoulder. "Don't you fucking *dare* think about coming in after me in here while I'm taking a leak or I swear to God I will bash your heads together so hard that you'll be unable to even remember your own names for a week. Got that?"

He didn't linger any longer for a retort and stomped inside the empty rows of cubicles to his expected moment of privacy. Like clockwork, the two men stood outside the door, backs to the wall, shoulder to shoulder.

A moment later, the door seemed to swing open by itself. Lars looked to his left at the door quizzically, but unable to explain the erratic occurrence, shrugged and continued looking imposing against any real oncomers.

Achilles was inside, looking at his reflection in the ceramic tiles above the urinal as he relieved himself, head swimming with dangerous ideas, when a disembodied voice came snarling over his shoulder, but only as loud as a whisper.

"You stupid fuck," Spiritwolf's voice growled with crystal clarity. "Damn you!"

"Holy fuckin' Christ, man!" the white wolf yelped, in a not at all dignified way. He looked over his shoulder, saw nothing, and yet continued to zip himself up with alarm. "What the hell!"

He was still staring in startled disbelief at the air when he noticed the door was being tapped open again. David stuck his head inside, chewing a stick of gum as he spoke. "Everything all right in here, sir?"

"What did I just tell you?" Achilles snapped, wasting no time in replying. "Stay the hell out of here! Do you two just share the one brain cell between you, and take turns, is that it?"

The bull blinked once, and then retreated. Achilles was glad that the new hired muscle was easy to control, if nothing else. He turned back to the bathroom, where he presumed Spirit was standing, when he was shoved backwards rather forcefully.

"Words cannot *describe* how pissed off I am with you right now!" the invisible wolf said, giving the singer a further shove. "You stupid, arrogant, meddling… *diva*! Just what do you think you're up to?"

Achilles batted the hand away, quietly hissing back in an angry whisper. "Just shut your hole, you bloody freak. Don't lecture me about arrogance! You're the one that abandoned me, right after you revealed your presto-disappearo routine. What did you think I was going to do? Just go along and continue to sing like nothing whatsoever was going on?" He lunged forward at the air, but found himself staggering into nothing. A swift punt to his shoulder saw him falling against the sink. He caught himself just in time to avoid a nasty fall; he knew the invisible wraith assaulting him was holding back, but that was of little comfort. "So I'm taking control! Deal with it!"

"This goes way beyond you. This is bigger than you can imagine. It's-"

"It's because it's your cure, isn't it?" The singer said, bracing himself, his ears prickling intently for the slightest sound of movement.

There was the tiniest moment of stunned silence from Spiritwolf that filled the room like an expanding bubble. "*What?*" Spirit was able to croak, after his heart skipped a few beats. The wind however was definitely taken out of his sails, and it showed as he began to try to regain his angry momentum. "You don't…"

"Oh, please," the white wolf sneered, dusting himself down, hoping that the tempest had been momentarily put at bay. "If this were anything else, you'd be at least acting rationally about this. You're too involved; you're too attached to what's at stake, without stepping back and seeing what's actually in front of you. You should be *thanking* me. I just gave you *Black Dust* on a silver plate. If he's on this tour, he'll have heard the song. At the very least, he'll show up just to find out what I know, and why."

"A fine theory." Spirit poked him in the chest, more for effect. The wolf's fur seemed to part of its own accord under his fingertip's pressure. "And what then? How will you capture him? How about the fact he's likely to kill you? Or every other mercenary who wants what Black Dust has, descending upon your location? God! When I said you were stupid, I meant it."

"I'm sure you did," Achilles said, moving toward the door. "But this is happening – with or without you. I think you and I both know it will go better if you're there too. But even if you're not, I'm getting Black Dust off my tour, one way or another. It's your call." He put his hand up to the door again, and nearly pushed it open before he was stopped.

"Wait," Spirit breathily interjected, reluctance flowing from his voice. "Where did you tell him to meet? In the song."

"*El Cuadrado Del Santo.* It's a plaza outside one of their old Catholic churches, in the western part of the city. You know the time." He cast his eye over the bathroom one more time, unable to know where to look. Inside he shuddered once more. "Find me there," he said. Whether it was a statement or a request, none could say.

And then he was gone. Lars and David took him away, and there was only silence that remained.

* * *

"We've got something, sir."

A sable dressed in black leaned over from the rear to the front passenger seat, and passed forward a flat tablet computer. Gareth Zirkowski took it in his white hand, and leaned back. The lights of the highway flickered orange over his eyes as they passed in bands overhead, making him look like a man of hotly glowing embers. He saw a video had been queued up for him; he sniffed once, and pressed play.

Immediately the screen was filled with a shifting, colorful scene from the concert, and the black SUV was filled with the tumultuous sounds of rock music from Achilles' concert. The polar bear saw that the title of the film he was watching was labeled: "*New song, Arenosa concert OMG!*" and quickly surmised he was viewing something that had been uploaded to a social networking site. The film itself was shot on a hand-held camera, seemingly by an audience member at the evening's show close to the stage.

"I am dust, I am dust, I am I am Black Dust… I am *dust*, I am *dust*, I am I am *Black Dust*…"

He leaned forward. His eyes seemed to glow hotter; though his face could not be read as the film ran to completion, he cocked his head, listening to the words. Absorbing. Contemplating. The other men in the vehicle cradled their semi-automatic guns stoically as they heard the film being played for a second time.

Gareth watched the screens behind the wolf. Heard the words. Put together the puzzle. Slowly he nodded, and passed the tablet back over his shoulder without even looking behind. The tablet was taken from him, and he cracked the bones in his neck with one discomforting twist, shaking out the lethargy of the journey from his body.

He leaned forward, and tapped the GPS on the driver's side. A holographic map of the city spread out on the head-down display. He looked at the area for a minute, then ran his fingertip in a circle over a square in an isolated area of the map. "Here," he said throatily to the driver. No other words needed to be said. The horse nodded, and made a turn.

Four other black SUV's followed in his wake. The convoy of the Merchant drove across the border of Arenosa like a hawk diving to a forest canopy, claws extended.

With the orange fire still in his eyes, Gareth leaned back and smirked. "Be seeing you soon, boys…"

* * *

Achilles was marched up the plush confines of the hotel corridors like a prisoner being taken to solitary confinement. The comparison was a fair one; the two bulls kept pace at either side of him as he walked, eyes scanning every portal with cautious regard. The fans waiting outside the lobby were rudely pushed aside; though the wolf wanted to do his usual meet and greet, he was swiftly denied.

"For your own protection," Lars had muttered, holding back a wall of people with the help of the hotel doorman. "Come."

"So what exactly has Regis told you about the nature of the threat to me?" Achilles ventured to ask sulkily, David spurring him onward as they crossed the lobby.

"You don't want to know," the younger sibling said, hailing the elevator. "It's fucked up." He slid his sunglasses down to reveal to the white wolf another glimpse of his baby blue eyes. "But if we see any giraffes, we're going to be giving them a wide berth tonight."

The rock star snorted and folded his arms as the doors slid open. "A giraffe? That's what he said? Please. Don't you see he's just set you two up with a reason to sit on me?"

"He pays the bills; that's enough for me," Lars stonily observed, giving the wolf an impatient prod inside the waiting elevator.

"Don't touch what you can't afford," Achilles growled, batting the hand away, but stepping inside regardless. He heard David chuckle slightly behind him; whether the younger bull was laughing at his brother or the singer, nobody could say.

And then, just like that, he was taken to his room.

The wolf flourished his card-key, fishing it out from his leather pants. "I suppose you're going to search the room for threats now, before you'll let me get a good night's sleep?" His voice dripped with sarcasm.

"Actually," the elder bull said, plucking the card from the wolf with irritating deftness, "we are." Without further ceremony, he swiped the card into the door, and let himself inside.

His back was a pillar of muscle as he blocked the entrance for the wolf, scanning the room this way and that. "Seems clear. Come on in," he invited, taking a step forward and finally allowing the wolf into the threshold.

"Look, guys," Achilles sighed again, looking at the clock. It was nearly one AM – the concert had finished late and the drive over had been slow. Just two hours remained to get to the rendezvous he'd arranged. "You like to be well paid. I get it. So I'll pay you *twice* what Regis is paying to buzz off. Okay?"

Lars snorted, coming out from where he'd been looking under the bed. "Were you just your typical wealthy banker we usually have to babysit, that *might* work – but you're not. You're a bona fide poster-boy, aren't you? A-list all the way. Or at least, B-list." He flashed his brother a grin. "Hard to keep track these days, ain't it? Anyway... we go away and something happens to you, everyone and their mother's gonna hear about it. That's our reputations and our careers blown to pieces right there – so no, we're not gonna leave ya. Not even if you're promising a million bucks." He fixed his eyes on the smaller wolf, and narrowed them considerably. "*Capisce?*"

Jaw hanging open slightly, the rock star regarded the bull for a moment, just taking in the condescension dripping from the bodyguard's voice. Then his face contorted into a mask of anger. "Go to hell!" he spat, nearly swinging his fist. David predicted the movement, and caught hold of his arm before he could move.

"Easy now. We're leaving, but we'll be right outside the door." He said, gently, but firmly. "Come on Lars," he said, giving his brother a pointed look that indicated he was used to his sibling pissing off the clientele.

"Mr. Achilles... goodnight," the elder bull said with one final, disinterested bow, before he shuffled out behind his sibling. The door closed behind them – and then a second later, the white wolf realized that Lars still had his key.

"Fuck!" The wolf angrily shouted to the empty room, his voice bouncing off the high white ceilings and cream painted walls. He paced for a moment, his brain trying to track the situation, before he ran back to his door. He put his ear flat against the surface, and listened; he heard their deep, bass-ridden voices right outside, talking in soft tones. It sounded like David was telling his brother off. Lars answered back in dull, impatient overtones. There was no denying they were going to keep to their word and keep him inside for the night though. Achilles used the opportunity to swear again and then he ran back into his bedroom, thinking, thinking, thinking...

I need a distraction, some diversion... something to get them away from the bloody door...

He eyed the smoke detector above his bed. *Damn. If only I were addicted to nicotine like the other half of the band, I could light one up...* He briefly surveyed the room for another way of making a fire; but unless he planned on causing flames by giving himself carpet burn, he was shit outta luck in the smoke department.

His mind danced over the possibilities again, head spinning as he looked at the clock again. Eight past one – he was running out of time. He retraced his steps mentally a couple of steps, examining the possibilities. *The other half of the band. Of course. Les!*

Swooping over to the telephone, he closed his eyes and tried to visualize which room the lizard had been put into. He would have seen it on the tour manifest when they'd checked in. *3005. That's it. I'm sure.* He lifted the receiver and hastily dialed. His heart was beating inside his mouth as he waited for a reply, the call-tone ringing ominously. Finally, someone on the other end picked up.

"Mmmmnyess?" came the lizard's slurred, tired voice.

"Les! Les, it's Achilles," the wolf blurted. He couldn't believe he'd woken the keyboardist up; he was a party animal. He went all night, every stop. He was probably sharing his bed with someone right now. "I need your help."

"Fuck... man..." the lizard said again, this time with a definite yawn following. "What's up?"

"I've got two goons sitting outside my room. A couple of bulls Regis hired to keep me in for tonight; I need them gone."

"So fuh... fire them," the musician drawled in reply, clearly not interested. "Isn't that what you usually do?"

"It's not going to work this time. C'mon dude... they're really hot. Just your type. I'm sure you could persuade one of them to step inside your room..."

"No!" Les' voice replied, practically jumping out of the speaker at Achilles. "What do you think I am, your whore of Babylon?" He sounded tired, and angry; it seemed a shift in his attitude had overtaken him for some reason the wolf was not aware of.

"I just... thought..." the white wolf began to reply, weakly.

"Yeah, and that's the problem," the lizard sarcastically replied. "I'm going back to bed."

"Les!" Achilles hissed, his temper flaring. "You've gotta help me here!"

There followed a snort of derision. "Good luck with the bulls," Les rasped, before the line went dead. The wolf held the phone against his head, listening to the static hiss, before he held it out before him, trying to absorb the rejection.

"No... nononono..." he moaned, then cursed, bashing the handle down upon the receiver again and again, his temperature rising even further. Then he pulled the phone out from the socket, and threw it against the far wall, where it disintegrated into a useless pile of plastic parts.

Once he had calmed down for a moment, the singer held his face in his hands, breathing tiredly. *Maybe I should trash the place. The paparazzi would love it; rock-star destroying his hotel room. Isn't that what we do?* He pulled himself out of his reverie, hands leaving his face, as he stared out and into his reflection in the darkened window before him.

Window. That's it; the only way…

Numbly, he walked up to the glass portal. He put his hand upon its cool surface, at first just looking at it. Would it even open? Most hotels in the States, the high-rise suites, you couldn't even open them. It was too risky; people would jump out, which was such a mess to clean up. But when he put his hand out and released the catch, the wolf found he was able to slide it up with ease. The night air washed over him; it wasn't overly cold, but it still made him shiver. He went back to his closet for his full-sleeved black polo sweatshirt, wriggled into it, and then crouched down, peering outside.

There was a solid white ledge running along the exterior of the building; its entire width couldn't be more than two foot-spans across. He looked over to his right, and five meters away his neighbor's window was an empty socket of black ink. He squinted, looking for a gap, but could see that it was shut. *No way in there. Let's try door number two…*

He looked to his left, hoping for a miracle; and he got it. The window was wide open. The room was dark but he could see the curtains ruffling in the breeze. But it was still so far away…

He looked down at the dizzying sight of the streets thirty floors below and shuddered, a sudden wash of nausea hitting him. *I'm not scared of heights though. I'm not. It's just one room over… I can do this…* He looked behind him, at the clock, the time now ticking past one-fifteen. *Shit. I have to do this…*

Sucking in a lungful of cold air, he exhaled three times, like when he was about to squat a heavy weight at the gym, and crawled out onto the ledge, palms first, crouching. He turned, gripped the lip of the window, and holding on for dear life he hauled himself into a standing position.

Oh God. Oh God ohgod. I'm doing this…

He closed his eyes for a moment, hands gripping at the wall behind him. He decided it would be better if he faced the other way; the smell of dry dust in his nose, he turned and put his face flat against the wall, for maximum surface contact with the only thing that was going to stop him from falling to his death below. He clenched his jaw tight, fought the jelly-like sensation threatening to overtake his knees, and turned his feet outwards, ready to make his move.

With the first shuffle he made, he could barely believe he was moving at all. *Still not too late to go back inside. Call off the plan,* one voice reminded him. His coward's aspect. *But no,* his stubborn, fierce side replied. *Can't let Black Dust get away with this. It's my tour. He has to go.* He moved another step and nearly turned back as a sudden gust threatened his balance. He recovered, though, and started again.

Inch by shaking inch, Achilles moved along the edge, as fast as he could make himself go. The wall was too smooth; smoother than he'd like. By the time he was halfway across, the other window felt like it could have been a million miles away. He couldn't make himself pull away from the wall far enough to see how close he was. He paused, listening to his terrible beating heart, his fear threatening to overwhelm his senses; and then he pushed on, sucking in lungfuls of air, fueling his muscles, making use of the adrenalin spiking through his veins.

When he touched the other window for the first time, he could have yelled with relief. *Stay calm. Just for a little longer; you can have your little victory dance once you're inside.* He fumbled for the window lip, and began to slowly inch his way into a position where he could shimmy the portal up the rest of the way, and get inside the room.

He'd just gotten himself into the crouching position when nature played one of her cruel tricks. Seemingly out of nowhere, an insect dropped out of the night sky, and landed upon his nose, right upon the very tip of his muzzle. And not just any insect, but the ugliest, most alien black beetle he ever did see. It buzzed and clacked its wings at him in petulant defiance, not caring one jot about the precarious position of the wolf. Achilles froze, and fought against his instinct to bat it off, staring down his muzzle at it like he was looking down the barrel of a gun.

It's just a bug, he reasoned. *You've seen beetles before. Thing's totally harml-*

He didn't even get to finish his thought, when it flew right for his eyes. His hand spun up instinctively to strike it away – by the time he moved, it was already gone, buzzing away, but it was the jerking of his feet that was nearly fatal. By only moving an inch, he felt himself lose his perch, and with a heart-wrenching loss of gravity, felt himself begin to fall.

A cry – guttural, frenzied and irrational – burst from his throat, and he was sure it was the last sound he was ever going to make. *At least I'm going to go out while I'm on top…* an irrational, burbling part of his soon-to-be-smashed psyche said, his vision filling with the stars of the night sky.

And that was when he felt hands grab both of his wrists and take hold of him in the moment that he fell from the ledge. The timing was impeccable; one second later and he would have gone beyond their reach. He heard his rescuer grunt in windless exertion as he strained to hold the white wolf's weight from inside the room. Felt, and heard, but did not *see*. It took him a moment of clarity from his near-death experience to realize that to his naked eye, it was as if he was being held by an invisible piece of string, though he could feel the hands taking hold of his wrists quite clearly, as he gripped back with death-fearing abandon.

"Sp… *Spirit!*" he gasped, kicking out, trying to find a way to prevent himself from slipping any further.

"You really are a stupid… guh…" he heard the unseen wolf's voice answer back, as the wrists gripped tighter and gradually he was pulled inside the room. "Just… shut up and don't scream like that again," Spirit hissed.

Never in his life had the white wolf been so glad to hear a ghost's voice. His knees scraped hard against the wall as he was hoisted, still somehow unable to quite grasp the sensations flooding his nerves. By the time he was fully inside the room, he was practically sobbing with relief. He was still shaking when a nightlight next to the bed in the room flicked on, and a groggy-looking businessman rolled over in his bed, just starting to stare in disbelief at the window.

"Wh… what? Who's there?" the puma mumbled, eyes opening wide like he thought he was dreaming.

Achilles heard quick footfalls as his savior crossed the room, toward the bed. "I'm sorry," he heard Spirit whisper. "Good night."

The next moment the guest seemed struck by a terrible blow, like an unseen brick wall had just landed atop him. He collapsed back onto the bed, groaned once, and fell back into his sleep. The singer shivered and patted himself down, just trying to make himself stand again. He guessed the wolf knew some kind of secret service knock-out punch. Who knew what other skills the invisible wolf possessed? He could be the perfect unseen assassin…

His train of thought broke when he was poked in the chest again. "You're damn lucky I was watching over you tonight." Spirit huffed, with exasperation. "Maybe I should have just let you take the fall."

"Then why didn't you?" Achilles snarled back. "You've already made it clear we're not going to get along."

"Made it clear – very funny," Spirit answered drily, padding away. "Because I need you now. You're the bait."

The singer folded his arms, looking unimpressed. "So you've decided to go with my plan, then?"

"Sounds like it," Spirit answered back with a grin – not that the other party could see it. "It may not be the opportunity I was looking for, but it *is* an opportunity. And I'm going to take it. Besides…" He came in close, close enough to allow the singer to reach out and touch him, which he did. Achilles put his hands on Spirit's broad shoulders as he finished his sentence. "Between you and me, I'm kind of pissed I didn't think of it myself."

"So – a truce then? I help you get the job done, and you stop being a colossal prick?" The white wolf found himself marveling at how he could feel the agent without seeing him again… and for a moment, how solid and muscular he felt.

"Sounds… acceptable," came the reply. Spirit moved away. "I was outside watching your room from the street you know, just thinking about how I could spring you out. You didn't need to put your life in danger. As soon as I saw you on the ledge, I knew I had to get up here. Good thing I did."

"Yes," Achilles answered, looking down. "Thank you."

Spiritwolf patted him on the shoulder. "Thank me later. Right now, Cinderella, we have to get you to the ball." He paused, and began to usher the rock star to the door. "Time for your best performance yet." Achilles blinked, and found a fedora hat being thrown over his head, followed by a trenchcoat, which floated out of the closet like something from a Disney movie.

"How did you even get inside this room anyway?" the singer asked, nodding in understanding as he put the coat on and bundled up into its recesses.

"Swiped the master key from reception," the poltergeist chuckled. "I may be invisible, but I don't have magical powers."

"Huh. And about your being invisible…"

"Not now. It's time to go." The door to the hallway creaked open of its own accord. "After you," Spirit requested.

Achilles complied.

He stepped out into the hallway, hat pulled over his head. Immediately he turned away from his own room down the hall, where sure enough the two broad bulls lay in wait. Lars was sitting in a chair outside, head bowed, already beginning to take his turn getting a bit of sleep in the night. David, on duty, gave the exiting figure only the barest glance before he resumed tapping away at his phone. He was texting, or perhaps tweeting, but at that moment it was beyond his reasoning that the figure in the coat now walking away from him could have been the wolf from inside the room he was guarding. Turning the corner to the elevator, Achilles couldn't help but allow himself time to chuckle, before another shove from Spirit reminded him that he was now well and truly beginning an undertaking where such mirth was not appropriate.

The agent was right; this performance was going to bring the house down.

Or, cost him his life.

He sighed, and pushed the button for the elevator. It was going to be a long night.

* * *

Greystorm looked up from his terminal, and stretched, cracking the bones in his neck. It was becoming a very long day. Taking another sip from his increasingly cold cup of tea, he looked over the desk into Zero's concerned visage. The bear was as deep into research mode as he was, poring over intelligence reports from the region, sifting through the vast amounts of data that poured into the TEA on a daily basis. As Senior Director, with all his other responsibilities, it was impossible for him to read every report from every part of the world in the utmost detail; he relied on the directors below him to consolidate the salient points into his Daily Brief and make sure that he had the necessary information to make the right decisions. But with the theft of the *SDS* algorithms now apparent, it seemed that there was something they'd all missed. And Zero was desperate to find out what. His eyes were running bleary from the number of pages he'd already read, but finally, just as Greystorm paused in tiredness, he clenched his fist and pointed at his screen.

"Grey, have you ever heard of this group – *Rising Force?*"

The snow leopard tilted his head. "No? They must be new."

"They are," Zero observed grimly. "So new, they slipped under my radar when I was reviewing the situation before sending Spirit in. Damn!" He banged the desk with his fist in frustration. "I've exposed him to more risk than is acceptable for his first mission back in the field."

The feline shook his head. "You're no seer. It's impossible to predict every eventuality… stop beating yourself up."

"And have we heard from him?" the Senior Director asked pointedly, even though he knew the answer. "Have we made contact?"

"Not yet, but he's probably in 'ghost' mode. You know how hard it is to get hold of him when he's like that, even before he changed. He's fine; just fully involved in the mission is all."

"Or he's already been captured by this group. I see now they have the means. Did you consider that?" Zero glowered.

"I try not to," Greystorm answered smartly. "You know, 'glass half full' and all that."

Zero snorted. "People tell me the British are supposed to be miserable, but here you go again showing me otherwise with your cheerful disposition. Every time."

The Sciences director nodded, fully appreciating the sarcastic compliment. "As I said – I try." He raised a half smile.

Zero nodded grimly. "You're going to do more than try. I'm sending you to coordinate in person with our top agents in Europe."

Greystorm appeared shocked. "Me? Why me? Don't you want your Operations director leading the charge, so to speak?"

"Corona's deployed in Alaska and I have a meeting tomorrow with some very angry people about my sudden billion-euro funding request, so you're the next logical person to go. I've asked Ixak and Inverno to meet you in Arenosa and from there we can figure out how to deal with Rising Force."

The snow leopard's eyes narrowed. "What about Spiritwolf?"

"He continues his mission to find Black Dust and the tablet. Don't get any ideas about helping him – he needs to do this on his own."

"Shouldn't we at least warn him that the algorithm was stolen and that people might be after him?"

Zero considered the request. "Only if you find him. Don't go out of your way to make contact with him – we need to follow standard mission protocols as well."

"Fair enough." Greystorm rose from his seat, scooping his datapad from the desk after transferring his work to it. "I'll leave right away, Zero."

"One more thing. Ixak knows about Spiritwolf – don't ask how he found out – but Inverno doesn't. So use discretion."

The feline nodded. "Understood. I'll call Ixak en route, maybe arrange to meet with him first."

"Good luck," Zero said softly and waited for Greystorm to close the door before resuming his analysis of yet another swathe of data, reviewing it slowly to make sure neither of them had missed anything.

Spirit, he mentally called. *Wherever you are now, don't do anything stupid. I need you to come back safe, and I won't forgive myself if you don't.*

* * *

As he stood beneath the outstretched arms of Saint James, the long dead apostle's statue lit up by wan orange light, Spirit realized that what he was doing was monumentally stupid.

If he had been the one formulating the plan, choosing the meet-up point, it would *never* have been this. In the field, half an agent's job is managing risk – the more time you have to lay down your defenses and ensure that there are no unpleasant surprises lurking for you in the wings, the less risk you're exposed to and the easier things will go. Meet with an enemy in the middle of a shopping mall during the day where there are clean lines of sight, lots of witnesses, and CCTV cameras, and you can be pretty sure you'll be able to walk away with your internal organs intact.

"Why on earth did you choose this place?" Spirit groaned, looking around at the exposed surroundings and all the places they could be attacked from. They were truly in old Europe now; behind the three meter tall statue of the saint, there was a darkened church; its silhouette a pointed finger to the sky. There were a couple of benches nearby, rubbish bins along building frontages, a few scattering sheaves of newspaper blowing along in the wind. During the day some kind of market was held here, but now it was empty. Across the square there were vacant office blocks constructed in a weird modern-medieval mélange around the turn of the twentieth century, their dark shapes were sculpted in stone with gargoyles and scrollwork nestled against the stars darkly. Any one of those bulges could have been a sniper on the roof. Probably was. The only illumination apart from the statue, its brass surface speckled with green weathering and pigeon droppings, was the face of the church clock-tower, now showing five minutes until the appointed hour.

Achilles shrugged. "I knew it would be abandoned at this time; give Black Dust all the more reason to come out and play. We'll have complete privacy."

"That's exactly what makes it so bad," his unseen companion moaned. "We can't do this." He looked over his shoulder, down the street behind him where the pedestrian area of the square ended and the road began. A few cars were parked against the curb in the darkness. They might have been empty, or they might not – there was no way to tell. "We need to get back to the occupied area of the city. Right now."

"No. You go, if you're so scared. I'm sticking around to see if he shows up. I have to know who he is."

"You have no idea that he'll even show up!" Spirit growled. "Listen to me. I've been doing this longer than you have; he's paranoid. The truly paranoid don't go to meetings themselves. They use a cut-out, someone unrelated to them hired to show a pre-arranged sign and deliver a message. You're more likely just to meet with a hired gun sent to end you."

For a moment the singer considered this, sticking out his bottom lip like a child. "But I have you here to protect me. They'll never see you coming. Someone will at least talk to me to find out what I know…"

"You hope. You *hope!*" the agent repeated, actually growling this time. "I told you before; I don't have super powers. I'm not a magic bullet. I-"

"Spirit!" Achilles interjected, giving the ranting agent a prod of his own. He was making enough noise; it wasn't hard to know where he was.

"You keep making excuses. Aren't you tired of playing defense? This whole time you've been pussyfooting around. Pretending to be my personal trainer; trying to sneak into the auction. You're always one step behind this guy. Are all you agents really so hesitant to act?" He shook his head and flashed the grin of a celebrity. "Sometimes, you just have to put yourself in the limelight and see what happens. It's how you get things done."

Momentarily at a loss for words, Spirit gaped. He was about to argue again for their retreat when, from across the plaza, a pair of headlights from an SUV w over them as it exited a hidden alley and turned their way before parking. Achilles went rigid immediately, his own words dying in his throat. In front of the vehicle, there were three figures. At first, they were just shadows, the light at their back making them look like faceless mannequins. Then the central figure took a step away from the black SUV and began to walk toward them; the wolf observed him as he strode, straight-backed and powerful. He noted the other two remained where they were, guns slung over their shoulders. Two more SUVs emerged and parked alongside; more people hidden within, no doubt. For the second time that night, fear gripped him by the throat. He didn't turn, but instinctively reached out to grip the invisible agent's arm. "Spirit…" he whispered.

"Don't move," the larger wolf whispered in his ear, squeezing the singer back and holding him steady. He came around until he was standing right behind Achilles, able to lean in and whisper without being overheard. "Whatever you do, don't run. They'll gun you down without hesitation."

"What do I do?"

"Keep calm," Spirit whispered again. "And from now on, just repeat what I say if you want to get out of this alive. I speak, you repeat. Can you do that?"

The man was getting closer; he was just about to enter their sphere of yellow light under the statue. Achilles was fixated on his approach. "Y-yes…"

"Good. Stay calm, you're doing fine."

The bear took one more step; he was still several meters from Achilles. He stopped, as if encountering a barrier none of them could see, and looked over the wolf with active interest. His fur was as white as the singer's, but his gaze was more serious and callous than could be imagined. "So you're *Black Dust?*" Gareth rumbled, his voice smooth with British disdain. "Or at least, you claim to be."

"Don't answer," Spirit hissed. "Ask him who he is."

"And who are you?" Achilles replied, trying to keep his voice steady. "I don't recall seeing your name on the guest list."

Gareth considered him again. He put his hands into his pockets, as if to seem less threatening. "Cocky shit, aren't you?" He chuckled. "I'm tempted to see how your humor lasts with a bullet between your eyes."

"Convince him he has to keep you alive! Tell him if he kills you-"

"You'll never get your hands on the tablet if you kill me, that I promise you," Achilles suddenly burst out, with more vigor than he'd intended. His nerves were showing. "So tell the black-tie-and-sunglasses squad back there to cool their heels. All right?"

The polar bear narrowed his eyes, and ground his teeth. "Very well. I'll play – what exactly do you want, wolf?"

"Good, he thinks you're *Black Dust* – or at least, is willing to consider it. Tell him your price."

"A… a… uh… *million* euros." Achilles replied.

He caught the bear's surprised look, and then a second later Spirit's elbow in his ribs with the hissed warning: "Too low!"

"…to start with," the wolf saved, as if that was what he meant to say from the start. "That's the price of the face time, tonight. The full price is…"

"Five hundred."

"…five hundred million. Once I know you're genuine."

Gareth rubbed his chin. "Interesting. Indeed." The next moment, he looked distracted. He held his hand up to his ear, and Achilles noticed that the bear was wearing a wireless earpiece. "Yes? Where? How many… ?" the bear was heard to ask.

"The enemy of our enemy could be our friend," Spirit whispered in the downtime. "We should use him to help us flush out the real *Black Dust*. Your plan hasn't worked; he's not here."

"How?" Achilles risked asking back in a low growl.

"I'm working on it, just-"

"So!" the bear erupted angrily, cutting off the secret dialogue. "This is getting *really* interesting. What angle are you working exactly?"

"What do you mean?" the wolf replied nervously, without being prompted. Suddenly, he had a sinking feeling in his gut. The men by the cars with the guns were raising them again. He felt Spirit's hands grip him tight.

"The people on the roof up there with guns on my team. Yours, I assume! You thought you could cross me?"

Filled with horror, Achilles shook his head. Spirit was heard to whisper "Oh shit…"

Up above, Clarice took her eyes away from the goggles. Darius, Brennan, and two others were by her side with assault rifles and semi-autos in position. "Shit!" she hissed, pulling back at the moment she saw the shift in the position of the men inside the SUV. "We've been spotted!"

Darius looked down, his own rifle pointed at Spirit's position, aided by the SDS-enhanced binoculars. "Can we still take him?"

"I think…" the tigress began to answer, but her next instruction was drowned out by the thunder of gunfire being opened up from the square below. Ducking behind a stone gargoyle, she howled. "Return fire! Engage!"

And that was when all hell broke loose.

The two enemy teams began exchanging fire like they were in a warzone. Achilles flinched and ducked back as both sides lay down their fire, for the moment leaving the two men standing alone. The bear produced a nickel-plated gun from a shoulder rig inside his jacket. "You and I are going to have a private and very *painful* conversation – and you're going to tell me *exactly* what is going on here!"

He pointed the gun right at Achilles, who held up his hands in surrender. The sight of blood spray across the square, coupled with the cries of Gareth's team as *Rising Force*'s bullets struck home, made his knees wobbly. "No, please, wait," he begged. He took a step backwards, and found that suddenly Spirit wasn't there.

The next second, Gareth cried out in shock as the pistol was knocked away. It discharged itself in a flash, the bang so loud it deafened the white wolf's hearing, the bullet practically whizzing past his ear – but thankfully not hitting his brain. The polar bear was still mouthing shock when he was struck with the full force of Spirit's fury and doubled over from the invisible combatant's quick blows to his stomach. With that assault, those not engaged with covering fire upon the roof began to turn their attention to Achilles' position, and across the square more bullets began to streak through the air.

Numb with terror, Achilles was still staring at Gareth's gasping form when he saw the pistol rise up again by itself, and his hand was yanked back toward the darkened street. "We have to get out of here. RUN!"

He was pulled along as the pistol cracked, firing again and again. Mostly it was just a distraction, but one bullet at least found its target, taking out a cheetah that was just unslinging his semi-automatic in their direction.

"They're getting away!" Brennan howled up on the roof, ducking behind a pillar again as the ricochets grew in intensity.

"We can't equal their firepower," Clarice hissed reluctantly. "Fall back. *Fall back!*"

"Run faster!" Spirit panted. He discarded the pistol once he'd emptied the clip.

They were just getting close to the road when the headlights of one of the parked cars switched on, and the passenger door was flung open. "Hey!" Achilles heard a familiar voice shout, over the crack of gunfire. "In here. Now!"

The vehicle, a blue BMW, roared to life by the time they reached it. Practically diving through the open door, Achilles thanked his lucky stars when he heard a cry of agony lance through the air right behind him. He looked back, but could not see anything. It all happened so fast. Their savior was already putting the car in motion as bullets peppered the vehicle; he didn't even notice as the rear passenger door was pulled open and something heavy threw itself inside as the car screeched away. Heart racing a million miles an hour, the white wolf had just processed that it was *Regis* hunched over the wheel and gritting his teeth as he floored it, before looking back and seeing the depression that told him Spirit was with them. But something was wrong. On the right side of the seat, a dark stain was spreading, like the fabric was absorbing some kind of fluid. "I'm hit..." he heard Spirit whisper.

"Well now," the elephant glowered. "Look who we have here." The car accelerated and *El Cuadrado Del Santo* and the gunfire were left behind. Streetlights flashed overhead. His eyes seemed dark and manic.

"Regis..." Achilles gasped, still trying to recover from the shock. "How are you... why... ?"

The elephant looked at him darkly. "Why do you think?" His tusks flashed ivory white, like fangs of ice. "I only saved you so I could thank you myself. For how much you've ruined and complicated things..."

Listening in the back seat, his invisible blood flowing out of his arm, Spirit tried to block out the pain and focus on what was happening. He wouldn't die from the wound – not right away. And yet there was a cold math to blood loss. The more he lost, the weaker he'd get. When you're on a clock like that, it pays to act, no matter how desperate your plan – because if he didn't, he might never get the chance. He clutched his wound, wincing, nerves sparkling with fresh jolts of pain, even as he felt himself wanting to black out.

"Goodnight, pop tart," Regis scowled, still driving. A small gun was nearly hidden at his waist and the elephant was trying to surreptitiously aim it at Achilles.

Spirit leaned forward and yanked the gun away. "Hello, *Black Dust!*" he suddenly cried, loud as he could, then choked the startled pachyderm from behind with his one good arm, rattling as they bounced over a curb.

"Oh *SHIT!*" he heard Achilles call in alarm.

The next second, the car was spun in a circle, colliding with a minibus coming the other way as they swerved across the lanes. The car accelerated and hit the side verge, where it lost contact with the road and gravity took over. Flipping onto its side, they were like socks in a tumble-drier as the car spun, windows shattering inwards with a shower of glass until finally they came to a stop. Crumpled against the roof of the backseat, Spirit winced, wondering how bad it was. He wanted to move, but then his already wounded arm took another hit and he began that familiar slide away from consciousness. His eyes closed and in the darkness, he heard the driver door being flung open, then footsteps running away. There were raised voices, horns blaring. His lifeblood still trickled from his arm and he tried to hold on to what remained of consciousness. "Spirit..." he heard Achilles' voice, quite near. "Hold on. Please. Oh God."

The next moment, rough hands were pulling him from the wreckage as the blaring of ambulance sirens grew closer, and then he vanished into oblivion completely.

Chapter Eight: Pieces

Gareth Zirkowski was one of the most imperturbable members of the intelligence community. Confident, in control, and a masterful tactician, the polar bear had rarely been beaten on the field of battle. Even temporary setbacks where it seemed like he might lose had led to backup plan upon backup plan, the end of which always resulted in a win.

Not tonight.

He stormed into the Arenosa apartment suite his group had rented earlier yesterday and fixed his icy glare on each of the startled CATS team members in turn. Several of them were surveillance and research, and had been in the room while the meeting had gone down. The field agents had trailed in his wake and now stood behind the others; they were equally subjected to the fury that blazed in his blue eyes.

"Will someone please explain to me what just happened?" he snarled at the room. "And tell me why the fuck the best covert operations team in MI-6… *MY team*… just got their asses handed to them?"

"Sir." A brown female wolf in the standard suit-and-black-tie 'uniform' raised her hand. An earpiece with a blinking blue light matched the one in the polar bear's ear, along with the rest of the team. She had a white-outlined black tiger insignia on her lapel, indicating her rank as third in command. Ferdinand, the sable who was the second in command, had been gravely wounded in the shootout and was on his way to the nearest hospital with the other injured agents. Events were still happening in real-time, though, and their wounded companions were put of their minds without a second thought, as they had been trained to do. "The satellite imagery picked up several heat signatures on the rooftops."

The director closed his eyes and pinched the bridge of his muzzle. "I ought to have you killed for stating the obvious," he said quietly.

The wolf blanched at that. "Sir. Analysis of the pattern of fire and the spent ammo indicates DAST involvement."

"The TEA?" Gareth frowned. "They have boots on the ground here? Without consulting us first?" A shiver ran down his spine, masked by his thoughtful expression. *Did Murdock alert them? Are they investigating us independently?* "Continue the debrief, Ardal."

"There were five of them, including one female that was heard to be giving the orders. We could have taken them easily, had our snipers been above ground level."

The bear's eyes narrowed. "Armchair quarterbacking, as the Americans would say."

"A suggestion for next time, sir." She nodded acknowledgement of his displeasure and spread her hands apologetically. "The plaza has no street cameras, of course, so we could not get a good read of the events at ground level, other than what's been reported by yourself and the surviving agents."

If she keeps needling, she'll be shortlisted on the next suicide mission. He ground his teeth. "What about the singer… Achilles?"

"We doubt he's Black Dust, sir, based on what you told us. Analysis of the audio telemetry showed quite a bit of stress in his voice as he was speaking. It's clear he wasn't used to being in that sort of situation. Maybe he was a lure set up by DAST?"

"That's not really their style. Given that, his presence is a discontinuity that still needs investigating.

"Yes, sir. And speaking of discontinuities…"

"What?"

She hesitated, looking for support from the rest of the team and getting none. "You say that there were only the two of you there facing off? Yourself and Achilles?"

"Of course!" Gareth snapped, losing his patience. "The heat signatures on your scans should confirm that."

"We picked up a third voice on the audio."

"So? A comm-link would account for that. Backtrack the source, or do I dare hope that you've already done that?"

Ardal shook her head. "The scan that Ferdinand took of the singer showed that Achilles only had a cell phone and it was off. No tablet, either." She paused for a moment. "It could be a new piece of tech that we've never seen before, but it would have to be using a new method of transceiving…"

"Wait." The polar bear held up a hand, which immediately silenced his subordinate. *A discontinuity. Something that hadn't ever been seen before.* He thought back to the confrontation, pictured the white wolf in front of him while everything else in the now faded to black. The stammering responses certainly could indicate he was taking cues from someone. He remembered his own amused, yet cool responses, as he wondered what was taking shape. Then the hurried warning from Ferdinand and the double-cross. He'd pulled his gun, intending to injure the wolf and take him in for questioning, but something had happened. Gareth slowed down time in his mind and pictured the next series of events.

Something had struck his hand. Hard.

The gun had gone off. Missed the wolf by a hair.

Something had hit his stomach. In his mind's eye, he could not see what was hitting him. At the time, he'd assumed one of the ambushers had approached him from behind and attacked, but now all he could see was himself getting punched and kicked by an unseen assailant. And the singer, staring stupidly at him.

Then the gun… HIS gun… had risen into the air and he'd heard… a male voice… yelled something about running. The wolf had been jerked back, as if being pulled by someone.

Something that hadn't ever been seen before.

"That's what it was!" he growled, startling half the room.

"What was, sir?" Ardal fidgeted.

The polar bear grunted. "Someone… unaccounted for. Listen up, people." His voice rang out like an army sergeant giving orders and the rest of the CATS immediately became attentive. "Our mission was, and still is, to find Black Dust… the real Black Dust… and retrieve the tablet currently in his possession. Your immediate task is to analyze the data we currently have available and add in street camera images for anything out of the ordinary. Follow Achilles and find out where he's going next. I'm sure Black Dust won't be too far behind," he finished with a smirk. Then he looked at his team, still waiting for him to continue. "NOW!" he roared and watched, satisfied, as they scattered like leaves before a tempest. He turned on his heel and exited the room, leaving them to their work.

He had an important call to make.

* * *

"You'd better have some good news for me. Wait." Blair Murdock shooed his security guards from his office with a wave of his golden-furred hand. He had come in early to be ready when the call came. When they were gone, he spoke into the phone again. "Do you have the tablet?"

"Not yet." Gareth's voice was uncharacteristically subdued.

"Sounds like failure to me," the lion said casually. On his computer, he pulled up the file and opened its contents. There was an image of doctored records from drug busts – missing money and weapons that the CATS had kept for themselves. Blair flipped through other memos of surveillance on MPs with a bored expression, changed over to his own notes of assassinations cross-linked with members of the CATS team, their aliases, false passports. And one very special report with an image of Gareth himself, executing two TEA agents using a high-powered laser rifle. Not long after, the TEA operations director had pulled the plug on joint operations with the CATS. "It's not too late to make the morning distribution, you know."

"Sir." There was a note of desperation in the director's voice. Just a sliver that few would have caught. "Black Dust is not Achilles."

"Mmm-hm. I recall saying as much."

"Yes. But I think Black Dust was giving Achilles orders."

"Oh? What did he look like?"

"I couldn't tell. He wasn't visible."

Blair Murdock straightened in his chair. "Say that again."

"He wasn't visible – the person didn't show up on our infrared scans, either. I know it sounds impossible but whoever it was used me like a punching bag."

The lion's eyes flicked toward the shadows and he opened his desk drawer. He stared at the improbable photograph inside, noting details afresh. "Here's what I want you to do, Gareth. Follow the singer; he's headed to Paris next. There will be a brown wolf with him – male, muscular, nearly two meters in height. That's Black Dust. He'll have the tablet on him, I'm sure."

"How… ?" Gareth was utterly confused. "How do you know all this?"

Murdock laughed. "The same way I know everything you've done on your climb to power. This is your last chance, Zirkowski. Do not fail me again. Better still, don't bother to come back until you've got what I want. Do you understand?"

"Loud and clear." The polar bear clicked his phone off and Blair Murdock carefully lowered the handset.

"You know what needs to be done," the voice whispered suddenly from the shadows in the alcove. As soft as it was, the tone was unmistakably firm, and more than a little impatient.

The lion nodded quickly. He picked the phone back up and dialed his assistant.

"Cancel my meetings for the next few days. We…" He paused and looked back at the alcove. "I'm going to take a working vacation."

It was time to put the backup plan into motion.

* * *

The short, stocky bat straightened the tie on his suit as he entered the lobby of the *L'Arbre Argenté* and smoothed back the coarse hair atop his head. It was empty of patrons, being the time between the end of check-out and the start of check-in. "Good afternoon, dear," he said cheerfully to the desk clerk, a tall gazelle who smiled in reply. "I'd like to book two rooms, please."

"Ah, no reservation?" she replied in a heavily French accent. "We only have suites available right now, sir."

"Fine, fine." The bat waved his hand. "I'll take them. Only for one night."

"Very good, sir." She typed a few things into the computer. "That will be seven hundred euros per room. With tax, it comes to sixteen hundred and three euros. May I have a credit card, please, and your passport?"

"Ah, my dear. I would prefer to pay in cash." He pulled out his wallet and gave her six five-hundred euro notes. "The extra will cover incidentals, as you're required to ask next. Since we will have no such charges, it can be yours as a tip." His eyes gleamed. "No passports, if you please. No names."

"Ah. Of course." She nodded and put the proper amount in the register while pocketing the rest surreptitiously, out of view of the security camera. She finished the check-in process and swiped two card-keys through the programmer. "Here are your room numbers, sir." She pointed to '2501' and '2502', written neatly on the folio. "Do you have a car?"

"Already parked. And don't worry, dear. I can get the luggage." The bat tipped an imaginary hat at her. "Ta." He sauntered outside and walked along the quay that fronted the Garonne River. Bordeaux was a favorite city of his, a source of many a fine wine he'd sampled over the years. But the time for pleasure would have to wait; there was business to attend to.

He turned into an alley and found his employer sitting casually at a table in front of the *Jardin*, a vegetarian restaurant, reading something on his laptop. "Got the rooms, boss." He held up the cardkey folio between two fingers. "Suites."

"Excellent." Regis put his laptop away and left a ten on the table. "Let's go." He picked up the large duffel and walked with the bat toward the hotel along the maze of alleys.

"So what's our plan?"

"Hmmm. Patience." The elephant continued on, letting his companion take the lead. "You're doing well on such short notice."

"It's why you're paying me the big bucks." The bat led him to a side entrance and paused before a pair of doors. "Need to blind something first," he murmured and pointed a short thin device up toward the camera. A short burst caused the circuitry to spark and smoke. "Clear."

Regis nodded and steered toward the service elevator. It was used for hotel laundry and had little trouble accommodating his bulk. The bat touched the '25' button and up they went.

The top floor was elegantly decorated with art and furniture that appeared to be from the time of Louis XIV. Dressed as well as they were, the pair looked exactly as though they belonged with the objects d'art.

The bat opened the corner suite first and looked around, pulling out another gizmo that would detect hidden transmitters. He checked the office area before moving into the kitchen, the living room, and then finally into the bedroom and bathroom. "All clear, boss," he announced upon returning to the door. "Visual sweep as well."

Regis nodded. "And your sonar?"

The bat grinned and tapped the side of his head. "Nothing to be heard, either."

"Perfect." The elephant carefully placed the duffel in the bedroom on the far side of the bed and set up his laptop in the office. "I want you to check your room as well, Pi."

"Of course." The bat cocked his head. "And when do I find out what's next? Hard to plan if I don't know what's going on."

Regis clasped his hands over his large chest. "There's not much for you to know, other than what I've already told you. However, I can tell you two things. First, we will be departing at two in the morning, so I suggest you turn in rather than party all night." The bat chuckled; his boss knew his habits well. Being up-front about what he did and making sure it didn't affect what the elephant wanted kept him employed. "The second is that we will have two more joining us when we get to our destination. Which, at this point, must remain secret."

"Sure thing." Pi nodded. "Anything else, before I fetch my own bags from the car?"

"See to it that I am not disturbed."

"Gotcha." The bat exited the room with a flourishing bow, thanks to the membranes under his arms.

Alone again, Regis scowled and loosened his tie before letting his bulk settle onto the couch. He was tired and instead of closing his eyes – which he knew would lead quickly to slumber – he turned on the large LCD TV and flipped through the news channels.

Stories about the sudden rally in the European stock markets barely held interest for him despite his net worth fast approaching a billion dollars. Reports of uprisings in the Middle East. *click* Basketball star Al Case calling out the refs yet again. *click* A poker tournament from last year. *click click click …*

He finally settled on a science program that was describing the latest satellite project, which would potentially generate terawatt-level power from solar energy collectors. The discussion of the special materials used in the construction of the collector array was a new technology that engaged his brain. He worked better when he multitasked, which was how he had managed to keep up his pretense as business manager of a rock band while working on his... side projects. His mind turned back the clock to the previous night, barely more than twelve hours ago, and started re-reviewing the events that had led him here.

Regis had followed Achilles to the plaza from the hotel; he knew that the wolf was stubborn and was going to find some way around the guards he'd gifted him with. Sure enough, the singer had shown up and nearly gotten himself killed trying to pretend that he was Black Dust.

Sudden arrogance flared and his temper went along for the ride. How dare that officious little prick attempt to impersonate him! Red colored his perception and he very nearly threw the coffee table at the wall in frustration. *Achilles. Damn him. The bastard had nearly ruined everything!*

And then a sudden thought cooled the edge of his anger. Why had the singer tried to impersonate him?

Given what he knew of Achilles, it must have been a ploy to get whomever he thought Black Dust was out in the open. Probably to get rid of him – Regis had tried to throw him off the trail by implicating Cain instead, but that hadn't lasted. Somehow, he'd figured out Cain wasn't really Black Dust. The elephant shook his head, returning his thoughts to last night. The lad might have gone about exposing him in the sloppiest way possible but the end result was his own making. He was sure he'd had the singer, giving the appearance of helping the wolf out of the jam he'd gotten himself into. But somehow, in the ensuing chain of events, he'd been thwarted in his attempt to shoot Achilles.

Which was another oddity, one which he hadn't realized until later. A loud voice had come from the empty back seat of the car, completely startling him. And then that invisible person had tried to strangle him, right before the car had hit the minibus. Despite the rasping tone, the voice had been quite familiar. Spiritwolf.

Regis had weighed his options during his flight on foot and had made his decision before getting back to the Oro. He would depart Arenosa and continue to his rendezvous without the band – there was no way he could keep tabs on a wolf who could just disappear at will. Packing hadn't taken very long; Regis had placed a call to Pi and had arranged for the bat to meet him with a sedan at a petrol station just outside the city. After picking up his other carefully stashed belongings, along with new identities and enough cash to see him through, they'd driven to Bordeaux. Pi was coming along to make sure Spiritwolf would not get the drop on him again in Paris.

Paris. The future. The road that stretched toward his destiny was taking a few twists and detours, to be sure, but it wasn't unnavigable. The important thing was to keep the goal in mind and be flexible enough to accommodate problems that emerged along the way. Regis leaned back and pictured the incoming bids, the announcement of the winner, then the exchange to conclude the transaction. Simple and efficient, it would be over soon. With this, he would establish his legacy as the world's premier black market dealer in exotic technology for all time. He was already set for life and could retire to anyplace he wanted; cash out and live out his days in security and comfort. Peace and quiet. No more deals, no more loose ends to tie up. It was the reward for someone as good as he was, having played the game as long as he had.

He let the moment linger for a few minutes before getting up and turning on his laptop. There were arrangements that still had to be made, not the least of which was to bring the other two into play.

Regis sent the encrypted emails, and then prepared to put the rest of the endgame into motion.

* * *

Clarice tried to ignore Darius while the crocodile finished his third cheeseburger with lip-smacking noises that brought looks of disapproval and condescension from the restaurant clientele. They were dressed as well as she; her boorish companion wearing jeans and a T-shirt that screamed 'American' to passersby. "Are you done yet?" she growled.

"Think so." He downed the rest of his beer – his fifth of the afternoon – and wiped his mouth on the cloth napkin. "So what now? Shouldn't we be searching for Mr. Elusive?" She had ordered him to not mention Spiritwolf or invisibility while in public, so he was finding creative ways around those constraints. Just to annoy her.

"Brennan is taking care of it." The tigress scowled at him and then the bill, letting one fang show. "The singer is nowhere to be found, either."

"But not for long. The Paris concert is tomorrow night, all we have to do is go there and let the mob find him for us again."

She smirked. "Didn't you hear? They've been delayed for a couple of days. 'Logistical difficulties', they said. So they are still in Arenosa until tomorrow."

Darius shrugged. "Yeah, okay. They'd do that so they could have time to find the singer."

"We must find him first, and quickly." Their waiter took the payment and nodded thanks when Clarice waved for him to keep the change. "Brennan has been in the Oro lobby and Michal is keeping an eye on the street. Benny is watching the concert tear-down. He has not shown up anywhere."

"Huh. Maybe your software's malfunctioning."

"It is working perfectly, as you saw last night." Her triumphant grin was all teeth.

"And what I didn't see, other than the obvious, was us bagging the prize."

The grin vanished. "*Ja*," she grudgingly admitted. "The new players in the game are part of MI-6. I recognized the uniforms – they are part of the anti-terrorism team."

Darius stared at her. "Shit. Are they after him, too?"

"Probably, and they may be after us. We cannot afford to think otherwise."

"Maybe we should just let this go. Y'know. Go back to DAST and the TEA before we're found out." He stood. "If I'd known this was going to go south so quickly, I would never have…"

"Sit down." Clarice said quietly. Danger stalked him from her eyes, and he obeyed. "There is no going back," she murmured. "No exit. I am sure that the TEA knows about us now."

Darius put his head in his hands. "How?" he groaned.

"When I stole the SDS, it left a trace. Unavoidable."

The crocodile looked up, fury blossoming across his face. "You meant to have him in your custody by now, didn't you? But that didn't happen. And now you're dragging ME down, too!" He hissed at her, which made several of the restaurant's patrons jump in their seats and glance nervously at their table.

And then he blinked; the soft click of a safety being disengaged under the table made him suddenly short of breath. "We are Rising Force," she said softly, with the eerie calm of pleasant conversation. "Either you belong to the team or you do not. Please let me know which. Right now."

"I'm on the team," he muttered quickly.

"Good." Another click released him from his near-death experience. Clarice's hands remained in her lap, or so he presumed. "From now on, you will take your cues from Brennan."

Darius grimaced; the bear was a greedy, bloodthirsty ass who wanted nothing more than to get her in bed. Sex, thugs, and rock'n'roll. *Why on Earth did I join this group, again?* he wondered.

Taking his silence as assent, she stood and slung her purse over her shoulder. "You will join him at the hotel."

He stood as well, short and stocky to contrast her lithe form. "What about you? Aren't you coming too? Part of the team?"

"Silly child," she said with a patronizing smile and left. Darius watched her go, tail lashing as his anger simmered after catching her parting quote.

"*L'enfer, c'est les autres.*"

Hell is other people.

* * *

He had lost track of time.

That was the first thing that came to Spiritwolf's mind. How many days had his count been at? Over a year, but after that? An additional month? Two? He felt groggy; everything was so far away. Probably a good thing; the light in the room that passed through his closed eyelids seemed to brighten gradually instead of blinding him like it had nearly every day since the accident.

The accident. Time. How long?

Through the slow-motion dullness came the realization that this was somehow familiar. Painkillers wearing off. Why would he have needed painkillers?

A voice was speaking. "Yeah, he's waking up. I'll call you back later."

The voice was familiar.

Spirit… hold on. Please. Oh God.

Achilles. He had been trying to save Achilles. What had happened? There had been so much concern in his voice – begging him not to die.

Die?

"Spiritwolf? Are… you awake?"

The white wolf was still worried. "Ugh. Yeah." He struggled but managed to sit up. Achilles was reaching out to help him, and then hesitated as the sheets tumbled down his chest to leave him covered only from the waist down. Nothing from the waist up.

The white wolf's uncertainty – that exact look he had on his face – was not the first time Spirit had seen it in the last year.

"I'm all right," he said gruffly. "Arm's sore." As if to underscore the lag in his thinking, he finally noticed the bandage coiled tightly around his right bicep, hanging in mid-air above the bed.

"You took a bullet. Seems to be just a flesh wound." British accent. The invisible wolf saw someone move from behind the casually dressed wolf. Grey and white fur, feline.

Greystorm!

"What are you doing here?"

"He is here at my request." The darker form in the corner resolved itself into Ixak as the beetle moved toward the bed as well. Spirit had vague impressions in his memory of the beetle's hands pulling him from something just as he lost consciousness.

"If you two are here…" Spiritwolf said with growing dread.

"Relax," Greystorm waved a hand nonchalantly. "I'm just here to coordinate with our European friends and pool our knowledge on Rising Force, as requested. Your mission's still a go."

"But… I've been shot."

"Winged, really. Don't be so dramatic. Blood loss was more of a problem." The snow leopard held up a used bag of type O and then sealed the biohazard container before stowing it in an unmarked cardboard box. His brow furrowed. "Unless you're giving up?"

"No, but…"

"Then you may return to your mission. You can probably take that off now." Greystorm peered through his glasses at the bandage and grinned. "I do good work, don't I?"

"You were checking up on me."

"Not at all. The Senior Director made it very clear that you're on your own with for this mission. Our European friend requested my assistance, so technically I'm still following mission protocols." The snow leopard nodded at Ixak. "He'll have to fill you in on what we've found so far – I'm already very late for my meeting with Inverno. Then it's back to the States. Best of luck, Spirit. We're all hoping for a successful conclusion to your mission."

"Thank you. For everything."

Greystorm picked up his duffel bag, slung it over his shoulder, and put the box under the other arm. He glanced once more at the bed. "I was never here," he said dramatically and then laughed as he left the room.

Ixak clacked emphatically. Spirit was starting to recognize some of the insect's 'intonations', which the voice-box resolved into, "And since your mission is still in progress, I will not disclose your status to alpha-bear, either."

"I appreciate it, really, but…" His voice trailed off. "Maybe it would be better if I stopped before I get killed. Seriously, you can bring in a team to finish things up instead of having me fly solo."

A long pause. "It is your choice."

My choice? "What do you mean?" The agent noted that Achilles had moved back, to be unobtrusive, but he was listening intently to the exchange.

"We are defined by our actions, our choices. If alpha-bear knew that you had been shot, he would put you into safe-keeping and you would never have the chance to complete your current mission. Trust in you would be lost. There would be questions of your ability to succeed under adverse conditions, whether, with your nature, you might choose in combat to flee to safety and leave your teammates to suffer."

"I would never… !"

"This, I know because of who you are. This, you must prove once again to everyone else." Ixak paused. "And you are not the only one who has failed. Agent Clarice Streifen has been discovered to be an operative of Rising Force. Inverno already told you that they are after you. What is worse is that she is also now in possession of the SDS algorithm."

They heard Spirit swear loudly.

"I am in agreement, agent. This happened under my command, so I am responsible. But I must continue with my mission, to correct my mistake. Unforeseen failures happen with our work, no matter how we may plan otherwise, so it is what one does after one fails that is important. A corollary to my earlier statement."

Who you are is defined by what you do, not what you are. That was what Master Song had been trying to tell him, if not beat into him. An unseen smile returned to his features. "Thank you. I understand."

"Yes. You do." Ixak gestured back to a laptop on the desk. "Because of your information relayed from Noir, we have created an integrating algorithm along the entropic range he specified. Our Eurozone listening network will detect Black Dust's transmissions and relay them to the laptop."

"The auction! I can find out when and where it will be!"

"Yes."

"Perfect." Spiritwolf felt much more upbeat. At least he had something to go on, now, even if he couldn't plan his way out of a paper bag. He needed more. "Okay, so, I've been shot and then patched up. Clarice is a double agent and she's gunning after my ass, apparently. What else did I miss? How long have I been out?"

"Fourteen hours and three minutes. You were in an automobile accident. This wolf was with you. He helped me get you back to your hotel."

"Thank you, Achilles."

Achilles nodded. "I had to tell the band that things got a little rough last night and to take today off. They were told you'd been injured and had to get some stitches. I called them, since I didn't want the bull brothers following me here." He frowned. "I'm worried about Regis, though. He isn't around anywhere and I still don't know why he ran from the accident. Since I can't be there, I've had to put Grant in charge of…"

"Regis is Black Dust!" Spirit blurted out.

Achilles stopped, his mouth unable to form words for the second time in recent days. Ixak began chittering. "Are you sure, agent? The elephant is the dealer?"

"That's not possible…" Achilles started to protest.

"It is," the invisible wolf said grimly. "He tried to shoot you in the car – that's why I tried to stop him. You couldn't see the gun, but I saw it clearly from the back seat. I'm glad he didn't hurt you."

Achilles nodded mutely and watched transfixed as the bandage unwound and fell onto the bed. Spirit tested his arm – it was incredibly sore, but he could manage. He'd certainly been injured worse in the field and had still completed his mission. Of course, he'd also been part of a team.

Meanwhile, Ixak went to the laptop and pulled out a smaller touchscreen computer, utilizing all four hands simultaneously. "I have transmitted his image to our organization and to Interpol," the director said a minute later. "I have also run an image check for him in Arenosa for the last twenty-four hours. There is nothing since the time of the automobile accident, other than a security camera that caught him re-entering the Oro at 3:48, ante meridian."

Achilles blinked. "That was quick of you."

"It is quick when one has more hands to do things with." Ixak put the tablet computer in a messenger bag, which he slung over his shoulder. The laptop remained on the hotel desk. "I must depart now." Spiritwolf believed he could hear the regret in the mechanical voice.

"Thanks again. For everything."

"You are welcome, agent. Good hunting. And be careful."

"Wait a moment… hang on!" Achilles barked at the beetle. "You can't just leave him like this. We were outnumbered in the plaza… can't you spare some other agents from your little secret organization to help him? I mean, he doesn't need to be taken to safety, but a little backup would help, right?"

This time, it was Spirit who answered. "No, Achilles," he said gently. "There's no way to know how many agents have been compromised by Rising Force. This will be an ongoing investigation for several weeks, maybe months. It's impossible for me to completely trust any agent he might assign. And I need to be able to do that or it won't work. It's also why sending in a team to replace me won't work either." Ixak nodded.

"But… your injury. You can't continue like this. It's still painful for you, isn't it? I can hear it in your voice."

Ixak regarded Achilles for several long, thoughtful moments. Then he clicked a short sentence. "You would go on stage to perform, even if you were badly hurting." Achilles' ears went back and he nodded, understanding the giant beetle's point. He would indeed do anything to sing. The passion burned so fiercely inside him; so, too, it would be for Spiritwolf. Ixak seemed to recognize the white wolf's acquiescence and without another word, he slipped out the door.

"All right, then." Achilles scratched his head. "You've got some really odd friends. I suppose it's par for the course for someone like you, isn't it?" He turned back to the bed, only to see it now totally empty of the invisible wolf's presence. "Shit," he said, backing toward the door and scanning the room with widened eyes.

"Relax, rock star," Spirit's voice came from near the window. The curtain peeled away from one side and then dropped back into place several moments later. "I just needed to stand and stretch."

"Ah, right." The white wolf rubbed the side of his arm, a nervous habit from his youth. "Are you all right?"

"More or less. The bullet went through cleanly, I'm guessing."

"That's not what I mean." Achilles kept his eyes and ears facing the sound of the other wolf's voice. "I didn't follow everything that was being said, but it sounds like you need to prove yourself, somehow."

"Sort of. It's my first mission after the accident."

Achilles frowned. "I remember you saying that you had been in an accident. Though you were trying to strangle me at the time."

"Sorry for that. I… I'm not used to people knowing about it."

"I'm pretty sure those two knew about it. Others in your organization seem to, as well." He folded his arms over his chest. "You don't have to worry about it with me, so lose the drama queen routine, all right?"

"I guess we did declare a truce, didn't we?"

Spirit's voice came from the desk, now. Achilles turned his head accordingly. "If it's not too much trouble," the white wolf grumbled, "would you mind putting on something so that I can keep track of where you are?"

There was no immediate response and Achilles was about to prompt the unseen wolf again when he heard "Yeah." Footsteps retreated toward the chair in the corner where Achilles had doffed the borrowed trenchcoat and hat. They rose into the air and, moments later, both articles of clothing hung in the air in a parodic semblance of life. "Better?"

The other wolf squinted. "I guess." He sat on the bed, studying the odd figure. "How does it work, anyway?"

"Can we not talk about it?"

They were both silent for a while.

"So what do we do now?" Achilles finally asked.

"What do you mean 'we'? You're not coming."

"Of course I am!" The white wolf folded his arms across his chest and glowered.

"No, you're not. You wanted Black Dust off your tour. Well, you got your wish. He's gone. Time for the rock star to go back to performing for millions of his adoring fans."

Achilles snorted. "And what are you going to do? Vanish your way toward capturing the bad guys? Please."

"Not exactly. Not if they have the SDS."

"What is that, anyway?"

"'Spiritwolf Detection Software.'"

"Are you joking?"

"That's – the snow leopard who just left – that's his sense of humor for you."

"You're not going to tell me his name? Or the insect's?"

"You know too much already."

Achilles shrugged. "More than I ever wanted, for sure. So, they can see you coming?"

"I'm capable of defeating them on my own."

"With your injury and no way to be undetected? Come on. And get off your goddamn high horse while you're at it. You need me." He held up a hand to silence the oncoming protest. "You do. You can't trust any of your fellow agents because they may have been compromised, remember?"

"What part of 'on my own' did you not comprehend?"

"The word 'my', actually," Achilles replied dryly. "Did you notice that both of your friends didn't seem to mind me staying here with you after they left?"

"Yeah. I was wondering about that." Spirit pulled the chair over and sat.

"They trust your judgment. And you trust theirs, right?"

"Of course. But that doesn't mean they think you should help me. Likely what it means is that they're leaving it to me to decide how I should keep my identity secret."

"Secret? But I already know…" If Achilles could have turned whiter, he would have. "You mean… kill me?"

The fedora tilted up slightly. "How many people in the outside world do you think know about me?"

"Probably not many." Achilles tried to keep his heartbeat from jackhammering through his chest. "You, uh, wouldn't… ?"

"Relax, rock star. I'm not going to kill you. I owe you for saving my life."

"And you've saved mine. Um, not that we should check the tally because I think I'm still behind on that score."

"But I've put you in danger. Though, you did that to yourself, too." That last sentence was spoken in a harder tone of voice.

"Hey, it was at least a plan," Achilles protested. "You didn't have one."

"The point is that you went off and did things on your own." Spirit leaned back and for a moment, it appeared as though the clothes had just been neatly arranged on the chair. "I can do that without much harm coming to me."

"Right. You just take off your clothes and go strolling around naked. You know, there's one thing I don't understand."

"What's that?"

Achilles pointed a finger. "You. You're talking about how you can just disappear on a whim like it was no big deal. And yet, I ask you a simple question about how it works and it's like you're embarrassed."

That seemed to catch him off-guard; the clothes stopped moving but Achilles could hear him breathing louder. The white wolf shook his head. "Forget it. Maybe you're right. Maybe the bug was right. I should go back to my singing, my music. It's what I'm good at. It's what I know. And it's not liable to get me killed. You can keep going just fine without me, right?" He stood; the motion didn't prompt any reaction from Spirit. "I should go," he repeated, looking at the door.

"Stay," the invisible wolf's voice was hoarse. "Please."

"Hey. Are you all right?" Achilles took a couple steps toward the clothes, then stopped.

"No. I'm not. I…"

Silence.

"What's wrong? Oh, crap… you're not bleeding, are you?" He hurried over, reached out a hand, put it on the coat's shoulder.

"No, it's not that. I just…" Achilles heard him sigh. "I hate asking for help."

Achilles nodded. "I can understand that. People tell me I'm a control freak," he added with a self-deprecating grin. "But sometimes, you just have to swallow your pride and ask."

The fedora tilted up to look at him; Achilles couldn't stop an involuntary shudder seeing nothing between the hat and the coat, then nothing *through* the coat. Up close and personal. He tried to imagine the wolf looking up at him. It helped only a little.

"Do you remember when I told you how I got my name?"

Achilles frowned. "Yes. But that was part of your cover, wasn't it? A lie?"

"Not all of it." Spirit took a deep breath. "The part with my friend telling me that I moved like a spirit through life, that was true. Some of the best cover stories come from the truth."

"Huh. That's interesting, but what does that have to do with asking people for help?"

"I wasn't willing to ask for help then, either. I… nearly made a bad decision. I thought I knew what was best for me. My friend showed me that I was wrong. Just now… you reminded me of that night. And that maybe I should ask you for help. But I don't want you to be harmed because I asked for your help."

Achilles nodded. "Tell you what. I'll follow your lead and if you think it's too dangerous for me, I'll do what you say. Since you're looking out for me and all," he added with a grin.

"I wouldn't want your millions of fans coming after me because I got you killed." The coat held up a sleeve – the left one. "All right. It's a deal."

The white wolf found the other wolf's hand and shook it firmly. "Right. So what do we do now?"

Spirit stood and Achilles stepped back, watching the coat and hat move to the laptop. "This is set up with an automatic trigger to record anything Black Dust transmits. Good." The hat and coat were taken off, then they floated over to Achilles.

"Are we going somewhere?" he asked, taking the clothes.

"The train station. I need to retrieve the stuff I stashed there. My clothes, my mask and gloves. And a few things that could come in handy. Including a certain laptop I picked up from the jackals the other night."

Comprehension dawned on the white wolf's face and he nodded. "Does this mean you have a plan?"

"Not as such." The door opened by itself. "But I think I have some ideas on how we can even the odds for our next fight." Achilles shut the door behind him and marched toward the stairs. "And in the meantime, I need to tell you a few things…" They went down and once outside, hailed a cab after walking a couple of blocks, all without realizing their exit had been carefully monitored.

Darius grinned and let the SDS-enhanced binoculars rest against chest as he pulled the van into traffic.

* * *

Two hours later

"Are you sure you want to do this?" Achilles asked.

"No." Spiritwolf was fully dressed again and carried his duffel bag slung over his shoulder.

"What about backup?" The elevator doors opened and they found the two bulls waiting.

"Look who finally showed up," Lars rumbled.

"We're not letting you out of our sight again," David added.

The wolves exchanged a grin. "You do realize Regis is no longer working for me?" Achilles asked.

"You can't fool us twice," Lars sneered.

"Once is all it takes, apparently." Spiritwolf handed him a folded newspaper. The front page of the entertainment section showed an article titled, *Business Manager On Achilles Tour Wanted For Questioning.* Both bulls' mouths dropped open.

"Now, my friend here," Achilles motioned to Spiritwolf, "is with an international task force working to apprehend him. He was going to take you two into custody, since you were hired by Regis." Lars and David looked very uncomfortable. "But I convinced him that you couldn't possibly have a clue about what Regis was up to," he added after a few seconds' pause. "The only way he'd let you two go would be if I were to keep an eye on you, as your employer. So, what do you say?" The rock star grinned, turning on the charm.

"Uh," was all Lars could say. He truly looked confused.

"We accept," David said quickly. "Please don't turn us in."

Achilles looked at Spirit, who nodded reluctantly. "We can discuss your pay rate later." Both bovines winced at that. "In the meantime, you two are to guard this floor and let no one out of the elevator without my say-so. Understood?" They nodded in unison and stood attentively, acutely interested in the elevator doors.

"Brilliant," Spiritwolf murmured and followed Achilles down the corridor.

"And for my next performance..." The white wolf fished out a keycard and slid it through the slot. They went inside when the light turned green and while Spirit opened the duffel and sorted through the items inside, Achilles pulled the new cell phone out of the package and flipped it open.

"Cain? Yeah, it's me. Everyone has their new phones?" He gave Spirit a thumbs-up. "Okay. I need everyone on the floor to go to the bar." He paused, listening. "Yeah, Diagonals. That's the one. Grab a late dinner. Drinks. Whatever they're serving. On me. And make sure no one comes back up here until I say so." Cain said something, causing him to reply with, "I don't know how long. A couple of hours should be enough." He checked his watch. "You guys need to get moving." He hung up on the protesting badger and turned back to Spirit. "Right. They're off to eat, drink, and be merry. What's all that?" He pointed at the various items laid out on the bed.

"Our backup," the agent said with a grim smile.

* * *

The bulls watched the last of the crew crowd into the elevator. "Celebrating the popularity of the new song," Cain said by way of explanation. "Concert footage went viral. You wanna come with?"

Lars shook his head and David responded with, "We're here for the duration. Have a few for us."

Cain nodded and David could have sworn he heard the badger mutter something about favors for assholes and princes but the doors shut before he could think of a comeback. Too bad – he thought the surly badger was rather attractive.

He was still lost in thought when the elevator doors opened again a minute later. "Floor's closed off," he said gruffly. "Even for room service."

The bear fired two tranquilizer darts from the gun hidden behind the cart. "It's all right, boys," Brennan drawled, passing by the sleeping bovines. He casually reloaded and smirked. "I ain't room service."

* * *

"Po'boy's in the house."

Clarice listened to the bear's crackling voice over the comm system. "Roger," she said crisply. "Everyone, sing to me."

"Father's good," Michal, the grizzled wolf, murmured. The sniper had his rifle trained on the window across the street.

"Captain reports clear skies," Benny the meerkat said from his position on the roof, many floors above the wolf.

"Smooth sailing below," Darius grunted. He hated his codename, Green. *So unimaginative.* And it gave the impression that he was wet behind the ears, metaphorically speaking. He peered down the sidewalk at the few fans who remained outside the front door to the Oro, still waiting for a glimpse of the singer. *Oh well. I gave them fair warning to clear out.* The street lights cycled the traffic to a standstill, allowing him to sprint across. He moved wickedly fast despite his bulk. He slowed to a brisk walk upon entering the lobby and made it inside the elevator before the doors closed.

"Very good work on the tail, Green," the tigress' voice purred in his ear. Rubbing it in. "Thanks to you, we're almost done." Fortunately, he didn't have to answer her; she had already moved on and was muttering some final orders to Brennan, which meant it was time for him to get into position as well. If this didn't go smoothly, he'd be in a world of hurt.

Yup. Almost done, he thought.

* * *

Brennan sidled up to the door and quickly scanned the hall. No one there. Not even that freak boy they were set to grab. The SDS overlay on his AR goggles supposedly worked but he was pretty damn nervous. He'd had electronics fail on him before, usually at the worst time, and this was one op where he didn't want that to happen.

He'd put in fresh batteries, just in case.

"Lights out," he murmured and slipped the master cardkey into the slot. The latch release clicked and he shouldered the door open, barreling into the room.

The room was empty.

The bear cursed and moved to the corner of the room, pivoting to look behind him. Still nothing. Wedged between the wall and the floor lamp, he noticed the small cylinder on the floor right as it went off. The mini flash-bang let off a thundering concussive wave in the room that translated back through the comm system, making the rest of the team wince. Roaring filled his ears as he staggered back; he couldn't hear a damn thing. What was worse was that the sensitive goggles overloaded, leaving him in a field of pure white until he was able to claw them off.

When he could see again, his field of vision was filled by the momentary image of a brown wolf already in the middle of a punch to his face. Pain exploded from his nose and teeth and as instinct made him raise his hands defensively, precise strikes to the nerve clusters in his armpit and elbow actually made the tough ursine grunt. Like the others on the team, he had been trained to ignore pain, but it was the kick that shattered his knee was what made him finally howl.

He dropped into a fetal position and never saw the wolf pick up his gun and shoot him with it.

* * *

Michal plucked the useless comm-link from his ear and threw it against the wall. "What the fuck is going on?" the Czech wolf growled. His left ear was ringing but fortunately his job relied more on his eyes than his ears. He sighted through the scope again. He had seen the flash a hair before hearing the loud pop, but now, the balcony and windows were dark. Still closed, too. Michal pointed his scope toward the street and didn't see anything out of the ordinary.

His comm-link buzzed. "What's going on, Po'boy?" Clarice was yelling, though barely registering in the lupine's good ear. "Brennan? BRENNAN?"

For a moment, he considered taking his eyes off the hotel long enough to retrieve the damned thing. Benny, his spotter, wouldn't be able to relay anything to him this way, and the tigress would have his head if the target eluded capture because of him.

Just as he was cursing his impulsiveness, the door opened. The Glock he'd pulled in response went back into his shoulder rig a moment later. "Would you mind getting that for me?" He thumbed at the comm-link and returned his eye to the scope.

He heard the soft pull of a trigger, then every muscle in his body suddenly cramped. His nerves buzzed much like his ear, only with more pain. The rapid clicks of a fired stun gun were the last thing he heard before he lost consciousness.

Darius ziptied the wolf's hands behind his back, then bound his legs similarly. Before he left the room, he picked up comm-link and began tinkering with the internal settings, grinning widely as Clarice's shouts were cut off.

* * *

Two hours ago
Still driving the van, the crocodile followed his targets into the train station. It was easy enough – the binoculars made the unseen wolf stand out clearly against the crowd even at a hundred meters. He was closer than that; still, Darius had to hurry to catch up to them after they detoured down a hallway that had been closed for maintenance.

He didn't see anyone in the stark white, fluorescent-lit corridor but he did notice an alcove about twenty meters down. He hurried down to it as quietly as he could; the binoculars bounced on his chest and he felt like a fool tourist that had just missed their train. Voices spoke softly on the other side of the door and he turned the knob carefully before pushing it open.

Inside, the white wolf whirled around like a kid caught doing something he shouldn't have. The room was a break room of some kind; there were a couple of tables with chairs, a sink, refrigerator, microwave, and coffee maker. On one of the tables was a large duffel bag – the zipper was open and inside at the top was a life-like mask in the shape of a wolf's head.

"Sorry, I didn't mean to trespass," the wolf said smoothly, in a voice that seemed to resonate in the room. "I just stowed my bag here to do a little shopping and now…"

"Where is he?" the crocodile snarled, shutting the door and keeping his back firmly against it. He couldn't hear any movement and took that as a good sign.

The wolf smiled, though there was some nervousness beneath the surface. "I'm the only one…"

"Like hell you are. Where's your invisible friend?" The crocodile took a deep breath, ignoring the sudden surprise on the wolf's face. "I want to talk to him. Now."

"All right," a voice said to his right. The reptile whipped his muzzle around; unsurprisingly, no one was there. He would have sworn the agent was standing right next to him. "No sudden moves. Keep your hands where I can see… keep them in front of you."

Darius complied with exaggerated slowness.

"Now, then. You've got my attention. So, talk."

The crocodile complied and took another deep breath. "My name's Darius. I work for the TEA. And I'm part of Rising Force…"

* * *

Now

Spiritwolf knelt and checked the bear's pulse. Then he strolled over to the closet and knocked on it. "Clear."

Achilles slid the other side of the closet door open, pulled out his earplugs, and blanched upon seeing the prone figure. "You didn't… ?"

"He's alive." Spirit stood and put the tranquilizer gun on the bed after first removing the ammo and stowing it in the hotel safe. The mirror was cracked and the furniture had been jostled about, scattering papers from the desk all over the floor. "Time to prepare for the next phase, before the hotel staff show up to evacuate us. There aren't any alarms going off yet, so I figure we probably have a few minutes…"

They both jumped when Achilles' new cell phone rang. The singer peered at the screen to read the caller ID. "Guess who?" he said grimly and answered it. "Yeah?... okay, sure." He held out the phone for the agent.

"Go," Spirit said crisply.

"Delivery went smoothly for me," Darius' voice crackled in his ear.

The wolf looked down at the bear. "My package got broke."

"What?"

"Relax. It's still under warranty. Just needs some repair."

"Still a go for the last two?"

"As planned." Spirit paused. "I need directions for my next delivery."

"Across the street, on the roof. Remember the handling instructions I gave you?"

"Yeah, I remember. And that leaves…"

"She's MINE."

The croc's snarl made the agent smile. "Give her a big kiss from me, all right?"

"I'll do my best. Call you after the whistle blows."

"I'll buy the first round." Spiritwolf shut off the phone and caught the bemused stare from the other wolf. "What?"

"Do all of you agent types talk like that?"

"Not all of us. Just the witty ones."

"Hm. You know, you were very quick to trust him."

"Jealous?" Spirit handed the phone to him.

"No. Just curious." He watched the larger wolf take out all of the items in the duffel bag and put them neatly on the bed. Then, as if changing his mind, a few items went back inside. The agent set the grey-furred mask and gloves aside, then changed into them.

"Call it professional courtesy." The brown wolf head and hands were given to Achilles. "His intel so far has been on the money, so I'm willing to give him some slack for now. Don't worry. I'm still watching for any sign of a double-cross." The agent looked at the rock star – maybe it was the white wolf's body language or his demeanor or some other vibe – but he was suddenly struck by how uncertain Achilles was with everything that was going on, things that were happening out of his control. Spirit had been like that, too, when he was younger, and it had led him down some very dark roads indeed. "You going to be all right?" he asked softly.

"Yeah." Achilles scowled. "I just wish we were going after Regis."

There was a pause. "We will. One thing at a time." Nodding once to seal his promise, he exited the room.

Achilles stared at the unconscious bear for a long minute, thinking. Then he picked up the duffel bag and left the room.

* * *

The meerkat had listened to Clarice rage long enough. "What's done is done," he said calmly as he monitored the hotel through SDS-enhanced AR binoculars. He was dressed in a jacket, polo shirt and slacks; despite being on the roof, any observer was likely to think that he was just another tourist looking down at the night life in Arenosa. "You and I are the only ones talking, boss. We should assume the worst and fall back."

"No!" Benny winced at a fresh snarl right in his ear. It was rather uncharacteristic of her to be this rattled. "We get the target and finish the mission."

He stared thoughtfully at the window where the target was. Was that a shadow darkening the curtain? It didn't matter; Michal was off-line and wouldn't be shooting. "I think the mission's been compromised."

"What? How?"

"I think Green set us up."

"How very astute." The voice from behind made him spin, but instead of doing a one-eighty, he turned and ran along the edge of the roof, firing blindly back toward the source with his Glock 19. He dove behind a rectangular vent and peered over the top. The silhouette of a wolf poked his head cautiously from the lighted interior of the stairway door.

"Definitely a set-up," he muttered.

"What's going on, Captain?" Clarice was calm again, but there was an urgency underlying her question.

"I'm being chased by our target."

"I'll be right there."

"Best if you didn't. I can take care of him." There was an all-too-familiar staccato burst in his ear, then silence. *Guess she's busy, too.* He peeked and shot a few more rounds before ducking back. The wolf hadn't moved from the stairway — it was good cover as well as the only way down, so it made sense to stay there and wait. *Good strategy*, Benny thought. Too bad it wasn't going to work.

"I can see you, you know," he called out.

"Yeah?" was the gruff response.

"I'm just wondering why you didn't try to sneak up on me." He reached inside his vest and pulled out a palm-sized box. "Seems like the sort of thing to do, with your talents."

"I already know you've got the SDS algorithm. Kind of pointless. Like this bantering. Why don't you quit stalling and give up?"

A couple of warning shots from the agent didn't faze Benny; his career in the Israeli Defense Forces had taught him to not panic under difficult circumstances. He touched a button on the side; the LED winked green and then turned off a second later. He removed the paper to expose the adhesive and slapped it on the back of his jacket. Earplugs went deep into his ears. "All right. You win. Don't shoot – I'm coming out."

Benny strolled toward the door in a carefree manner. The wolf was still mostly behind the door and motioned down. "Drop the weapons and stay back." The meerkat obliged, laying his Glock and the earpiece on the ground, along with a knife that he pulled from his boot. He made sure to face the door so that he wouldn't give away the presence of the booby trap on his back.

The door opened a little wider and the wolf silhouette came around the door. The roof creaked just to the left of the meerkat and he idly wondered if it was built to code. "You're not quite as built as I thought you were," Benny observed with a smirk.

A sudden shove from his left sent the Rising Force agent tripping over something and he landed face-down. Before he could detonate the sonic screamer with the command word, it was ripped off his back and thrown over the side. Then his muzzle kissed the roof, hard.

"Don't move, smartass," a voice growled from above him. Despite the tears in his eyes, he watched the wolf by the door pull off the brown mask, revealing a smaller, white-pelted lupine head underneath. Coupled with the weight pinning him in place, it wasn't hard to figure out what had happened.

"Looks like your plan worked." Achilles brought the duffel bag over and then stepped back to block the doorway. Benny's hands were brought behind his back. A pair of cuffs floated from the bag and fastened to his wrists. Only then did the meerkat feel the heavy weight lift from his back.

"Yeah. Good thing Darius warned us about this guy's little devices." Rough searching of the meerkat led to the discovery of two more shivs and three compact boxes. He watched the invisible wolf dress using the clothes that had been stuffed into the duffel, and then he was hauled upright.

"Freak," Benny muttered.

The larger wolf snarled and punched his stomach. At the last second, the meerkat dodged the blow and head-butted Spiritwolf right in the sternum. The surprised agent sailed backward and landed hard; Achilles landed on top of him two seconds later. Benny flew past them and rushed down the stairs. He worked his wrists free by popping his thumbs out of joint and then back in. *Painful, but effective.* The earplugs came out as well.

The sound of pursuit came all too quickly. His brain processed lightning-fast what he heard: only one person and just a few floors above. *That damn freak's on my tail already. Time to go*, he thought and poured on the speed. With his hands free, it was easy to leap over railings and land nimbly on a narrow stair before vaulting down again – the most basic parkour move learned on day one. He noted with grim satisfaction that the thudding from above grew more distant the further he went.

He exited on level fourteen and tore through the hallway. He and Michal had stationed themselves in the Sunrise hotel, across the street from the Oro. The wolf was up on level thirty-two, but Benny had heard him get zapped and didn't want to risk running into the croc or any other TEA agent that might be around. He had to disappear quickly.

Benny pulled the fire alarm.

Warning sirens immediately screeched and he slowed to a walk, forcing himself to breathe normally even though his heart pounded and his lungs screamed for more air. He pretended to tie his shoelaces and waited for guests to pour out of their rooms before rising again and shuffling along as though part of the herd.

"Can you believe this?" he grumped to a rumpled husband-and-wife rat couple who had hastily thrown on the barest of clothes.

"Yeah, fucking annoying," the male said in an American accent. He was dressed in boxer shorts. "I hear there's a science fiction convention in the hotel… one of those assholes probably did this."

"Well, be sure to ask for compensation from the hotel staff," Benny replied sympathetically. "They'll lay into the organization, for sure. Say," he added. "You're probably cold. Why don't you take my jacket?" He took it off and handed it to the rat.

"Oh, I'll be fine. It's warm enough out."

"I insist," the meerkat said, grinning. "I would feel bad if you got sick because you caught a cold. Besides, I still have a shirt on." He pointed to his tan polo. "Don't you agree, ma'am?"

"All right," the male said, gruffly taking it before his wife could say anything. They all slowed down and melted in with the throng of taller folks congregating at the stairway door opposite from the one Benny had emerged from. "Thanks," he said and led his wife down the stairs.

"My pleasure," the meerkat murmured and let a family of bears go ahead before following. Blending in with the crowd was easy enough to do, especially given his height. He hunched his shoulders forward and stooped his back a little, like his father had been in his later years. With his muzzle and ears downcast, he gave the appearance of being twenty years older than he was.

Benny emerged from the stairwell and vigorously rubbed his face to further obscure his identity. He ruffled his fur on his arms and his head – presto, he had just been awakened from a sound sleep. He lingered in the thick of the gathering crowd, surreptitiously glancing between people to see if he'd been spotted. The white wolf wasn't there and Benny obviously didn't know whether the invisible wolf was about, but as long as he stayed where people were packed in, there was little chance he'd be found without noticing folks being strangely shoved aside. More than likely, the lupines had gone back to the roof to try and spot him, but there was a still chance the unseen agent was outside, lurking. He had to leave, while he was still anonymous.

Or, he could try to lure the invisible wolf to him.

As tempting as it was to finish the mission, the practicality of it just wasn't there. He had none of his gizmos on him. He was at a distinct disadvantage in a physical fight. His team couldn't help him; he didn't even know whether the tigress had been captured. His only real option was to keep going, avoid capture and report back to the others. Wailing sirens in the distance added another layer of concern.

Benny stepped cautiously toward the street and glanced around. A fox couple to his left, a dingo to his right, and the family of bears again in front. Behind was a grumbling river otter holding hands with an older, much more cheerful golden retriever with square-rimmed glasses. No one appeared to have noticed him. So he took a few more tentative steps, then slow-danced his way past a fennec and a weasel. The meerkat thought he heard breathing in his ear, but when he turned, it was only a fat bull, exhaling with a rumble that set his overlarge stomach in motion.

"I'm bored, let's go DO something." Curbside, a college-age otter was tugging his two friends – a hyena and a burly jaguar – toward an idling taxi. Benny approached them cautiously and overheard the jaguar mumble something about doing too much in a resort town. The meerkat grinned and looked back over his shoulder at the shuffling crowd.

A loud shout caught his attention and he saw the male rat with his jacket suddenly get bowled over. His wife screamed and began swinging her purse wildly around. One of the swings, Benny noted, appeared to hit something and the purse rebounded back to the surprised woman's hands.

The meerkat dodged around the waiting trio and in a flash, dove into the taxi. "The Salamander Club," he snarled at the driver, an elderly wolf. The bespectacled eyes studied him momentarily then the vehicle merged smoothly into traffic. Benny's heart raced and he peeked through the back window as they departed the scene. Nothing out of the ordinary now but he knew what he had seen. Two blocks further and after several shifts from one side of the cab to the other, he finally began to relax.

His swirling thoughts coalesced. He had, to all appearances, escaped intact. At the club, he could bide his time until he could get a ride out. He'd have to make a few calls, but there were agents in the IDF still around who would help their former fellow soldier. And if Clarice had somehow managed to survive, he thought with a smirk, maybe he would convince the Rising Force leadership that he was best suited to lead their team. After all, he could provide a first-hand account of the target's abilities and weaknesses. All she had to show for their efforts was the capture of two and the betrayal of a third teammate.

If she hadn't survived, the convincing would be much easier.

Benny was combing through strategies of how to defeat the target when the taxi pulled up to his destination. The Salamander Club was in the seedier end of town but the women inside were still of superb quality, so it attracted a robust clientele despite its location. He handed a credit card to the driver; a swipe and a quick signature later, it was handed back to him. The meerkat exited and waved to the bouncer, an overly large rhino in a dark suit and shades, then brushed aside the red curtains made to look like flames. He found a table that had a large plant partially blocking line-of-sight to the entrance and a clear path to the rear exit – perfect for his needs.

Benny sat and watched the nude vixen bend over and give the crowd a shake of her breasts before somersaulting and stopping on her back with her legs in a wide 'V'. The roar of all the males in the place kept swelling with each pose of simulated sex she struck and Benny used the noise as cover to make the call on his cell. He'd be out of town by morning.

A white-furred hand closed over his wrist and twisted; he dropped the phone and was about to counter but he stopped when he saw who was holding him.

"Long time no see," Gareth Zirkowski growled. Benny was about to protest but one look at the polar bear's bared teeth shut him up. A quick assessment confirmed his instincts – *he's stressed underneath the pissed-off expression, best to find out what he wants first.* Zirkowski and the two male CATS agents that flanked him – an otter and a serval – were all dressed to the nines and he could see the outlines of their weapons.

"And speaking of that," the director continued, "you're going to tell me everything you know about a certain wolf that you've been after…"

* * *

Thirty minutes ago.

"Sir! I think I have something!"

Gareth grunted and padded over to Ardal's monitor. His mood had deteriorated with no leads after nearly eighteen hours. "What?"

The wolf pointed to the screen. "Satellite picked up someone on the roof of the Sunrise Hotel, across the street from the Oro."

"Yeah? Is it the wolf?"

"No. It's a meerkat. Someone we're familiar with." She closed her fist in front of an adjacent terminal and mimed throwing an object toward hers. A window disappeared from the other screen and reappeared in front of her.

Gareth studied the new records in the window next to the satellite image. Honorable discharge from the IDF five years ago, provided advanced technology consulting to a number of defense agencies for three years after that, including the CATS, and then off the grid until now. His history went back through college, then high school, and grade school – he was a prodigy, no surprise there. The polar bear peered at the numerous projects he'd worked on during his IDF days: sound-based weapons, shaped charges and other explosives, energy shield technology, cyberwarfare, even some biological and chemical weapons research.

"Good work," Zirkowski rumbled. Then he straightened up and began speaking in a voice everyone could hear. "Ladies and gentlemen, we have a new secondary target – Benyamin David Anhalem." Gareth pressed a button on Ardal's keyboard; the meerkat's military ID photo appeared on the wall-to-wall screen behind him. "He's ex-IDF and extremely dangerous. Orent, you and the rest of your team set up a tight net, five block radius minimum." A rail-thin rabbit toward the back nodded and began gathering his operatives in one corner of the room. "Faisal, you've got point. Lock in on him and don't let him out of your sight." A dark brown fox with short curly hair and devious black eyes grinned. "Everyone else, monitor video and comms for the hotels, adjacent areas and all transportation. Trips will be coordinating and will liaise with the field personnel." The ebon-furred panther stepped into Zirkowski's place and took charge of the remaining CATS.

The polar bear put a hand on Ardal's shoulder. "And you, my dear," he said in a hushed voice, "are going to be keeping a much closer eye on our primary target…"

* * *

Now

Darius knew he shouldn't have gone with a direct assault, but Clarice had been on the move since Michal had been taken down. He had used their comm system to backtrack her to an American-style shopping mall just west of the Oro. The mall was closed for the evening; entry had been gained by picking the lock on a delivery door.

When he finally found her, she was in a conference room in one of the corporate offices, staring out the window and talking to Benny. The croc had whipped out his gun and fired but she had seen his reflection in the window and dove behind the long mahogany table. Glass shattered noisily into a million shards that flew everywhere. Darius knew to not remain in the doorway admiring his work and so he took off down the hall as bullets tore through the drywall behind him. He shot the lock on a security door and sprinted toward the mall proper – the end of the corridor seemed much too far and it was too soon that he heard his pursuer's footfalls.

"You TRAITOR!" he heard her snarl from the corridor. "This is all your fault!" She emptied the rest of her clip at the zigzagging reptile, who somehow managed to avoid intersecting her line of fire.

"Damn right, bitch!" Darius taunted as he rounded the corner and dove for the sheltering alcove of the first store he saw. His belly took most of the impact but he stifled a groan and spun around to his back and faced the corridor. As he did, he glimpsed the sign above the store; it was a "BNC" – Books and Coffee – megastore. *I couldn't have found a sporting goods store, could I? Of course not, because that would have been helpful.* He aimed his gun carefully at the alcove opening leading back into the corridor.

Clarice didn't appear.

"Fuck," he swore and slowly got up, hugging the wall like a long-lost friend, and carefully listened. Nothing… not even breathing, as far as he could tell. He peered at the BNC's glass windows to check the store across the way but they weren't angled right. So he squatted back down and crab-walked the few meters back to the corridor and looked for himself. Very empty.

He got up and swept his gaze across the upper level as he tried to puzzle out where the tigress could have gone. It only took him a dozen seconds to figure it out and after checking a mall directory, he began jogging through the deserted mall toward the east wing.

How did it ever get to this? Darius looked longingly at a bakery as he passed by. *I mean, it's not like I'm even friends with the fre… Spiritwolf.* The wolf had been part of the super-secret Ultra team, or so the croc had learned upon joining Rising Force, when some kind of accident during a "lab grab" had rendered him invisible. The psych profile he'd been given indicated that the wolf occasionally went rogue during an op (though usually for good reason), had borderline insubordination issues with his superiors (idiots, by his reckoning). But he was smart, honest, and stuck up for his teammates. He had integrity. Despite her claims of team play, Clarice suffered from a severe lack of the same. Her threat in the restaurant had brought that into sharp focus. She was smart and had a hot body, but damn, she was arrogant. And ambitious. The bitch would stop at nothing to get what she wanted, no matter who was in the way. And so the conclusion Darius had reached was that he probably matched up with more of Spiritwolf's traits and less of Clarice's. Besides, he didn't take threats to his life at all lightly – one of his own personal quirks of character – which had led him to pursue the previously unthinkable. Welcome to now.

That wolf had better keep his word. Darius approached his destination, the main security room, and stopped to calm his breathing. Security took up residence in one of the corporate offices at the other end of the mall from where he'd been. And of course, anyone inside would have access to the feeds from numerous cameras throughout the mall. Thank goodness this was Europe – only police officers would be armed at a shopping mall, not the security guards. Darius suddenly realized just how useful Spiritwolf's talent could be, while looking at a CCTV camera aimed right at him from across the way.

Shit. The croc casually walked out of the camera's field of view toward the next office over. *How the hell am I going to get in without being seen?* He waited, pointing his gun back at the door. *Maybe she didn't notice. Nah, that can't be right. The bitch must have seen me. But she's trapped in there, too, right?* He wished he had an interior layout of the place. Darius took a quiet step forward.

He wasn't sure whether he heard the gun go off before or after he felt the searing pain in his right shoulder. The croc twisted from the impact and his own gun dropped from his useless hand before he could yell, which he did loudly along with several choice curses. "Silly child," a cold, familiar voice tsked behind him. Darius leaned heavily against the wall, barely standing and eyes shut tight to keep his tears from showing. The pain was overwhelming; the bullet had probably broke his arm. A strong leg shoved his backside indelicately and he toppled over like a drunk at 4 A.M. He nearly threw up, too.

"So, you think you can play with the big girls?" Claws raked the back of his neck, shredding through scales easily. Then a hard-booted foot came down on his head; a decent stomp that nearly shattered his skull. A hand grabbed the back of his neck and lifted his head up; this time, there was thick fluid oozing from his nostrils. The hand turned his head around and he stared up at Clarice through nearly closed eyes.

"It is far too easy to out-think you," she hissed and spat in his face before grabbing his head and driving it down again into the carpeted floor. The tigress unleashed several vicious kicks to his ribs; through the growing fog of pain, he was still glad that his family jewels were somewhat protected in the fetal position he was in. The fight was gone from him, though, and he was growing tired with each new beating his body took. *Please, God*, he begged. *Make it stop. Let me die.* He would die trying to do the right thing, to atone for his mistake to Spiritwolf. Spiritwolf. The invisible wolf… had to be nearby. Just waiting for the right time to come in and save him. He hoped.

"…pathetic waste of space," she was saying. Then his vision exploded into stars; she had kicked his eyes. Or tried to – he couldn't feel anything anymore. *It will be over soon*, he told himself. There was nothing left in him, now. Not even surrender.

He heard a soft whisper. It caught his attention – was it Spiritwolf, come to save him? Or was he already dead? Darius couldn't hear anything.

"…you still with us… ?"

Someone was gently touching his face. Tapping. "Spirit… wolf?" he croaked.

"No."

The croc opened an eye, just a crack. A white fox was examining his face, lightly touching the broken bones, tracing the bruises and wiping away the blood. "Where… she… ?" His breathing has some burbling to it. The pain was fading… they must have given him the really good shit.

"In custody. Where you will be as well, soon enough." The fox worked grimly but there was an underlying gentleness in his touch. "My name is Inverno."

"What… ? How… ? Aren't you… part of the… group in Rome?"

"Best not to talk. You've been beaten badly, you're concussed. I'm sure you have internal injuries. We'll be taking you to the Arenosa Medical Center – they have a fairly advanced surgical bay there. You're going to need it." Inverno motioned to someone outside of Darius' field of vision, which was frighteningly tiny. Then the croc heard, "One, two, *three!*" and he was floating, coming to rest gently on a gurney. Only then did he see the prone body of Clarice sprawled inelegantly on the floor. *She's… still breathing. Can't win them all.*

"I flew up for a meeting. Spiritwolf called and gave me your cell number so that we could track you. He told me you were part of Rising Force, said you helped him despite that, and that you'll cooperate with our investigation but he didn't fill me in on what you were after." The fox looked askance at him with a curious look of concern. "If Spiritwolf is still in danger, you need to tell me. I can help him."

Darius closed his eyes and giggled under the influence of the painkillers. "Nothing... can dooz... gon... na... help... himmmm..." he slurred and then lost consciousness.

* * *

"I'm glad he's all right." An hour later, Spiritwolf was comparing notes with Inverno in the alley behind the Oro. Brennan was already safely secured – and still asleep – in an unmarked van that also held the tranquilized bodies of Clarice and Michal.

The white fox was studying him. "And you say you didn't catch the meerkat?"

"I failed at that." Spirit had figured out Benny's plan as soon as he'd heard the fire alarm go off. He had nearly panicked, surrounded by the throng of hotel guests outside; in his haste, he'd mistakenly gone after the rat. The rat's wife had scored a direct hit on his injured arm with her heavy handbag, nearly causing him to cry out in pain. He'd had no choice but to retreat after that and try to find his quarry from someplace other than in the middle of the crowd. He finally gave up after the crowd had dispersed.

Inverno nodded. "Well, four of five is still a job well done. We'll deal with them and find out what they're all about."

"Sounds good." Spirit hoped that Zero and Ixak would put a stop to anything that led back to him. Or the other surviving Ultras. "Like I said over the phone, Darius will tell you what you need to know about Rising Force."

"In all honesty, I am rather surprised that he is cooperating. How did it come to that?"

"Something about hating the tigress, I think." The wolf looked at the traffic, still heavy even for being this late in the evening – still early for those who played in Arenosa. "Time for us to part ways, I think. It's been quite the day and my arm's still healing, too. Thanks again, Inverno."

"Of course." The fox hesitated, then held out a hand. "I hope we get the chance to work again in the future, *amico mio*."

Spirit smiled and shook it. "Just like old times." Inverno nodded and grinned before getting back in the van and giving instructions to the driver. The agent watched them go and sighed. *Just like old times, except that things have changed.* If Spirit were to come calling, odds were that some kind of very serious trouble wouldn't be far behind. It was something he wouldn't want to expose Inverno to. Or anyone else, for that matter.

Achilles, unfortunately, was already in it deeper than Spirit wanted. But the agent had no choice – there wasn't anyone else he could trust that knew of his secret. Heck, the rock star had already been privy to more information than most TEA agents knew about. Spirit idly wondered whether Achilles would make a good agent, given the proper training.

Nah.

Spiritwolf set his musings aside and went back into the hotel lobby, where the white wolf was waiting for him. "How did it go?"

"Nothing unexpected. Handed over our friends and then said goodbye." They walked to the elevator. "Thanks for your help. You did a good job."

"I guess I did, despite getting bowled on top of you. Can't argue with the results, though." The elevator doors closed. "What about the meerkat?"

"We'll keep an eye out for him. And since too many people know your itinerary, I think it's time we took a different route."

Achilles frowned. "I still have a tour to run, and without Regis, it's going to be very slow going."

"What about… what's his name? Grant?"

"He's still wet behind the ears. Though he's not half-bad," Achilles admitted. "I absolutely need to be present for the equipment transfers and checks. Other than that, well, we already had to cancel our charter flight to Paris because of Regis' departure. I haven't re-booked anything yet."

Spirit nodded. "Excellent. I'll procure our transportation. How many are coming with us?"

"There's a dozen of us in the 'inner circle', now, if we include the new bodyguards. Twenty more crew, but they travel separately. Grant can take care of rebooking them."

"All right." The doors opened and they went to Spirit's room. "I need to check in with the folks back in the States," the agent said once the door had closed. "And I still need to work on the jackals' laptop."

"What about Regis? Is there anything on that special laptop that the… uh… bug left?"

Spiritwolf went over to the desk and ran a quick check. "Nothing yet. I'll let you know if I find anything."

Achilles nodded. "Fine." He paused. "We're not planning to work out in the morning, are we?"

Spirit laughed. "No. I think we're a little beyond that."

Achilles smiled. "Pity – I was starting to enjoy them. Well, maybe we could do one when this is all over."

"I think that could be arranged. Get some rest, rock star."

"You do the same." Achilles left the room and went up to his floor, where he found David and Lars finally beginning to wake up. *Things have certainly changed*, he mused and approached them.

They quickly got to their feet. "We... we were shot by the room service guy," Lars blurted. "We need to go find him!"

"Don't worry – my friend already took care of him." Achilles looked them both up and down and shook his head. "Your first job for me and you were taken down? You certainly don't have a strong position to start from for your salary negotiations." They both looked crestfallen and Achilles sighed. "Stay out here and make sure I'm not bothered."

"We won't fail you again," David said and motioned for his brother to follow him down the hall. They took up position on either side of his door like twin columns framing the entrance to a building from ancient times.

Achilles rolled his eyes and was about to follow them when he heard the elevators open again. Cain was the first one out and the smile on his face vanished upon seeing the singer. "How was Diagonals?" the wolf said cheerfully.

"Peachy." The badger shrugged and didn't say another word. *Things have indeed changed.* But ever since the old lion had caught him doing after-hours recordings in school, he hadn't ever bothered to look back and reflect; he just kept moving forward. Everything had come to him so quickly – fame, fortune, new friends, partnerships – all of his successes had made him into the person he was.

Had he unknowingly discarded something along the way that which could have made him even better? And did that mean he had failed, because he wasn't that better person?

Others came out from the elevator as he stood there in silent contemplation, laughing and essentially ignoring him in their drunken stumbling down the hall to their rooms. Garrick had returned to his reclusive self, slinking quietly along. Les and a well-muscled ram were sharing their own amusements. The lizard saw Achilles and gave him a haughty sneer before tugging his catch of the evening into his room.

Failure. The word buzzed in his head like a testy neon sign. His muzzle curled angrily. If Spirit had never shown up, he'd be having a great time with his band, tearing up Europe with a tour that would make the music gods take notice. No... if Regis had never become his manager... He couldn't even say that. Some of the problems were his own doing, like Spiritwolf had said. They all shared in the blame for this tour going askew.

Achilles rubbed his head. It was like someone had taken the jigsaw puzzles of their lives and mixed them all up. It would be nearly impossible to sort out all the pieces, separate them, and get things back on track. It was an awful mess that had landed in his lap and he needed to deal with reality, not the fantasy of invisible agents and black market tech dealers.

"I'm going to Diagonals," he called back to his bodyguards. "Stay here. I'll be back later." He stabbed the down button and suddenly realized he was very thirsty.

* * *

Two hours later, after a brief phone call with Zero where the bear had done little more than listen before saying "Good work, keep going," and disconnecting, Spirit had finally cracked the encryption on the jackals' laptop's hard drive. He scanned through the directory structure and found a folder called "Survey" which turned out to have information on him and his association with the TEA. It also had an electronic copy of a CATS memo stated that they were to monitor but not engage in any action unless in defense. The memo was signed by their director, Gareth Zirkowski.

Spirit leaned back in his chair. He'd heard of Zirkowski – a well-respected and feared leader within the intelligence community. There had been several joint operations between the TEA and the CATS over the years and at least one had ended very badly, with the deaths of two TEA agents. Some had claimed a set-up and Zero had gone so far as to withdraw offers of support for further joint operations. Nothing had been proven, though, which meant that the bear had dealt with it in the most efficient way possible – eliminate further problems by exclusion.

Why must things be so difficult? He rose and took off the rest of his clothes; he'd taken off his mask, contacts, and gloves as soon as Achilles had left. Invisible again, he formed a wolf-shaped indentation on the bed as he relaxed and let his mind wander. While training to become an Ultra, Greystorm had suggested the technique as a means to let his brain process the huge amounts of sense data and reading material that was part of his everyday life as an agent. The creative, associative part of his brain could then go to work and make nonlinear associations and leaps of logic that connected dots his linear, mathematical side missed.

Your invisibility is a part of you, but it does not define you. Master Song had said that and Ixak had reinforced it. Spirit realized that he was getting comfortable with his unique nature but it hadn't controlled him. The temptations had, with one exception, been reined in and for the most part, he'd used his advantage judiciously. The discipline he'd learned with the TEA, with the world-class martial arts lessons, had kept him on an even keel. And his friends, old and new, kept him grounded. He would succeed on all fronts of his mission.

Soft beeping made him scramble toward Ixak's computer. The agent clicked on the playback button and listened to a scrambled version of Regis' voice announce…

* * *

"Congratulations to the bidder on this frequency. You are the winner of the auction for the tablet that was formerly the property of Conway National Labs. The transfer will be at *l'Ossuaire Municipal* in Paris, at the Crypt of the Sepulchral Lamp at 10:04 P.M., the day after tomorrow. The details of the rules of engagement for the exchange have already been made clear, but there are several important ones that bear repeating. You may bring up to two witnesses with you. No weapons of any kind are permitted. The payment will be to a Swiss bank account via computer transfer. After the exchange, my team shall depart; your team will wait fifteen minutes before departing. Again, congratulations, and I look forward to the exchange."

The elephant concluded by selecting the "Quit" button, which reset the modulation and cut off the transmitter. He shut off power to the oblong box and looked at the trio watching him. Pi was lounging on the couch, martini glass in hand and feigning disinterest. The black wolf called Ramsden was sitting across the desk from him with a huge grin on his muzzle. He was shirtless and wore only thin cotton shorts, having just returned from a workout at a nearby gym. The third member was Hikiwake, a percheron horse whose muscularity rivaled Regis'. He stood with his back to the wall, his mane done up in a topknot in the style of the ancient samurai. He even looked the part, wearing a white cotton robe. His grey eyes narrowed – the only hint of emotion on his otherwise solemn demeanor.

"Gentlemen," Regis said. "Welcome to the endgame."

* * *

The security entourage got off the business jet first and only when one member of the wall announced "Clear" did the VIP step down the ladder and head to where the limousine was waiting.

"Well, boys," Blair Murdock announced. "I think I'll start my vacation by taking in some of the sights that this lovely city has to offer. I hear the Catacombs are just lovely this time of year," he added with a deep laugh.

* * *

Achilles stopped talking when he heard the light knock. The white wolf was standing by the door and he glanced toward the window, making a shushing motion. The coastline was speeding by quickly as the clacking train finally reached its cruising speed. When the room was silent, the white wolf opened the door.

"Sorry to disturb you, sir." A lovely brown-furred wolfess had a food trolley in front of her. "I was wondering whether you and your guest might want something to eat?"

"Oh, you must be mistaken. I'm quite alone, as you can see." Achilles stepped back and let her see that the rest of the room was indeed empty.

"But…" she said with a cute pout. "I thought I heard you talking to someone."

"Oh, that. I like to bounce ideas around by pretending that I'm having a dialogue with a friend." He smiled charmingly. "You'd be surprised at what gets thought of."

She nodded and blushed. "My mistake, sir. Would you like anything to eat?"

"No, thank you. Free hotel breakfast, you see. I may stop by later, though, if I'm feeling peckish."

"Of course. The dining car is available for the entire trip to Paris. Thank you, sir." The white wolf closed the door and Ardal smiled as she pushed the trolley toward the next room.

Chapter Nine: Dust to Dust

In a dark room underground where all light was stolen, Gareth Zirkowski stood with his back to the cold stone wall, expectant fire in his eyes. In his hand was the smoldering remains of a cigarette; by his left shoulder was the outline of a toothless skull, embedded into the cobbled surface. This grim visage was not alone in its watch; all around the small room, planted into the dark surfaces, were the blank scalps of the dead of every species, all looking upon the polar bear with the blank expression of those sleeping the ageless sleep. The silence was broken only by the gurgling of a hidden aqueduct buried in the stone, channeling a hidden spring or sewer away from the area. The whole place had a gloomy, dank quality; an ossuary of irrefutable age and importance. The Catacombs of Paris; *l'Ossuaire Municipal*. And for the bear, something else; the place of meeting.

He blew out a puff of smoke that disappeared into shadow and considered the bones for a moment, the piles upon piles of dead that lay here. These men and women could have been anything; paupers or princes, bankers or bakers. Whatever they had been in life, however important or unimportant they had been, was now lost. All that was left were their dry husks, forever interred in a mausoleum beneath the feet of a city that had seen centuries come and go. Stared over by countless tourists; nameless. Shameless.

The white bear's eye flicked up to the eastern arch that led into the room, looking upon the inscription again. *Arrête! C'est ici l'empire de la Mort.*

"Halt…" he whispered, translating aloud, his voice gravelly and alone. "This is the empire of Death…"

"Truer words were never spoken," came a familiar, distinguished voice from the darkness of one of the many other portals that accessed the room.

Immediately the bear drew himself to attention, flicking the cigarette away, and brought himself around to face the man whose footsteps he had been expecting and dreading.

"Blair…" the director growled in recognition, dusting down his cuffs as a golden lion in a well-pressed suit emerged into the bone-ridden room. "It's been too long."

The feline did not so much enter the space, as puncture it, setting all the shadows into sharp relief with his outline, his presence. The lamp that illuminated the space seemed to flicker for a moment, even though it was electric. Blair Murdock stood against the opposite wall to the bear, hands in his trouser pockets. Half his face was in darkness; the other half was so alight with inscrutable enmity that he could have been mistaken more for a demon than a lion. And yet he placidly smiled, assuredly, and nodded to Gareth expectantly. "Yes… it was over a decade ago when we were last face-to-face, wasn't it? How time flies…"

"You've always been content to pull the strings of your web from afar," the ursine answered, his own British accent sounding ragged and common next to the regal overtones of the lion. "Spider that you are."

The lion smirked. "Spider, am I? Goodness. If it wasn't so apt, I might almost take that as an insult. Are you trying to insult me, Gareth?"

"I'm not going to dance with you, Blair," the bear answered, drawing himself up to his full height. "Insurance or not; stop prevaricating. You don't just fly into the middle of this without a reason. You don't summon me here without a reason. So cut to the chase."

"You think you can give me orders now?" Blair snapped. "My, my. Something *has* made you bold." He stepped closer, taking his hands out of his pockets finally. Gareth had expected a gun, but they were empty. His own weapon was an obvious bulge in the corner pocket of his suit, a comforting weight. "You think you have something," Blair continued, staring deep into the bear's eyes, as if reading him. "Something that gives you power over me."

Gareth gritted his teeth, intending to keep his cards close to his chest. "Maybe." He rumbled, eyeing Blair up carefully.

"Oh, don't be so coy," the lion charmingly replied, extending his hand for a moment as if in admiration. "I know all about the power of information. I know how tiny little secrets keeps people in their place… the power of control." He stepped back to his original position facing opposite, and raised his eyebrow. "Yes, you're a sucker for information, just like me." He purred, rolling his shoulders. "Shame. I don't like that trait in people that work for me, but I do respect it. But yes, Gareth, I *am* here for a reason, a reason that should be obvious; you've failed me."

"Cut the crap. I can still get the tablet, and you know it. I haven't-"

"*Could* get it; but you *should* already have it," Blair interrupted. "And as I was sitting in my office I thought to myself… if I send my PA to grab me a coffee, and she takes longer than the task requires… I don't put up with it." The eye illuminated by the dark suddenly flashed with menace. "I get a new PA."

"I know about him!" the bear hissed, taking on board the message. Revealing his card at last. "I know everything now. It's not the tablet you want; it's him." He gritted his teeth. "I'll get him for you…"

"No," Blair countered, unimpressed. "You really won't." As quick as a cobra strikes, he raised his hand and gave one click of his claws, which echoed like a bullet throughout the dusty passages. Immediately, six red dots appeared upon Blair's chest, dancing like fireflies. From the six different entrances, the laser-targets of the unseen gunmen pointed their weapons upon the director.

Too stunned to grab his gun, Gareth stepped back. "What is this? Ardal, you were supposed to warn me of an ambush!" Heart pounding in his chest, he lifted his hand up to his left ear to check that the speaker was working. There was nothing but crackling silence. Where was his team? He never came to a meeting like this unprepared. It shouldn't have been like this…

"Ah yes…" Blair purred, pleased at the reaction, tail twitching. "Ardal. Ambitious girl; I think I'm going to like working with her." He stepped over to Gareth, dominating him completely, and disarmed the bear by casually retrieving the gun from inside the bear's jacket. He saw the hatred in the deputy director's eyes and laughed, feeling in the mood to impart some final nuggets of wisdom. "Oh, Gareth… there's just one thing men like us have to watch out for when we gather our facts, one thing you are going to painfully learn now; who gives you the information is as important as the information itself…"

"So, she's betrayed me," the bear gravely observed.

"Only as much as you thought you could betray me by taking the invisible agent for yourself and trading him for the leash I have around your neck!" Blair roared, shaking his head, his mane shifting. "I always thought you were better than that. You make me feel sad, Gareth." He lifted the bear's gun, pointing it at the director.

"Stop this," Gareth pleaded, his options limited. "You've made your point. I'll give you my prisoner, the meerkat. Leave it to me and I'll grab this 'Spiritwolf' for you. When Black Dust comes here tomorrow night, he'll be here. Then we'll say no more about it."

"He's already *my* prisoner," Blair growled, his face looking sickened by the plea. "Ardal saw to that. But don't worry, you're going to help me in your own way."

Gareth's eyes locked with the predator's in a deadly embrace. He saw his end written there. "How?" he asked, knowing full well he would probably never ask another question again.

Blair smiled. "You're going to send a message," he purred, as the red dots coalesced into an angry pattern between the bear's yellow eyes. "One which Paris will never forget."

* * *

A little while later, far removed from the horrors below, a white wolf stirred from fitful sleep, waking to a room he did not know, from a nightmare he could not remember.

Achilles looked about the Parisian hotel room, shivering. The tour had crept into the city in the small hours of the night. In a state of near exhaustion he'd made it into his bed, desperately needing sleep but unable to drift off, feeling the fingers of danger still squeezing about his throat. First light was only just breaking now upon this part of the world and the first thing he noticed, sitting up, was the fluttering curtain of the window next to his bed. Mumbling something, he rose, gingerly, and nakedly walked over to it, pulling it closed without too much noise.

Over his shoulder was the ornate chamber decorated in typical French Rococo style, as only the old hotels of Europe were possibly able to provide. Luxurious and suffocating both with its gilded mirror frames, hand-painted wall panels, and dried flowers in vases. Slumped in a chair by the door, Lars sat half-snoring, beefy arms folded across his chest, sleeping in his clothes, upright. His brother David would be on the other side, awake in the hallway. He understood that through the night the pair would exchange places, taking turns between sleep and keeping watch.

And yet Achilles felt one tenth as safe with them keeping watch, as he would have with Spirit keeping guard.

The wolf looked over the room, still half-asleep. "Spirit…" he whispered into the dark corners. "Are you there… Spirit?" Hopeful. Wondering.

When no reply came, he sighed and looked out the window again. The soft light from the east was just now starting to barely illuminate the buildings; he heard gentle rumblings below from the occasional car; the city starting to turn back to life. When he looked upon it all, all events coming to mind, he shuddered. He'd always thought there was something just a little off about Paris, something off-putting, unfriendly, just beneath the surface of civility…

As he dragged himself back to bed, hoping to catch a little more sleep, he couldn't shake the feeling that he was about to have his opinion about the city confirmed… in the worst possible way.

He put his head down upon the pillow, closed his eyes, and sighed.

* * *

Not too long after, at the very heart of the old metropolis, a shocking discovery was made.

Monsieur Bertrand was an unremarkable man, the aging stoat small and disheveled in the early morning light, completely disconnected from the eddy of events even then swirling about the city like a gathering storm. He was of no importance, save for being the first to witness a bizarre scene that would send shockwaves throughout the fragmented intelligence communities of the old powers of Europe.

From his tiny rooftop apartment he emerged, skulking along the slowly disappearing shadows, feeling the nip of settling cold upon his fingertips, his mackintosh grey and weather-beaten like the fur on his face. He stood upon the rooftop of the Louvre; the museum beneath his feet centuries old in prominence and size. It felt like he had been its caretaker for nearly as long – mending the gates, sweeping the corridors, polishing the railings. Everybody who worked there knew him; nobody acknowledged him. He was just Bertrand, of no importance, caring for the building he loved.

He cared for the old more than the new, that much was certain; and as he went about his daily ritual of feeding the pigeons – an act he performed always in spite of his better judgment – his thoughts turned again to the Louvre Pyramid, an ugly construction of metal and glass that had blotted the courtyard of the old building since 1989. No matter how often he looked upon the glass building, no matter how beloved it had become in the heart of Parisians, to him it was always an eyesore. From his rooftop perch, he seemed to turn, and regard it angrily again, like it was a bothersome fly flitting about the edge of his vision, instead of a building.

Yet, for a second, he sensed something different about it that morning. Something unexpected. A difference. His hand dropping to his side, still clutching the birdseed, he turned and walked over to the edge, hands touching the cold surface of the rooftop barrier, peering intently at the structure in the middle of the courtyard. Right to the top, where instead of ending in a point… there was a kind of shape sitting atop it. The light was still too weak for him to make it out properly, but it almost looked like…

Now the birdseed tumbled from his hand as he hurried over to his telescope, normally reserved for his lunch break when he spied upon the flocks of tourists below, marveling at their silent, unknown stories. Muzzle dry, he squinted, pointing it away from the plaza, dizzyingly following it up to the very tip of the Glass Pyramid.

The sheets of glass shimmered out of sight, as he found himself looking in the dawn at the most incredible, sickening thing. "*Mon Dieu...*" he whispered, staring into the cold, dead eyes of one Gareth Zirkowski.

The broken bear's body slumped over the very tip of the pyramid, placed there by means that would be speculated over intensely in the hours and days to come.

Monsieur Bertrand was an unremarkable man, but he was the first to call in the body… and the first to announce his retirement, the very next day.

* * *

It wasn't just Paris that got the message.

On the other side of the world, where night had just recently descended from the sky, a different bear, very much still alive, was walking down a startlingly luminescent corridor deep underground. Zero nodded to a fox in a white lab coat that passed him by, taking his time as he walked, deep in thought. It had been a long day; on top of his other work, he had been spending considerable time working on the *Rising Force* incursion. Even for a secret organization, prisoners still generated paperwork, and there was plenty flying his way now. The fact that Clarice had been behind so much of it was particularly troubling; after Ixak and his people had finished his interrogation, the bear intended to extradite her to American soil, where he personally could get to the bottom of how she had gotten away with so much, particularly the theft of the SDS algorithm.

That was to come; for now, he was thinking about getting some shuteye, with the hour growing late. But there was someone he had to visit first. Reaching the end of the corridor on level 11, the director came to a large steel-plated door that was several inches thick. Still brooding, he put his hand upon the palm-reader to the side of the portal, waiting patiently as the machine scanned his thick ursine digits. A welcoming hum sounded; with a pneumatic *clank* and a hiss of air the lock parted, and he walked inside a familiar room.

Clinically white, the space, some six meters across in every direction would have seemed spacious were it not for a large, sarcophagus-like structure in the very center. It rose from the floor like a large coffin; at its base was an array of panels and a small monitor that displayed vital signs. Stark naked light panels in the ceiling shone down upon its mirrored, strangely metallic surface. Letting the door close behind him, Zero walked softly around the outside, running his hand over its cold surface, perhaps thinking about the person within. All was silent, except for the small hum the deprivation tank gave off as it maintained its basic operation. The only other thing in the room was a large blank television screen embedded into the far wall.

Coming over to the far end of the sarcophagus, the brown bear paused for a moment, then pushed a large silver button marked 'CALL' upon the access panel of the curio. Then he waited, hands clasped together. He knew that inside, a soft green light would have appeared to gently let the occupant know that they had a guest. Whether or not they responded to the call was up to them. With a thought, they could make the light go away and sink back into numb solitude, or…

The metallic surface of the tank shimmered, flickered, and then faded away into a translucent surface as the call was answered. Through a now transparent, seemingly plastic surface, a woman was revealed floating in a body of water. Her golden mane-like hair spread like sunshine in the water, the lioness was dressed in an all-in-one dark blue wetsuit that clung to her feminine curves, showing her beautiful form, but also how much muscle she had lost in her recuperation. Nonetheless, as Zero stood over her tank, she managed a dreamy smile, and the director couldn't help smiling back, the faint crow's feet at the edge of his eyes crinkling.

"Hello, Topaz," the bear said, having pushed the button that said 'SPEAK'. "How are you today?"

The lioness was looking up at him, but her completely white eyes gave nothing away. She remained silent; it was to be expected. From the progress reports he'd been reading, she was still seeing people in multiple time-streams, multiple conversations and possibilities happening at once. Part of the same fateful team that had given Spiritwolf his own curse, the lioness' own forced evolution had been much, much more crippling. Her predatorial instincts had been heightened to the point where she saw the future itself; precognition. For many weeks after the accident, she had been catatonic. Eventually they figured out that the reason she would not respond was because she could not respond to the overwhelming number of stimuli and possibilities her mind was having to process; though her neural pathways were constantly reconfiguring to try to process the new information, they could not grow and change fast enough to take in the sheer amount of it flooding her thoughts. So, they built her this tank… and eventually, she awoke. Or seemed to; it was often still very hard for her to understand which moment she was living in, how far into the future she was seeing, or could see. There had been fragile moments where she seemed to comprehend the present and what had happened to her, when she would talk as the Topaz of old, and it seemed her core self was still intact, but it was so easy for her to slip away into visions of the never. Functionality was a long way off yet, it seemed; Dash and Greystorm were currently trialing a series of experimental cognitive drugs that they hoped would taper down her ability to a level where she could function in the outside world again. They theorized that if they were to get her precognitive scope down to ten seconds into the future, she should be able to balance that with enough of the present to begin venturing into the outside world again, like a toddler learning to walk. The only time she left the tank currently was for physical therapy, to ensure her limbs did not completely atrophy... the television they played to her for short bursts – just the news – to retrain her mind and keep it on track with which reality was real, what events had passed, and those that had not...

All this sad information was going through the bear's mind as he looked down upon the stricken agent, wondering if today was a good day or whether he should let her be when her smile returned and she answered him: "Hello, big bear." Her voice crept through the speaker on the intercom on the other side.

"T... Topaz!" Zero replied, a hint of surprise in his voice. "It's been awhile since you called me that."

"I think... the treatment is starting to work. And yes."

"Yes?"

"You were about to ask if I felt like talking. You still feel guilty."

"Well, I-"

"Mmm. I'll tell you so many times not to blame yourself but... how are the others?" Her sightless gaze shifted as she became more conscious, out of the dream world of the tank.

Zero sighed. "So Morey is-"

"Still in a tank as well, I see," her ears flicked back and forth, as she listened to words that had not been spoken. It still took some getting used to; she could carry a whole conversation by herself, asking a question and then responding to an answer that had not been given yet. "Canis... Bal... all my boys..." she said, forlornly. And then something seemed to catch her interest. "What? Spirit is in Europe?"

"His first assignment," Zero blurted, glad to have the opportunity to talk. "He's doing well so far. He's just put to bed a new terrorist cell called *Rising Force*. And-"

"Turn on the television," Topaz interrupted. "Something's happened." She pushed a button inside the tank and the top of it hissed and slid open, letting her sit up. As she did so, the colored wires around her forehead that monitored her brainwaves fell across her shoulders and down her back like technological hair weaves. On the panel, a light winked from green to yellow.

"What?" The senior director said, still one step behind.

"Big bear," the lioness answered, turning her head fiercely. "*Now.*"

Fumbling, Zero looked down at the control panel for the room, looking for the one that turned on the screen on the wall. Even as he did so, he noted the change in lights that monitored the agent's condition and frowned. He hit the switch and looked expectantly up at the screen, just as the lioness did.

In a second, the panel flickered to life, already tuned to a 24-hour news network. BBC world service. The bear got a sinking feeling in his stomach as the breaking news story punctured the room, filling it with its drama and noise.

"...it's a remarkable scene here at the Louvre this morning, where just a short time ago the body was discovered," an avian reporter was jabbering; a large, distinctive glass pyramid was in the background with tiny black figures dotted along its edges. "The police haven't given us any information yet, and the entire plaza has been cordoned off as the authorities consider what will have to be one of the most bizarre crime-scenes in the history of the city. We do not have an identity for the deceased yet, but eyewitness reports that the body at the top of the pyramid appeared to be a white male polar bear, somewhere between his mid-to-late forties..."

Zero knew that so much... activity would be too overwhelming – he didn't want to trigger a relapse for Topaz. He found the button that muted the report and just stared at the images of the body, a white bear that somehow seemed familiar...

"Who... ?" was the only word the director could muster. His throat felt dry – he didn't know how this was connected to Spirit, yet somehow he knew it was, of course. It had to be.

"He's coming to tell you," Topaz sighed, clutching the side of her head. She looked away from the screen, bowing her neck. On the panel, the yellow light flashed to the next level, amber. Just below red.

Ignoring the screen again, Zero turned to address the lioness with concern, but the next second the large steel portal slid open again and the unmistakable form of a snow leopard recently returned from Europe prowled into the room, clutching a tablet computer.

"Zero…" Greystorm began, coming up close. "I came… Topaz, you're awake?" He, too, came to the lioness' side, from the very first moment noticing the readout on the panel. He knew better than anyone what the colors meant because as the Sciences director, it had been he who oversaw the sarcophagus' construction as well as its monitoring systems. He knelt by her side. "All right, you're over-stimulated. You have to go back inside," he said with concern, his original reason for coming forgotten along with the bear.

Topaz shook her head. "Just… give me a second… tell him… he needs to know." She closed her eyes and let her hand point at the tablet the snow leopard was clutching.

The bear's expression was grim. "Is it this?" he said, pointing at the silent news report on the screen. "What's just happened? Who is that?"

The snow leopard considered the lioness for a moment, before letting out a big sigh. He wanted to give her his attention, but it seemed the news he carried was just as pressing. "All right. Look, here," he handed the tablet to the bear. Zero turned it over, and instantly looked at a dossier on a man he now recognized. "Gareth Zirkowski…" he mumbled, thumbing down the page, then looking back up at the television screen. "That's him? Deputy director in charge of MI-6's CATS unit?"

"Seems so…" Greystorm said, looking over Topaz' monitors, frowning. "The whole intelligence community is alight with it. Nobody can work out why, or who did it. They don't even know why he was in Paris in the first place." Topaz had gone silent, watching the news report, considering it quietly with her knees halfway drawn up to her chest in the water.

"I can hazard a guess," Zero growled. "It's where Black Dust is conducting the trade; Spirit's on track to stop him in just a few hours."

"You don't think…"

"That Gareth got in the way, and Spirit took care of him?" Zero chewed his bottom lip, as if considering the question painfully. "Maybe. But he wouldn't… do something so reckless with the body…"

Greystorm seemed to nod, even as he looked down at the floor. "Well. Nobody knows how the bear got up there. No witnesses."

His heart sinking further, the bear gave his best poker face, turning to face his Sciences director completely. "As if he'd been placed there by an invisible hand… was that what you're implying?"

The white feline's tail twitched. "I wasn't implying anything. But Spirit…"

"Sp… Spirit… !" Topaz suddenly exclaimed, her hands gripping the side of the tank. Her voice was strange and broken as she continued to stare at the screen. The two men turned to look at her; there was a second of calm before all hell broke loose. The tank sounded a shrill alarm, even as the light turned from amber, flashing red, a critical point seemingly reached as the lioness suddenly yowled, her back arching, neck twisting as she closed her eyes in the outbreak of a spasm, water sloshing from the tank.

"Topaz!" Zero cried out, reacting instantly. He gripped her hand, not knowing what else to do.

Greystorm was already moving, swearing, turning the television off first, throwing off his lab coat to reveal a T-shirt as he raced behind the lioness, supporting her as she gasped and thrashed, hooking his hands under her arms so she didn't go under the water. "Shit! In the cabinet at the other end of the tank, Zero, get the needle, *now!*"

"What's happening to her?" Zero barked, not understanding the situation as well as he would have liked.

"She's seizing; more than that… there's an… unbounded aspect… to her… ability… She's fighting it…"

The bear moved quickly, flinging open the cabinet to reveal a stockpile of syringes containing a blue liquid. He retrieved one and brought it to Greystorm, who was even then desperately holding on to the thrashing, choking lioness, her eyes flashing open and closed. "Tell me."

"It could kill her, she's too weak…" The muttering feline was still focused on Topaz; one hand held her in place while he pulled off the syringe's safety cap with his teeth and spat it out. "Grab her arm. Turn it over," he instructed, carefully positioning the needle in his one free hand. "This'll put her under, hopefully stop what's coming."

"What is it? What's coming, Grey?" The bear moved to grab Topaz's arm, but before he could do so the lioness' hand snaked out and grabbed his wrist. For a split-second she was still again, her milky-white eyes piercing Zero to the core as his gaze met hers. She grabbed him and pulled him close, whispering in his ear. Just three words she uttered, in a haunting, deep voice that seemed not to be hers. Zero's heart seemed to stop for a moment as he heard her speak… and then Greystorm found a vein and pierced her skin. She was still as the drug entered her, and then she started convulsing again, worse than before. With horror, Zero let her go, scooting back across the floor even as the snow leopard took firmer hold of her and whispered in her ear.

"Shh… shh… stop now… go to sleep… it'll be all right… sleep…" She moaned, cried out once, and then all of a sudden stopped, like a marionette whose strings had been cut. The shrill beeping continued for a moment, and then stopped, leaving the room in silence save for the sound of lapping water as the tank slowly sloshed with the ripples still within. The indicator was shining green once more.

Panting, his heart beating hard in his chest, Zero looked her over, even as Greystorm turned her head to rest on the edge of the tank. "Is she… Grey!"

"Sleeping," the director replied, a hint of blame in his voice, as if he thought Zero had endangered her by even waking her up. "Mercifully. She should recover from this. We'll have to monitor her for a while to… to make sure no permanent damage was done. She's never gotten that close before."

Standing, his clothes wet, Zero nodded, feeling guiltier than ever before. Of course, he'd exposed her to too much. He shouldn't… "Close to what?" He rasped, still panting. "What is it? Why haven't you told me about this?"

"We're still learning about her," Greystorm replied sadly, stroking the side of her face comfortingly. "She's seeing a multitude of futures, so many possibilities all colliding at once… the true and the lies… like many patterns of light, all scattered across the spectrum of her vision…"

"Yes, I know that," Zero replied irritably.

"We've extrapolated her ability to its ultimate extent," the scientist continued. "We think she can create… a sort of… destiny lock, for lack of a better term."

The bear's brow furrowed. "I'm not sure I follow."

"It's similar to wave function collapse, quantum decoherence, but as a kind of positive feedback loop, which is why it's so damaging. The future coalesces for her… normally she skims across the more probable timelines, but the more closely she examines a particular one, the more into sharp focus it becomes… until the future becomes an inescapable, unchangeable path of causality."

Listening, Zero shuddered. "I don't want to hear that right now."

Greystorm looked puzzled at first, then remembered the senior director's interaction with Topaz. "Sir, what did she whisper to you… ?"

The bear straightened his back. He took a deep breath and sighed.

"She said… 'Spirit will fall.'"

* * *

"How do I look?" the lean white wolf said, emerging from the bathroom, half-stretching, half-flexing, making the black lines upon his arms dance, rippling musculature underneath. Achilles was wearing a sleek white cotton shirt, could have been Armani except they didn't come in the sleeveless variety. A pair of designer sunglasses was hooked into the V of his neckline, and he completed the ensemble with a pair of sandy-colored cargo pants – from Barney's of New York – laden with pockets. He tried to make the remark with casual assurance, but he could tell the bull was staring.

"Like a rock star," David replied, swallowing. The bodyguard's light blue eyes caught the light as he stood inside singer's suite, just in front of the closed door. "Are you sure you wouldn't prefer room service? With everything that happened in Arenosa…"

"Quite sure," the wolf replied. "Are we ready?"

On the other side of the door, footsteps could be heard approaching. Through the wood, Achilles heard the muffled scrape of wood as Lars pushed his chair back, presumably standing to attention as the visitor approached. Then he heard the following muted exchange from the heavyset bull on the other side. "Hey… not so fast," Lars could be heard to command. David's ears twitched, and he cocked his head, as did Achilles. "Just wait a sec… no! AH!" The next second they heard a thump, like the sound of someone being brought to their knees. David reached for his gun.

And then there was a knock on the door.

"Achilles. Open up; it's Spirit," the unmistakable wolf's voice said from the other side.

"What in the world?" Achilles muttered, pushing past David, making him get his hand off his weapon as he squeezed past. Without hesitation, he opened the door to find the nearly comical scene of Spiritwolf – clothed and dressed in his gloves and brown mask – standing before the door, holding the bull's hand by the wrist, which was bent back into a position that it ought not to be bent to. While the wolf looked perfectly calm, Lars, brought to his knees, practically had tears in his eyes, being careful not to move and exacerbate his situation.

"He tried to touch me," Spiritwolf said by way of explanation, stepping inside and letting the poor bull go. The large bovine winced and shook his wrist, getting himself back up, all the while glaring daggers at the two wolves. David, flustered, couldn't even look his older brother in the eye, seemingly embarrassed to find him like that.

Shaking his head, Achilles sighed. "I did tell you Spirit was part of an international task force, Lars," he said, as if admonishing a child. "Now you know why."

Spirit turned his head toward his former prisoner. He stayed silent, but nonetheless looked pleased with himself.

Lars spread his hands apologetically. "Sir, I-"

"Oh, be quiet. Outside, you two. Wait for me like good muscleheads, and we'll be coming for breakfast shortly." He pointed to the door. Sheepishly, David retreated and joined his brother on the other side. Just before the portal closed again, he was caught giving his sibling a look that said *Really?* While the reply was shot back, equally silent, signaling: *Don't.*

Achilles turned around, for a second half-expecting to find the wolf had shed his disguise and vanished just to play with him, but there Spiritwolf stood, looking as muscular and assertive as the day he first laid eyes upon him. Which seemed so very long ago now… another time, when all he'd been was a singer, and all Spirit had been was a personal trainer…

Whatever else, they were totally beyond both of those roles now.

"What's the news?" Achilles inquired. He padded over to the kitchenette and poured himself a glass of water. "Was your superior pleased with your report?"

"He was short on words, as ever. All he said was 'good work, keep going'. And yes, there's news." Spiritwolf padded over to the end of the bed, looking down to where the television remote had been discarded. He picked it up, but merely held it in his hand. "Black Dust – Regis – has signaled where he intends to make the exchange, at last. It'll be tonight." He turned over the remote in his hand, looking the white wolf over in the morning light. "It's nearly over; you must feel relieved."

"Wait, tonight?" The singer answered, after swallowing from his glass, ignoring Spirit's last statement. "When? The concert is…"

"Same time as the concert, actually. It's perfect."

Achilles put the glass down. "How is that perfect?"

Spiritwolf sat on the edge of the bed, casually. "Because you'll be up on stage, where you belong, out of harm's way… and I can take care of the final problem and get what I came here for. What I was trained to do."

As if lost for words, Achilles nodded. He silently padded over to the end of the bed too, then sat down alongside the larger brown wolf. "I see," he said, so softly it could have been a sigh.

"What's wrong?" the agent asked, cocking his head. "I thought this was what you wanted. The old tour back."

"I know…" the white wolf rumbled, shaking his head. "It's just… after everything that's happened… what we've been through together… I guess I had hoped to be there at the end. You know… when you brought Regis to justice."

Spirit raised the corner of his muzzle into a smile. "That's not for you, and you know it. You've already seen and done enough; hell, you helped me bring Rising Force down, which is a heck of a lot more than anyone else not on my team has ever done. You go; you sing. You're not in any immediate danger any more, and if you still feel hung up about Regis, when it's over I'll give you a jail address to write to, or a gravestone to visit."

Achilles managed to chuckle and shake his head. He punched the wolf's solid arm, feeling playful. "You think you're so bad-ass, don't you?"

"That's because I am," Spirit replied cheekily.

"Right," the singer snorted teasingly. "But what about that bear... the one who showed up at the trap I laid for Black Dust..."

His playful expression cast aside, Spiritwolf swallowed his humor to look serious again. "That's actually the other thing I came here to show you. I don't think he's going to be bothering us anymore. Look here," he said, flipping over the remote in his hand, now turning it to the television at last. The channel flipped to a local French station, which was just broadcasting the morning news. While the narrator spoke in a fast stream of Gallic, the camera was panning around a helicopter view of the Louvre square, showing the giant glass pyramid, and then something being removed in a body bag from on top of it. The next shot showed a black and white archive photo of someone all too familiar: Gareth Zirkowski, now identified by the press, and very much declared dead. *Mort*, as the caption beneath the photo read.

"He's... dead?" Achilles wonderingly said, staring at the picture.

"Mmm-hmm. He was found on top of the pyramid this morning. Right at the very top. Seems like he failed somebody important when he tried to take the tablet for himself," Spiritwolf said, pleased.

"Why would they put him there?" Achilles said, horrified.

Spiritwolf shrugged. "They wanted to send a message; a message to all that work for them, about the price of failure. Or something like that... these underworld types are hard to read sometimes. Anyway, they don't come any higher up the food chain than Gareth... if he's gone, that's it," the wolf said assuredly. "We don't have to worry about them anymore. All that's left is the elephant." He cracked his knuckles as if already relishing the thought.

Achilles turned the television off again. "But... he'll be waiting for you," the wolf said. "I mean... he'll be expecting trouble."

"He won't be expecting *me*," the wolf said, again with complete confidence. "I can take him down. I'll be ready for anything he has to throw at me."

"You're not a superhero, Spirit."

The brown wolf snorted, leaning back on the bed. "I never said I was. But you must believe me; I can do this. It's what I've been trained to do, as much as you know how to sing."

Achilles turned to face Spirit, leaning over, concern writ large in his eyes. "I just… feel like I should be worried. For some reason."

"Don't be. Really."

"I don't want you to get hurt."

"I won't…"

The singer didn't realize it, but as he sat next to the large, masculine presence of Spirit upon the bed, he'd been drawing nearer and nearer, and for a confusing moment, he wondered what it was he was feeling, listening to the agent assure him of his plan and abilities, he felt concern, he felt trepidation… and something he could no longer deny, though he had felt it every time they shared a moment of danger together:

Attraction.

"You'd better not…" Achilles exhaled, before surprising them both by leaning in and putting his lips against the side of Spirit's muzzle for a brief, chaste kiss.

The moment of surprise continued as the two wolves looked at each other in mild, dazed acceptance… and then Achilles leaned in again, this time planting a proper kiss on the front of the agent's muzzle, lips indicating the depths of his concern. Spiritwolf's first instinct was to nearly recoil – his promises of 'never again' after his night with Les resurfaced strongly, and then he remembered Achilles already knew the secret he had to hide so carefully from everyone else. The walls came down again; old habits took over and he soon found himself returning the emotion and the gesture, closing his eyes and huffing softly.

The kiss was broken a moment later, and Achilles sat back, looking the brown wolf over, seemingly unable to believe he'd just done what he'd just done.

"Wow…" Spiritwolf said, breaking the silence first. "So you're…"

"Yep." Achilles answered, tail twitching into a half-wag.

"And you just…"

"I did."

"…why?" Spiritwolf said, standing to his feet. Flustered… he could feel his temperature rising, as if he were somehow embarrassed… not that he should be… but his condition… and Achilles, he…

"So you'd look after yourself I guess," the white wolf answered, pawing at the fur on his arm. "Call it… a kiss for luck."

"Is that all I get?" Spirit found himself answering, his normal attitude resurfacing through rattled tones. "A kiss?"

"For now," Achilles smirked, walking over to the door. "Tell you what – get this mission behind you and… maybe we could go out and get a drink afterwards?"

The brown wolf blinked. "A drink…" he repeated, as if those words were foreign to him. "Are you… asking me out on a date?"

Achilles rolled his eyes. "No. I'm asking you out for a *drink*. Don't be so American." He answered though his own heart was beating fast, and finished his sentence with a wink.

* * *

Paris had a natural rhythm that was as timeless and enigmatic as the city itself. From the bustling joy of the morning, where all avenues were seemingly beset by crowds set upon the freshest bread, the finest produce, all full of destinations and trades, there came an hour when the streets calmed, as if the very buildings themselves were breathing a sigh of relief. Even the *Avenue des Champs-Élysées* was not immune, the thundering vein of cinemas, cafés, luxury specialty shops at the heart of the city suddenly calming for a moment around noon, when Parisian appetites demanded lunch and leisure in equal measure.

At the foot of this prestigious street, upon the *Place de la Concorde*, in the heart of one of the oldest luxury hotels in the world, a lion who had come upon the city like an invader from a foreign land was sating his appetite in his own way.

Ardal watched him eat, her spine straight in her chair, as if painfully aware of the performance she had to give and the way in which she had come to be sharing Blair's company. The brown wolfess had a small Caesar salad in front of her, picked over, and barely touched. The golden lion meanwhile was surrounded by a graveyard of mollusks; one pile of *escargot* drowned in garlic and butter to his right, another pot of *moules marinière* to his left, the discarded shells of mussels and snails alike littering the plate in front of him. With a perpetual smirk upon his features, while they chatted the mogul had been dining, requiring no fork but merely hooking out the tender flesh from the husks with one immaculately sharp claw. He ate with aplomb, making even such a potentially messy feast seem like a perfectly executed example of dignity and relish, not even a splash of sauce upon the crisp lines of his grey tailored suit. When he drank from the glass of wine accompanying the meal, something hideously expensive and old from the cellars of the eminent *Hôtel de Crillon*, it was as if he were an emperor holding court at Rome.

"Lost your appetite my dear?" he purred, putting down his glass, examining his newest acquisition – the woman who would be taking Gareth's place as his lever inside MI-6's hidden reaches. She was wearing a black suit, the white shirt now missing its tie, the top buttons undone revealing a very feminine figure underneath.

"I shouldn't have ordered the salad," Ardal replied, coldly. She lifted her own glass, the tip of her muzzle sniffing out the delicate aromas within. "I'm a predator, after all." Not once daring to tear her gaze from the lion, she tilted back her neck, and drank.

"You certainly are. Particularly when you're shooting a man on my command." The feline replied, an impressed growl in his voice.

"Don't give yourself too much credit," she shot back, seemingly holding her own. "I've wanted him out of the way for years. All you did was provide me with the reason and the assurance that my bid to replace him would be successful." She pursed her lips, trying to look fierce.

Blair laughed, softly, in the English way. "So you're saying our arrangement is mutually beneficial. I see. How very... *predatory*."

"Mmm," she replied, falling into silence and looking about the opulent surroundings again. They were sitting in one of the grand hotel's reception room; once a former ballroom of the Count de Crillon, it was a resplendent example of the Louis XV style, complete with white marble marquetry, crystal chandeliers, and frescoes of heaven upon the ceiling. In this sunny afternoon, they had the entire room to themselves, the pair a portrait of Blair's wealth and egotism, commanding an entire chamber all to himself in one of the most expensive hotels in the world, all for the sake of what he called a 'casual chat' to get to know Ardal better. At the edge, nervous waiters hovered, seemingly understanding that to get too close might be to hear things beyond the pay grade of anyone who valued their life or livelihood.

"So," the broadly-built lion intruded, bringing her attention back to the table. He dabbed purposefully at the corner of his mouth with his napkin, as if signaling the time for eating had passed. "Tell me about the train."

"The one I took from Arenosa to Paris with Achilles, you mean? What do you wish to know?"

Blair smiled. "Tell me what you *think* I want to know."

Tilting her head a little, the wolfess had her hand upon the stem of her wine glass again, but failed to raise the vessel to her lips again as she considered this. "After the intelligence we garnered from the Israeli meerkat, the link between Achilles, the tablet, and this hidden agent couldn't have been clearer. Gareth wanted to find out more."

"Go on."

She rotated the glass a little. "I was placed on the train in deep cover; my assignment was to first confirm the link."

"Which you did, as I recall. And second?"

Ardal narrowed her eyes. "Take Spiritwolf into custody, if the opportunity presented itself. When we grabbed Benny, we were able to recover the SDS algorithm – it would have been easy."

"An opportunity you passed up. That's when you contacted me." He leaned across the table, his mane shining in the sunlight. "That's what I wanted you to tell me about; the moment you decided the treachery in your heart should be given in to."

"Why?"

"So that I can look right into your eyes to know the birth of it; so that I may recognize that look for myself if the day ever comes you decide to turn on me, as you did the bear." He finished his sentence with a twitch of a claw upon his fingertip.

Only now did the wolfess lift up her vessel, forcing out a chuckle herself before knocking back the last of the expensive vintage like it was cheap vodka. Then she looked deep into Blair's eyes, as if she were trying to seduce him, and replied with a soft growl. "It was a simple decision to make; fifteen minutes out of Paris, I watched Achilles excuse himself and visit the restroom. Spiritwolf was alone at last, no idea he was being watched. And as I looked at him I knew that if I took him for Gareth, I would never be rid of the bear, he would always be above me. His incompetence, his womanizing, his… arrogance." Her eyes narrowed. "I let Spiritwolf go then, vowing that when I took him it would be for the right man, someone with real power, rather than the power loaned to him from afar." She raised the corner of her muzzle into a happy image of mirth. "He was like the moon, and you the sun. One stealing light from another."

"How poetic," Blair snapped, seemingly unimpressed. "You surprise me."

"Then you tell me something," the lupine intruded, nodding gently as an eagle with a shaking claw cleared away the disappointing meal in front of her. "I have a question of my own."

In stony silence, as if offended by the waiter's presence, Blair merely looked upon her like he had found a dropping upon the bottom of his shoe.

"Why did you place Gareth there? And how?" she asked, undeterred.

"How?" Blair grunted, his shoulders deflating, his expression changing instantly. "You ask how, the most tedious question of all? Oh, Ardal, now you disappoint me. How is irrelevant. It means nothing." He flashed her an ominous, toothy grin, like he could have eaten her up. "Nothing other than the fact that enough money can buy you anything. Even a body impaled upon the top of a glass pyramid."

"Then answer my other question."

"Ah... yes, you think you can dare to understand my motives. I said it was a message, didn't I?" The wait-staff had retreated again, and now it seemed the lion felt free to expound and grow ebullient again. "But a message to whom, eh? That is the question. Perhaps there are others out there on my puppet-strings and I wished to remind them of the consequences of contemplating betrayal. Or perhaps I wished this secret agent to feel that the danger Gareth posed was eliminated so that he would relax, grow sloppy. Or perhaps I'm a lover of modern art, and wanted to donate a new piece to the Louvre to remember me by." He looked across the table at the wolfess, his voice rising in volume as he spoke. "Or perhaps it's none of your fucking business!" he suddenly roared, dangerously.

As if undeterred, Ardal met his gaze, trying to pretend that she wasn't rattled. She merely put her lips together, tightly.

Blair jabbed his hand at her. "You don't get to ask *me* why. You might think us equals because we had an exchange; but no, my dear, *we are not*. I own an empire, and you are just one tiny, small part of the game. Whatever my reasons are, you will never know them; but rest assured, I am one step ahead of Black Dust. One step ahead of Spiritwolf. And certainly, above all else, one step ahead of *you*."

Only now did the wolfess narrow her eyes at him, as if feeling a surge of hatred. Then, her gaze softened, and she bowed her head meekly, obediently, the animus hidden as quickly as it had come. "Of course. My apologies. I won't ask again."

The lion took a deep breath and smoothed the back of his mane, putting down the hairs that had gotten out of place in his momentary scolding. "Forget about it," he answered, crisply. "It's a lesson everyone has to learn at some point. Now, I want to discuss the plans for tonight. There's still work to be done here before I let you go back home to your new, bigger office."

"Yes," the agent replied in a matter-of-fact way as they ventured onto a topic she was more comfortable with. "The rendezvous. As the winning bidder, I'm sure Black Dust will be pleased to meet you."

"Me? Meet Black Dust?" Blair scoffed. "Don't be ridiculous. I won't be anywhere near that exchange. I don't even need to send anyone in my place to fetch it."

Ardal wrinkled her brow, a fluttery feeling of uncertainty rising in her chest. "But... the tablet..."

"Will be mine, as planned," Blair chuckled, standing and buttoning the bottom of his suit, signaling the end of lunch. Outside in the Avenue, the rest of the city responded in the same way, the rhythm resuming. "And Agent Spiritwolf will be the one to deliver it to me. You'll see..."

* * *

Lines.

There were so many lines; lines in the paper in front of him, black and white, depicting the network of tunnels underneath the city; lines that had been crossed, between the singer and himself, a boundary of familiarity that could never be replaced; and a line in the sand, the one he was drawing for himself now, the point where all retreat, all games were finished, and only Black Dust's fall remained.

Spiritwolf was sitting, naked, in his hotel room. All his belongings had been packed away, including his mask and clothes. He was ready to leave, it was now three in the afternoon, and before long he would go underground to begin preparing for the exchange. This was the most crucial part of the operation for him; gathering all intelligence, drawing up scenarios, contingencies…

The power of information.

It was a quiet, peaceful moment. The sun was filtering softly through the curtains, the window slightly open, letting a cool breeze wash over the invisible wolf and his fur, giving him goosebumps he would never again see. But he could feel it. He put down the map of the tunnels for a moment to rub at his arm.

The door behind him clicked open and he turned around, instinctively freezing, half-expecting to find the entrance of a maid; instead he was greeted by the always unforgettable sight of a giant beetle entering the room, its antennae twitching, hard black carapace glinting the moment the light hit his shell.

"Agent Spiritwolf," Ixak's voice-box buzzed after closing the door. "I hope I'm not interrupting."

"Number one," the wolf slowly replied and stood to face his visitor. "I'm surprised you found me; this isn't even my room. Have I been careless?"

"No," the insect replied assertively, mechanically. He walked over to the desk where the voice came from. "But I have my ways." He looked through the wolf, onto the pile of papers before him.

"Fine. Number two – what do you want?"

"All ready for the mission?" Ixak chirped, deflecting the question. Spiritwolf noted that the beetle was carrying some kind of dossier under one of his spindly arms, which immediately piqued his interest.

"I'm getting there," the agent grumbled. Despite his nature he couldn't help but feel… scrutinized, somehow, by the insect. Perhaps it was those compound eyes… so alien… so alone. He had no idea what the insect could be seeing. Could the beetle detect things others couldn't? Uncertainties aside, he decided to be more direct. "You got something for me?" he asked, his hand tapping the dossier.

Immediately, Ixak turned from him. "I do," the beetle replied, equally direct. "But first, let's take a walk." He headed to the door.

"Excuse me?"

"You heard me, agent. Walk with me now."

The wolf hesitated, looking to his packed case.

Ixak immediately detected the pause. "You desire your disguises, yes? A pity. No time for that now, agent. You may either come with me now, or you will not be armed with all the information you need." And then Ixak exited the room, leaving the wolf to make his decision.

It only took a moment, and by the time he caught up with the director standing in the carriage of the elevator, he could have sworn he heard the insect give a shrill buzz of amusement. He had no thought of making remark on it however, as the carriage was also occupied by a slim female crocodile in a white business two-piece suit. She was looking at Ixak with a mixture of nervousness and curiosity, the kind of expression people give when they don't think they are being watched. Ixak had his back to her, and Spiritwolf gently slid inside before the doors closed, his heartbeat already pounding. He was close enough to detect her perfume; absorbed as the reptile was with the insect, she suddenly straightened up and looked to her left where Spirit stood, as if she were faintly aware of another presence inside the elevator.

The invisible wolf considered her uncomfortably for a moment, before the doors opened again and Ixak stepped out, into the lobby. Spiritwolf took a deep breath and quickly followed, leaving the crocodile behind. As he walked into the foyer, he was already tracking the movements of everyone in motion in the space, considering all angles of possible collision, moments where paths might cross. People had a certain way of walking that didn't take invisible obstacles into account that gave someone with the agent's condition a lot to think about at short notice. Ixak must have been aware of this but for some reason chose that moment to start talking again.

"This has been a most interesting experience for me," he clicked, stepping over the polished marble of the floor. "I must say I am very glad to have met you."

"This isn't going to be much of a conversation if I'm like this," Spirit hiss-whispered to the director as quietly as possible. And yet as they walked, he noted how the whole room seemed to be staring at them – staring at *Ixak* – as they passed by. Porters stopped walking with their bags. Receptionists on telephones trailed off sentences before coming back to their train of thought. Spiritwolf even caught one Asian fox getting out her camera-phone and taking a couple of discreet pictures. The hair rose on the back of his neck, and he felt suddenly dizzy. Being the center of attention was the antithesis of his nature, and yet just standing next to Ixak changed all that. Finally, the front door opened, and they were standing outside on the pavement.

The streets were blessedly quiet for the time of day; nonetheless the parade of curious Parisian eyes continued, as the insect ambled off in the direction of the municipal park. "You are acting very skittish, agent," Ixak continued. "Is there something the matter?"

"Why are you doing this?" Spirit scowled, talking a little louder now that they were outdoors, his mind still racing trying to keep track of the different pedestrians hurrying to and fro. "Just give me the files!"

The director suddenly stopped. He turned to address the spot he last thought of the agent as standing, which actually wasn't far from the mark. "I am attempting to show you," the director continued. "One last time before we part ways… how fortunate you are." His antennae twitched rapidly. "I… cannot put on a mask to hide who I am. Like yourself, I am a rarity. A freak. I am less than one per cent of one percent of the population. I cannot even go outside without people taking notice.

He extended a claw, motioning for Spirit to join him on a nearby bench. "And then there's you; you can go wherever you want without being seen. Even Achilles, in his heart, would yearn for that kind of anonymity again."

"He chose that," Spirit growled. "I didn't choose-"

"But you *are*," Ixak's voice-box countered. "And when you want to re-join society again, all you have to do is put on a mask. You choose which world to walk in! I have no choice. My future… is already written. As much as I like to enjoy this world, sometimes I must remind myself it is not mine. It is yours."

"Huh?"

Ixak waved his claw. "I fear sometimes this box does not interpret my words as well as I would like it to. But I am grateful for the technology, in the same way I hope you are grateful for the invention of the disguise that lets you be seen. But we must never come to rely on these devices too much. That is one reason why I had you walk here. You will be alone tonight, Spiritwolf, in a way you have not been alone for a long time."

"What… do you mean?"

The insect's large eyes seemed to glint for a moment. He reached into the dossier, and pulled out the first sheaf of paper. "Let's start at the beginning. Take this; tell me what you see."

Spiritwolf gingerly took the sheet, careful to see if anyone was watching, and laid it flat on the bench in front of him. He looked over it intently for a moment. There were several photos of the elephant taken covertly; Regis doing things he probably shouldn't. He examined the data, which listed the pachyderm's background, amasses of intelligence, stolen phone calls. Code names. Links to Conway technology. And there… the name.

Black Dust.

"It's a file on my target," Spiritwolf said, saying it as if it were something unremarkable. And yet, something wasn't right. His eye was already drifting to the corner of the page…

"And then there is the detail," the insect chirped, encouraging his instincts.

Just there, in the corner, there was a date. Such a small detail; but it rocked the invisible agent to the very core. "The… the *hell?*" Spirit suddenly snapped. "This says the file was collated… two months ago… *before I even got here!*" His hand scrunched around the paper, and then he thrust it at the insect. "You… you *knew* who Black Dust was from the very beginning! Before I even arrived! And you didn't… *you didn't tell me!*"

"That is correct, agent," Ixak answered coldly.

"Does… is Zero in on this too?!"

"No," the director replied. "This information was mine alone. And yes, I held it back from you, Zero, all of you. I am sorry, agent. I had to know…"

Spiritwolf so badly wanted to scream right then. Instead he had to hold himself in check as a couple riding their bike tandem passed them by. The second they were gone however he let out a loud blast of air he'd been holding in his lungs, his voice a chill, throaty snarl. "You… explain this to me *right fucking now!* Because from where I'm standing, you're a traitor if ever I saw one!"

Ixak quietly smoothed the paper and put it back in the dossier. "Do you recall how I knew about your invisibility from the moment you arrived, agent?"

"Even though you weren't supposed to? You bet I remember."

The insect put his claws over his stomach, looking serene. "I have a talent for gathering information. I am not omnipotent. But I am, as has been observed, a 'bug'. We know things; we see things. And so I came to hear of the Ultras. Oh yes, not just you, but all of you. Transformed by your accident. Topaz; Canis; Bal; Morey. All of you. And I know that Zero has been quietly keeping this a secret from the rest of the TEA and DAST leadership. For now."

"Except for Vayana. He already knows."

"Yes. And yet he has not said anything in over a year, letting secrets remain secrets. I am concerned what his intentions are, how he will behave when Zero informs the other senior directors."

"He's going to tell them soon. Hasn't… hasn't he convened a session in Phoenix next month for that purpose?"

"He has," Ixak answered. "But while you have been the 'special project' of the Americas' senior director, his will is not indomitable. He and the other senior directors act as a council and when your existence is made known to the others next month, the issue of what to do with you all will be of paramount importance."

"What… to do with us?"

The voice box buzzed. "Alpha-bear may have to turn over control of the surviving Ultra team members to the rest of the council, if it comes to a vote. It is even possible the World Nations committee would re-assert their authority. Worse, Vayana may attempt to claim you and the remaining Ultras for himself."

Spiritwolf absorbed this information quietly. "So what does all this have to do with keeping your intelligence on Regis a secret from everyone?"

The insect clicked once something untranslatable before his voice-box began replying. "When I discovered the secret Ultra files, I was not sure what to do with this information. I had no need to confront Zero about it. But when I learned of Regis and the commodity he possessed relating to the Conway accident, I knew he would be making a move. Sure enough, you arrived. While I was capable of taking Black Dust into custody myself with the information I had, I know that it is very, very important that *you* be the one to capture him and retrieve the tablet, on your own merits. Not just for your sake, but for Zero's and the other team members as well."

Spiritwolf's goosebumps returned. "What? Why?"

"Because if Zero is to maintain control and keep you out of Vayana's hands next month, there *must* be a success he can point to. An example that shows that the team, under *his* guidance, is capable of not only recovering from the accident, but also exceeding expectations." Ixak looked down at his claws again. "I like alpha-bear. I do not like Vayana; the weasel is always scheming and lacks character. I want Zero's plan to succeed. So I swore I would help you from the sidelines, even before alpha-bear asked me to keep an eye on you. He made me promise not to tell you that, you know. He is playing everything so delicately, like a master tactician." Ixak's eyes stared directly at the empty spot next to him. "He must keep control. He *must*. So you, agent, must prove him right and capture Black Dust. *Alone.* This is, and has always been, about more than just you proving yourself. You are validating the continuation of the Ultras in service as well."

The wolf had been listening to all this quietly for a moment. Although the insect couldn't see it, the wolf had slowly begun to hold his head in his hands, taking it all in. When the insect stopped talking, all he could do was meekly utter, "…fuck me. You really know how to pile the pressure on. You know that?"

The insect buzzed. "I am sorry. But it was better you know. I only wish I could have helped you more; when you were momentarily taken into custody by the police in Germany, it was I who helped spring you from that van. But for all of my information gathering, I was still blind to the way that Clarice betrayed me. I only hope there is nothing else of importance I may have missed. Here."

He handed Spiritwolf the rest of the dossier. "In here you will find a complete intelligence report of all the men Regis has hired to be with him at the exchange tonight. Pi, Ramsden, Hikiwake. They are all in there… get to know them, Spirit. I am sure by now they will know, and be expecting, you."

That said, the insect rose, standing to his feet and brushing down the dust of the bench from his leg. "Good luck, agent."

"That… that's it?" Spirit uttered, not daring to stand himself, keeping the dossier flat on the bench. "You're done?"

"I am done," Ixak repeated. "I have done all I can. Any more and I risk jeopardizing alpha-bear's plan. But I believe in you, Spirit. You will succeed, I am sure of it now."

"But how am I supposed to get these files back to my hotel without being noticed?"

The insect paused and for the last time, gave one his unmistakable buzz-chuckles. "I am sure you will find a way. Go on, agent… exceed my expectations. Exceed everyone's expectations. It is, after all, what you were sent here to do."

* * *

Achilles stepped out of the limo and into the mist of rain that had descended upon the city. A light shower of nearly imperceptible particles of water dancing through the air as the clouds moved in. But for now, the sun was still shining – somewhere, he was sure, there would be a rainbow.

He craned his neck, turning his attention to the outside of the stadium. This was going to be the largest gig on the tour; the ultimate, the climax. There was even going to be a full-on camera crew recording the show for a concert DVD to be released early next year. Regis had apparently arranged it despite his order to cut the tour staff. Looming up beside him came Lars and David, the bovine brothers looking somewhat less fresh than they had been when they'd first joined the singer in Arenosa. As if they hadn't gotten much sleep lately.

"Big place, boss. Sure you can fill it?" the younger one said, squaring his shoulders.

"Sure I can," the white wolf replied, his thoughts elsewhere. "Let's go."

They stepped over the pavement, and headed inside the stage door. They were met inside by a meerkat from the crew. Grant flicked aside his cigarette, took his boss' bag, and began leading him down the network of corridors toward the dressing rooms. The place was so quiet, so peaceful. Tonight, it would be thrumming with energy and chaos as the hordes descended. But for now, it was a monolith at rest. In the distance, the sound of heavy equipment could be heard groaning and shuffling as the rigging and instruments were put into place. All these sounds were comforting to Achilles; he let himself be led on, and finally found himself at the door to the dressing room.

"Sound-check's scheduled to begin in thirty," his new manager said. "Stage is easy to find – just down there on the right. We'll see you there?"

"You will," the singer said perfunctorily, taking back his bag before letting himself inside. As the door opened, the two bodyguards leaned in for a look at the room's occupants before, with satisfied nods, they stationed themselves at either side of the entrance, giving Grant a 'hey, it's a living' look before the meerkat made himself scarce.

The wolf closed the door and was greeted by three familiar figures who had seemingly been waiting for his arrival. Les, Garrick, and Cain turned around from their huddle, and gave him expectant smiles. His band, together again to perform in style, as they always did.

"Fashionably late, as ever, aren't you?" the lizard said with cheeky aplomb. "Don't tell me – you were doing your hair?"

Achilles casually flipped his keyboardist off and walked over to the chair reserved for him, slinging his bag down. In reality, he'd been delayed because of his time with Spiritwolf. Not that he could tell his buddies that.

The cheetah, Garrick, said nothing but he brushed his neon fringe out of his eyes for a moment before handing Achilles a can of *Red Stripe Energy Drink* and staring at the white wolf thoughtfully.

* * *

The short, stocky bat straightened the tie on his suit, and gazed directly into the empty sockets of the vacant feline skull in the wall in front of him. "Hello, gorgeous," he cooed, as if chatting up a prospect at a bar. "What's a lean piece of meat like you doing in a mausoleum like this?" He asked, his fangs glinting in vampiric mock delight.

"*Ossuary*, Pi," Regis snapped, correcting his employee. "Now, if you're quite done cracking jokes, are we ready?"

The bat turned, wiping the smile from his face. A damp droplet from the dark stone roof above him fell upon the end of his muzzle, the water scattering in the dim light. "Just so, boss," he replied, taking out a small device from his pocket. "Best grid I ever installed – at such short notice."

The elephant crossed his arms over his chest, his trunk twitching. "Let's see it."

The leathery mammal used a black digit to push a button on the object he held. Instantly, flickers of red light sprung up around them, a dazzling array of red lasers pointing every which way down the corridors that led to the main ossuary chamber, like a network of spider webs, receding well into the distance. The devilish light licked over the faces of the dead in the wall, highlighting them in the hues of ghoulish gore, momentarily making the scene even more gothic than before. The light also highlighted the other living souls in the room: one rough-looking black wolf, and the huge, granite-like form of a colossal percheron.

If the horse was impressed by the light show, he didn't indicate it, but Ramsden began to applaud in slow, echoing claps. "*Wunderbar*," he said, sounding impressed. "This is the way to catch the *fliegen*."

"That's just the visuals," Pi said, hitting another button and turning the beams off again. "They're running even when you can't see it. Best motion-detection software money can buy. Heat sensors too. A moth could flap its wings in there, and I'd know about it."

"It isn't moths I'm worried about," Regis interjected, standing at the center of the group. His voice had a tense, stressed edge to it. "But at least we won't be having any surprises. Time?"

"Nine-fifty, boss."

"Soon, then. Hikiwake, go sweep the perimeter and check the east gates. We wouldn't want any tourists looking for a night-time thrill to find more than they bargained for."

The percheron nodded, his steel-grey eyes glinting, and he moved out down the corridor to his left without saying a word. His white robe entered the gloom, and then he was gone, topknot and all. Pi's device began to vibrate angrily, alerting him to the movement down the corridor and Ramsden watched in fascination as the bat pulled out a tablet that displayed a map of the ossuary complex. There was a tiny dot that indicated the horse's movement, moving away from their position.

"He creeps me out," the black wolf muttered, once he was sure the horse was out of earshot. "How come he never talks?"

A sly, almost delighted smirk spread across Regis' face. "He's the best damn swordsman alive today; he was trained by the great Yamato Takeru himself. Legend has it that a young, foolish Hikiwake dared answer his master back one day during a lesson. As punishment, the old man removed his student's tongue." As he spoke, the elephant stared directly into the wolf's eyes, as if relishing the telling of the story.

Ramsden stared hard, for a moment his muzzle hanging open in awe. Then he closed it again. "Bullshit," he said dismissively.

"If you say so," Regis said, smirking again. He pulled out the object he'd been playing with in his pocket, staring at it for a few moments. "But believe me, there's information on here that makes such a tale seem tame…"

The tablet seemed to glimmer in the dim light, as if hinting that its secrets would belong to someone else very soon.

* * *

Achilles closed his eyes and sang. The same words, the same songs. He knew them all. The crowd before him was wild with delight, the music throbbing through his blood, coming from both outside him and inside him at once.

Lights flashed; cameras, spotlights, pyrotechnics. His world was alive with color and glare, but his mind was elsewhere. With someone else. For all the patterns on display, for all the chaos and commotion, he was instead imagining a very dark place, down beneath the city, where something important was happening without him.

From one of the VIP booths at the side of the arena, hungry eyes were watching him intently through a pair of binoculars.

"He's getting tired," a voice growled against the cacophony of noise, watching the white wolf pant between breaths. "He'll go offstage after the next song. Be ready."

Ardal put down the binoculars, and smirked with predatory intent.

* * *

The horse practically filled the corridor as he strode down it, eyes moving back and forth inside the thin slits they had become as he peered into the gloom ahead of him. Bare-footed, he found the cold stone comforting somehow, as if something so ancient and worn were familiar to him.

He passed by an alcove that contained a grisly stack of skulls piled atop one another. Hikiwake stared at them thoughtfully for a quiet moment. He felt a breeze coming up the unlit corridor toward him. He stared openly for a moment and then put his hands to his sides. His ears swiveled and flicked atop his head, breathing steady as he closed his eyes.

In a sudden flash of speed, he swiveled, with blind purpose, and struck out at the seemingly empty space behind him. His open hands momentarily took hold of an unseen furred pelt, before he was sparring with an opponent who could not be seen. He fended off fierce jabs to his nerve-points, counter-blocking, grunting in silent control as he struck back against the air itself. His fists connected with solid fur, taking hold for a moment before being blocked, redirected, countered. Their dance together was as silent as it was intense, the horse giving no cry for help or surprise, only focused on using his ears to fight, to defend. He punished his opponent with a brutal jab to his muzzle, giving him enough time to unsheathe his katana at last. The blade sang as it pierced the air, swinging out to cut into the ghost. All the steel found, though, was empty air; the surprise assailant seemingly vanished.

"They told me about you," the equine rasped, speaking rare words. His English was clipped, laced with the accents of the east. "Hidden wolf. I did not believe. But I hoped."

Spiritwolf regarded the samurai cautiously, still in a crouched stance facing opposite. Hikiwake would never know how close he'd come to gutting him. He didn't respond, instead calculating how to bring the horse down now that his surprise assault had failed.

"You are wise to remain silent. I know the value of it myself. But – hidden wolf – you betray yourself. Those special nerve strikes? You are a student of a certain fox. Master Song has taught you well."

Spiritwolf's eyes widened. He hadn't expected his moves to be pinpointed with such accuracy. The percheron seemed to be looking right at him as he continued to speak. "He is a great warrior; my master thought of him most highly. Until the day the fox killed him. I owe him for that..." He growled and leveled his katana again. "But killing his student will have to do."

Hikiwake struck out, quick as a wasp. Spiritwolf rolled backward, his eyes watching as the blade passed by mere centimeters from his pupils. He gave a round-house kick, which was ineffective against the horse's mass, but gained a second's respite as the swordsman had a momentary wobble. He continued to weave around the cutting arc of the equine's deadly blade, every passing second coming that much closer to being struck. Forced ever backwards, the agent found himself on the defensive, no weapon of his own. This was not an even fight.

The percheron, seeming to sense victory against the ghost, pressed his advantage, and came at Spiritwolf in a rush. The wolf had been expecting this, and in a moment of unseen grace, pivoted his body sideways, his hands striking the horse's sword arm as he executed Master Song's valued Biting Talons technique. It was the perfect move for disarming an overconfident opponent, one the wolf had used many times in sparring. For a second, he felt victory, his grasp finding the horse's nerve-points upon the thick arm.

That second was short-lived.

The wily samurai was fast as a snake as he sprung his trap. His blade clattered to the ground as he released it to twist his arm, pivot his whole body in fact, as he punished Master Song's over-eager pupil by turning the technique against him, one that he had expected. It was so fast, so sudden, Spiritwolf could hardly comprehend how it had happened as he found the horse taking hold of his invisible arm – the one that had been shot – and with a twist of sharp, agonizing pain he found the horse had him right where he wanted him. He couldn't help but cry out as his face was forced into the cold stone wall, a noisy drainage pipe rumbling next to his muzzle, his arm twisted up with exploding pangs behind his back.

"So predictable. So disappointing," his opponent nickered, twisting the arm again, testing how much the wolf could endure. "Tell me where to find Master Song and I will ensure your death is quick. Or I can make your demise linger so long, you *beg* for the end."

Spiritwolf's heart thumped; he wanted to retaliate, but the pain was so great he felt on the verge of blacking out. The horse was surely set to break his arm.

Hikiwake growled. "You have all of the fox's tricks, but none of his guile."

"His tricks… aren't… the only ones!" the wolf said, hissing, finally speaking, as his free arm reached out and grabbed the drainage-pipe, yanking it from the wall with all the upper-body strength he had left.

A sibilant spray of effluent black water burst from the pipe under high pressure, striking the gloating warrior in the eyes with a force that stung. Blinded and crying out, it was Hikiwake's turn to be surprised and Spiritwolf used the momentary release of pressure upon his arm to deliver a backwards kick to the horse's groin. Stunned and blinded by the water, the horse found that his grip upon the invisible agent was gone. He didn't have much of a moment to regret the mistake when the wolf used the piece of pipe he'd torn from the wall to club the horse across the cranium.

There was a solid metal *thunk* as it connected, echoing loudly through the complex of corridors. The equine's muzzle twisted into a final 'O' of consternation before he fell backwards, unconscious. A puddle of muddy-brown, stinking water soaked his once-white robes.

Panting, shaking dry his now-damp fur to regain his invisible state, Spiritwolf looked down upon his beaten opponent with a satisfied relish, dropping the pipe as the water continued to pool around his feet. "Master Morey taught me that one," he gloated, then winced as he willed himself to ignore the pain from his arm. He looked down the corridor, where he'd stashed his tools and weapons earlier in the day. He had time to zip-tie this one before going after the others.

One down, three to go.

* * *

The bear was sitting with his back to the door of his office, brow furrowed, looking down into the amber of his glass. He wasn't much of a drinker; as a high-ranking official of the agency, he was used to being gifted expensive bottles of fine spirits, as if having such luxuries on hand was expected of him. As such, Zero had accumulated a nearly-untouched collection of aged cognacs, scotch, and whiskies in a cupboard under his desk, that even his powers of re-gifting had failed to diminish. He'd only poured himself a glass from the collection twice in all his years as director and senior director; the night after the aftermath of the Conway incident, and today.

He was so deep in thought as he looked down into the golden world in his glass, that he did not even hear the footsteps approaching his door. When he heard the entrance click open, all he could muster was a glance over his shoulder, watching Greystorm sneak in before he turned his attention back to the glass again.

"You're drinking?" the Sciences director observed, closing the door behind him. "Must be serious."

"Thought everyone had gone home for the night," Zero replied, swirling his glass. "Got some things on my mind."

"I can guess," the snow leopard said, seating himself in the chair opposite the brown bear's desk. "After what happened this afternoon…"

"Right," the senior director sighed and turned around. "Dash was of the opinion that perhaps Topaz was just overwhelmed. That what she said about Spirit could mean anything. Could be something a long, long time away…"

"…but?"

"But her saying 'Spirit will fall' isn't going to mean something *good*, no matter which angle you look at it. Damn." He gave another sigh, as if he were carrying a heavy burden.

"You're thinking about calling him and aborting the mission, aren't you?"

The bear put down his glass. "Thought about it. Can't. He wouldn't listen anyway, not when he's so close; stubborn bastard, you know him..."

"Heh, that he is," the feline agreed with a conspiratorial grin. And then his face became more serious as he leaned in and tapped his hand on the desk. "He's going to be okay, Zero."

"I hope so. I had to pull some strings, get approvals quickly for..." The bear suddenly stopped talking.

"For what, exactly?"

"I said too much, Grey. Forget it." He sighed and shook his head. "You and the others, you've probably wondered a lot of things about this mission. Why I sent him in on his own. Why no support or resources, only limited tech. Why... when we're not sure he was ready..."

Greystorm cleared his throat. "I'd be lying if I said no. But... we've guessed it has something to do with directorial politics..."

"Mmm," the bear replied, neither confirming or denying. "Directorial fucking politics..." he growled and cracked his knuckles. "I shouldn't even be here. But... I pushed Spirit into this, it was already risky enough. And now this; Topaz's warning. It put me on edge. I don't like it."

"None of us do," the cat replied, standing up, knowing when to leave his friend and superior alone. "But we're all managing to do what we can with what we're dealt, all the same. Spirit, too; he'll be fine. You never know, he might just be in for a trip when he tries to tie his shoelaces..."

"Let's hope so," Zero said, eying the phone again, as if waiting for it to ring. "I'll let you know as soon as I hear from him."

"Be sure that you do," the leopard replied sagely, letting slip for a moment his hidden concern. "I'll be in the lab should you need anything."

"Understood."

The door closed, and the bear was alone again. He looked at the clock, poured himself another shot from the amber bottle, and let out one final sigh.

* * *

"Hikiwake's stopped," Pi said, breaking the silence in the central chamber where the other three were waiting, the cold already starting to seep into their bones.

"Stopped?" Regis rumbled, stomping over to the bat's tablet display. "What do you mean, stopped?"

"Unless there's any meanings to the word I don't know about, it means he's bloody ceased moving!" the bat said and flicked his ears back toward the tunnel. "I can't hear any more fighting, either."

"Maybe we should have gone after him instead of staying here, *ja?*" Ramsden rumbled and glanced at the elephant. He shifted the weight on his submachine gun, sucking on his cigarette.

Regis ignored the wolf and watched as the dot stayed still for a few tense minutes – and then vanished.

"Pi..."

"That means he's now at a *complete* standstill," the bat hissed. "He's no longer moving even enough for the sensors to detect him..."

The crisp sound of Ramsden loading his weapon filled the air. "We're under attack," he growled, gun pointing down the corridor the samurai had taken.

"It's Spiritwolf," Regis said, taking out his own piece of 'personal protection', the small CFN-38 he had almost killed Achilles with.

The black wolf stood on edge for a moment, flicking his cigarette away. The next moment he was completely baffled as a sudden trickle of dark water began to flow across the stone floor, looking nearly like blood in the dim light. He looked down the black, unlit corridor where the water was coming from, suddenly feeling ill at ease, as if he could sense a presence down there, coming toward them like an unstoppable force. The thought of an invisible assassin gave him the willies.

"Pi!" Regis grunted. "Tell me what's going on. Your grid should be onto him! What about the heat sensors?"

"I don't know," the bat snapped, feeling betrayed and panicked. "They're state of the art, even if they couldn't see him move... a guy like that has to give out *heat*, right? I set it up based on what you told me!"

"He's not taking it," Regis said, holding the tablet close to his body. "I won't let him have it. Ramsden!"

"Fuck it," the German canine spat, almost certain he heard a footstep ahead of him. "Bullets don't need to see!" He yelled and began to fire his weapon blindly into the corridor. The room was lit up with the thunderous echo of his weapon discharging, casings of shells clattering to the wet floor, his face lit up in manic bloodlust and fear.

"Stop firing!" Regis yelled. Next to him, the bat had his fingers in his ears, his senses particularly jarred by the gunfire in such a tight space.

Eventually, the wolf ceased his mindless assault upon the air. He looked down the corridor ahead, smirking, sure he would have cut anything down there to ribbons with the hail he'd just laid down. "Got ya, freak," he said, satisfied and sure.

He had no sooner spoken his words however than a small, egg-shaped object suddenly lobbed itself out of the darkness from a different corridor, bouncing into the room.

"FLASH GRENADE!" Pi screeched, already putting his wings up around his face and eyes to form a protective cocoon. Regis had moved the second he saw the object, taking off like a coward down a different tunnel. When the blinding, loud flash shook the space, it was Ramsden who bore the brunt of it, grunting as his world exploded into dissonant white, his hearing ringing as he staggered against the wall.

"Got *you*, dog," Spiritwolf spat, slamming Ramsden's skull into the stonework as he pounced into the space like a vengeful poltergeist, following the grenade as surely as fire follows smoke. Not that the German could hear the insult, swiftly being knocked unconscious by the bash, the blow dislodging dust and old bones as he fell to the floor.

Spiritwolf's teeth were set on edge by a strange tingling sensation along his fur as he spun, turning around to face and disarm the bat. He was somewhat shocked to find the chiropteran had a gun trained directly on him, pointing with intent and accuracy. Instinctively he went to move to his left, to get out of the way, but Pi acted first, shooting directly into the wall next to Spirit's head.

"Don't. Fucking. *Move!*" the sharp-suited bat instructed, narrowing his eyes. Spiritwolf took a moment, in his confusion, to notice that aside from talking, Pi's lips were pursed, as if whistling.

"Sonar," the agent growled, now understanding the weird feeling. There was obviously no need for silence with this one. "Of course."

"You bet your ass," Pi responded, in clipped tones, his ears twitching. "Why do you think Regis came to me first? Now. Nice and slow." He reached into his pocket, pulling out a pair of handcuffs. He tossed them over to the agent, who let them fall at his feet rather than catch them. "Put them on or I swear, I'm going to put a bullet in your brain before you can even blink."

"You sound rattled," the wolf said, being seen to pick up the cuffs as they floated up from the floor. "Stressed. Why, I wouldn't even be surprised if you felt a little nauseous…"

"Shut up!" the bat barked. "Cuffs on."

The metal links unfolded themselves, and seemed to close themselves around something, hanging in the space where the wolf's wrists would have been, had he been visible.

"Funny thing is how many tests they ran on me before they let me loose," Spirit growled, his voice echoing through the chamber as his voice remained perfectly calm and in control, even as he could see Pi swaying, beads of sweat upon his brow. "...boy, was that ever a pain in the ass. But you know, I kind of appreciate it now. With how many useful things I learned..."

"U... useful?" The winged man said, having trouble focusing.

"Mmm. See, your sonar doesn't *quite* work on me. You must be feeling... mighty motion sick." The cuffs came closer, as Spirit stepped forward, his words neutral. "It's the disparity between what your sonar senses, and what your eyes see. Cool, huh?"

"Fuck..."

"Mmm. That ol' sonar of yours almost slides right around me... gives me a buzz, too... which means *you're* in deeper shit than you realize."

Suddenly, the cuffs dropped out of mid-air; Pi grunted and let off a shot, but it went wide of the mark as the wolf, who had never restrained himself in the first place, launched himself fully at the leathery mammal standing in his way.

"Christ!" was all the man had to say, feeling the full 250-pound weight of a naked wolf pile-driving him to the cold stone floor. It was an odd sensation, he came to realize upon reflection, once he had come to several hours later. All that muscle and fur, exposed, unseen, and pressing upon him. If he'd been thinking rationally, his best move would have been to kick his assailant in the balls. And yet, he reached for his gun anyway, trying to fight the agent off.

"Time to say goodnight," Spiritwolf hissed, snatching up the very same pistol Pi was reaching for, and then slamming it into the man's temple. The bat squeaked one last time, then went out like a light, sinking into the same stinking stream of water that Hikiwake and Ramsden had fallen into before him.

The wolf rose, victorious. All the pawns were off the board now.

Now it was time to take the king. Growling anew, he sprinted in pursuit.

* * *

The applause was thunderous; Achilles stood there, bathed in the glow of the lights and their praise, and for a moment forgot about his troubles. Everything that had happened in the past week was beginning to slip from his shoulders and for a moment, it felt like things could be normal again.

He raised his arms in a cheer and salute, panting, eyes wild with the thrill of performance. So many lights. This was what it was all about, wasn't it? Putting on a good show, having a good time. This was his world, not the crack of gunfire, nothing secret, everything bright and out in the open. After this gig, there would be an after-party, and it would be glorious. He might even go to it. Get drunk. Forget.

The boom of a drumbeat came from his left, as Cain began pounding the skins, readying the first salvo of his scheduled drum solo. Garrick and Les hopped away from their instruments, slinking away to the left wings of the stage, already grabbing towels and a quick refreshment. The badger's solo was the perfect midpoint of the gig to take a couple minutes' breather for the rest of the band while the mustelid entertained the crowd and got to show off. Achilles grinned and headed for the right side of the stage; most of the roadies and crew were on the left, but even here among the cases of equipment and leads there were a few stashed bottles of water.

The white wolf grunted and flicked the lid off a crisp flask of Evian, swigging gratefully and retreating into the shadows of the wings for a moment, out of sight of everyone else. He hated being babied during the middle of a set; he just wasn't one of those kind of stars. His crew knew this rule too, so when he heard the sound of a footstep coming up behind him, he was somewhat surprised and annoyed.

"Don't need anything guys..." he said, turning around. What he saw instead was a female wolf in a sharp black dress, smirking at him. "Who the fuck are *you*?" he said with agitated surprise, thinking a groupie had somehow gotten backstage.

"Oh, honey. I'm your new biggest fan!" Ardal said, stepping forward and ramming a stun gun into the wolf's neck.

Achilles didn't even have time to cry out as another shape came out from the shadows and placed a cloth bag over his head as the paralyzing device did its work. The burly wolverine assisting Ardal secured the star's head, picked him up in a fireman's carry, and proceeded to follow the wolfess toward the stage door with military efficiency.

The drums were beating loudly as they made their escape through the backstage area, soon reaching the door to the stadium corridors. There were a couple shouts of confusion as they swept past roadies who were more paying attention to what Cain was doing to notice the moment their boss had been grabbed. As soon as they were into the open, they broke into a run.

"FREEZE!" a booming voice suddenly yelled at them, the door bursting open again from behind. The two large angry shapes of Lars and David came into view as Achilles' bodyguards gave chase.

As one, Ardal and the wolverine turned, drawing out their guns with deadly intent.

Lars' own pistol was in his hand, but he was too exposed. The first bullet from the wolfess cut him down instantly, slamming into the bull's chest. David got off his own shot, but he was no sharpshooter – and in return, he got his own bullet to the knee.

The corridor was filled with blood and screaming as the two bulls went down. One would never get up again.

The two kidnappers were long gone by the time anyone could make sense of what had happened, and by then the whole stadium was in chaos.

Spiritwolf was not the only one removing pawns that night.

* * *

Regis was fumbling with a padlock when Spiritwolf found him.

"Fuck… FUCK!" The elephant was snarling, his voice shaking. His pistol glinted comically in the low light, looking very much like a toy compared to the weapons being toted by the others. Above him, through the metal gate, was the night sky – a crisp clear sight of the stars and full moon but not one the former manager would make in time.

"I took the liberty of changing the lock," the agent said from the shadows of the catacombs behind. "I figured you'd try to run."

Regis turned, eyes wide with horror, and began firing blindly at the darkness. He kept firing until the chamber was empty, at which point he kept squeezing, hopelessly, listening only to the dry clicks.

There was a pregnant pause as the sound of the gunfire died away, and he stood there on the steps that led up to the outside world, panting, horrified. And that was when Spiritwolf stepped out of the shadows – now fully clothed again, wearing his mask and smirking.

"Y… you're supposed to be invisible!"

"A friend of mine once told me I don't need to always rely on that. And he's right. I sure as hell don't have to be invisible to take down a piece of work like you. It's over, Black Dust." Spiritwolf squared his shoulders, his gun pointing at the elephant in case he tried anything. "And speaking of which, I have to know. Why the hell did you ever choose that name?"

The elephant sneered. "No one would ever think of me upon hearing 'Black Dust,' would they? Unlike you, 'Spiritwolf.' And just how did you become invisible, hm? Was it perhaps some kind of lab experiment gone freakishly awry… ?"

"Can it!" The wolf roared. "Give me the fucking tablet. Your men are all captured. You've got nowhere to run. This is the endgame."

Regis slowly put his hand inside his jacket pocket. It came back out with the precious piece of technology that the agent had been chasing this entire time. "You fool," the pachyderm hissed. "Endgame? This isn't even *close* to the end. You take this now… there are still people after this. I know there are. Whoever the buyer was… he's not just going to let you walk away with it. He's going to-"

The elephant's words were stolen from him as the agent sprinted up and punched Regis square in the jaw, snatching the tablet away. "That isn't your concern any more. You've been beaten. Now you have a choice to make."

Scowling like the Black Death, the grey-skinned fellow picked himself up. A cut was starting to well up on the bottom of his jaw. "What choice?"

"It's very simple, really," Spirit said, tucking the tablet into his jacket pocket, gun still trained on the elephant. "Now you've lost the thing that made you so valuable… I'll imagine there are a lot of toes you've stepped out there in the black market, belonging to people who you really shouldn't piss off. Not to mention your 'buyer'. If you think he's going to come down on me, what do you think he's going to do to you? I could let you go – but you'll be a dead man, Regis. You know you are. You'd have to be on the run for the rest of your life. Always looking over your shoulder…"

"Then shoot me!" The elephant scowled. "That's what you want to do, right?"

"That's one option. The other is you come in, cooperate. Tell us what we want to know and we'll protect you. Keep you alive."

"That's not much of a fucking choice."

"It's the only deal on the table right now. Choose." Spiritwolf growled blankly, raising his eyebrow and his gun.

Regis stood there for a long moment, his mouth working uselessly. Finally he threw his hands up in the air, clenching his fists. "You think you've won? Well, you haven't. I'm going to make you pay for this. I swear it." Yet his head drooped in defeat.

"Atta boy," The wolf said, pulling out the cuffs that Pi had so helpfully tossed at him before. "Turn around nice and slow, now. You're about to take a trip to the good ol' U S of A."

* * *

Cold eyes looked down at Achilles as the bag was removed from his head at last. Gasping for air, the white wolf turned an even paler shade of white upon seeing a gun pointed at his head.

"Thank you for joining us on such short notice," the owner of the gun purred to the bound star. "Ardal? Make the call. It's time we put this bait on its hook."

Chapter Ten: Blackest Night

Out of the darkness, Spiritwolf staggered.

The moon was a full beam upon his blank features as he turned and locked the gate to the catacombs behind him, padlock in place. He looked down into the pit where Black Dust and his men had been conquered, and still displayed no emotion as he turned again, taking a few steps into the deserted backstreet.

He seemed to sway as he walked. Drunk on a feeling that he could not contain. Finally, after a couple more steps, he leaned against an old brick wall, putting his back to the stone, head bowed. He reached into his pocket, and brought out the small, unassuming black shape of the tablet he had fought so hard for. His face was a perfect mask as he turned it over in his hand, studying it, appreciating every facet of its exterior. It was so small, like a PDA used to be. So valuable.

And now it was his.

Finally, at last, a small smile broke upon his face. He could not seem to stop it as the small upturning of his muzzle became a full grin of victory. *Beat you, Black Dust. Fucking beat you!*

He had been waiting so long for the end of his mission, to have finally reached the end, to have what he came to Europe for, he felt like he was in a dream for a moment. Then his training kicked back in, the smile faded, and his mind was full of the things he would have to do next. His prisoners were secure in the catacombs for the moment; he'd have to contact the agency to get them taken into custody, make arrangements for Regis and himself to fly back to the States. The tablet would have to be secured too, not to mention the reports to be filed. Paperwork. And… he'd promised a certain wolf a drink, hadn't he? The smile showed a hint at returning as he slid the precious device back into the inner pocket of his jacket, getting his phone out of another in the process.

He studied it for a moment. Who to call first? Zero would want to know that Spirit's first post-accident mission was a success, of course. But, the wolf reminded himself, the prisoners had to be extracted before the police or any other public agency showed up, and he would need local TEA boots for that. Ixak would be the one to call before anyone else, though Spirit wondered whether the beetle already knew of his victory. He cocked his eyebrow after punching in the number, cleared his throat, and pressed dial. He lifted the phone up to his ear, and for one last moment got to appreciate how beautiful Paris, the City of Lights, looked at night.

A momentary crackle of silence, and then the clear click of someone picking up on the other end. "Agent Spiritwolf reporting," he began. "Clearance Ultra, verifying code Two Charlie Victor-"

"Sp... Spiritwolf!"

The voice that answered was so unexpected so... unlike the person it belonged to, the agent felt another lurch of unreality, punching him square in the gut. He visibly boggled as his words were cut off. "A... Achilles?"

"Spirit!" The shaking voice said again on the other end, the singer sounding... so different. So *afraid*. "Listen to me. I... I'm with some people. They... they want me to deliver a message to you."

"What's going on? Why are you on this line?"

A moment's pregnant pause. "They said... your equipment was compromised when... when you were in the tunnels with Regis. They... they know you have the tablet. They... they have me, Spirit. They want you to follow my instructions."

"Who has you?" the agent said, trying to stop himself from shouting. His heart was beating so hard he thought his ribcage would get bruised. *This can't be happening.* "Talk to me yourselves!"

"He... he said...'not yet.'" There was the sound of the singer swallowing, more mumbling as he was told what to say next. "They're going to kill me, Spirit. They want to exchange me for the tablet." This bit was on, and said quietly. But suddenly, the line went loud as the white wolf was heard to scream. "But they'll do it anyway! You can't give it to them! Just fucking forget about me, just-"

There was the sickening sound of a jarring blow, and then Spiritwolf didn't hear the singer any more as he stood there, listening to his own breath for a moment. "Achilles..." he said, the word exhaled from his muzzle with blank expectation. Then the line was picked up again, an unfamiliar female voice – British – on the other end of the phone.

"Agent Spiritwolf. Our man is coming down the street toward you now. He is a messenger; he is unarmed. He will escort you to where the exchange will take place. For both your sakes, I would recommend leaving him unharmed. We *will* kill the singer, should you refuse. All we want is the tablet."

"We'll see about that!" the agent barked in return; but the line already went dead, a click on the other end of the phone signaling the end to the negotiation. The wolf's head suddenly snapped to the side as, true to the woman's word, he could make out the silhouette of a figure in a trenchcoat moving down the alley toward him. His hand immediately went for his gun, which he pointed with deadly intent at the newcomer. "Hey! Hands where I can see them! Not *one* fucking step closer!"

The figure froze, his face hidden in the shadows. He slowly raised his skinny arms above his head, mute. The agent kept his pistol ready and pointed as he prowled forward, his muzzle full of the bitter taste of robbed victory. Finally, he stopped short and peered at the man before him... the messenger turned his face slightly, finally letting the wolf see who he was dealing with.

"It... it's *you*," Spiritwolf said with dismay, recognizing the meerkat from Rising Force who had gotten away from him.

"I did not expect to meet you again either," Benny said, not moving. His face looked bruised from beating. "Not like this; this night must be full of many surprises for you."

"I want to know what the fuck is going on, *right* now. Who is behind all this? They're playing a dangerous game."

"More dangerous than you realize, agent. I... would reveal to you who wishes to meet you so badly, but it seems he wants that pleasure for himself. I'm wired; he'll be listening even now."

The wolf shook his head, sadly. "I can't. Doesn't he realize I *can't*? Achilles... I'm... I'm so sorry he was dragged into this. But..." He swallowed hard, steeling his heart for what he was about to say. "Even his life... as much as I like him... I can't exchange the tablet for him. It doesn't fucking work that way!"

"Yes," the Israeli meerkat rasped with displeasure. "He anticipated your saying that. That is why he has sent me. You must... open my coat, Agent Spiritwolf."

The brown-furred wolf looked upon the smaller man in disbelief as he listened to the words. Suddenly he realized how bulky the trenchcoat was... a stupid detail to have overlooked, now of all moments. He stepped forward, and undid the zipper of the shaking former-terrorist's garment. Halfway down, he saw the wires and the bundles of C4 that made him truly aware of how screwed he was.

"Please," Benny said, meeting Spiritwolf's gaze with his own. "Even if you do not care about my life – we are both in this together. If you try to run now, he'll detonate me before you get two paces. We'll both go up."

"And his precious tablet as well," the wolf spat, his whole body quivering. He felt sick.

"If he can't have it, no one can," Benny said mechanically, repeating something he was being told in an earpiece. Yet there was an undercurrent of absolute revulsion, rebellion in the man's words. He hated this as much as Spiritwolf did. The great Benny Anhalem, reduced to this, a mere messenger boy. A walking bomb. "He would have you come now. It's time you met."

"Seems I have no choice," Spiritwolf said, muzzle curling. He put his gun up against Benny's chin in sheer frustration for a moment. "You fucking coward. You're just a puppet on his string now!"

"Let's just fucking get this over with."

"He's going to regret this," the wolf said, shaking his head. "Go on… lead the way." Spiritwolf sighed. His shoulders slumped, giving off the impression he was co-operating and defeated.

In reality, his mind was already thinking of the ways he would tear this new player apart once he got him in his sights.

* * *

"We're here," Benny announced, coming to a stop.

"You have got to be fucking kidding me," Spiritwolf rejoined, looking up at the skyline. The Eiffel Tower was a golden monolith against the night sky, a fat, round full moon sitting upon its tip. Around them, in the center of Paris, nocturnal citizens were wandering to and fro with no concept of the walking bomb that stood in their midst.

"Afraid so. Come on. This way…" the Israeli agent huffed, making for the southeastern side of the famous landmark. Crossing the cold stone slabs gingerly, he came up to an unimpressed-looking panther, the suited and booted feline apparently standing guard by a private elevator doorway. Above the entrance, in gilded letters was stamped the name of the establishment that lay upstairs. *Le Restaurant Jules Verne.* The meerkat gave the guard a nod, then patted Spiritwolf on the back. "Up you go. Good luck," he hissed in a low whisper, even as the panther swiped his key in the electronic lock to make the lift doorway slide open silently.

"Not coming, huh? Figures…" the agent said, coldly.

"I'm supposed to wait down here. Insurance. You wouldn't want the tower and everyone around to go up."

"No. Just you." He glared at the smaller man one more time, then stepped inside the elevator. He turned, facing outwards as the lift doorway shuddered closed again. The last thing Benny saw was Spiritwolf mouthing him the words "I'm coming for you," before the portal clanked closed again, and the winch began to turn.

As soon as he was alone, he exhaled sharply. The option of hitting the elevator's emergency stop when he was partway up, escaping the capsule, and getting the tablet somewhere safe was still on his mind. It was, after all, his mission, his top priority. Yet he knew that option had consequences; Achilles would pay. So would Benny. And other innocents too, if this new player detonated the bomb. He wasn't so cold as to be blind to that; besides which he had an opportunity to meet with this new adversary and dispose of them at the first blush. It certainly seemed that he knew enough about their operation to remain a thorn in their side, if left unchallenged.

He rolled his shoulders and scowled, mentally preparing himself for what was to come as the carriage glided upwards.

When the doors opened again, he was met by a scene of unparalleled luxury; a plush red carpet led out to a stunning restaurant, heaving with white table-cloths, waiters in suits, chatting diners, even a coyote playing a piano in the corner. It was an intimate space, taking up the entirety of the second level of the tower; every side had a window which presented the most stunning view of the city, lights twinkling in the distance, cars far below moving like fireflies.

As the door opened and the large wolf stepped out, a cream-colored feline in a tuxedo stepped forward to meet him. "*Bon soir, monsieur,*" the maître d' began to purr, ready to receive him and take his jacket.

"Go away," Spiritwolf growled, scanning the room for the man, the threat that had brought him here.

The fellow sniffed stiffly. "Ah. Monsieur Spiritwolf. Pardon. Monsieur is expecting you." He turned on his heel, and beckoned the agent to follow him.

Cocking his head, knowing he was dressed inappropriately for the swanky establishment, the wolf tailed after, giving all of the ordinary patrons a fierce glare if they even so dared look at him. Finally, he was brought up to a table at the very center of the room, and came face-to-face with the man who had been pulling his strings all along.

The lion was ready for him, too.

Blair held a glass of red wine in his hand, swirling it casually as the agent approached. "Right on time," the feline purred, giving him a cold glance. "I do so admire punctuality. Have a seat, agent."

"I'm not here to dine with you," Spiritwolf growled, even as the maître d' pulled out his chair for him.

"That wasn't a request," Blair said, cocking his eyebrow. "Unless you want to get this over with quickly, in which case the next time the singer makes an appearance, it will be as a serve of tartare coming out of that kitchen." He spoke pointedly, flicking out his claws. "And, well, if you wanted that to happen, you wouldn't even be here. So… *sit*."

Keeping his face a blank mask, revealing nothing, the large wolf stiffly sat down in front of the lion, the chair creaking as he went. The waiter went to put a napkin over his lap, but the agent reached out, grabbed his wrist, and put just enough pressure on it to make the man squirm. "Leave us," he growled. "Now."

The man blanched and nodded his head in recognition, and scurried away. As soon as he was gone, the magnate sitting opposite burst into a delighted, callous laugh. "Look at you, giving orders. So confident. Almost like you still believe you're in control of the situation." He took a sip of his vintage and addressed the wolf over the rim, smirking. "I can see now why you have been such an asset to the Ultras program."

Spiritwolf's glare intensified. "Who are you and how do you know so much?"

The lion put his glass down. "Both questions, while obvious, should be of small consequence compared to the real question you should be asking – how is it that *you* know so *little*?" He spread his claws again. "No mention of me in your mission briefings, no clue as to where I came from, who I am, or why. That must really trouble you, agent."

"I'll admit to being mildly surprised."

"Mmm. Mildly…" the lion said with a smile.

"But, well, at least I now have an answer for who was responsible for putting Gareth on top of the pyramid." He smiled back and showed the lion all his veneered teeth. "They hate loose ends upstairs, you know."

"So I've been told," the lion said. "I'd wager they hate losing valuable technology even more. But, well, that's the way the cookie crumbles, so to speak."

"If you think I'm going to hand you the tablet, right after I took down Black Dust and all his men, you really don't know me as well as you think you do," Spiritwolf threatened. "I'd sooner jump across this table and take you out now. Your men might take me out, too. But you'd be gone. Is that what you want?"

"Charming as your offer sounds, I will have to decline. My men put their guns on you the moment you walked in. I sincerely hope you can do better than that, agent," the man chided, as if he were playing a game of chess with an opponent who had already lost.

"You seem like a man of status," Spirit quipped. "I doubt you are prepared to commit a murder in front of a room full of eyewitnesses," he hissed, eyes casting over the rest of the room.

The lion rocked back in his chair, closing his eyes. "And you are so very right about that," he crooned, finally, softly. "So, it is probably best I resolve that problem for you now." His voice dripped disdain as he leaned forward again, golden hand reaching out for a tiny, unassuming little silver bell that rested next to his napkin. Relishing the moment, he picked it up and gave it a singular, charitable, shake.

A dainty ring rang out, cutting through the hubbub and chatter for all to hear. The seasoned agent couldn't help it, but a chill went down his spine as the entire restaurant dropped into deathly silence, as if a secret signal had been made. Suddenly the room was full of sound and motion again as if a spell had been broken, chairs scraping across the carpet, forks being put down and glasses clinking against each other as all the diners rose in unison, saying nothing, unwilling to look Spiritwolf in the eye. The white-jacketed staff melted away like ghosts into the kitchen while only some of the patrons filed for the elevators and stairs; the rest took up positions around the room's edge, pulled out their weapons and pointed them as one at the wolf. The two men remained a central, still point; Blair's smile had gotten all the more pleased as this went on until they were left virtually alone.

"A man of status, like you say," the lion announced proudly once the performance was done. "Now, shall we get this over with?"

The brown wolf openly glared, taking a deep breath. "All this and you presume I even have what you want on me." He cocked his head at the feline. "You really should have had Benny check, before you walked me all the way over here."

"Enough games, agent," the magnate snapped, starting to bristle. "All I require is a simple exchange. Ardal," he said, calling over his shoulder in the direction of the kitchen. "Bring him."

The brown wolf sat rigidly in his chair, spine perfectly straight as the swinging doors burst open, and two figures marched out; there was no mistaking the treacherous wolfess, dressed up to the nines in a black dress and pearl earrings, like she'd come to the restaurant for dinner instead of business. Ardal wore a smirk on her face as she held her considerably less well-dressed captive by the arm, bringing him over to the table, the man limping.

The singer, still clothed from his gig from which he'd been abducted, was shirtless still, only his body was now marked with bruises and cuts from where he'd been beaten at some point in his capture. The dark marks created blotches around his signature tattoos, marring his well-honed frame. He had a black hood on his head, like he was being led for execution, his hands bound by rope, which he was holding very tight and close to his body, like he was protecting something. Spiritwolf noticed, as Achilles was forced to his knees directly next to the lion, that the singer's leather pants were marked with frost and the singer was helplessly shivering.

Ardal stood back, arms folded across her chest and seemingly waiting for what was to happen next. As the hood was removed, the two wolves locked eyes, reunited under duress. The white wolf's face was a mess too – his bottom lip was cut and puffy, his left eye swollen shut with blackness. It looked as though somebody really went to town on him, perhaps after the phone call when Achilles had shouted his warning.

"You shouldn't have come…" was the first thing the singer croaked.

"Didn't have much choice," Spiritwolf somberly replied. "I'm sorry." He looked up and glared at the lion. "What the fuck did you do to him?"

"Went a couple rounds with a guy who was jealous of my good looks," the captive answered before anyone else could, spitting dark blood that had congealed from the cold. "Then they shoved me in the walk-in freezer until you got here."

The lion swirled the last of his wine, sighed, and finished it. "What can I say?" he said, almost apologetically. "We don't always get the best performance from those who work for us – a fact your American superiors will soon understand." He put down the glass purposefully and began to make his final offer, his voice laced with relish. "So, agent, here we all are at last. Give me the tablet and this fine, promising artist doesn't have to die." He smirked. "I'll even let you go afterwards. How's that?"

"Useless," Spiritwolf growled. "Even if I agree, I have no guarantee you won't kill us both."

"You're running out of time, agent," Blair warned. "Choose your next words carefully." He flicked out a claw. The end of the game was drawing near.

The agent stopped listening; his predatory mind had already formed a plan; first, he would overturn the table, shield himself from the fire, hopefully; then grab the lion's gun – he saw the magnate was packing personal protection, the concealed holster was unmistakable to him – exchange fire, do his best to eliminate as many as possible, escape… but before he could act, someone else beat him to it.

"Fuck you!" the singer said, suddenly rising, moving as quick as a venomous snake, his bound wrists suddenly of no consequence as he revealed something he had been concealing – a long shard of white, sharp as a dagger, holding it to Blair's throat before anyone could react, least of all the lion. "Nobody move!" Achilles barked, pressing the bone shard so closely to the lion's throat, all it would take would be an ounce more pressure to tear it open. "Or your boss eats it."

"Achilles – no!" Spiritwolf said, getting to his feet. Ardal had her own weapon out, and was pointing it at the white wolf's head. The guards meanwhile, two of them, stepped out of their shadows, having been covering the agent so closely they were left useless as the singer made his move. One of them was now keeping Achilles in their sights, while one clearly had his pistol pointed at Spiritwolf, preventing him from making any further moves. "Nobody shoot, please!" the agent pleaded with everyone.

"Interesting," Blair crooned, barely able to swallow. "I assume you've thought this through?" he growled. "Because you just signed your life away, whatever happens."

"You should never have stuck me in that freezer," the white wolf said, bitterly. "With all those frozen rib-bones. They make perfect shivs when you shatter them; one to cut the rope with, another one to stick you with."

"Achilles, you're not trained for this, you don't know what you're doing!" The agent barked. There weren't many options left to him now.

"Shut up – I knew I was a dead wolf either way. At least now you have a chance," the canine holding the weapon to Blair's throat answered, locking eyes with him again. "You're going to get out of here – you and the tablet. You can't let this monster have it. It's too important."

The lion began to chuckle, but Achilles pressed the bone in deeper, silencing him.

"No…" Spirit tried to argue, though he knew the wolf was right, in his heart.

"Blair," the white wolf hissed with the intent of a man who knows he has nothing left to lose. "You tell your men *right fucking now* to let Spiritwolf walk out of here, or I'm going to cut you open like the bag of meat you know you are. We'll go down together."

"…un-fucking-believable," the magnate rumbled, for a moment sounding deflated. Before he roared, "That you think I'd roll over and surrender to a mutt like you!"

"Achilles, get his gun. It's in his left pocket. We can both get out of here," Spiritwolf pleaded. "*Now.*"

The wolf looked shifty-eyed, his composure starting to weaken now the lion had refused to give the order. He didn't know how much longer he could keep this up, painfully aware of the gun Ardal was pointing at his head. The wolfess was saying nothing, but her pose said it all. She was ready, all right, for the smallest opening the singer gave her to eliminate him.

All eyes were on Achilles. It was now or never. "I'm… I'm sorry, Spirit," the wolf said, meeting the agent with his gaze, his arm starting to waver.

"Interesting party," an unexpected voice said, cutting through the tension and the moment like a knife through butter. It came from the direction of the elevator. "Let's make it more interesting." A familiar Israeli accent was wrapped around the words. The focus of the room turned, shifted, and alighted upon the sight of the meerkat, walking purposefully toward them. He'd lost his coat, the bomb that was strapped around him plain to see now for all the room, the red light at the center of his chest glowing a dire warning for all to see. He seemed to have pulled some wires out from the main circuitry, held tellingly in his hand.

"Benny?!" was all Spiritwolf could say. One of the guards covering the brown wolf turned his weapon onto the agent, but the smaller mammal had him in his sights right away.

"You'll not be shooting me," he warned. "This bomb was wired to a dead-man switch from the beginning." He came ever closer, until he was standing right next to Spiritwolf. "And now I have control," he said, indicating the wires he held. "So… unless you want to meet a fiery end, everybody relax." Spiritwolf was looking in disbelief at the meerkat, who simply smirked and explained. "You leave the bomb expert alone with an explosive around his chest, you're going to have a bad time."

"What are you doing here?" the agent asked, not knowing whether to feel relieved or more alarmed than before.

"My thoughts exactly," Blair said, still with Achilles on him. He narrowed his eyes. "Someone was supposed to be watching you. You were to be dealt with later."

"You – and your man – got sloppy," Benny said, picking up a roll that was on the table between the tense parties and munching it like he didn't have a care in the world. "Ah, look at that," he said, picking up the bottle of red, seeing some still left within. "Chateau du Breuil… this will make a fine last drink…"

"…last?" Achilles said, looking as though he might faint.

"I'll take it from here, kid. You and your invisible friend scram." Benny waved the wires for effect, to all of the lion's men. "And nobody's going to stop them, or else… well, you know what's going to happen," he announced. "All I have to do is make the connection and everyone will be singing with the angels."

Spiritwolf risked standing, even as the meerkat took a long swig from the bottle. Achilles couldn't hold his composure anymore and let Blair go, the bone falling from his hand. Stepping into the shadow, Ardal began backing away, her gun pointing at everyone she considered a threat.

"Why… why are you sticking your neck out to save us?" Spirit wondered. "You were trying to capture or kill me, not so long ago."

"That's before this fucker got involved," Benny said. "I owe him. Nobody straps a bomb to Benny Anhalem and gets away with it!" He glared at Blair. "So, yeah. You take yourself and whatever thing it is he's after and get gone. One time offer. I'm going up with him; I don't have to take you with us, but I will if it comes to that." He became solemn in his expression, yet behind his eyes he looked crazed. "I never imagined I'd be the one martyring myself for the cause."

Achilles had limped his way over to Spiritwolf; his brief moment of heroism and mad sacrifice taken from him, he looked scared and keen to preserve his life again. "Is he for real?" he asked, voice cracking.

"Undoubtedly," the agent answered. He grabbed hold of Achilles, helping him walk as they made their way to the emergency exit. There was no way Spiritwolf was going to trust an elevator with a bomb in the building. "We're going."

"This isn't over, Spiritwolf," Blair spat. "You'd better run because I won't be far behind."

"Shut your mouth," Benny growled, getting angry. His hand twitched. "Before you make me do something we both regret."

Achilles burst through the door, already limping down the cold, metal stairwell. Spiritwolf paused on the threshold, taking one last look at the meerkat. The guards were regarding him venomously and helplessly both at once. The agent narrowed his eyes. "Thank you," he said sincerely before he followed the singer down the stairs.

"Don't mention it," Benny whispered, alone in the dining room at last with all eyes upon him with loathing and fear. "Well, guys," he announced in a loud voice, as if he were making a toast at a wedding. He used his free hand to raise his wine bottle. "Any last words?"

* * *

On the stairwell, the two wolves ran like the hounds of hell were upon them. Achilles didn't get far before he found himself stumbling against the wall, grabbing his side painfully. Spiritwolf was with him in an instant.

"C'mon, don't stop. If Benny detonates…"

"Sorry... sss... I think they cracked my rib... look... go on ahead, disappear. I'm just going to slow you down."

"Oh no," the brown wolf said, hooking himself under Achilles' shoulder, starting to help him down. "You already tried to sacrifice yourself for me once, I'll be damned if I'll have you doing it again."

Achilles winced and began stumbling on again, having to use Spiritwolf for support, their progress considerably slower than before.

"What the hell was that, anyway?" the agent asked, unable to help himself. "You're supposed to be an entertainer, not a secret agent. Next time, leave the heroics to me."

"You're welcome," Achilles grumpily replied. "Look... I just... I know what I do isn't important, but you—"

"Cut that out!" Spiritwolf barked. "The things I do... what I am... it'd all be meaningless without something to do it *for*. I do it so the world – *your* world – can carry on as normal. People can go to concerts, enjoy life, do all the things I can't do, without terrorists, corporations, or governments getting out of hand..."

"Heh..." Achilles said, wincing. "Only my world... doesn't seem so normal any more..."

Before the agent could reply, above them they heard the sudden, but unmistakable muffled sound of gunfire. They couldn't help but freeze for a second.

"...not an explosion?" Achilles whispered, the words hanging in the air.

"*Definitely* not an explosion. MOVE!" Spirit said, already fearing the worst.

* * *

It was the gunfire that had put an end to Benny's gambit, sure enough.

The lion was watching Benny intently, looking serene and neutral as the contemptible Israeli drank the last of his wine and swanned about like lord of the manor after the two wolves had left. "Never imagined Paris would be my last stop," he quipped. "Still, neither did you, I'm guessing. I trust you have your newspapers ready to print your obituary?"

"As a matter of fact, I do," Blair said, suddenly deciding to rise out of his chair. "But only because I prepare for all eventualities."

"What are you doing?" the meerkat said, turning on him. "You think I am bluffing, like the wolf? I am not." He brought his hand up, the two wires perilously close.

Blair slowly turned his head. He looked to the kitchen door, and Benny couldn't understand why until Ardal emerged from it a moment later. She'd slipped away without him noticing. His expression began to change from confidence to dismay.

"How did you get on with the remote deactivation?" the lion asked casually, as if he were merely asking to see the dessert menu. "The app makes it a breeze, doesn't it?"

"Just like you said, sir," the wolfess said, waving her smartphone. "No more dead man switch and no armed bomb."

"Always good have a fail-safe in case things go sideways," Blair said and turned to face Benny; the meerkat's arm drooping, the wine-bottle he was holding falling from his grip. It splashed red all over the floor.

"*Ben Zona…*" he muttered, even as the lion raised his eyebrow.

"You said it," the magnate replied, even as the bullets cut through the air, ending the meerkat's part in the drama once and for all.

* * *

The two wolves reached the doorway, even as bullets began flying down the stairwell toward them, down the spiral shaft. "Exit, exit!" the agent barked, barging through the door, bracing himself as he met with a cold wind, and the night sky. They'd burst onto a maintenance platform of the famous tower, steel and railings surrounding them. It was as big across as a concert hall at least, cover provided by steel pillars that reached up into the structure. Spiritwolf didn't quite know the layout of the place, but he knew there had to be another way down, and as he ran with Achilles limping on his shoulder, he raced to find it.

"Now you have to leave me!" the singer pleaded. "Complete your mission. Just… take off your stuff, leave me here, disappear! You could do so easily!"

"You're dead if I do," Spiritwolf panted, pausing long enough to consider it. "…no, I can't. We… we still need to go grab that drink together, right?"

"Yeah, right… you were never going to come to that anyway…" Achilles huffed as they crossed over from one side of the platform to the other, still urgently looking for the stairs. "I saw the look in your eye, back there. That's why I knew I had to make my move…"

"What are you talking about?" the agent growled, feeling distracted.

"When Blair brought me out and offered you the exchange," Achilles answered. "You weren't going to take it. You were thinking of some way to get under him and fight your way out. But you weren't thinking about what was going to happen to me."

Suddenly, Spiritwolf heard the door they'd come from, a short way behind them, burst open, and footsteps echoing on the steel platform. He didn't have the time, or the heart to reply to the singer and let him know just how right he'd been.

"Well, I'm thinking now," he said breathlessly. He grabbed Achilles, and set him, pushed him down with his back against one of the large steel girders that made up the larger structure, into the recess of it, into the shadows. "Stay here," he hissed insistently. "They won't spot you," he said, standing again. "I'll go and draw them away. You wait until they've gone; then you head *up*, back to the restaurant. Benny's dead and they'll have disarmed the bomb, so it'll be okay. They won't be expecting you to double back, they'll be covering the exits. You hide there until the police come…"

"Spirit…" the singer said, lost for words. "It's madness…"

"Then I'm mad," the larger wolf huffed, kicking off his boots to reveal the nothingness seemingly supporting him. "Now, stay and be quiet!" he rasped.

Taking off before he could hear any words to the contrary, he ran up the platform, shucking his jacket as he went. His heart pounding in his ears, he felt intensely… liberated and determined as he yanked up his t-shirt, now just a collection of floating hands, head, and legs attached to a central, unseen point. In his right hand, he clutched the precious tablet.

Sprinting, he heard footsteps all about the platform as the men frantically searched for him. It was time to end this. Running toward the center of the structure, under the main archway, he finally found the main stairwell, only to find Blair himself blocking his path.

The lion's mane looked considerably less well-groomed in the open air, and his hard-won controlled countenance starting to fray. The pistol in his grip seemed to suit him poorly.

"Not one step closer," Spiritwolf said, pulling back his arm holding the tablet. "Shoot me, try to stop me, I'm tossing this thing over the edge. You'll never get your hands on it."

"You fool," the lion said, growling contempt. "It was never just about the device," he said, advancing. "If that was all I wanted, I could have had the elephant brought to his knees, brought to *me*, without even needing to leave the office." He glinted coldly, calculatingly at the agent, the surreal appearance of the half-invisible wolf seeming to throw him not one bit. "What I want, what *he* wants, is the same thing everybody has been after. *You*."

"Me? Who… ?" Spiritwolf said, getting ready to unleash his full fury on the lion. Were it not for that one question, he would have done so already.

The lion smirked. "An old colleague of yours… he who now lies in the shadows. You'll be meeting him again, soon enough."

"Spirit!" Achilles' voice suddenly called out, across the platform. There was a moment's distraction, as the singer stole attention from both men, and then Spiritwolf lunged at Blair, knocking the gun from the lion's golden-furred hand. But, to the agent's surprise and dismay, the feline fought back, hard. He parried Spiritwolf's next blow, and then hit him in the jaw with the hardest, most brutal punch the wolf had ever received. The tablet clattered uselessly from Spiritwolf's grasp, and then slid through a gap in the plating beneath them, seemingly lost.

"I was the boxing champion at Eaton for three years!" the lion roared. "I will *end* you!"

"Not if I end you first!" Spiritwolf shouted, fighting back with everything he had and cursing the fact that Achilles hadn't listened to him. The men exchanged blows, the fight moving from the center of the platform out to the exterior. The cold wind tore at the men as they grappled with one another; the view of Paris a couple hundred meters below just a few missteps away. Spiritwolf thought he had the lion in a hold, but the brute head-butted him, almost cracking a sensitive bone at the base of his muzzle. There was a primal rage in this fight now; Blair's well-mannered exterior had fallen to reveal the beast, the temper that lay within, and he used that fury to land a flurry of punches on the agent. Wave after wave came without a moment's respite; all Spirit could do was try to defend himself. A lucky shot found his temple and then dizziness took hold of the agent; he'd been trained enough by Master Song to know when a fight was about to become a loss. They were at a section of the platform with only a small railing separating them from dark oblivion; on a tourist level, this never would have been the case. The fight brought them to the very edge of it.

"You can't have me," Spiritwolf said, gasping and using all his strength to hold back the lion, whose perfect fangs were centimeters away from his face. "No one can."

"Then you know what to do…" Blair snarled, making his last threat. "Or you know what will happen. But you won't…"

"Spiritwolf… SPIRIT, NO!" Achilles screamed, his legs not fast enough to stop what happened next, as the invisible wolf made a final, determined growl, a hair's more pressure as they fought, grappled…

And the two combatants went over the edge of the railing together.

Thinking his heart had stopped, the white wolf ran to the edge, sinking to his knees, for a moment not daring to look at the dark black void the wolf and lion had tumbled into, the flickering lights mixing with tears in his eyes as he imagined the agent falling to his death below. But then, mercifully, he saw a brown hand, just clinging on for hope at the edge. Achilles instantly threw himself onto his belly; the searing pain that shot through his body from his cracked rib meaning nothing as he shot out his hand, taking hold of Spirit's own, just as it slipped, losing its grip on the structure.

"I got you!" he barked, thankfully. But the moment he took the weight, he knew there was something very wrong, the heaviness too great for one man alone. He looked down and saw Blair, hanging with fury onto Spiritwolf's leg.

"Shake him off!" the singer gasped, trying to hold on. "I can't... he's too..."

"His men are coming," the agent said, his voice cracked, but unable to let the white wolf know his fear. "You have to let go!"

"I can't... you can't... Spirit, *fight*, damn you!" Achilles implored, even as he felt a kind of... slipping of the hand... like a glove coming off. Spiritwolf felt it too and knew it was the bio-glue of his disguise... finally giving way, just like when the old woman had grabbed him on the bus, seemingly a lifetime ago, when he'd first begun his mission in Dresden.

But this time, he knew it wouldn't last.

He looked up, fixing the white wolf with a soul-penetrating stare. "It's going to be all right. Forget me, Achilles... I'm already gone," he uttered. Below, Blair hissed, his eyes widening to portals of absolute rage.

"No!"

There was a moment's fragile pause, as if all of time stood still to observe the moment, and then there was a sickening, wet *snap*, as the glue finally became unbound and suddenly Achilles wasn't holding on to Spirit's hand any more. He was holding on to an empty rag of skin, something artificial. The wolf, the thing that had filled it, giving it warmth and life, was gone.

He stared at it for a moment, horrified, then looked desperately over the edge, only seeing the lion falling, screaming obscenities. There was nothing he could see of the agent, and yet, he heard a stomach-turning sound of impact a second later.

He scooted back from the edge, holding the empty hand like it would do something, perform some miracle. But it was done. It was over.

Spiritwolf and Blair Murdock were gone.

* * *

It was no coincidence that the paparazzi found Blair first; in the aftermath of the singer's disappearance from the stadium, the whole city was in an uproar wondering where the star had gone. All it took was one report, one hint that the singer had been spotted up the Eiffel tower by someone with a telescope, to send the photo-hungry hounds in the direction of the monument.

The lion would have appreciated the irony as flashbulbs illuminated his smashed corpse; those doing the photographing instantly recognizing the man many of them would have hoped to be paid by. Back home, calls were made, files pulled, obituaries readied. And newspaper editors across the continent struggled to fathom the right way to make a headline to report upon the death of the man they had feared above all others.

After the paparazzi came the police. Once they gained control of the scene, their search began in earnest. Finding the brutalized singer was only the first surprise of the evening. In their custody, on the ground, Achilles looked on with vacant, expressionless eyes as the lion's corpse was covered over. An officer was talking to him, trying to get a statement as he sat on the step of an ambulance, flashing lights of every hue surrounding him.

He barely heard the man asking questions. Instead, he was looking on, sadly, as an officer within the taped-up crime scene used a pair of rubber gloves to pick up something he'd found on the ground.

"Looks like some kind of... Halloween mask?" he said, curiously, holding it up. The loose, brown wolf's head seemed to stare at Achilles with empty eye sockets moments before it was sealed into a clear plastic bag and taken away.

Epilogue: From Darkness and Ashes

It was late afternoon that found the bear and the fox walking along the gently sloping path. Its arc descended gradually toward a worn wood bench that was distinctly out of place compared to the relatively new buildings behind them. The bench overlooked a grove of pine trees clustered at the far end of a clear circular pond. The trees sighed together as though whispering gossip carried by the warm southern breeze. The fox, despite being blind, tapped the way forward for the both of them with his cane, causing amused fondness to break through the bear's perpetually gruff exterior. The bear was the one who usually did the leading and ordering about. Not so, here, it seemed.

"I'm worried about Spiritwolf," he finally said, pulling up beside the fox.

Master Song had stopped just behind the bench. The martial arts master appeared to be surveying the water, as though he were able to see every last detail along its shores and across the rippling surface. "You needn't be," he replied, calmer than the pond and the pines. "You shouldn't be. But you are. Why is that?"

Zero also looked at the beautiful scenery, then up at the clear blue sky overhead. "Someone… Topaz… said that Spirit would fall."

"Topaz. Ah, of course," the fox murmured and bowed his head. "She saw his death, then?"

"No, and I know where you're going with that. Exact wording and such. Now or in the future." Zero ran his hand along the top of the bench, as if expecting the invisible wolf to be sitting there, listening. "But he hasn't checked in for almost thirty hours."

"His body was not recovered with the lion's?"

Zero blinked. "How did you… ?"

"Corona was kind enough to tell me."

295

There was no chastisement in the fox's voice but Zero still felt a rare moment of shame. His trenchcoat rustled as he shrugged his apology. "It was not recovered at the scene. The paramedics did find his mask; Ixak persuaded them to turn at least that over to him."

"And you are worried that Spiritwolf could be injured or incapacitated, invisible, and unable to call for help."

"Yes."

Master Song flicked his ears and nodded. "As much as I would like to visit Paris and help search for Spiritwolf, I do not believe that is necessary." He smiled. "The wolf is resourceful, and more resilient than you realize. I am sure he will be fine."

Zero looked sideways at him. "And have you now acquired Topaz's ability to see possible futures, as well?"

The fox abruptly quarter-turned left to face him and, in one perfect move that reminded Zero of the first time seeing him spar, spun the cane so that its head came to rest on the bear's chest, over his heart. "This is how I see Spirit's future," he said in a clear voice, firmly tapping. "And, my friend, it is something that you have forgotten about him."

Zero looked down at the fox, then at the point where the cane touched him. "And something I needed reminding of," he said, chagrined twice in as many minutes.

"We all must think with our hearts as well as our heads. Otherwise we risk losing our identity, our very being, in the face of what we are fighting." Master Song withdrew his cane and grinned. "That is why you have me here to help you."

"One of many reasons," Zero quipped. "Thank you for the lesson. But I have to leave. There's a meeting in five minutes that I must attend."

The fox waved him off. "Don't worry. I can find my way back."

"All right." The bear indulged a final moment to appreciate the quiet and serenity before trudging back up the path toward the main complex.

Master Song stood silently for several minutes, contemplative and listening to the quiet movement of air around him, its ebb and flow in simple and complex rhythms that afforded a deeper understanding of nature for those who took the time to do so. It was a form of meditation that the martial arts master had learned almost from the time he could walk and even now, at his old age, he was still a student and still learning. At least now he knew enough to be able to teach the technique to others.

A subtleness of the pattern made him smile once more, and say, "Do you plan to ever wear clothes again?"

A soft chuckle. "How long did it take you to figure out I was here?"

The fox turned to his right. "I will admit, young wolf, that it took longer to discern your presence than before. That tells me that you have learned much since you have been gone."

"I have."

The fox tilted his head. "There is the sound of regret in your voice."

Silence intervened for a short time and Master Song pictured the wolf grasping for the right words. "I think it's safe to say that we all… accumulate at least some regrets as we move through life by learning the lessons we need to learn."

* * *

Twenty-five hours earlier, 12:05 AM, Paris, CEST

Spirit looked down at a tiny white dot from the highest maintenance platform, near the very top of the Eiffel tower. *Even from this height, he's so distinguishable from everyone else. So noticeable. And so very much not like me.* The agent had been on stage with Achilles, that night in Arenosa. He had felt the thrill knowing that a couple hundred thousand people were looking in his direction, if not directly at him. Screaming in joy, and not in horror or fear or disgust. It was as though he had been welcomed into the singer's world. He had been liberated from his fears, felt accepted.

And what had he given Achilles in return?

Paranoia. Betrayal. Death. A glimpse into the struggles of a small group of agents the rest of the world knew nothing about, and would never know a thing about their sacrifices so that lives could be lived in peace and with the freedom to make choices in their quotidian routines. A secret world that was invisible, save for the occasional removal of the veil that obscured the agents' lives from normal people. A veil of necessity where normal people would never, could never, be the same again after having seen what lay behind.

A cold wind gusted. The invisible wolf shivered, not from his naked body's exposure to the chill, but due to something else.

"Crikey, but you're heavier than y'look. Oh, er, sorry, mate." The person next to him was stretching his left arm, shaking off the pain. Spirit found forgiveness of the words uncharacteristically easy for him to reach. Saving him from falling to his death kind of helped – that, and the assistance in taking out Ardal and the rest of Blair's goon squad quietly, before they could ever get near Achilles. It was easy to do when one was invisible and the other could fly – more like glide at high speed, really. But the fight had tweaked his own right arm and he rubbed the area where he had been shot in Arenosa.

"No apology necessary, Antis." The Australian bat had leaped from a lower platform and had caught Spirit while Blair Murdock continued the last moments of his life below. The wolf had thought he was being attacked by Pi again and had managed to remove the few remaining articles of clothing before realizing that this bat was on his side. They had been very lucky; the strength of the bat's wings were significantly reinforced by the high-tech glide-suit he was currently stripping out of, but even so, Spirit had nearly caused them to plunge to their deaths. Just carrying another person had been extremely difficult for Antis. Spirit had lost his mask during their struggle, while the remaining glove, the fake teeth and contacts, and the rest of his clothes were already in the flying mammal's waist-pack. They had, thankfully, also recovered the tablet from a lower platform. "Hell of an introduction to your new partner."

"Fair dinkum. Never met an invisible person before, didn't know what to think when Zero told me that. Good thing you had at least some clothes on so I could see ya falling."

Ah. The importance of being seen, Spiritwolf thought.

"Anyway, the clothes help with… with being… able to…" The bat was already shaking his head slightly as though disoriented after a long nap. "What the…?"

"My looks are doing a number on your sonar, Antis. Try to not use it, if you can."

"Hard to turn it off, mate – part and parcel for us bats, y'know."

Spiritwolf sighed; it was an unseen breeze. "I know what that's like." A spattering of flashbulbs from below caught his attention; Achilles was being led toward an ambulance. *He's going to be checked out and then probably just released. He didn't seem to have any significant injuries, not if he's walking around.* He watched the police talk with the singer for several minutes while the EMTs examined him and wrapped bandages around his chest. Then the police departed and the white wolf climbed into the ambulance. More flashbulbs went off; a meerkat came over and started yelling at them, shooing them away. The doors closed and the ambulance drove off, slowly making its way through the crowd with a limousine following close behind. Achilles was safe; he would soon be back to his world of music and screaming fans, and Spirit would fly off to his world as well. The veil would drop back into place and that would be the end of it.

"I think it's time for us to be going," he told the bat.

"Right. The car's over on the other side of the Champs de Mars. We'll drive to our base in Tousson, where the transport's all fueled up and ready to go."

"That's not what I meant. We're staying for a bit longer."

Antis scowled at him. "That's not our orders, mate. We've got the tablet, you're in one piece… er, far as I can tell, anyway."

"Yeah. I am."

"All right. So Zero was rushed on the phone but I remember him saying he wants us back stateside yesterday."

It's not like Zero to make rushed decisions, Spiritwolf thought. *Like pairing me up with a bat who's going to get motion sick during every mission. Maybe this is just a temporary thing, or maybe Greystorm's come up with some kind of fancy anti-emetic…*

"You don't want me to get fired for breaking the rules on my first assignment with you, right?"

Spirit leaned over and put a hand on Antis' shoulder. Where another person might have flinched from the surprise of a sudden touch with no forewarning, it did not bother the bat at all. The wolf took note and smiled to himself before replying. "If you're going to be my partner, Antis, you'll have to get used to breaking a few rules. I've got unfinished business with someone. We'll discuss it on the way."

"Bloody Yanks," the bat muttered and followed Spirit's descent to ground level.

* * *

Three hours later, Le Monde Bar, 03:15.
One last drink.

The white wolf glanced at the note that had been left in his pocket and then entered the place. Like the rest of the hotel, it was modern and top-notch trendy, decked out in the latest European lounge stylings with high chairs at the bar proper; tables of various sizes and shapes where food was being ordered in addition to drinks; and larger chairs and sofas that were designed for long conversations. The music complemented the babble-talk nicely, filling in gaps between words and sentences, laughter, and subtle murmurings. The rhythm was a little too down-tempo and predictable – boring, really – for his tastes, as were the hue-changing lights, but the place seemed good for just kicking back and relaxing with friends.

Achilles tentatively stepped into the place and combed his hair with nervous fingers. A few people noticed him, letting their glances linger before returning to their previous conversations and what not. He wasn't sure whether their behavior had been out of respect for the bruises he sported across his face, or if they were allowing him his privacy, or whether they just didn't give a damn. It was a strange feeling for the singer; he'd become so used to being noticed in public wherever he went, so used to the fans screaming and yelling after him, that the perceived lack of recognition was just so… different. It was calm, but on another level, it left him feeling momentarily lonely. He imagined… it was almost like… being like *him*. Was it, really? He'd never know for sure. He didn't have the same… hadn't gone through… what the other wolf had gone through, survived through, and had lived every second since the accident. Yes, it was at the other absurd end of the axis that their lives had been separately lived on, until a little over a week ago.

He stood there lost among the disjoint of his thoughts and, for several seconds, did not know whether to go forward or back, left or right. And then he spotted a vaguely familiar-looking grey wolf sitting alone at a table facing the window and staring out into the rainy night. Was it *him*? It… seemed to be. He had the same build, a similar demeanor, the same overall look, ironically. It was practically impossible that it could be him. There wasn't anyone else it could be, if this was the same wolf he'd first seen in the hotel lobby in Arenosa.

Achilles made his way cautiously over to the other wolf, keeping his eyes on him the entire time and not wanting to disturb what could easily have been mistaken for a dream. He paused by the table with held-in breath; the wolf still hadn't noticed his arrival and the singer's sense of surety was quickly diminishing to match the lights that had changed from sunset orange to twilight blue. "Hello," he exhaled quietly.

The wolf finally turned from the sheeting rain and smiled. It was a different face but that smile was the same. "Hello," he replied, just as softly. Same voice, too.

"Mind if I join you?"

"I'd like that."

Achilles settled into the opposite chair and angled himself so they were both looking out into the night. They were silent for a minute while the music wove its way longingly between them. "You're alive," the singer finally said.

"Still am," the green-eyed wolf said with a chuckle. "I seem to have a knack for it."

"I'm sorry."

Another soft laugh came from the wolf next to him. "Not sorry for me being alive, I hope?"

"No." The singer shook his head. "I'm sorry I… couldn't hold onto you. I wasn't strong enough. It was my fault that you fell. I couldn't save you like you saved me. Back in Arenosa, I mean."

"Achilles," the other wolf chided gently. "I wasn't expecting you to." He continued after the rock star's look of shock had faded. "You're not trained for that sort of thing. Don't blame yourself, especially if I'm, you know, alive." He tilted his head. "If anything, I should be the one apologizing. For bringing you into this mess of a world I live in."

The white wolf looked out at the rain again. "It's all right," he murmured. "I'm… glad I was able to be a part of it, for a little while. And I can hardly blame you for wanting the chance to be… to have your former self back." He noticed the other wolf's movement. "Did it work? I mean, you have the tablet now and…"

"No." Gently, firmly, the word was said and Achilles' ears went down. "The data… it's encrypted. And it appears to be unbreakable. We have our best experts working on it but…" He shrugged. "For now, I'm still who I am. Still Spiritwolf."

"I'm so sorry. All this, then… it was for nothing?"

"I've been thinking about that, about futility and failure. It may seem that way, on the surface. But I wouldn't have met you otherwise, so I would say something good came out of it." They paused their conversation as the waiter, a bulky raccoon, came and took their drink orders. "And I'm buying," the agent said. "It's the least I can do."

"As I recall, you quit, and I'm down one personal trainer. You owe me more than a drink!" the singer shot back good-naturedly. For a few moments, it was as though the pain of the last day – the weirdness of the last week, too – had never existed. "And I intend my compensation to be paid in full," he said coyly.

"Oh?" Spirit sounded amused. "What do you mean by that?"

Achilles put a hand over the agent's. The other wolf twitched ever so slightly at the touch. "I know I can't ask you to stay, because you won't. Because of your line of work, and your… unique situation."

"I hope you're not asking to go with me and become an agent," Spiritwolf said with a soft chuckle. "The paperwork alone would destroy lesser men. I've seen it myself."

The white wolf tsked. "I make music. I'm quite happy with that, in case you weren't aware."

"Then what is it?"

Noticing familiar movement, Achilles looked off to his side. "In a mo'. Our waiter's back with our drinks." The raccoon deposited the caipirinha with the agent and a craft beer in a frosted mug opposite. "What shall we toast to?" the singer asked.

Spiritwolf raised his glass. "To being alive."

Achilles returned the salute. "To living life to the fullest." They clinked glasses and took a long swallow of their beverages.

Spirit looked at his drink with admiration. "Oh. That's good."

Achilles nodded. "Mine, too. As I was saying, what I would like… is to know you. The real you."

"Why? Why would you want to know who I really am?"

"Because soon we'll have to go our separate ways, get back to our lives. And I want to know more about the man who saved my life."

Spirit smiled. "The man who saved your life is right here, rock star."

Achilles took another long swig. "So he is. But you're not a personal trainer."

"You're aware of what I actually do for a living."

"I know that people shoot at you… they want to kill or capture you. I know you live a dangerous life. But who are you?"

The agent stared back at him and for a moment, Achilles felt like he was back in the alley in Arenosa with the seething wolf ready to throttle him. And then the moment was gone and in front of him was only the muscular gym trainer, hesitant and unsure of where he fit in. "I've been trying to figure that out, believe it or not."

The singer nodded. "I can imagine. I spent a while doing that, myself. A teacher of mine – he helped me, told me to go out and be who I was meant to be. And I've done that."

The other wolf looked into his glass. "Teachers have done that for me, too," Spirit said softly. "Master Song. Ixak. Zero. Greystorm. The others… they were all helping me to find out who I really was. Beneath the exterior, the façade that hides… what I've become." He looked at the white wolf. "I help people. I protect innocent civilians from those who would use technology to harm them. Spiritwolf… that is who I am and it's all I need to be."

Achilles put his hand over the other wolf's again. "Stay with me tonight, Spirit," he whispered urgently. "Please."

The agent fidgeted. "Um…"

"Oh, for…" The white wolf rolled his eyes. "Really? Why is it that you Americans are always thinking of sex?"

"Then what were you thinking of?"

"That it's possible to spend a night with someone and not have sex?"

"Is it because of my… because I'm… ?"

The white wolf punched him lightly in the arm and then winced. "Ow. No, you silly wolf, it's not because of that. Not at all. It's because… ah, how do I say this? It's because I want to feel… safe… and secure for just one more night. And that's how I feel when I'm with you."

Spiritwolf cupped Achilles' hand in his. "All right then, rock star," he said with a slight smirk. "Tonight, I'm yours."

They finished their drinks quickly, and paid the tab. Spirit kept his promise with a fifty euro note, and left without another word. They were almost to the elevator when the agent's phone rang. "I have to take this," he said with a laugh and hurried over to an alcove. He was back a minute later. "All clear... let's go," he said cheerfully.

"Who was it?"

"My partner, reminding me yet again that we're overdue to depart back to the States. As if I didn't hear him the first twenty times."

"Your partner?"

"Brand spanking new. Nice enough guy. Don't worry... he's not coming along with me tonight. I'll meet him in the morning. Or maybe afternoon, given the current time."

"Okay, but..." Achilles blinked. "You were supposed to have headed back already?"

"Yup. I have the tablet and Regis... Black Dust is in custody."

"But you're here... aren't you going to get in trouble?"

Spirit chuckled. "Yeah. What else is new?"

"You stayed... for me?"

"Kind of hard to say a proper goodbye if you think I'm dead."

Achilles was silent for several moments. The elevator finally arrived and they got in. "You know, that was what you'd told me when we first met," he said, swiping his room key and pressing the button for the top floor. "You don't like authority. I guess that much about you is really true."

"What, you hadn't figured that out by now?" Spirit teased. "I think that's why we get along, you and I."

"Yeah, we're practically twins, aren't we?" They exited the elevator at the penthouse level and made their way to the furthest corner of the floor where a duffel bag was waiting for them in front of the door. "You knew you'd be up here?" the singer said, amused.

"No. I had my partner drop it off when I spoke to him."

"So he's nearby, then?"

Spiritwolf nodded. "Sixth floor. As I said, he's not chaperoning, but we're supposed to be traveling back together. Tomorrow."

"I guess you needed your kit for tonight?" Achilles swiped his card key again.

"Yes." They entered Achilles' hotel room and shut the door. Spiritwolf sauntered past the white wolf and whistled. "So, a suite in this hotel is basically a small apartment, then?"

"Yes. We're leaving tomorrow to cut down on tour costs, so this is my last night in the room."

"You sure know how to show a guy a good time." Spiritwolf quipped. He followed the white wolf into the bedroom and set his bag down near the door.

Achilles approached slowly, his tail swaying. "I certainly hope so," he said and wrapped his arms around the agent's broad torso. Spiritwolf did the same and dipped his head down to kiss the shorter wolf. Small, gentle pecks at first, then a surge toward a longer, needful kiss as familiarity settled in.

"Mmm," Achilles murmured when they finally parted. He looked up breathlessly at the agent, who was gently panting. Smiling at him. The singer smiled back and began unbuttoning the agent's shirt. Whatever hesitation Spirit had before was now gone; he stood patiently while Achilles undid the row and opened the shirt.

Achilles pressed a hand against fur-covered muscle he couldn't see, arresting progress toward the back side of the shirt. He brought his other hand around and felt along the other wolf's chest. Spirit's heartbeat pulsed back. "Here's the real you."

"Not completely." Spiritwolf stepped back and pulled off the shirt entirely. He hung it over the back of a chair, then did the same with his pants after using his feet to tug off his shoes. Socks peeled off invisible feet and the head and forearms of the agent dipped toward the bag, which opened. Contacts and veneers went back into their vials, and the fake fur elongated before they were pulled off and deposited inside the duffel.

Achilles looked toward the bag. "I repeat what I said earlier about Americans," he grinned.

"You wanted the real me, here I am!" Spirit's voice retorted good-naturedly. A small piece of paper floated up from the bag; Achilles tracked it as it moved over to the bed, hovering above it as the edge of the mattress curved down.

"What's that, Spirit?"

"Something you'll like."

Achilles nodded. "All right. Be right over." He pulled his own shirt up and then gasped as the pain suddenly sharpened. "Oh, damn. That hurts."

"Let me help." Spirit's voice was right in front of him; the paper was on the bed, sans indentation. Achilles nodded and let the shirt gently roll upward, taking great care around his ribs and other bandaged bodyparts. "I'm so sorry about this," the other wolf said. Gentle pressure yielded only a slight flare-up.

"I'll be okay." The pressure traced along his chest; the wave of flattened fur followed the tribal pattern. "And I'm sure my tattoos will be okay, too," he added sardonically.

"How about your lower body?" His pants unfastened but Achilles batted away the unseen hands before they went any further.

"Everything's fine down there, thanks," he said, to airy laughter. He slowly removed his pants and then his shoes, socks, and underwear. Almost immediately, he was swept up into another hug pressed tight against the other wolf's muscular form. Their naked bodies finally parted and Achilles found himself grinning at nothing in particular. "Nice. Now, then. What was that thing you wanted to show me?"

"Over on the bed." The white wolf followed the sound of padding feet and joined his invisible friend on the bed. The paper floated into the air again and from this distance, Achilles could see it was a photograph.

"When I gave you my cover story and told you how I got my name," the agent began, "Most of it was true, believe it or not, though it was from the perspective of the organization I'm part of. There was something that happened, before I became invisible. Something I did… it was… Anyway. I disconnected, was having difficulty trying to go on by myself. And then a friend… he helped me. Helped me begin to rediscover myself and move forward. He was the one who gave me my name."

Achilles searched for the other wolf's broad shoulders and put his arm around them. "I'm so sorry, Spirit. I won't pry, but I'm glad you told me."

"I'm glad I'm able to share the real story with you, rock star. You wanted to know me? This… is me. What I used to look like."

The photo floated into the white wolf's hands, and he cradled it as if it were the most precious thing on earth. He studied the image of the bear seated across a diner table (not unlike the one in Dresden) from another white wolf. The young lupine seemed barely an adult and yet, despite looking relieved about something, he had such a haunted look to his eyes, as though he were decades older. Achilles had seen it before, when he'd visited hospitals for charity. It was a look born from a firsthand encounter with death, or at least some kind of experience with it, but how it had come to be seared across Spiritwolf's features, he did not know. Nor did he need to.

"Thank you for letting me see this, Spirit, for sharing it with me," Achilles finally said and handed back the photo. "You're very handsome. And a white wolf, too!" He grinned.

"The last thing I was expecting to happen that night was to have my picture taken. It's a captured moment in time, from my past." The photo returned into the duffel and then Achilles felt the wolf's hand on his shoulders, a quick kiss on the top of his head. "And for tonight, you are my present."

The rock star smiled coyly. "I've already unwrapped my present. Let's see what else I'm to be gifted with." They embraced again and, after a long while, they drifted off to sleep under the covers, still snuggled together and safe from the pouring rain outside.

* * *

The old fox shifted his position slightly. "And you have learned the lessons you need to learn, then?"

"As much as I could."

"That is the best you can do, of course. Regrets, though." Master Song sighed, a soft, sad noise that Spirit had never heard from him before, nor would ever hear from him again. "The best you can say about them is that they are all based on what happened in the past. You can never have regrets about the future." He turned his head toward the invisible wolf and spoke with a harder edge to his voice. "You understand?"

"Yes, sensei."

"Good. Tell me about Hikiwake."

Spiritwolf did a double-take. "I never told you that I encountered him."

"Nor did you tell me that you fought him. And yet," the blind fox smiled in that sly way characteristic of his species, "it is readily apparent to me that you did."

"What? How? Did you feel some kind of spiritual tremor, or something like that?"

Master Song smiled even wider. "No. I was informed of his capture."

"Funny. Well, his technique was flawless. And he knew my technique was based on your teachings."

"As any experienced person should. I am sure he recognized the way you struck at him, particularly the nerve strikes."

"He knew where I was even though I wasn't wearing anything. It was like I was sparring with you, Master Song." The fox nodded. "And… he said that he owed you for killing his sensei. What did he mean by that?"

"Exactly as he said."

When the fox didn't elaborate, Spiritwolf asked, "But what happened? What did you do? And does this mean he's coming after you?"

Master Song looked as though he'd bitten into a lemon. Then he punched the air, connecting solidly with Spiritwolf's stomach. As the invisible wolf doubled over, trying desperately to remain upright, the fox led his stern rebuke with, "I have spoken all I desire on that matter. You missed that subtlety in my reply, so I have provided a more direct means for you to understand that."

"Yes… yes, sensei." Spiritwolf struggled to breathe normally. "I'm… sorry."

"Well, it appears you have lessons to learn yet. But, I am impressed with the result of your mission."

"Thank you, sensei." For Master Song to compliment anyone was a high form of praise.

The fox flicked his cane up the path. "As, I believe, is Corona."

Spirit turned and saw the muscular tiger marching toward them. "He doesn't look impressed. He looks pissed."

"Yes. Perhaps you should have informed them of your return, after all."

"What, and miss out on a few last moments of freedom?"

The Operations director approached the fox, nodded a greeting, and then looked around guardedly. "You really shouldn't play these sorts of games, Spirit. It's what got you into trouble before."

"Sorry, Corona. I just wanted to have a chat with Master Song before I went back to confinement."

"Confinement? Hardly. You've been put on full-time active status again. First of the remaining Ultras to get there. Congratulations." The tiger put out his hand.

"I've fallen for that trick once before. Never again."

"Oh, for the love of…" Corona scowled and rolled his eyes. "Just shake already. I won't put you in cuffs. Unless you really want to go back to inactive status again." He smirked as an invisible hand quickly closed around his own. "Zero pushed through the paperwork as soon as you called to say you had the tablet. And he thinks he'll be able to convince the World Nations committee and the other senior directors to bring back the Ultras when they're ready. Might be a while, though," he added soberly.

"Yeah." Spirit thought of his friends, those who had died on the day he and the other surviving members of the team had been changed. And the dark days that had followed. But now, it seemed as though things were truly starting to get better. And they would continue on that path into whatever the future held for them.

No regrets.

"So, Spirit, get your ass back to your room. I pushed several case files to your tablet for you and Antis to study. And by the way, put some clothes on. You're out of uniform. Afternoon, Master Song." The tiger nodded again and turned on his heel, marching back the way he'd come.

"I guess no one appreciates nudity these days."

The fox grinned. "Not anymore. Now, agent Spiritwolf, you must go back. I will remain here for a while yet. But before you go, I will offer my congratulations as well. You have earned what you have been given."

"Thank you, sensei." He bowed, as did Master Song, and then he began the short trek toward the main building. He looked over his shoulder after a minute and saw that the short fox was staring out over the water. Spirit smiled fondly and headed back to where Antis had stashed his duffel bag, per their earlier agreement.

Spirit put on a hoodie, sweat pants, and sneakers and walked up the path he'd come down invisible. On the way back, he paused near a small stone dais. Someone had put a fresh bouquet of flowers in the urn next to the marble plaque that listed the names of the Ultras who had fallen – his family. He stepped up and stood before it reverently, thinking back to all those missions and the good times they'd had. He'd been the youngest but now he felt like he was the oldest, the first of the surviving team members to have completed a mission. In some way, he felt like it was his responsibility to carry their shared legacy forward into whatever might lay in the future.

He bowed his head in silence for a minute before turning back to the path and walking up to the main building.

He made his way down the corridors uneasily at first, unsure of what to expect. The first few people he encountered said hello or otherwise nodded respectfully to his empty clothes as he passed them by, and he began to relax. *Maybe things aren't so bad after all.*

A familiar cheetah in a lab coat rounded a corner at the same time as he, nearly colliding with the agent. "Sorry… sorry… Oh, hey, Spirit. Didn't know you'd returned."

"Hi, Dash. Yeah, I just got back a little while ago."

"Right. Hey, Greystorm and I are going to Elm's birthday party at eight. You're gonna be there? He invited you but you may not have seen your email yet."

"Well, I was thinking of just catching up on sleep. I'm still on Central European time." The cat nodded. "But, maybe I can make an appearance for a little while. So to speak."

"Great! See you there." The cat sped by him, no doubt in the midst of some analysis or experiment. Spirit chuckled and headed in the opposite direction. When he got to the elevator, he saw the new voice module and then looked up at the special SDS-overlay camera that had been added in his absence.

"Agent Spiritwolf, access code Seven-Eight-Zeta-Alpha-Five." The doors opened and he pushed the '7' button, then repeated his code. *Looks like my active status is official. You never really know for sure until the security system lets you in.*

He opened the door to his 'apartment' and stepped inside. Everything had seemed smaller before; the claustrophobic side effect of being cooped up – confined – in the building. Now it was smaller for a different reason. He had gone out into the world – an invisible wolf hidden by the exterior layers of clothes and fake fur with nobody the wiser – and for the first time in… in over a year, everything had seemed normal. And with that taste of freedom had come the belief that he wouldn't go back to being a captive, for all intents and purposes. There was so much now that he could do, and he would make the most of it. Within the rules, of course. Well, the ones that made sense, anyway.

"Speaking of 'making the most of it,'" the agent said to himself. He began perusing the files Corona had left for him, quickly taking note of various persons of interest and associated data contained within. He paused on one that showed a huge scowling bison who had escaped custody. The picture of the DAST person who had originally captured him showed a handsome, smiling grey wolf, maybe a couple of years younger than himself. A handwritten note from Antis stated that the person, Tymber, had already recaptured the bison, which meant that the case was closed for all intents and purposes. And he wasn't even an agent!

Duly impressed, Spirit closed that file and then moved on to the next one.

* * *

I must confess that I had my doubts about Agent Spiritwolf's ability to succeed in his assignment. We all did, I am sure, just as I believe that we all wanted him to be successful. This is the reason for the clandestine help from his team, despite orders to the contrary. The loyalty that he inspires in his companions, whether he knows it or not, is another reason for his success. Of course, his invisible nature also played a part, as it must. The changes to his physical form are an asset and he has now fully adapted to them, integrated them into himself to allow him to become the person he was meant to be.

Just as I must become who I am meant to be.

The case of Black Dust has been more than a mere single point along the path that must be charted. Agent Spiritwolf has learned much during these past days. This much he knows. But he will also learn much more that he is not aware of yet. It is the way of things.

As for I, much work remains to be done and yet the time of reckoning is drawing ever closer, ever faster. But I am not as I once was. I have grown, I have changed, I have… evolved.

How do I continue the work that I had set out to do when I am not the same person I was when the work had started?

Who am I?

Ixak stared at what he had written on the screen. His antennae twitched violently like twin thin snakes whipping sinuously even as the rest of his body was completely still. It was a display of emotion alien to all of the other mammals that inhabited this world; it did not seem like much, but to another insect, it spoke volumes. The voice-box interpreter sputtered and popped as though it wanted to say something further of its own accord, without vocalized orders from its master. A quick flip of a hidden switch silenced it and let secrets remain secrets.

Ixak forced himself toward calm, dispassion, and steadiness. Down here in the shielded darkness he was just himself. He could be himself, at peace. He closed the journal and moved the file back into the encrypted folder that had just one elegant, almost poetic phrase for a title that the casual observer would not understand but meant the world to him.

Unbeknownst To the Butterfly

* * *

Cain walked along Canary Wharf. He had no idea why he had decided to come here but it felt right. Being back in London. His office wasn't too far away now. He had to get there, retrieve a few precious articles from the wall safe and then transfer all of Blair's assets into private, secure accounts before the lion's funds were frozen. Only then could he leave and continue his work by "starting fresh." It would look as though someone had embezzled everything, which he supposed was true. But first, he had to get to his office.

"My... office?" The badger rubbed his head tiredly. "I don't have an office. What's going on? I was in Paris, and..."

Cain looked at his reflection in the building's window. The drummer was haggard, unshaven, his eyes bloodshot. Dressed... differently than he remembered. In a business suit, instead of his usual cutoff T-shirt and jeans. And then something flickered, a tiny spot of light like a distant torch. He pressed his hand against the cool glass and looked deeper.

The badger felt it before he saw it. "No," he whispered. "No, no no nononono..."

A black shadow surged from the reflection and traveled up his arm, covering him in inky darkness that brushing, clawing and even biting couldn't stop it. Cain knew with preternatural certainty that he and only he could see it; it wouldn't do to scream, as it would make him seem mad to anyone around him. Madness was his last thought as the darkness finally entered his eyes, nose and mouth, reasserting the control over the badger it had momentarily lost.

"Much better," the badger murmured, smiling toothily. Practice made perfect; it wasn't too different from learning to drive or ride a bike, really. Soon he would be able to do so much more; the only way he had been able to overcome the impotence of incorporeality was by developing vast reserves of patience. And practice. Cain was easy to work with but Blair had been somewhat difficult to control for stretches at a time – the man's lust for power, his ego, had been distasteful in the extreme. Those traits had warred with his own desire to keep the mission going and so he'd had to develop backup plans. Still, he hadn't quite expected his Rising Force operation to have crossed paths with the CATS and Black Dust. Somehow, Spiritwolf had beaten them all, as well as his former host, Blair Murdock, and had recovered the tablet.

"Spiritwolf," the badger murmured. The agent was a force to be reckoned with, now that he was invisible. He admired the young wolf's resiliency but additional precautions would still need to be taken.

First things first, though.

He adjusted his business suit and entered the building that had once belonged to Blair Murdock. The male gazelle behind the security desk returned his smile when he politely asked what floor the lion's office was on, even though he already knew. The badger agreed that yes, the news of the lion's death was tragic, but he was actually there to see Murdock's secretary about an evening engagement. Cain stared at the male, who was ringing the office to confirm the engagement, and realized that his impatient, ravenous appetite had returned once more.

The badger shook his head and sighed, quietly walking around the side of the security desk. *First things first, indeed.* Biology was a force that just could not be denied.

Thankfully, the lobby was devoid of people who could have witnessed the killing, and it was several hours before the facilities engineer entered the generator room and found the security officer's red, wet remains in a trash bin. By then, Cain was long gone, having accomplished everything he'd needed to do, including vigorous showering, brushing and flossing the fleshy bits out of his teeth, and changing into fresh clothes not soaked in blood and gore. And some cologne, to mask any remaining odors before he got on the plane traveling back to the United States.

It was time to return to where it all started.

And now, a sneak peek from the next book, Reflections

Chapter 1.0: And The Light Shall Touch Me No More

The bear code-named Zero sat quietly behind the desk, lost in troubled thought as he looked out the window into the stormy darkness beyond the transport airplane. Rain was usually a soothing friend, tapping a lively, rhythmic connection to nature that renewed his spirit. Tonight, the energy was different; the heavy drops driven by the howling wind were a staccato migraine. He couldn't concentrate on the paperwork he'd set out to finish, so he had loosened his tie and turned away from the attempted distraction, frowning at what he could not see outside.

"Not a good night." he murmured. The latest rumble of thunder seemed to prove his point.

The rapid knocking on his office door didn't surprise him. The white hare entering his office without permission, however, did. As well as speaking before he turned around.

"Sir…"

"If you're here to give me a weather update, Marzo, you can get the hell out right now." His irritation at the disturbance belied the cold prickle he felt in his spine even before his response had been uttered. Urgency overlaid the British lagomorph's normally placid tone.

"Sorry, sir, but…"

"And didn't I tell you not to call me 'sir?'"

"You did, sir. And I told you I can't stop that. It's automatic, second nature, as it were, since my family…"

Zero growled.

"Anyway, your comm-link's not active…"

"I didn't want to be disturbed."

"…and Corona's been trying to reach you. It's the Ultras." Marzo's voice grew soft. "Something's happened to them."

Zero turned from the window, stood, and leaned over the desk. The director's looming presence would have cowed just about anyone else but the agent merely raised an eyebrow and waited. Marzo's earpiece blinked green once every five seconds, indicating that it was in standby mode. Zero's was completely off, unlit.

He probably shouldn't have done that, in retrospect.

"Corona's the Operations lead for the mission," he rumbled.

"Yes, sir. There was an explosion several minutes ago at the complex. From the chatter, it sounds like they walked into a trap."

"A trap?" Zero slammed a meaty fist into the desk, which shuddered in sullen complaint. This time, the rabbit was startled enough to step back. It wasn't often that the bear's temper was given physical release. "How did this happen?" he growled, his brown eyes smoldering.

"They're still piecing that together. Corona had only just established a containment perimeter when I spoke to him. Control space encompasses a hundred kilometer radius."

"A hundred… !" That would extend well beyond the site and both transport airplanes. Hell, it included several small towns and went right up to the reservoir. And it was a huge area to patrol, even if it was in the middle of nowhere. "Are you sure?"

"Yes, sir. Corona said local sensors and satellite telemetry showed that nothing was released into the environment, as far as we can detect."

The bear grunted. "That's one positive. Why the large area, then?"

"I was not privy to the reason, sir," Marzo shrugged. "But Corona told me to tell you that protocol Ultra-Zero has been initiated. I presume that has something to do with you?"

The bear's eyes narrowed. Without answering Marzo's question, Zero walked around the desk and retrieved his trenchcoat and fedora from the door hook. He quickly exited the office with the stunned rabbit trailing in his wake as he hurried along the upper deck. Zero's gaze scanned the clustered workstations below as he proceeded down the stairs but none of the operatives was the snow leopard he was looking for. "*Private channel, Greystorm.*" His comm-link came to life and double-beeped an error message in response moments later.

"Greystorm's comms are off and I don't know where he is," he called back over his shoulder to Marzo. "Find him. Tell him what Corona said and then tell him that *I* said he needs to be there ASAP. Pull him away from whatever he's working on. And tell him to bring *all* of the gear this time. He'll know what that means." The rabbit nodded and immediately began speaking into his earpiece. He swerved off to the side and disappeared into a tight corridor.

"Ultra-Zero. Damn." The bear bounded down the next set of stairs more like a controlled fall than a safe descent. He barreled past a surprised analyst in the hallway and slammed his fist against the big red cargo bay door release button. With hand on hat, he sprinted to the remaining black SUV, gunned it to life, and zoomed into the pouring rain before the door had completely lowered.

They'd cleared the back roads of civilians and the local police before the operation, but that was only for forty klicks. Zero didn't care; he drove like a maniac toward Conway National Laboratories, preparing himself for what he needed to do when he got there.

"*Incoming private channel from agent Marzo,*" the earpiece's default voice told him pleasantly.

"Sir." The hare's voice crackled. "Greystorm is on his way and he's already coordinating with the Sciences team at the site. ETA is five minutes after your arrival. Shall I contact Corona and let him know you're coming?"

"I'll do it myself. Call me if there's anything else."

It was unusual for a Director to venture into the field, but Ultra-Zero required that he take charge in person. It meant that the agents that comprised the Special Operations' "Ultra" Team were all incapacitated or dead, or possibly affected by whatever technology they may have encountered on their mission. Any command decisions regarding their status needed to be made directly by him. Corona would not have made the call lightly.

A stray memory bubbled through his chaotic thoughts, his last conversation with one of the Ultras before sending him and the rest of the team on the mission. A friendly chat without the foreknowledge of disaster. Had he known… The bear burst the thought bubble with a mental pinprick and focused on keeping the speeding SUV from hydroplaning off the highway. He took a deep breath and said, "*Corona, private channel.*"

The private channel was anything but. Frantic voices filled his ear with yelling and cursing, Corona's loudest of all. "Shut UP!" the tiger finally snarled, killing a lot of the background noise. "It's a mess here, Zero. The explosion nearly took out a fusion generator that our intel didn't pick up." The bear's eyes widened. There was the reason for the hundred kilometers; control space would prevent anyone from entering the blast zone, with margin. "I've got to go back and tell these idiots that it's pencils down for the preliminary assessment. See you when you get here." The channel clicked off abruptly, leaving Zero alone with the driving rain.

"Not a good night at all," he murmured as he tuned into the primary Ops channel to try to make sense of the chatter during the rest of the drive.

The lack of any law enforcement en route was a testament to Corona's ability as the Ultras' Operations lead to quickly establish a containment perimeter of that size. The research compound was in the middle of nowhere, Wyoming, which helped keep large groups of civilians out of their way. This particular middle of nowhere was on a large mesa in the Rockies; the storm cell that had blown in unexpectedly was rapidly moving out of the area by the time Zero arrived at the installation.

The security gate was bent and barely hanging on its hinges, indicative of the haste with which the support team had come in to control the situation. Four agents with high energy electrolaser pistols had been left to guard the entrance and their leader waved him through while talking on his comm-link; Zero heard her inform Corona of his arrival over his own earpiece. He followed the road for another mile and parked amidst some smaller office buildings at its end. Agents swarmed around in a chaotic dance of soaked uniforms, gesticulating and speaking harshly into their comm-links. The Ops lead was nowhere to be found.

"*Location, Corona.*" Zero noted the distance and bearing that suddenly sprang into being on the windshield overlay and then got out and went to go find him.

The rain was tapering off but water still sluiced off the front of his fedora by the time the bear stepped inside the mobile command center – an unmarked eighteen-wheeler that had been brought by the second transport airplane. He spotted the large tiger at the data fusion console, directing other agents while windows on the console displayed UAV patrol feeds of the control space as well as satellite and sensor telemetry. Between people, he caught brief glimpses of slow motion playbacks of video feeds from the team's suits. As tempted as he was to barrel his way to the front and watch what had happened to the team, Zero waited for the Ops lead to finish and then motioned him outside.

"We're still trying to piece together exactly what happened, Z," Corona rasped. He had probably been yelling non-stop since the explosion.

"Have you heard anything from any of the Ultras?"

"No. All of their comms went off-line several minutes before the explosion."

"Tell me what you know," Zero said. "From the beginning."

"Not much to tell so far. One moment, the Ultras had fanned out and were moving through the labs, making their way toward the back of the building. The next moment – well, a couple of minutes later, actually – we lost the video and audio from all of them. Then the telemetry from their uniforms went haywire – their biometrics all suddenly spiked into the red like they were all having some kind of seizure. Another five minutes or so and we lost the signals completely. Ten seconds after that… boom!" He pointed to a large chunk missing from the back left side of the building. "That's the area that Nightshade, Lightning, Azure, and Dev were in."

"Dammit." Zero closed his eyes and ground his teeth. "What about the rest? What happened to their vitals?"

"Don't know."

"What does that mean? Are they dead or aren't they?"

"Like I said, we lost biometric telemetry from everyone just before the explosion, so there's no way to know for sure. You know as much as we do."

"And you declared Ultra-Zero without knowing exactly what happened?"

"It sure as hell looks like something fucked with them and I didn't want whatever 'it' was going uncontained after the explosion tore the building a new one." Corona glared at him and his tail thrashed behind him. "Based on what little we do know, there's some decisions that will need to be made that are above my pay grade, so I'm pretty sure you need to be here."

Zero took a deep breath. "Sorry. I didn't mean to question your judgment. You made the right call."

Corona nodded. "No harm, no foul, Z. Everyone's on a short fuse around here. You as well, by the sound of it."

"I'm just worried about the Ultras."

"Tell me about it. I hate walking into an ambush."

"Sending others into an ambush is even worse," Zero brushed the water from his face. "Is it safe to retrieve them?"

"The fusion generator appears to be off-line, so there's no threat from that, thankfully. I'm worried that whatever affected the Ultras is still active inside, where we don't have eyes or ears. I wasn't about to send more agents in to find out." The tiger squinted at the large shadowy building on the hill. "Greystorm's mini-drones ought to give us a better picture, so to speak."

Zero nodded. "He'll be here momentarily. If he gives the all-clear, I'm heading up there myself."

"I figured as much." Corona nodded and reached inside his coat and pulled out a small flashlight and a tablet computer. "I'm going with you, Zero.

The bear gave him a tired smile. "Why, Corona. That's not per protocol, to have more than one ranking agent going into a hot zone."

The tiger scowled. "Don't tell Greystorm I said this, but sometimes… fuck protocol. I need to find out what happened to my team, so I'm coming."

"Wouldn't have it any other way. And speaking of, here's Greystorm." His thumb flicked toward a paramedic's truck that was speeding toward them. "That makes all three ranking agents, then."

Corona nodded. "In for a penny…" he murmured and then spoke into his comm-link to let his support staff know where he was going. Meanwhile, the wiry snow leopard was frantically pulling equipment from the cabinets on the sides of the truck and stuffing the larger items into a frame-pack. Smaller items disappeared into the pockets of his cargo pants or his vest jacket.

Zero called to him when he had finished. "Can you send the mini-drones in for a look-see, Grey?"

"Certainly." The British director of the Sciences division popped open a tube in the side of the truck and keyed in the launch sequence on his own tablet. Six round spheres the size of tennis balls shot from the tube and unfolded their propulsion system before zipping off toward the building, following the directions Greystorm continued to tap into the command interface. "Should have a basic assessment in a minute or so." He pulled a few more items from the truck and cinched up the frame-pack before maneuvering it onto his shoulders.

"Great," Corona rumbled upon joining them. "Mind telling us where you've been?"

"What's this, then?" The snow leopard buckled the pack around his waist just above his long tail, looking very much like he was embarking on a camping trip. Or caving, with the head-lamp strapped around his forehead. His green eyes peered up at the taller men through rimless glasses as he approached. "Oh, right. Sorry. Was thinking about something else just as you were talking. Would you mind repeating?"

"Greystorm," Zero prompted in a surprisingly patient tone, ignoring the tiger cursing under his breath about discipline and attention. "What took you so long to get here after the explosion?"

"Umm… I was busy trying to figure out what happened to the Ultras."

"From back on the plane," the tiger rumbled. "You should have been doing that here. With me."

"My on-site team are perfectly capable of handling things, if that's what you're implying. Anyway, I was at my workstation – which has several PFLOPS more processing power than the equipment you've got out here combined, by the way – that was when everything had gone haywire…"

"We lost their vitals," Corona prompted. "After they suffered seizures."

"Yes, right, along with all the other fluctuations in their biometrics. About that. My team mentioned the same thing and after I examined all of the data, I believe I may have come up with a theory or two about what happened..."

"Do tell," Zero said after the snow leopard began thinking again.

"What? Sorry. Keep getting distracted."

"No shit," Corona muttered.

The snow leopard waved his hand dismissively. "Never mind why I didn't get here sooner – that's not important. Here's what is: the Ultras. So, their suits are keyed to their DNA, right? There are two likely scenarios that I can conceive of, given the signature and timing of the events. Either there's a huge EM field in there somewhere causing massive distortions and interference – damping, if you like – or their DNA has been altered. Given that the electronic devices out here are working, it's likely the latter."

Zero and Corona looked at each other.

"DNA-keying was kind of my fail-safe to indicate the presence of a fast-acting mutagen or retrovirus. Anyway, you can recalibrate the suit's sensor array to remove the agent's default template, which I just figured out how to do remotely as we've been talking." He swiped the tablet from the stunned tiger and, after several keystrokes and sliding motions, handed the unit back. "There you go. I really ought to write a user's manual for these apps." Greystorm repeated the keystrokes on his own tablet.

"Yeah, and make sure you write manuals for your other gizmos, too." Corona fiddled with the softkeys on his tablet and then peered at the circles and corresponding annotations overlaying the map of the complex. "Looks like Bal and Topaz are still with us. Maybe Canis, hard to tell. The sensors aren't picking up the others, just their suits. Sorry, Zero." The tiger put a heavy hand on his shoulder. "It's not looking good."

The bear nodded grimly. "Greystorm, is it safe to enter the building?"

The snow leopard studied the readings. "Elevated levels of aromatics and ammonia, consistent with explosives. Picking up some RDX and no PETN, which means probably C-4 was used. Other than that, the minis aren't picking up anything unusual."

"All right, then. Let's get going and see if we can save at least two of the Ultras."

"Hooah," Corona murmured.

Greystorm piped up again. "Um, Zero? Shouldn't we be in full hazmat gear for this?"

Corona rounded on him. "Why? Don't you trust your own mini-drones and sensor arrays?"

"Yes, but this could be something completely new. Besides, I can't think of everything in advance all the time, you know."

"Obviously, or else we wouldn't be in this situation!"

"Says the on-site Operations lead. Feeling guilty, hm?"

"Coward."

"Stop, you two, RIGHT now," Zero cut in. "Felines, I swear! Corona, he's no more a coward than you or me, and he's smarter than both of us put together. Shut up and have him network your tablet with his." The tiger wordlessly handed it to the snow leopard, who obliged and gave it back. "Greystorm, we're close enough to that gaping hole in the building," he pointed at the left side, "that anything that might have escaped detection by your various devices means we're already fucked, all right?" Both cats looked distinctly disconcerted by what he said. "This is not the time to be sniping at each other, so let's keep our focus on our friends."

"Sorry," Corona offered to both of them. "You're right, Zero."

"And apologies from me as well," Greystorm murmured, abashed.

"Accepted. You wouldn't happen to have another tablet, would you, Grey?"

"In the pack, third side pocket on the left." The bear found it and handed it to Greystorm for activation. "OK, it's networked with Corona's and mine. Sensors are working." He passed it back to Zero and turned on his head-lamp after taking a deep breath. "Ready."

"Sir?" Marzo's voice crackled into the bear's ear after they took a couple of steps. "I can see you via the feeds from the mini-drones. You're not all going in there, are you?"

"*Broadcast*," Zero commanded, and the comm system obliged, widening the output stream to include everyone in the operation. "Agents and other personnel, this is Zero. By now, everyone should be aware that the Ultra team is down and there has been an explosion. That's what we know for sure, but it is obviously just part of the story. We have initiated an emergency protocol to seal off the site and protect the surrounding area as best we can. The protocol also puts me directly in charge and I have decided that the best course of action is for Corona, Greystorm, and I to head inside to investigate and see if we can save any of our friends who might be still alive. Outside of the Ultras, the three of us have the most experience in dealing with exotic and dangerous technology. I'm saying this to be up front with everyone and, quite frankly, because this isn't open for discussion or debate, or even questions. These are my orders. Be ready in case we find anyone alive; otherwise, keep the analysis and investigations moving forward. We'll be in contact again soon. Until then, Marzo is in command. You are the best of the best and we are counting on you. Especially the Ultras. Zero out."

The bear took a deep breath and set his jaw. "Let's move."

The tiger nodded agreement and pulled his electrolaser pistol from his jacket. Greystorm was multitasking between monitoring the mini-drones, sending out directives to his Sciences team and batched a few more jobs to his various analyses of the team's biometric data. The two cats flanked Zero as they continued up the hill. Several agents paused to watch the trio trudge silently toward the dead building in the misting rain that had replaced the earlier downpour.

About the Authors

Invisiblewolf

Invisiblewolf spends his days in a day job and, like all good writers, would like nothing better than to be writing full-time. He spends much of his spare time writing, reading, traveling, and enjoying other endeavors related to creativity. He has lived in many cities in the U.S. and has visited several other countries. He currently lives in the Midwest, not too far from his real-life Tymber.

Achilles

Achilles is a British ex-pat who has resided in New Zealand for over a decade; upon gaining his BA (Hons) in Creative Writing from the University of Bedfordshire, he promptly left for a new life down under. Still cranking out the occasional bit of literature when he's not working his businesses or at the gym, he is looking forward to the next chapter in life's great adventure in Australia.

About the Artist

Ifus

Ifus is a freelance artist who lives in central Illinois with her husband. She has a bachelor's degree in Illustration with a minor in Animation. She's been doing art as a job in the fandom for over 10 years and loves every minute of it!

About the Publisher

FurPlanet Productions

FurPlanet is a small press publisher serving the niche market that is furry fiction. We sell furry-themed books and comics published by us and most major publishers in the community. If you can't get to a furry convention where we are selling in the dealers room, visit *www.FurPlanet. com* to shop online.

www.ingramcontent.com/pod-product-compliance
Lightning Source LLC
Chambersburg PA
CBHW051636050726
47502CB00011B/561